Praise for
WEAPONS OF CHOICE
Book One of The Axis of Time
by John Birmingham

"Birmingham hits the ground running and accelerates through the first half of the novel, before slowing down enough to let the reader and characters consider the implications of what's going on. Quick-paced and very clever alternate history."

—DAVID DRAKE, acclaimed author of *The Far Side of the Stars* and *Redliners*

"An excellent combination of near future military SF and alternate history, and a riveting story to boot."

—ERIC FLINT, author of *1632* and *1634: The Galileo Affair*

"This book has everything: time travel, the British royalty, things that go boom, and unrelenting action. Read the opening at your own risk: you won't be doing anything else until you finish it."

—SEAN WILLIAMS, coauthor of *Heirs of Earth* and *Star Wars: Force Heretic: Reunion*

"Smart munitions meet smart writing in a military-grade action-adventure that's impossible to stop reading."

—GARTH NIX, author of *Sabriel* and *The Ragwitch*

BY JOHN BIRMINGHAM

THE AXIS OF TIME

Weapons of Choice

Designated Targets

*Final Impact**

*forthcoming

DESIGNATED TARGETS

DESIGNATED TARGETS

★ A NOVEL OF THE AXIS OF TIME ★

JOHN BIRMINGHAM

BALLANTINE BOOKS / NEW YORK

A Del Rey® Trade Paperback Original

Copyright © 2005 by John Birmingham

All rights reserved.

Published in the United States by Del Rey Books, an imprint of The Random House Publishing Group, a division of Random House, Inc., New York.

DEL REY is a registered trademark and the Del Rey colophon is a trademark of Random House, Inc.

LIBRARY OF CONGRESS CATALOGING-IN-PUBLICATION DATA
Birmingham, John
Designated targets / John Birmingham.
p.   cm.—(The axis of time ; bk. 2)
ISBN 0-345-45714-5 (trade pbk.)
1. World War, 1939–1945—Fiction.   2. Time travel—Fiction.   I. Title.
PR9619.3.B5136D47 2005
813'.6—dc22   2005049371

Printed in the United States of America

www.delreybooks.com

4 6 8 9 7 5 3

FOR MY PARENTS,
the first storytellers

ACKNOWLEDGMENTS

A big tip of the propeller hat is owed to the usual suspects. Cate Paterson and Brianne Tunnicliffe in Sydney. Steve Saffel and Keith Clayton in New York. I'm abashed by and indebted to Steve Stirling and Eric Flint, who took precious time away from their own, much superior work to give me advice on mine. If I were a better listener, this would be a better book. A special thanks goes to the lads in soc.history.what-if who responded with scarifying enthusiasm to my off-topic requests. You know who you are.

Finally, love and thanks go to Jane, Anna, and Thomas for putting up with me while I'm on deadline. It's not a good look. I owe them a treat.

DRAMATIS PERSONAE

MULTINATIONAL FORCE COMMANDERS

Francois, Major Margie. USMC. Combat Surgeon and Chief Medical Officer, Multinational Force. (USS *Kandahar*)

Halabi, Captain Karen. RN. Commander Deputy Commander Multinational Force. Commander HMS *Trident*.

Jones, Colonel J. L. USMC. Commander 82nd Marine Expeditionary Unit. (USS *Kandahar*)

Judge, Captain Mike. USN. Commander USS *Hillary Clinton*.

Kolhammer, Admiral Phillip. USN. Task Force Commander. OIC Special Administrative Zone. (California)

Willet, Captain Jane. RAN. Commander HMAS *Havoc*.

Windsor, His Royal Highness Major Harry. Task Force Commander British SAS contingent. OIC Special Air Service Regiment. (Training cadre)

MULTINATIONAL FORCE PERSONNEL

Ivanov, Major Pavel. Russian Federation Spetsnaz.

Nguyen, Lieutenant Rachel. RAN. South West Pacific Area HQ Intelligence Liaison.

Rogas, Chief Petty Officer Vincente. US Navy SEALs.

Müller, Captain Jurgen. European Defence Force. Reassigned Special Operations Executive.

MISC

Duffy, Julia. *New York Times* Feature Writer. Embedded 82nd MEU.
Natoli, Rosanna. *CNN* Researcher/Producer. Embedded 82nd MEU.

1942 ALLIED COMMANDERS

Churchill, Winston. Prime Minister, Great Britain.
Curtin, John. Prime Minster, Commonwealth of Australia.
Eisenhower, Brigadier General Dwight D. US Army. Head of War Plans
Division. Appointed Commander of US Forces, European Theatre of
Operations, June 1942.
Hoover, J. Edgar. Director Federal Bureau of Investigation.
King, Admiral Ernest J.USN. Commander in Chief of the US Fleet and
Chief of Naval Operations.
MacArthur, General Douglas. US Army. Commander Allied Forces, South
West Pacific Area. Headquartered Brisbane, Australia.
Marshall, General George C. US Army. Chairman of the Joints Chiefs of
Staff.
Nimitz, Admiral Chester. USN Commander in Chief US Pacific Fleet.
Roosevelt, President, Franklin D. 32nd President of the United States of
America.
Stephenson, William. Personal Envoy of PM Churchill, Head of British Se-
curity Coordination Western Hemisphere.

1942 ALLIED PERSONNEL

Barnes, Brigadier Michael. Commander 2nd Cavalry Regiment, (Australian
Army).
Black, Commander Daniel. USN. Senior Military Liaison, Special Admin-
istrative Zone. (California)
Curtis, Lieutenant (j.g.) Wally. USN. Military Liaison, Pacific Fleet.
Kennedy, Lieutenant John F. Commander PT 101.
Mohr, Chief Petty Officer Eddie. Transferred to Auxiliary Force Develop-
ment, Special Administrative Zone. (California.)
Molloy, Able Seaman Michael "Moose." PT 101.

MISC.

Cherry, Detective Sergeant Lou. Honolulu PD Homicide.
Davidson, Fmr. Able Seaman James "Slim Jim." CEO Slim Jim Enterprises.

O'Brien, Maria. USMC Captain. (Legal Services) (retd.) Chief Counsel
Slim Jim Enterprises.

SOVIET COMMAND

Josef Vissarionovich Stalin, Secretary General of the Communist Party and
Premier of the Soviet Union.
Laventry Beria, NKVD Chief and head of Special Research Programs.

AXIS HIGH COMMAND

JAPAN

Yamamoto, Admiral Isoroku. IJN. Commander in Chief Combined Fleet.
(HIJMS *Yamamoto*)

GERMANY

Göbbels, *Reichsminister* Josef. German Propaganda Minister.
Himmler, *Reichsführer* Heinrich. SS Chief.
Hitler, *Reichschancellor* Adolf.

AXIS PERSONNEL

Brasch, Colonel Paul. Senior Consulting Engineer. Ministry of Armaments.
Hidaka, Commander Jisaku. IJN. Chief Aide, Admiral Yamamoto.
Philby, Harold "Kim." Fmr SIS officer. NKVD temporary liaison to Skor-
zeny.
Skorzeny, Colonel Otto. Waffen SS. Personal bodyguard to Adolf Hitler.
Commander of Special Operation Section.

DESIGNATED TARGETS

1

TUPELO, MISSISSIPPI

Lordy, thought the boy. *It's a miracle for sure.*

He was seven and a half years old—the man of the house, really, what with his daddy being away in Como, and he had never seen anything like the fearful wonder of the newly chiseled monument.

HERE LIES JESSE GARON PRESLEY.
DEEPLY BELOVED OF HIS MOTHER GLADYS, FATHER VERNON,
AND BROTHER ELVIS.
A SOUL SO PURE, THE GOOD LORD COULD NOT BEAR
TO BE APART FROM HIM.
BORN JAN. 8, 1935,
TAKEN UNTO GOD JAN. 8, 1935.

Despite the unseasonable heat of the evening, gooseflesh ran up his thin arms as he read the words again. Whippoorwills and crickets trilled their amazement in the sweet, warm air. With a pounding heart, the boy inched forward and muttered hoarsely, "Jesse, are you here?"

The stone was cut from blindingly white marble that fairly glowed in the setting sun. The inscription had been inlaid with real gold—he was almost certain of that. He ran his fingers over the words and the cold, hard stone, as if afraid to discover that they weren't real.

It must have cost a king's ransom . . .

An enormous bunch of store-bought flowers had been placed upon a patch of freshly broken earth that still lay at the foot of the monument. Hundreds of tiny beads of water covered the petals and caught the last golden rays of daylight.

He dropped down on his knees as if he were in church and stared at the impossible vision for many minutes, heedless of the dirt he was getting on his old dungarees. He remained virtually motionless until one hand reached out and his fingers again brushed the surface of the headstone.

"Oh, my," he whispered.

Then Elvis Aaron Presley leapt to his feet and ran so fast that he raised a trail of dust as he sprinted down the gravel lane, away from the pauper's section of the Priceville Cemetery, a-hollerin' for his mama.

"He'll probably get his ass whupped, the poor little bastard." Slim Jim Davidson smiled as he said it, peering over the sunglasses he had perched on his nose.

"Why?" asked the woman who was sitting next to him in the rear seat of the gaudy red Cadillac. You didn't see babies like this every day. Slim Jim had seen to the detailing himself. The paint job, the bison leather seats, everything.

"For telling lies," he said. "Headstones don't just appear like that, you know. They're gonna think he made it up, and when he won't take it back, there'll be hell to pay."

The woman seemed to give the statement more thought than it was really due. "I suppose so," she said after a few seconds.

Slim Jim could tell she didn't approve. They were all the same, these people. They'd bomb an entire city into rubble without batting an eye, but they looked at you like you were some sort of hoodlum if you even suggested raising your hand against a snot-nosed kid. Or a smart-mouth dame, for that matter.

And this O'Brien, she was a helluva smart-mouth dame.

She'd kept her trap shut, though, while they'd been watching the Presley kid. In fact, she seemed to be fascinated by him. They'd been waiting in the Caddy up on Old Saltillo Road for nearly an hour before he showed. Long enough for Slim Jim to wonder if they were pissing their time up against a wall. But the kid did show, just as his cousin said he would. And he'd heard O'Brien's stifled gasp when the small figure first appeared, walking out of a stand of trees about two hundred yards away.

"It's him, all right," she said. "Damned if it's not."

Slim Jim had grabbed the contract papers and made to get out of the car right then and there. He'd had enough of sitting still. His butt had fallen asleep, and he was downright bored.

But O'Brien shook her head. "Not here."

He'd bristled at that. His temper had frayed during the long wait. Long enough even to make him feel some sympathy for the cops who'd had to stake him out once or twice. But he took her "advice" because it was always worth taking.

Her advice had cost him a goddamn packet, too, over the course of their relationship. But along the way, Slim Jim Davidson had learned that you had to spend money to make it. Problem was that up until recently, he didn't have no money to spend. None of his own, anyway. And spending other people's money had sent him to the road gangs.

Mississippi was a powerful reminder of those days. The air tasted the same as it had in Alabama, thick and sweet and tending toward rotten. The faces they'd driven past in town had brought back some unpleasant memories, too. Hard, lean faces with deep lines and dark pools for eyes. The sort of uncompromising faces a man might expect to see on Judgment Day. They'd sure looked that way to Slim Jim when they trooped in from the jury room.

Well, that felt like a thousand years ago. Now he could buy and sell that fucking jury. And the judge. And his crooked jailers. And the whole god-damned state of Alabama, if he felt like it.

Well, maybe not the whole state. But he was getting there. This Caddy was bigger and more comfortable than some of the flophouses he'd crashed in during the Depression. He had an apartment in an honest-to-goddamned brownstone overlooking Central Park back in New York, and a house designed by some faggot architect overlooking the beach at Santa Monica, out in L.A. He had stocks and bonds and a big wad of folding money he liked to carry in his new buffalo-hide wallet—just so's he could pull it out and snap the crisp new bills between his fingers when he needed to remind himself that he wasn't dreaming.

Hell, he was so rich now that when those C-notes lost their snap, he could give them away and get some new ones.

Not that he ever did, of course. *Ms.* O'Brien would kill him. And she was more than capable of it. No doubt about that.

She'd insisted that he pick up the Santa Monica house as a long-term investment, too, even though he thought it was kind of down-market, given his newly acquired status.

"You can stay at the Ambassador if you don't like rubbing shoulders with your old cell mates down on the piers," she'd said. "Believe me, Santa Monica will come back, and you need to diversify your asset base. Waterfront property is always a sure bet."

Yes, indeed, and Slim Jim was fond of sure bets. After all, they'd made him richer than God. They'd also delivered him a conga line of horny babes, a small army of his own hired muscle, and the slightly scary Ms. O'Brien.

Thinking about the slightly scary Ms. O'Brien sitting next to him there in the Caddy, however, led naturally to thinking about the slightly scary Ms. O'Brien sliding her body over his in a king-size hotel bed. But that was a dangerous line of thought, he knew. Because Ms. O'Brien wasn't inclined to get anywhere near a bed with Slim Jim Davidson, naked or not.

He'd tried feeling her up once, and she'd nearly broken his arm for it. She'd snapped an excruciating wristlock on him without even breaking a sweat, no doubt a party trick she'd picked up back when she was a captain in the Eighty-second MEU. And she'd kept him locked up, gasping for breath and nearly fainting away, while she explained to him the facts of life:

One, she was his employee, not his girlfriend.

Two, she would be his employee only for as long as she needed to be, and she would *never* be his girlfriend.

Three, she could kick his scrawny ass black and blue without bothering to lace up her boots.

And four, she . . .

"Mr. Davidson?"

Slim Jim jumped, feeling guilty and worried that she might have figured out what he was thinking. But no, luckily she was just dragging him out of his slightly bored daze.

"Elvis has left the cemetery," she announced. She said it in a singsong way, and it seemed to amuse her more than it should have. But Slim Jim had given up trying to figure her out.

"Let's go over it one last time, just to be sure," she said, pulling out a flexipad.

"Oh, please," he begged. "Let's not."

O'Brien ignored him, and his shades suddenly flickered into life. Windows opened up on the lenses and seemed to float in the air in front of him. Some carried photographs of the boy they'd just seen. Others were full of words. Small words in large type. She'd learned not to burden him with too much text.

Bitch thinks she's so goddamned smart . . .

Slim Jim sighed, and read through the briefing notes again. Some of his reluctance was for show, though. He never really got tired of the amazing gadgets these guys had brought with them.

"Elvis Aaron Presley, age eight and a half. Mother's name, Gladys. Father's name, Vernon," he recited. "Dead brother, Jesse. Attends school at East Tupelo Consolidated. Father jailed for fraud. Asshole tried to ink a four-dollar check into forty . . ."

O'Brien shot him a warning look, but he hid behind the shades, pretending he couldn't see her.

"Daddy's out now, away in Como, Mississippi, building a POW camp for the government. Mama takes in sewing when she can get it. Local yokels call 'em white trash behind their backs . . ."

Slim Jim laughed out loud, glancing out across the ragged fields of corn and soybean that stretched between the cemetery and the edge of the town. "Ha! There's a fucking pot calling a kettle black if I ever—"

"The *notes*, Mr. Davidson. Just review the notes," said O'Brien.

Slim Jim returned to the readout for what felt like the hundredth time. He'd heard about some big-time grifters who worked like this. Getting so far inside the heads of their marks that they knew what was going on in there before the chumps realized it themselves. He could sort of see the point.

O'Brien had helped him close some amazing deals these last few months. But *damn*, it was hard work. Nevertheless, he plowed on, reciting most of the notes from memory even though the words still hung there in front of him.

"Gladys drinks in private. She finds her comfort in the church. Her first love was dance, her second music. But she's kind of a fat bitch now so . . . Sorry! *Sorry* . . . She gets around in bare feet and old socks so her kid can have shoes. Elvis, he's aware of his family's low standing. It eats him up and he wants to rescue them. It always tickles him when his mama says she's proud of him."

In spite of himself, Slim Jim couldn't help but warm to the little prick. They'd listened to his music all the way down here, and you had to admit, the kid had a gift. *Or would have.*

Then again, maybe he wouldn't. If Slim Jim bought him a ticket out of Tupelo now, gave him enough money for a comfortable life, maybe the kid would never sing a song worth a tinker's crap. Not that the thought really bothered him. Those songs were recorded by an Elvis from another time. No, this was all about who was gonna get paid for them.

Not some asshole called Colonel Tom Parker, you could bet on that.

Nope. "Slim Jim Enterprises" would be latching itself on to this particular money tit. And if the kid never became an actual recording star, just because he grew up rich instead of poor, well, who gave a damn? Slim Jim had grown up in a town a lot like this, with a daddy a lot like Vernon. And if some asshole had turned up on their doorstep, offering to buy them out of poverty, Daddy would have been trampled to death by the entire Davidson clan rushing to sign on the dotted line. And to hell with the consequences.

Slim Jim was only vaguely aware of the deepening dusk as he sat in the Caddy, chanting his way through O'Brien's notes like some kind of mad priest. *Yeah, Tupelo is a lot like home.* Besides the two main roads in the center of town, every street was a strip of dirt or gravel. Clouds of dust would rise from them in summer. They'd turn into rivers of mud during the spring rains. Most folks would have worked the Roosevelt program during the Depression, cutting brush, fixing roads. Most, like Gladys Presley, wouldn't ask for handouts, but would accept what was offered. The men would all be factory workers and sharecroppers.

Now most of them would be in the army or working in the war industries. Poor but honest, they'd think of themselves. *Screwed and stupid* was how Slim Jim would have put it.

A guy like Vernon Presley he could understand. He knew the type. He'd have had good intentions, but not enough character to see them through. Slim Jim wished they could deal with Vernon rather than Gladys. It was a laydown that they could sneak a signature out of old Vern, just for a crate of beer and a hundred bucks.

But O'Brien had been a real ballbreaker on that particular subject, even more so than usual. There'd be no grifting the Presley family. They'd get the industry standard percentage, and Slim Jim would take the industry standard cut. It was a shitload of money to be tossing away to a bunch of dumbass crackers, at least to his way of thinking. But she'd given him that stone face of hers again, and he'd buckled. She was a scary bitch—and bottom line, he was rich because of it.

"And then Vernon told Elvis he was responsible for his mama's ill health because of the bad birth . . . ," he continued, only half his mind on the task.

"No," O'Brien said. "We don't know for sure that that's happened yet, so it's better not to bring it up. But it's supposed to happen around about now, so just keep it in mind."

"Right." He nodded. "So are we gonna fuck this puppy or what?"

His lawyer rolled her eyes, but she leaned forward to tap on the glass partition that separated them from the driver.

"Okay," she said, raising her voice. "Let's roll."

It was a short drive from Priceville Cemetery to East Tupelo, a pissant little rats' nest of meandering unpaved streets running down off the Old Saltillo Road. A couple of creeks, two sets of railroad tracks, some open fields, and a whole world of dreams separated the hamlet's beaten-down inhabitants from the good people of Tupelo proper. Slim Jim wasn't bothered none driving into such a place.

Nor, he noticed, was Ms. O'Brien. He figured it was just another one of those things about your dames from the future. Not much seemed to rattle them, unless you tried to cop a feel without being invited.

"That's it," she announced.

She indicated a small wooden frame house, a "shotgun shack," they called them. This one stood about a hundred yards up the street they'd just entered. Dusk was full upon them now, and the car's headlights lanced through the gloom and the dust and pollen that always seemed to hang in the air, even at this time of year.

"You sure you don't want to do the talking?" he asked, suddenly nervous for no good reason. That wasn't like him at all.

"You'll be fine," O'Brien assured him. "It's just business. Be sure and treat them with respect."

"But . . ."

"No *buts*. You'll nail it. I've never known such a rolled gold bullshit artist. If you'd been born any luckier, you could have been a senator or a televangelist."

Slim Jim wasn't sure what she meant by that, but she didn't seem to mean it as a compliment.

His driver pulled over into the gutter. As soon as he stepped out, the smell took him by the throat. Sour sweat. Outdoor toilets. Woodsmoke. Corn bread, grits, and boiled spuds. The smell of his childhood.

He could tell, without needing to check, that dozens of pairs of eyes had settled on the back of his newly cut, lightweight suit. Some of the bolder folks would have wandered right out onto their verandas—an awful fancy name for a thin porch made of raw pine boards, roofed in by scraps of tin, and supported at each corner by sawed-off bits of two-by-four. Others would be hiding in their front rooms, twitching aside sun-faded curtains, if they had any, peering out suspiciously at the Presleys' unexplained visitors.

And if they thought *he* was something, he wondered what sort of ripple went up and down when Ms. O'Brien emerged from the car. East Tupelo wasn't used to women like that, not yet. Hell, neither was the rest of America. That skirt of hers would surely send tongues wagging, showing off so much leg above the knee as it did.

But it was time to get into character, so he pasted a harmless, well-meaning expression on his dial. A neutral grin that said to the world he was hoping he'd found the right address.

Slim Jim took in the details of the kid's house in one quick glance. Again, he didn't need to stare. It was all old news to him. There'd be only two rooms running off one corridor. You could shoot a gun clean through without hitting anything, hence the name. The kid would probably sleep where Slim Jim himself had for years, on an old sofa in the front room—which did double duty as a kitchen, and a parlor when guests came a-calling. Every stick of furniture would be someone else's cast-offs, but it'd most likely be clean. Gladys would make sure of that.

The water would be pumped by hand, from a well out in the backyard. There'd be bare boards on the floor and walls. No little comforts or luxuries. Not a blade of grass grew in the brown dirt that substituted for a front yard. Even in the gloom, he recognized the scratch marks of a homemade dogwood broom in the hard-packed earth, and the telltale prints of chicken feet. He bit down on a sigh. It was going to be like a goddamned oven in there.

He really missed his brownstone.

2

LOS ANGELES, CALIFORNIA

He'd expected some changes. Even so, after an hour or more in Los Angeles, Chief Petty Officer Eddie Mohr felt like his head had been turned inside out. Sort of like an old sock.

He felt awkward as hell in his new "twenty-first" uniform. Figured people woulda been staring and pointing at him like he was some sort of carnival freak as he walked through the train station. But it was Mohr himself who had to resist the urge to stop and gawk, while nobody else gave him as much as a second glance. Most didn't even notice him the first time around.

He'd stood on the concourse at Union Station for a long time, ever since he'd painfully uncurled himself from one of the hard, cheap seats on the *Super Chief.* The station was roaring with foot traffic. Sailors from what they were calling the Old Navy lounged around in their best whites, clearly in no rush to get away to the South Pacific. Hundreds of civilians swarmed over the bright mosaic floor, too, their shoes clicking and scuffing on the tiles. Many of them were of fighting age, but none seemed to be bothered that somebody might front them about why they hadn't signed up yet. Or been drafted.

Mohr wandered through, hauling the dead weight of his duffel bag as if it were a side of beef. Occasionally he'd spot a uniform like his own, the coloring slightly different from the local rig, the cut a little more stylish. At least that's how some fairy from New York called it.

His old man had read that article from the *Post* out loud, howling with laughter, tears streaming down his face. *"Lookit this, Ethel,"* he'd yelled out to the kitchen. *"Lughead here's standin' at d' cuttin' edge a fashion."*

Maybe that's why Mohr was rolling and twitching his shoulders so much inside the new uniform. To steady his balance. Meanwhile, he did his best to avoid catching the eye of anybody else who looked to be headed out to the

Zone, to the raw, sprawling settlements and industrial "parks," as they called them. Not a one of them looked much like a fucking park to Eddie Mohr, though. Just a bunch of big sheds and warehouses with a few scraggly fucking eucalyptus trees for shade. Some of them, they didn't even seem to have workers inside. It was like the machines ran themselves.

He scowled then, and remembered Midway. Machines running themselves—that's what had caused the whole class-A fuckup to begin with. That's why he never went out near the factories if he could avoid it.

He'd seen that movie, the one with the muscle man in it. A kraut, and he'd been the goddamned governor of California, if you could believe it! In the movie, the machines had tried to take over the world. He felt like it was about two minutes from happening whenever he set foot in some of them factories out in the Valley.

Somebody bumped into him then, knocking the duffel bag off his shoulders. "Sorry, mac," the guy called out as he hurried away, not even bothering to turn around.

Some long-haired gimp. Mohr snorted in disgust. Probably wearing an earring, too.

He found himself standing in front of the station's Harvey House restaurant. It was full of officers and their dates. Freshly minted war brides some of them, to judge by the painfully happy smiles and that just-been-fucked glow about the cheeks. And a fair swag of gold diggers, too, if his suspicions played true. They were probably dizzy with the prospect of the ten-grand GI's insurance they'd pocket if their "dearly beloved" got himself shot to pieces along with old Dugout Doug.

Mohr's whole body ached with fatigue, and his fractured skull—or at least the cracks they'd fixed up with some sort of plastic cement—throbbed in a dull, far-off kind of way.

His train had left Chicago early, and he'd rested only fitfully on the long haul across the continent. He thought about grabbing a sit-down sandwich or a burger at Harvey's. He could see they ran a desegregated joint—a lot of places in California seemed to these days. There were a couple of uniformed Negroes and some Chinese-looking fellas eating in there. Even had some white folk with them. But he thought he could still detect a sort of no-go area around them. The place was packed, but a few empty chairs seemed to be scattered around their table. Still, they were being served, and left in peace.

That wouldn't have happened six months ago.

He propped himself on the arm of a big leather chair for a moment. If he weren't so tired, he would have marveled at the thing. It was a much flashier piece of furniture than had ever graced the Mohr family home, and here it was stuck in a goddamn train station. Somebody had left behind a crumpled copy of the *L.A. Times*, and he flicked through it idly while he waited for the bus out to Fifty-one.

Bad move.

Right there on the second fucking page was a picture of that fucking idiot Slim Jim Davidson, grinning up a storm!

He had some poor kid tucked under one arm and some flint-eyed dame who just had to be twenty-first lurking at his shoulder. In his other hand, he was waving around a giant cardboard check written out for twenty thousand dollars.

Mohr felt a wave of acid rise in his gut, and he hadn't even gone for the burger yet. He tried not to read the story, but he couldn't help himself. Davidson had bought himself another singer, name a' Presley, and a whole bunch of this kid's tunes were gonna be released over the next six months. Mohr snorted when he read that a "significant" percentage of the profits was being channeled straight into a war-bond drive. It'd be one tenth of 1 percent of fuck all compared with the bribes that little weasel had paid out to get himself taken off active duty and assigned to "special services" with the USO. Mohr bitterly regretted not hammering Davidson flat when he'd had the chance back on their ship.

On the *Astoria*, he'd had the little crook under his thumb; now he was just like everyone else—reduced to following the adventures of Slim Jim in the papers and the newsreels. Mostly that involved watching him getting richer and richer. But Davidson was a sneaky little shit, and it seemed every time he fell ass-backwards into a pile of someone else's money, he made sure to donate a big whack of it to some war widow or an orphaned kid, or some dogface with his dick shot off. So now everybody *loved* Slim Jim Davidson. Walter fucking Winchell wouldn't shut up about the jerk.

Mohr felt a twinge of sympathy for the Presley kid, though. He looked like some poor dumb rube who'd gone to bed on a dirt floor and woken up in the Ritz. He wanted to warn the boy not to hold on to that check too tightly, or one day he'd find Davidson had chewed his arm down to a bloody stump trying to get the thing back.

He angrily reefed the page over and tried to lose himself in some other, less aggravating news. He half read some piece about a delegation from the NAACP and the Congress of Industrial Organizations visiting Kolhammer. His old man would have been interested in that. He still kept up with the union news. Next, Mohr skimmed a report out of London about all the invasion fears, and he was actually getting interested in a bit on some guy called McCarthy who would've been some kind of heavy-hitting senator one day, 'cept that he got himself killed by the Japs down in Australia.

Then he heard the police whistle.

The roar of the crowd died away to a buzz, and he could suddenly hear music coming from somewhere nearby. A twenty-first number, for sure—a duet about this dame called Candy. It sounded like it was being sung by some drunk on laudanum and a Texas bar whore.

Then everyone turned, the way a crowd will. Mohr turned with them and heard the whistle again. He got a quick flash of a dark-skinned figure in a uniform like his—

Ah, shit.

—being tackled by two guys who looked like LAPD, until he moved a little closer to discover they worked for the Union Pacific line. They were older than your average beat cop. And fatter. But by God, they could swing a nightstick just as quickly.

Mohr cursed under his breath at the sound of polished hickory smacking into flesh. He'd once stood on a picket line with his old man when it had been broken up by private muscle using ax handles and brass knucks. The sound of the nightsticks took him back there, and he started to trot. Nobody else within thirty yards of the assault was moving. A few women gasped and turned their faces away—they wouldn't have been from the Task Force, then. A few of the men looked on meekly. Some green kids in army uniforms, who'd been so full of themselves just a minute earlier, looked queasy now. A couple of sailors snickered and pointed.

Mohr glared at them as he picked up speed.

"What the fuck is going on here?" he roared in his fiercest gun-deck voice.

The guy they were hitting, a young kid, a greaser of some sort by the look of him, actually flinched as much under the lash of the chief's voice as he had under the rain of blows. He was a Mexican, in what had been a new Auxilliary Forces uniform, until it got all torn up and bloodied.

"None of *your* business, salty," snarled one of the railroad cops. He had his billy club raised for another blow, and he suddenly seemed to become aware of it hanging up there. Mohr could tell that for a split second he thought about whipping it down one last time, but a cold, fixed stare stayed his hand. The man lowered the weapon uncertainly.

A spell was broken. The tableau on the station concourse began to move again as a furious buzz of conversation started up and spiraled out and away from the confrontation. The kid, a newly minted private, still lay where he'd been taken down. Violent shudders ran through his body as he struggled to choke off sobs and whimpers that wanted to turn into full-blown howling. Mohr willed the kid to keep it together as he bent down under the hostile eyes of the UP cops and gripped him by the arm.

"Suck it up, kid," he whispered fiercely. "Get on your feet, and cut out the sniveling."

"What do you think you're doing? He's coming with us."

Mohr turned to confront the guy. His partner hadn't spoken, and to judge by how he was shrinking away, Mohr didn't think he would now. "What makes you think he's going anywhere with you?"

"He's a thief," came the retort. "We got a report that he stole a pair of sunglasses."

The tendons all along Mohr's jawline stood out as he ground his teeth together. "You—got—a *report*?"

He freighted the question with about as much contempt as it could carry, which was a fair fucking load. When he'd transferred into the Auxiliaries, he'd expected to take a lot of shit from his old buddies—and he did. But it was basically good-natured. Some of the guys he'd served with on the *Astoria* were even thinking about making the jump, too. They'd seen the time travelers' weapons up close, and that was a powerful enticement to swap uniforms. In the end, though, most didn't. They couldn't come at learning a whole new set of rules in the Zone.

Mohr regarded the UP cops with cold scorn. It seemed they weren't so keen on learning the new rules either. It was becoming a real problem all over the city.

"Some asshole loses his fucking *sunglasses*," said Mohr, "sees this kid nearby, so you figure to beat him to death in front of a thousand people. Is that what you're telling me?"

Mohr was *this* close to hauling off and decking the big ape when a new voice shorted out the dark current that was building up between the two men.

"My brother Lino, he bought these glasses for me when I joined up."

It was the kid—PRIVATE DIAZ, Mohr now saw from the name tag on his shirt. Diaz smiled anxiously. His teeth were stained fire-engine red with his own blood, and when he spoke, it was in a stuttering, apologetic voice. The sunglasses, which had been damaged beyond repair, dangled from one shaking hand.

"H-he is working with m-my family out on the Williams ranch. He could t-tell you."

The railway cop dismissed the suggestion with a look that just verged on becoming a sneer. "You assholes couldn't lie straight in bed. Why would—?"

Whatever he intended to say was cut off when Eddie Mohr's hand shot out and grabbed a fistful of shirt. Several onlookers gasped and backed away. Mohr leaned in close and ground out his next words through gritted teeth. "Check out the kid's story, or pay him for the shades and let him go."

As the cop squirmed in Mohr's grip, his partner moved toward them, but a murderous look from the navy chief stopped him dead.

"I mean it," growled Mohr. "A pair of glasses like that, a farmhand'd work two weeks picking fruit just to buy 'em. You fucked up. You broke 'em. You bought 'em."

Diaz was about to speak again when someone else rode in over him.

"Chief. Do we have a problem here?"

Eddie Mohr didn't relax his grip, but he swung around fractionally to take in the speaker. When he saw the commander's uniform and the man wearing it, he did let go. But he didn't back down. "One of our men just took a licking from these goons, sir," he said, standing straight.

"Did he deserve it?" asked the officer. Two other figures Mohr recalled seeing at the table in the Harvey House restaurant came jogging over at a fast clip.

"No, sir. Not that I can see," answered Mohr, triggering a brief but muted demonstration of outrage by the two cops.

"Good enough, then," Commander Dan Black said with a tone that drew a line under the issue. "Marine, you need to clean yourself up. You carrying a spare uniform with you?"

Private José Diaz, who looked like he'd just witnessed a vision of the Blessed Virgin materialize in a pool of his own blood, nodded quickly. "Yes, sir. In a locker, sir."

"Chief, you want to make sure Private Diaz gets changed without further incident? If you're waiting for the trolley out to Fifty-one, perhaps he should wait with you. It's a big city. I wouldn't want him to get into any more trouble."

Black smiled at the crestfallen railroad officers, but his eyes remained cold.

"The marine appears to have suffered some damage to his personal effects. I'm sure Union Pacific will have a procedure for making good the losses. Is that right, Officer?"

"There's probably a form to fill in," the man agreed unhappily.

"There always is," said Black, "and I'll be following up personally, to make sure it gets done."

SPECIAL ADMINISTRATIVE ZONE, CALIFORNIA

The twenty-three-inch flatscreen looked incongruous sitting on the old wooden desk. Admiral Phillip Kolhammer wondered if he'd ever get used to the collision of past and present that now surrounded him. Mil-grade flexipads and crank-handle telephones. Quantum processors and slide rules. Holoporn and Norman Rockwell.

Probably not. He was a good deal older than most of the men and women in his command, more than twice the age of many of them, and he was way past going with the flow. When the pressure of his work abated for a short time at the end of each day, he still ached for his wife and his home and even, surprisingly, for his own war—as savage and stupid as it had been.

He had no real home to retire to at day's end. There was a bungalow he'd rented in Oak Knoll, but he rarely made it back there. Most nights he just bunked down "on campus," the hastily erected complex of low-rise plywood-and-particle-board offices just off the 405, where Panorama City would have been laid out in 1947. It was pleasant enough at this time of year, a mild autumn without anything like the smog of his era to suffocate the entire basin. But he found driving through the baking farmland and emerging gridiron of future suburbs to be depressing. It wasn't how an admiral should spend his days.

The big screen beeped discreetly as his PA ushered out the labor delegates. Multiple tones, telling him that the message-holding command had been removed and dozens of urgent new e-mails had arrived. One vidmail had come in, too. That was less common. They just didn't have the bandwidth to support it anymore.

He knew he'd *never* get used to that. In his day, California had been bathed in an invisible electronic mist, 24-7. Nobody even thought about bandwidth. It just wasn't an issue. Now, the ramshackle comm system they'd clipped together from scavenged Fleetnet equipment just about did a half-assed job of *nearly* meeting their needs in the greater Los Angeles area. But that was all. There was no such thing as full-spectrum access to the National Command Authority in Washington, and there wouldn't be until the cable came online, God only knew when. Maybe 1952.

He didn't get anything like the vidmail traffic he'd once had to wade through, which was a blessing in some ways. So the distinctive ping of a new message arriving caught his attention. He had a few minutes before the engineers from Douglas Aircraft turned up, and the small avatar of his liaison chief, the newly promoted Commander Black, floated in virtual 3-D right in front of him, demanding attention. Kolhammer clicked on the icon, and Black's image came to life. It was a recorded message, captured by the small lens in the officer's flexipad. There was enough depth of vision for the admiral to recognize Union Station in the background.

"I'm sorry to bother you, sir," said Black, "but we've had another incident downtown, between a Latino guy called Diaz and a couple of railway bulls at Union. I saw it myself. That's over two dozen so far this week for the wider city. We may want to pull our guys back to Fifty-one and talk to the locals again. I just got a feeling things are about to light up here. Thought you'd want to know ASAP.

"Over and out."

Kolhammer indulged himself in a smile at the arcane terminology. Dan Black tried hard, but he still seemed to have as much trouble dragging himself uptime as Kolhammer did shifting down. The smile faded, though, as he thought about the message. This was a hell of a business, messing with history the way they had. He knew there was no such thing as a grandfather paradox, but Einstein had spoken to him about something he called "deep echoes." At first it sounded a lot like the CIA's idea of blowback, the law of unintended consequences. But the Nobel winner had waved that away with a flourish of his pipe stem. It was more like history trying to right itself, having been knocked off its axis by the Transition, if that made sense. It was sociology, not physics.

Kolhammer sighed deeply. *None* of it made sense. Not the accident that had brought them here, or the seemingly infinite number of consequences that had since flowed on. None of it. It was barely four months since they'd arrived, and far from kicking fascist butt, the Multinational Force seemed to have fucked everything six ways from Sunday. There was a whole Japanese Army Group fighting in Australia now, three German Army Groups massing in France to attempt an invasion of England, and old Joe Stalin had proved himself to be a worse ally than the fucking Malays that Kolhammer had escaped back up in twenty-one. The old bastard had signed a cease-fire with Hitler and withdrawn from any hostilities against the Axis powers, suddenly freeing up the Nazi war machine to have another try at Great Britain. Christ only knew what was going through his mind. He may well have doomed the whole world.

Kolhammer shook his head clear. Other people were getting paid to worry about Stalin. He had more than enough to keep him up nights right here. He made a brief note to do something about Black's vidmail, and brushed the flatscreen with a fingertip, touching an icon that told Lieutenant Liao that he was ready for his next visitors, the design team from Douglas. Without having to be asked, the young officer sent him a set of schematics for the Skyraider ground-attack aircraft, which wouldn't have been built in this time line for another four years.

In the bottom left-hand corner of the screen, another window, surrounded by a flashing red border, outlined his schedule for the rest of the day. With a few keystrokes, he flick-passed about a dozen minor tasks, sending them to his production chief, Lieutenant Colonel Viviani. She could deal with the usual FAQs on steerable parachutes, body armor, MREs, penicillin, grenade launchers, claymores, and the rest. He was due to have a serious talk with General George Patton about the wonders of reactive armor and the need to make some drastic changes to the thirty-one-ton mobile crematorium known hereabouts as the Sherman tank.

A delegation from the navy was scheduled to politely ignore him while he told them to fix the torpedoes on their submarines. And another group from the army would soon arrive to rudely ignore him while he tried to convince them of the benefits of issuing a basic assault rifle.

He really wished Jones could have been around for that one, but the last time Kolhammer had checked, the commander of the Eighty-second was all tied up getting swarmed by a couple of Japanese divisions. And anyway, Colonel Jones wasn't the sort of officer who inspired confidence in your 1940s army types. He was a marine, and he was black. About the best that could be said of his visitors today was that they were equally prejudiced against both.

When Kolhammer wasn't trying to bang heads with people who refused to see the benefits of 20/21 hindsight, he had to juggle the competing demands of his new role as the sovereign lord of the San Fernando Valley. This meant dealing with everyone from disenfranchised citrus farmers to L.A.'s downtown power elite. Labor unions, land developers, minority rights activists, Hollywood moguls, industrial combines, and local home owners all hammered at his door without respite.

And at the very end of the day, he had a deniable back-channel meeting with William Stephenson, the Brits' top intelligence man in the U.S. Yet another fruitless attempt to deal with the ugliest pain in the butt he'd ever had to endure—a pain so severe, it surpassed even the nationally televised three-day cornholing he'd taken from Senators Springer and O'Reilly at the Armed Services Committee hearing regarding the Yemen fiasco. That occurred just after he'd first made admiral, and Kolhammer had been secretly grateful for the experience. He'd figured that nothing outside of close combat could ever be that bad again.

But of course, at that point in his life he'd never had to contend with a vengeful and paranoid cross-dressing closet-case like the legendary FBI director, J. Edgar Hoover.

The express trolley carrying Dan Black out to the Zone took its own sweet time covering the distance to the city's newest center of power. "Travel through eight decades in just one hour," or so it said in all the brochures. And people did, by the thousands. Tourists and rubberneckers passed through, wanting to catch a glimpse of the future—even though at the moment it was mostly just half-dug foundations and unfinished factories. Volunteers and recruits poured into the barracks of the Auxilliary Forces, which were growing like topsy around the core of the original Multinational Force.

Representatives from the "old" armed forces came to learn what they could as fast as possible, and not always with good grace. Engineers and scientists traveled there from all over the free world. Students bussed in from across the country. Factory workers and their families streamed in to fill the plants and production facilities, which were starting to sprawl across the Valley floor, chewing up thousands of acres of orange groves and ranchland. They filled the constellation of fast-growing, prefab suburbs known collectively as Andersonville so quickly that they threatened to outpace the contractors who were building the vast tracts of cheap housing. Indeed, most were still living in tents, like itinerant workers during the Depression.

Still, they came whether or not there was a bed or a job waiting for them. Riding the overcrowded trolley back to the Zone with about a hundred new arrivals, Commander Black wondered how Kolhammer could possibly hope to manage the explosive growth of his strange new world.

It reminded him a little of the California he'd known in the thirties, when waves of nomads from the dust bowl states had fetched up on the western shore of the continent. Glancing up from his flexipad, he could see that about half the passengers fit his recollection of those days. Families clung tightly together around rotting cardboard suitcases held together with twine. They swayed back and forth as the tracks carried them eastward, forcing them to retrace some of the last steps they had taken on their long trek to the coast.

To Black, they didn't look any less desperate than the thousands of Okies and chancers who'd poured into the state during the Depression, but for one small difference: hope burned a little brighter in their eyes than it had in his own when he'd lit out from Grantville. Even now, months after the world had adjusted to the fact of the Transition, the newswires still hummed with developments taking place in California, be they dry stories in the business pages about new manufacturing techniques, or yellow press hysteria about the "perversions" and "moral sickness" that were widely believed to be rampant within the confines of the San Fernando Valley. Some days it seemed to Black as if half the country wanted to drive the time travelers back into the sea from which they'd appeared, while the other half would sell everything they owned just to purchase a ticket west, and into the future.

Eddie Mohr and that Mexican kid Diaz were a good example of the latter. Black had no idea about why the chief petty officer had opted to transfer from the old navy to the AF, but he wasn't alone. The applications list ran to tens of thousands of men and women, all wanting to get out of their original units and into new Auxilliary Force outfits that, for the most part, existed only on paper—or data stick, he corrected himself. Sometimes, Dan knew, they were simply drawn by the lure of flying rocket planes—which hadn't yet been built—or sailing in missile boats—ditto.

Diaz, on the other hand, was like any number of hopefuls who had been seduced by a single promise. When they set foot on that relatively small patch of turf, which had been established by a narrow vote of Congress as the Special Administrative Zone (California), their skin color, gender, religion and—most controversially—what they did in their own bedrooms, ceased to be a factor in determining the path their lives would take. Once inside the Zone, they became subject to the laws of the United States of America, and the provisions of her Uniform Code of Military Justice, exactly as they existed on the morning of January 15, 2021, the day of the Transition.

It meant, for instance, that nobody could call Diaz a wetback or a greaser, at least not without incurring significant legal penalties. It also meant, however, that they couldn't drive without a seat belt, smoke in public spaces, or "cross a public roadway while immersed in a virtual reality." Not that much of that sort of thing went on just yet, anyway.

Black couldn't help but smile a little smugly at the warm self-regard the uptimers had for themselves and their many personal liberties. To him, they looked like people who'd been freed from heavy iron shackles—only to bind themselves just as tightly in a million threads of silk.

As the trolley line swung up through Cahuenga Pass, the old wooden 800-series interurban slowed noticeably. Pacific Electric had recommissioned dozens of the cars to handle the extra traffic flowing into and out of the Valley. They seemed to wheeze and groan beside the sleek red-and-cream 700-series "Hollywood" trams, which fairly zipped along the new track, laid at breakneck speed by the company that had a lucrative contract to provide mass transit services into the Zone.

Glancing out the window, Black noted that as quickly as the PE engineers could lay track, the road gangs still seemed to be outpacing them, adding another lane to the Hollywood Freeway. There had to be two thousand men out there working on the link that would stretch between the Valley and Santa Monica. Personally, he didn't have a view about it, but he'd seen fistfights break out among the uptimers when talk turned to the new freeways. It was a hell of a strange thing to start throwing punches over, if you asked him.

But nobody asked. And anyway, he'd learned to keep his opinions to himself. Julia had smacked that much sense into him, at least.

He was tempted to close the file he had up on the flexipad screen and sneak a peek at the home movie Jules had shot for him the last time they'd stayed together in New York. But he could tell that about half the carriage was still staring at the device in his hands, and they really didn't need to see his fiancée do her pole-dancing routine on a four-poster bed at the Plaza. So instead, he tried to concentrate on an epic dissertation from a Captain Chris Prather about building a better Sherman tank.

You'd have thought, being a navy man, he'd be safe from the likes of Prather. But General Patton was set to come calling today, and Black would have to shepherd him through the visit. He knew from recent experience that Patton would cut him no slack at all. Navy or not, he was Kolhammer's chief liaison to the old forces, and so he was about to become an instant expert on the care and feeding of Shermans.

Before he could help himself, he wondered idly what Julia was up to. He shut down the thought before it could go any further. She was somewhere on the east coast of Australia, covering MacArthur's defense of the Brisbane Line.

And apart from that, he really didn't want to know.

3

SOUTHWEST PACIFIC AREA, THE BRISBANE LINE

The last mortar round nearly fucked her video rig, but Julia got the little Sonycam back online by slamming the data stick into its port a couple of times. It wasn't a recommended fix, but it'd worked before. A small window in her battered Oakley combat goggles flickered into life again, the scene around her in the foxhole emerging from a blur of white noise.

Five men lay in the shell crater, protected from most of the Japanese fire by a huge granite outcrop halfway up the slope of Hill 178. Two of them were dead. Unable to directly target the rest, the Japanese had been dropping mortars all around, but the rock formation would provide just enough overhead cover to protect them for a few minutes—until the odds caught up with them.

One of the men had died when a nearby eucalyptus tree had been shattered by the blast of a small mountain gun; a foot-long splinter of wood had speared into his throat. The other guy, they had no idea. He was just dead, and he didn't have a hole in him.

Julia let her gaze slide down the slope, the Sonycam zooming in and out, taking in the wreckage of the shattered company. Less than two minutes earlier, over a hundred marines had been creeping up through the darkened scrub, toward the Japanese positions just below the crest of the hill. They had moved silently and with a speed that had surprised her, calling to mind a platoon of Gurkhas she'd once covered in Timor.

These marines were 'temps, fighting without body armor, remote sensors, or tac net. Three rifle platoons of older prewar volunteers. She'd interviewed many of them over the past few days, and now, in the space between two ragged breaths, their lives passed before her eyes. At least a third of them were dead, and near as many so badly torn apart by the Japanese claymores as made no difference.

She breathed out against a wave of overpressure as another packet of high-explosive bombs bracketed their hideout. Shrapnel rattled against the granite overhang, and the familiar scramble to check for wounds mechanically repeated itself, with each man who was able to instinctively patting himself down where a superheated shard of metal might have tugged at a sleeve or sliced so cleanly through living tissue that no pain or shock had yet registered.

Each quickly cupped his balls, she noted, in fear of the Wound.

Cocooned in her titanium-weave reactive matrix armor, her own responses deadened by ten years of this bullshit, Julia Duffy logged the screams of the dying for recall as she checked her machine pistol. No damage. The best part of a full clip jacked in, alternating penetrators and dumdums with a single tracer round three from the bottom to warn her when it was time to reload. She'd taped two clips together, for grease. A little trick some of the marines had quietly copied from her.

She sucked a mouthful of chilled Gatorade through a rubber tube that emerged from the padded collar of her coveralls. Something heavy fell into their midst, and Julia nearly jumped out of her skin.

It was a koala, its fur burned to black tar and weeping red skin. It keened pitiably as smoke curled from its charred body. The marines regarded it, and her, with horror as she drew her sidearm, a SIG Sauer P226, and put one round of Nytrilium fragmentable hollow point into the animal. It blew apart like an overripe tomato.

"Jesus Christ," someone croaked.

She looked at the men and essayed the faintest of shrugs as a furious eruption of small-arms fire broke over them.

In the distance on the slope above them, someone gave a shrill shout. *"Banzai!"*

"Ah, shit."

Julia glanced quickly in the direction of the sergeant who'd just cursed, measuring his likely response to what was coming. She didn't know him. The chaos and madness of the ambush had thrown them together. The man looked to be a good deal older than his two buddies. She couldn't guess at his actual age, though, through the gore and dirt, but his eyes looked like pools of dead water.

"You ever shoot anything besides a stuffed toy?" he spat at her with unexpected vehemence.

She didn't reply, but moved her selector to three-round bursts, unsafed the weapon, and drew her knife from its scabbard. Satisfied that she could get to it in a hurry, Julia sheathed the evil-looking blade.

The crescendo of Japanese rifle fire seemed to build in an infinite curve that merged with the *kiai*-scream of the charge and the cries of the shattered marine company on the hillside below. It was a vision drawn straight out of Hell. Small groups of men huddled around blasted tree stumps, the momentum of their advance completely spent. The false promise of safety offered by the scraps of cover was enough to fix them to the spot where they were soon to die. The dead lay everywhere, closely entwined, their bodies grotesquely violated by blast effect and speeding metal. One man still moved. He tried to drag the top half of his body back down the slope, clawing at the scorched earth to heave his torso away from the red smear of rag and bone that had been his legs. Julia's eyes took in the information, the shreds and tendrils and obscene tailings that dragged from the stump where he now ended—but no part of her connected it to the humanity of the dying creature. She wondered if she knew him.

"*Banzai!*"

"Fuck fuck fuck!" cursed the sergeant in the hole with her.

He was shaking like a frightened dog, and what little color had been in his face drained away now.

"Cover me!" he yelled as the leading edge of the charge appeared where they could see it from their shelter. He stripped four grenades from his belt, primed them, and pitched them into the descending horde. The grenades detonated in a condensed drum solo, ripping a thirty-meter hole in the Japanese line, which staggered almost to a halt.

Julia smacked one of the other two marines on the shoulder and gestured for him to turn around and cover their rear, before training her Sony-cam back on the sergeant just in time to see him scramble from the shell hole and rush at the enemy. He fired long bursts from a Thompson submachine gun, and plucking still more grenades from his webbing, he threw them into the ranks of Japanese, bizarrely reminding Julia of a rioting anarchist outside a Starbucks.

"Come on! Come *on*! Get moving!" he called back at the small knots of marines farther down the hill.

Julia was struck by the scene of this one, aged, slightly potbellied white man, surrounded by dozens of stunned Nipponese soldiers. It could have lasted only half a second, but it looked like something out of an old movie, as if the enemy were standing completely still, just waiting to be mowed down.

Then she realized her own weapon was up and pouring fire into them, as well. Shouts reached her from below, but of a different pitch and timbre to the sounds of terror that had come from there before. Rallying cries gathered more survivors than she thought possible as the light of more grenade explosions glinted off the steel of at least two dozen American bayonets, suddenly moving at speed again toward their targets.

Julia stayed hidden behind the rock so she could remain fixed on the vision of the sergeant, who had run out of ammunition and was swinging his machine gun like a club, staving in the heads of two enemy soldiers just before his left knee disintegrated in a dramatic spray of blood. He dropped with a strangled scream, and instantly two more Japanese were on him, their improbably long rifles raised like farm tools, the bayonets aimed at his body.

Julia zoomed in on the attackers. Her goggles read the microlight targeting dot square in the center of the nearest man's *T*, and she squeezed the trigger. The gun coughed three times in rapid fire, the recoil dragging the muzzle up slightly, as she knew it would. All three rounds hit. Two dum-dums and a penetrator.

Enormous gouts of lumpy red mist exploded from the soldier's back, spraying his comrade, who was also hit and was spinning around under the impact. The penetrator had passed clear though the rib cage, lungs, and spinal cord of the first man, beginning a supersonic tumble as it exited, before striking the left shoulder of the second. As the second attacker fell away, Julia flipped the selector back to single shot and drilled another round through his head. The body jumped in that heavy, lifeless way she knew all too well.

"Hey! *Hey!* Over here!"

The shouts came from close behind and were almost consumed in the roar of rifle fire. Duffy spun around, losing sight of her subject, some deeply buried instinct causing her to flip the selector to full auto. The other two marines were emptying their magazines into a platoon of Japanese that had appeared on the far side of the giant rock. The muzzle of her gun swung up and began to spit long tongues of fire. A dozen men shuddered under the impact of the augmented ammunition. A streak of yellow light shot out, the tracer, thumping into the chest of an officer who had been racing at them, brandishing a samurai sword. He effected a near-perfect backwards somersault, a little Catherine wheel of smoke tracing his path through the air.

Julia popped the dry clip, flipped it, and snapped home the loaded magazine. Her heart beat like a jackhammer. It seemed impossible to draw breath.

She fired at the swarm of their attackers again, her arms aching from the tension in her rigid muscles. The attack faltered and broke, and then dozens of marines slammed into the survivors. Their full-throated roars mingled with her own snarls and the *kiai* of the enemy. She distinctly heard the wet, ripping thud of a long knife spearing into human flesh, but could not place it anywhere in the mandala of blood and savagery that swirled all around her.

A cry, a scream with a familiar tone. A Jap was in the hole with them, scrambling on top of one of the marines. They wrestled like large, awkward children in the dirt. Raking and biting. The other American thrashed beside them, trying to reattach his mangled jaw. Julia was on top of the intruder without knowing how she'd crossed the distance, the knife already in her hand, her thick gloves gouging at the eyes of their would-be killer. Wrenching back his head to expose the throat. She stabbed the blade in to the hilt, and her world disappeared in a red wave as hot blood jetted out onto the goggles, leaving her just one small window in the upper right-hand quadrant of her visual field—the feed from the Sonycam, on which she watched herself slaughter the man who struggled in her hands like a wild animal.

Two thousand meters away, Colonel J. Lonesome Jones was crouched over in his command bunker, a cramped dugout with a roof of logs and rammed earth, the interior lit by glo-tubes and two dozen computer screens feeding tac data from the drones circling high above.

The battalion was stretched thin, covering an area of low hills and light scrub at the western base of a soaring tabletop plateau with sheer granite sides. Forward observers for the Crusader guns had been choppered up there along with a small security detail. Between the 'temp forces, the Eighty-second's ground combat element, and the Australian Second Cavalry Regiment to the northwest, Jones had bottled up the advance of three Japanese divisions on MacArthur's headquarters in Brisbane.

It had been a turkey shoot at first. Thousands of enemy soldiers had ridden down the thin two-lane "highway" on bicycles. They'd done something similar in Malaysia, if he recalled his history correctly. But in Malaysia they hadn't had to contend with a battery of computer-controlled howitzers firing time-on-target along their precise line of advance. After losing the better part of two regiments to the Crusaders, the Japanese had got off their bikes and begun to press forward on foot through the bush.

They had died in there, too. Surveillance drones picked them out of the background clutter, and a fearsome nighttime barrage by three hundred antique howitzers—American, New Zealand, and Australian guns under MacArthur's command—chewed them over. It was a vindication, said MacArthur, of his Brisbane Line strategy.

Jones's men and women were paying for it now, though. Thirty-seven KIA so far, some from hand-to-hand, but mostly through the inevitable fuckups. Two days ago, a squadron of Liberators had bombed them by mistake, wiping out the better part of a platoon at the edge of his base area. That had finally and irrevocably poisoned an already strained relationship with MacArthur's command. In response, Jones could only say his prayers to thank the good Lord that the 'temps—as they called the contemporary forces—missed most of what they aimed for, although he did tell Mac-Arthur, off the record, that in future any contemporary air assets that came within five thousand meters of the Eighty-second without clearance would be target-locked by his air defenses as a precautionary measure.

It hadn't been a pleasant conversation.

His intelligence chief, Major Annie Coulthard, broke into the memory. "Colonel, we have movement in the scrub to the northwest, eight and a half thousand meters out, across a one-thousand-meter front. I make it a regimental force, advancing on a direct line toward the New Zealanders on Hill One-forty-nine."

Jones could see the advance on a bank of flatscreens, some carrying real-time drone footage, others displaying schematic CGI with tags identifying the disposition of friendly and enemy forces.

"We got an envelopment under way?" asked Jones.

The S2 worked her touch screen, zooming out, dragging the focus box to either side of the red column that was advancing on the small hill held by the depleted Kiwi battalion. Jones could see the place in his mind, a shattered landscape of gray ash and blackened tree stumps where everybody was coated in a layer of dark charcoal that gave both the Maori and white pakeha soldiers the appearance of black ghosts crouching in their gun pits. They were going to have a hell of a time holding off a frontal assault by a Japanese regiment.

"Here we go, sir," said Coulthard. "Two clicks farther west, sir. Another column. Five-hundred-and-fifty-meter frontage, give or take. Battalion-sized force, moving on the double. Probably hoping to infiltrate through that blind valley along the creek bed."

"No prep fire?" asked Jones.

"None yet, sir. I think we took them all out. But it's a laydown that they'll set up those dinky little mortars as they get closer. Maybe even one of their mountain guns."

"Okay. Give 'em a heads-up over on One-forty-nine. The bush has already been burned out over there, so we can hit 'em about . . . here," he said, tapping the screen at a couple of natural choke points. "Set up some close air support just in case. And stay sharp, Major. These fuckers just will not stay ass-whupped. Could be they're shooting for a divisional envelopment. If they knew the limits of our coverage, they'd go for it."

"Yes, sir."

The tempo in the dugout picked up, background chatter rising, the snap of fingers on keyboards quickening as the effects of Jones's orders spread out through the command post. On a screen to Coulthard's left, he could watch a video feed of ground crew around his own attack helicopters as they suddenly picked up their pace. A virtually identical scene repeated itself over at 2 Cav, except that the gunships were Arruntas, not Comanches. There was no cam coverage of the aerodrome at Brisbane, but he knew that as soon as word passed down the landline, the same burst of frenetic activity would take place there, except this time the aircraft would be old Kittyhawks and sad little Wirraways, refitted for ground attack using napalm; just one more ghastly development that had arrived before its time.

Jones turned away from the small drama that was about to play itself around Hill 149 and took in the theater-wide view. It was nothing like he'd been used to back in 2021. Drone coverage was minimal, and there was no satellite feed, of course. No satellites. He had access to two AWACS birds, safely lurking a hundred miles or so in the rear. A couple of long-range SAS patrols and Marine Recon were buried deep behind the Japanese front line and reporting by microburst. But that was about it.

He felt naked, even though he knew, or at least he hoped, that his own view of the battle was godlike compared with that of his opponent, General Homma. He could never really be certain what technology had leaked across to the enemy, but they were running a full ECM suite, and Homma didn't seem to be packing much beyond a few flexipads used for communications. The encryption software seemed to be commercial and dated, at least by his standards; some Microsoft piece of crap that had been hacked to death about ten years beforehand, subjectively speaking. The pads had probably been used for games or VR porn on the *Sutanto*.

Still, even without the war-fighting technology that Jones had at his disposal, the Japanese were still here, weren't they? As Lenin once said, quantity has a quality all of its own, and three months ago they'd poured enormous quantities of men and material first into New Guinea and then into northern Australia, using MacArthur's island-hopping tactic before he had a chance to use it himself. Jones doubted that they could have been stopped were it not the rapid deployment of the Multinational Force's ground combat element to bolster MacArthur's defenses. As soon as the first reports sorted themselves out, it was obvious the enemy had finally decided on how to respond to the strategic shock of the Transition. They were going to try to swarm the Allies with sheer weight of numbers. The Germans looked to be preparing for something similar in Europe, having shifted the bulk of their forces west after agreeing to terms with Stalin.

Jones had more immediate problems to deal with, however. High strategy could wait. Six large flatscreens had been linked to provide a workable video wall that displayed theater-wide data, and it wasn't family-friendly viewing. There were seven divisions of Imperial Japanese troops infesting the eastern coast of the Australian continent, four of them pressing down on MacArthur's much-vaunted Brisbane Line. Jones didn't think they'd break through, and the *Havoc* had cut off any chance they had of reinforcement, but when the killing was done with, he didn't imagine he'd have much of a force left, either. Both his guys and 2 Cav were starting to run uncomfortably low on war stocks, and although they brought other strengths to the field, when you ran out of bullets, you weren't much of a soldier anymore.

Jones had been hoarding matériel for weeks now, farming out tactical and even strategic strikes to the 'temps, who'd been strengthened by a long list of quick fixes and catch-ups, such as those napalm tanks now slung beneath the local ground-attack aircraft. It was a two-way street, though. He'd just read a report of a marine company cut to ribbons by a string of claymores a few hours earlier. They'd have been completely wiped out if one of their sergeants hadn't rallied the survivors and charged right into the enemy force, which was racing downhill to finish them off.

The command bunker had gone very quiet for a minute when the microburst packet from that reporter's Sonycam had filled one of the screens on the video wall. Every marine in his Battalion HQ had at least four years' combat experience. Most of them had a lot more. There'd been some unkind talk about what a bunch of pussies and amateurs the 'temps had turned out to be, and Jones was certain he could feel some embarrassment in the room as the footage of that unholy, disorganized blood swarm filled the screen.

It was every bit as bad as anything he'd known in Damascus or Yemen. And these guys, with the exception of the embed from the *Times*, were fighting old school. No body armor, medevac, spinal inserts, or tacnet. It was like something out of the Dark Ages.

As he watched now, the thunder of massed artillery rolled over them; that was the barrage he had initiated just a minute earlier. Hundreds of old-fashioned high-explosive shells screamed through the air, their firing sequence controlled by an old laptop computer and designed to drop the entire load simultaneously. Hearing that rumble, he nodded in satisfaction. Air control had three dozen planes stacked up, ready to drop on the Japanese like hawks as soon as the artillery was done fucking with them. Hopefully, the New Zealanders wouldn't have much to do beyond picking off the survivors.

They'd given up investing much energy in trying to grab live prisoners. These guys had turned out to be worse than Hamas jihadi. It was like every one of them kept a grenade in his loincloth, just to avoid capture and to take a few gaijin with him.

The ground shuddered as hundreds of shells struck home.

Jones stifled a sigh as a bone-deep lassitude swept over him. It had nothing to do with sleeplessness and fatigue. Not a fatigue of the body, at any rate. He was tired in his soul. As the first flight of Kittyhawks dived away to unload their shiny new tanks of napalm on the unseen, screaming survivors of General Homma's shattered envelopment, Jones fought an urge to just walk away. For the briefest moment, the only thing keeping him at his post was a replay of Julia Duffy's video package on a small screen at an untended station.

Jones couldn't help but stare at the sergeant who had saved his entire company from annihilation. The commander of the Eighty-second Marine Expeditionary Unit was certain the man would earn a high honor for his actions. Perhaps the highest. The evidence of the video was irrefutable. He had turned that small battle from a disaster into a most unlikely victory. But that wasn't what caught Colonel Jones's attention. He knew that man from somewhere. He just couldn't place it.

A quick scan of the theater-wide threat boards informed him that nothing was about to go pear-shaped in the next few minutes. He pulled out his flexipad and called up the brief report from the action on that hill about two clicks away.

Nothing.

Oh, well. Time's a-wasting. He grabbed his G4 and helmet and called over Sergeant Major Harrison, his senior enlisted man. They were due to tour the perimeter, but the image of that 'temp sergeant, swinging his old Thompson machine gun like a baseball bat, just would not leave him alone. He'd lay money on the barrelhead that they'd met before. Christ knew where, though.

"Sir!" barked Harrison, who had been chewing the ass off a corporal from B company, no doubt for some minor sin. Aub Harrison was nearly as enthusiastic about ass-chewing as his battalion commander, which made the Eighty-second a very dangerous place to walk around with your ass hanging out for no good reason.

"Grab your shootin' irons, Aub," said Jones. "It's time for us to take a stroll."

He threw a glance back at the screen as they left. The sequence was replaying, and the marine was heaving a couple of grenades up the hill again, firing his machine gun from the hip with his other hand.

He looked angry, and Jones had that infuriating feeling that he was *this* close to remembering where they'd met. But then he was out the door and into the light of the day.

CANBERRA, AUSTRALIA

There would be a terrible drought in the 1980s. And another at the turn of the century. El Niño they called it, although why you'd name a drought was beyond understanding for the Australian prime minister.

"It's not the drought, sir," his adviser offered helpfully. "*El Niño* refers to the weather pattern which apparently causes our droughts."

Paul Robertson, the former banker who'd been recruited to the PM's staff, thought the old man looked very ill, as bad as he'd been when he'd recalled the Sixth and Seventh Divisions from the Middle East back in March. They knew now that he would die in July of 1945—or at least he would have in the normal run of events. A doctor from the Australian component of the Multinational Force had run all sorts of gizmos over the PM, and had even inserted some kind of pellet under the skin of his right elbow that was supposed to help him cope with the stress of his office. But to Robertson, John Curtin looked like he might not make it through the night. No matter what wonder drugs they gave him, he was being eaten alive by the war.

"I suppose the Japs will find this information useful when they take over the place," he muttered bleakly, dropping the briefing memo back onto his desk. "Although I'll be buggered how they expect to grow rice here."

"They won't be growing any rice here, Prime Minister. You know that," said Robertson. "They'll be beaten here. Driven back through the islands. And burned alive in their own cities. Probably a lot quicker than would have happened originally. We had that uranium dug up and shipped off to the Yanks double-quick. They're working twenty-five hours a day on this A-bomb of theirs. And they're not going to waste time running up blind alleys like they did—or would have—the first time. They have a room full of computers now. It could be less than a year before they test the first warhead."

The prime minister, a former journalist, sketched a thin, humorless smile. "Everybody is working overtime to build their own bombs, Paul. I don't imagine for a second that Hitler and Tojo haven't stripped all the computers off the ships they found. And I think the Japs are here partly because they covet our uranium—"

Robertson made to object, but the PM waved him away.

"Oh, I know, I know. They're going hell-for-leather to deny the Americans a launchpad for their counterattack in the Pacific. They can get uranium from the Russians now, anyway. Neither they nor the Germans can hope to compete with the Yanks in the end. They just don't have the industrial base needed to win a race to the bomb—" Curtin rubbed at his red eyes with a shaky hand. "—but they are here, on our soil, killing our people."

"We're beating them."

"No. We're killing them. But we're not beating them yet. They're not in retreat from MacArthur's bloody Brisbane Line. They're dying on it. But there's a hell of a lot of people trapped behind that line, and I'll wager pennies to pounds that they're dying a lot harder than Homma's men. It's not even propaganda that the Japs treat their captives worse than animals. It's history now."

Robertson couldn't argue with him on that. It had proved impossible to suppress the knowledge that had come through the Transition, and after a couple of futile attempts by the Commonwealth censors, they hadn't bothered trying any longer. For once they hadn't had to invent stories of the bestial nature of their enemies. The Nazis and Imperial Japan already stood condemned by history, and even by the testimony of their own descendants.

He had seen newsreels of some of the English-speaking German and Japanese personnel who'd arrived with Kolhammer. They were touring the U.S. on a war-bond drive, and had proved themselves to be more than effective campaigners against their own countrymen. The Germans in particular, as he recalled, attacked the Third Reich with almost messianic zeal. The two Japanese sailors were a little more restrained, but no less emphatic that the militarist government of their homeland had to be defeated and replaced with a modern democracy.

It made Robertson's head spin every time he thought about it, and he was grateful to be so busy. He wasn't responsible for giving Curtin military advice. Originally he'd been assigned to the PM's office to help smooth the transition from a state-based to a federal taxation system. But that had been temporary, and now he'd agreed to a permanent appointment, helping the government deal with the economic implications of the Transition. His brief covered everything from planning for future droughts, through to simple trademark issues. Before joining the PM in his surprisingly small, dark office, he'd been on the phone to the American ambassador, trying to convince their cousins across the Pacific to prosecute some five-star grifter by the name of Davidson who'd lodged patents for more than half a dozen inventions that would have been developed by local businesses.

It was a hell of a job, dealing with the monetary implications of an invasion one moment, and with a crook who was trying to steal the plans for a self-chilling can of beer the next. But when nobody was watching, Robertson had to admit to himself that he was, just occasionally—well, not having fun exactly, but he'd never been as excited by the challenge of his old job in the bank. There he'd made money. Here he made history.

"Prime Minister, you *cannot* give up hope," he insisted. "They surprised us with the landings in Queensland because it was *insanity*. They lost half their troops just getting ashore, a disaster by anyone's measure. And yes, they've rolled over dozens of small towns, but as soon as they hit MacArthur's defensive line, they stopped dead—literally. They have *no* chance of reaching our main population or production centers. They're terrified to the point of impotence of engaging with Spruance's fleet because of the *Havoc* and the *Kandahar*'s battle group.

"Yamamoto is like a drowning man desperately grabbing at anything to stay afloat. He—will—lose."

Curtin's tired, watery eyes glared defiantly up at him over the rims of his glasses. "Then what are they doing here?"

4

MOSCOW, USSR

The killer was well known, at least to his most important victims. Blokhin was the man's name. He had served under the Tsar in the Great War, but had switched his loyalties to Lenin's Bolsheviks by the early 1920s. He had been a secret policeman ever since, rising to head the *Kommandatura* Branch of the Administrative Executive Department, a rather bloodless title for the lord high executioner of the Soviet Union.

Nikita Khrushchev, who would now never become the Communist Party leader, groaned as the heavy iron door swung open and Blokhin entered the room. Through the sweat and blood that clouded the vision in his one good eye, he could make out the hem of the leather butcher's apron that was nearly as legendary as the ogre who wore it. It was said to be so heavily stained with the blood of the thousands of Polish officers Blokhin had personally executed at Katyn that it could never be cleaned. There was probably more life in that filthy tunic than remained in Khrushchev's entire broken body.

Blokhin spoke to a couple of NKVD guards, his flat, Slavic features hardly moving as he did so. The pair stomped over to where Khrushchev lay on the cold concrete floor and pinned him beneath their boots. The agony of their hobnails grinding into his already tortured flesh and broken bones summoned up screams the former Politburo magnate had not thought he would be able to voice. His throat was already raw from what seemed like a lifetime of screaming.

He was dimly aware of Blokhin's heavyset form as it advanced on him, and for one irrational moment he wondered if he might have lived had Stalin agreed to liquidate the executioner, as Beria—the head of the NKVD—had once desired.

But that was madness. The Soviet Union had no shortage of executioners.

After all, Yezhov—that poison dwarf—had tortured and killed unknowable numbers of enemies, only to be killed in turn by Beria. He had died begging and screaming and thrashing against his fate, and all Khrushchev had left was a determination that he would not go out like that. He knew there was no return from this very special section of Lubianka. Best then to consign his shattered carcass to the release of death with what little dignity he could muster.

Naked, covered in his own filth, nearly toothless, his face a bruised ruin, one eye gouged out, nubs of broken bone poking through torn flesh at half a dozen places on his body—the very concept of dignity was ludicrous. But he would not beg for his life. He would—

A small sting in his neck. He wouldn't have noticed it amid the blizzard of pain, were it not for the fact that Blokhin had grabbed one of his torn ears just before he jabbed the needle in. This was unexpected. *Death by injection.* It was not standard. It was . . .

A trickle of soft, indescribably sweet pleasure. No, it wasn't that, either. It was . . . an absence of pain. It spread from the site of the small sting, flowing down his spine and out along his thin, scabrous arms and legs. It was like slipping into a warm bath. Even his mind, which had been as badly abused as his body, found itself floating on a summer breeze, drifting away from the horrors of his torture. The beatings remained in his memory, but now he felt so disconnected from them that they were as easily endured as the thousands of beatings and murders he himself had ordered over the years. Other people's misery, he'd learned, was a much lighter burden than one's own.

Even when the guard flipped him over roughly, so that his skull hit the floor with a crack and the glare of the cell's naked lightbulb shone into his dying eye, he did not care.

"So, Nikita Sergeyevich, you have lost weight. The regimen here agrees with you, *da*?" That was a new voice. A familiar one.

Khrushchev blinked the tears from his eye. He tried to wipe them away, forgetting his broken fingers, but the guards still pinned him to the cold floor. Each crushed a wrist beneath one boot, and they held long rubber truncheons in their hands. He didn't care. They could do as they pleased. *It's a free country.* The thought made him chuckle in spite of himself.

"Is there something funny, my friend. Why do you laugh so?"

Khrushchev coughed up clots of dark blood and a few broken pieces of his teeth as he regarded his latest visitor across a gulf he could not fathom. Beria stood there like a snake in human form. He had stepped from behind Blokhin, appearing without warning.

His former friend, now chief tormentor, wore a general's uniform and carried a small cosh. Khrushchev recognized it from previous beatings. Early on, in this new phase of their relationship, he had repeatedly wet himself when it had appeared in Beria's thin, white hands. Now it was just a curious artifact. He didn't even flinch when the NKVD boss took three long strides toward him and bent down to smash him across the jaw with it. An awareness of blinding pain flashed through his thoughts, but at no stage did it connect with his concerns. Then the pain faded, and he did not care that it had been visited upon him.

Nikita Khrushchev, despite the fact that he was teetering on the edge of mortal existence, found himself fascinated. What on earth were they doing to him?

Beria just smiled. "I can see that you are intrigued, comrade. But before I can satisfy your curiosity, I wonder, would you mind signing this confession for me? I know it has been a matter of some difficulty between us. But I thought I might seek your indulgence one last time. The *Vozhd* is pressing me for a resolution. You understand, my friend."

Khrushchev did. After all, they had known each other for years. A few years anyway, which counted for something in the charnel house known as the Soviet Union. It was Beria who had warned him off his friendship with Yezhov, just before the perverted little monster had been snatched up and fed into the meat grinder. Why, that made him closer to the NKVD chief than poor Blokhin over there, who had once served loyally under Yezhov, and nearly died for it.

As Beria squatted beside him and motioned for one of the guards to step off Khrushchev's arm, the fallen Communist felt something that was akin to love well up within his breast. It was suddenly very important that he make a gesture of good faith for his old friend.

What did it matter what had passed between them? He didn't care that he had been made to lie in his own excrement while Blokhin and Beria beat him on the soles of his feet with iron bars. He did not care that they had tied him to a chair and beaten his legs until they were black masses, then returned to beat the bruises so that it felt like boiled water had been poured over them. It was no longer even a concern that Beria had gouged out his eye with a gloved thumb, and then crushed the ruined eyeball as it hung on his cheek.

He didn't shudder as he recalled the memory. He had seen worse, and had ordered worse things done.

"What is it I'm to sign?" he croaked.

"You forget?" asked Beria. He seemed disappointed. "It is your confession. That you worked as a German agent to undermine the defense of the Southwestern Front."

Khrushchev's thoughts moved as slowly through his mind as a child's balloon in the air of a hot summer's day. He recalled the rout and encirclement at Kharkov only dimly. It was from his past life. Before Lubianka.

"I do not remember so well, Lavrenty Pavlovich," he confessed. "But I am quite certain I was not a German agent."

Beria smiled, a gesture that fell on Khrushchev like a shaft of spring sunlight. "It matters not. Will you do me this favor anyway? Will you sign this for me? For the *Vozhd*?"

Sinking deeper into narcotic lassitude, Khrushchev was ashamed of himself for quibbling. With a great effort he took the confession in the broken claw of his free hand. The weight suddenly came off his other arm, and a fountain pen appeared. He could not concentrate sufficiently to read the document, but he had seen enough of them over the years. He knew it mattered not.

His signature was barely legible, and he smeared blood on the paper.

A dreamy, almost happy indolence had taken hold of Khrushchev.

"Fascinating," Beria said quietly as he turned to leave.

Khrushchev felt himself forever tottering on the edge of blessed sleep, but he never quite tumbled over. With a great effort he managed to rouse himself to speak. "Tell me, Lavrenty Pavlovich," he croaked at Beria's retreating back. "When your time comes, will you be able to withstand the pain?"

The NKVD chief stopped and turned, regarded Khrushchev with the flat curiosity of a viper sizing up a small meal. "This *is* my time," he replied. "It has already come."

Blokhin moved to bar the door, and the two guards hoisted Khrushchev up by the arms. He knew without being told what was about to happen. He would be taken from the cell and placed in a Black Crow, driven a short distance to the killing house in Varsonofyevsky Lane and into the courtyard where stood a low, square building. The floor was concrete, just like his cell. It sloped down slightly toward one wall constructed of thick wooden logs. Taps and hoses were provided to wash away the blood. He would be placed against the wall and shot in the back of the head by Blokhin, who personally undertook the most important executions. Then his body would be placed in a metal box and driven to a nearby crematorium. Most likely his ashes would later be dumped in the mass grave at the Donskoi Cemetery.

He didn't care. Nothing mattered any longer. Not Stalin. Not Beria. Certainly not the Party or the revolution, or the tens of thousands he had sent to be killed by men like Blokhin. As they dragged him down the narrow, damp corridor he could raise neither self-pity nor hope, anger nor terror. Nothing really interested him.

Not even the odd sight of a woman in a naval uniform with a British insigne sewn onto the shoulder. She was being dragged, unconscious, out of a cell three doors down from his. At first he thought the woman had been beaten black and blue like him, but then he realized she was dark-skinned. However, her swollen, battered face did testify to a number of savage assaults, such as he had endured.

He supposed he should have wondered at her presence. What with everything that had happened. But the closest he came to curiosity was a very brief, almost preconscious moment of trying to recall what the letters *HMS* stood for in the name HMS *Vanguard*. He read that on a small cloth tag on her uniform as they passed. It reminded him vaguely of the initials *VMN*, standing for the "Highest Measure of Punishment." Somewhere in Lubianka there was a file with those letters written next to his name, probably in Stalin's own hand.

By the time the executioner fired a single round into the back of his head half an hour later, Nikita Khrushchev had forgotten all about her.

Natalya found her father in a remarkably good mood for a change. She could not tell him, for to voice her fears would be horribly unpatriotic, but she had been very worried about him. He had lost so much weight in the months after the Nazis invaded that sometimes, coming upon him by surprise in their bare, small four-room apartment, she didn't recognize him for a second. Not until his haunted, sunken eyes lit upon her. Then they lost that hooded darkness and became the same kind, honey-gold color that she remembered from so many happy days at the dacha, or friendly meals here in their modest apartment.

Papochka was teasing her again, flicking orange peels into her soup bowl, laughing as she squealed in delight. It was a game he often played, one she remembered from the earliest days of her life. He was wont to flick whole scoops of ice cream at her sometimes, even when her friends were at dinner. If fact, *especially* when her friends visited. He seemed to revel in the embarrassment his childish behavior caused her. But even blushing furiously and wishing he would not tease poor Martha so, she could not help but love him. The same way she adored his hugs and kisses, even though his mustache bristle scratched her skin, and he always smelled of foul tobacco.

He had been so kind since mother died. As she grew into her teenage years, Natalya came to understand how hard that time must have been for him, with so many responsibilities to take him away from the family.

"*Papochka*, will we have a holiday this year?" she asked.

Her father waved over their housekeeper, Valechka, to clear away the dishes. "You do not like it here?" he mocked his daughter gently. "You would have me send you away again?"

"No, but we have not been on holiday since the war started. And you have sent all of my books away. The apartment is very dark, and it always feels so empty. Can't we go to the seaside, like we used to? The fascists have gone, haven't they?"

"*Da*, my little sparrow," he said, suddenly looking tired again. "They have gone, but they will come back again. And you would want your *papochka* to be ready for that, wouldn't you? We must all be ready for them."

Natalya was reaching the age when she would soon be able to fight, just like her brother—well, hopefully better than her brother, who was a hopeless lout and a drunk, from all she'd heard. But she knew better than to broach that subject with her father. Since the news of the miracles, he swung between periods of black depression and unrestrained bouts of fevered joy. She worried that it was another symptom of his weariness with the war. He had even turned his legendary temper on her once, storming into the apartment one evening, slapping the homework from her hands, and shaking her violently, shouting, "*What were you thinking? What were you thinking, you stupid little girl?*"

She had no idea what he was talking about, but the outburst terrified her. So many of their friends and relatives had disappeared that she feared she may have said something irresponsible or ill-considered, something that might have been overheard by a zealous informer. Her father's rage seemed tainted with a fear that she had never known before, and like the little girl she had once been, she found her parent's terror infectious. Within minutes, she was shaking and blubbering and begging him to tell her what she'd done. The fire had gone out of his eyes immediately, and he'd collapsed into a chair, awkwardly pulling her down with him, onto his lap, where she had sat for so many hours as a child. He'd held her tightly to him, wiping her hot tears away.

They had never spoken of the incident again.

Her father's eyes clouded over now as he spoke about the Germans, and she wished she hadn't mentioned them. He held a piece of black bread in his hands, which he had probably been meaning to throw into her soup. Now it seemed forgotten.

"I received a very good mark for my essay on *The Lower Depths*," she ventured, but his mind was gone from the room.

A phone rang, and was answered by Valechka. She said a few words and hung up. "They have called for you," the housekeeper reported.

Natalya's father nodded, and the change came over him. He stood up, patted her on the head, and apologized for leaving before dinner was over. "I have important work," he explained, and he shrugged.

"I know, *Papochka*," she said. "Do not worry about me. I shall help clean up, and then I shall study my Gorky some more."

Josef Vissarionovich Stalin, general secretary of the Communist Party and premier of the Soviet Union, pushed back his chair and smiled absently. "I sometimes miss Gorky," he said. "He was a great loss. Study hard, Natalya. You will have to make your way alone in this world when I am gone."

He shrugged on a heavy trench coat and walked out of the apartment.

The office was located in the same building as Stalin's apartment, in the old Senate building, sometimes called the Yellow Palace. In the time line from which the Multinational Force had arrived, it remained the center of Russian power. The Cabinet still met there, where the Politburo had reigned. Presidents Putin and Dery had both governed from the same building; Putin's chief of staff and Dery's national security adviser actually working at the same desk in the same converted corridor that had once housed Stalin.

Beria was privy to all this information. As were Malenkov, Poskrebyshev, and, of course, Stalin himself. The researchers who had compiled the data from the *Vanguard*'s computers also knew, of course. Or rather, they had known. They were all dead now.

As Beria waited in the anteroom, he wondered idly at his own fate. The air between him and Malenkov, who sat in another armchair as far away as possible, was frozen with malice. It was a fact that Malenkov would betray him, conspiring with Khrushchev and Molotov to charge him with anti-state activities. Beria would have been executed in 1953.

Well, Khrushchev was no longer an issue, and before long, Malenkov and Molotov would join him. Just as soon as Beria could convince the *Vozhd* to lift his halt on the great purges that had consumed the state since the discovery of the British vessel. It was like 1937 all over again. No, it was worse. Because now there was real evidence. And all that evidence pointed to a great tumor of fear and paranoia feeding on itself. It seemed sometimes, from the electronic files they'd found, that apart from maybe half a dozen stalwarts, there was nobody in this damned traitors' nest of a country who wouldn't turn on them, given half a chance.

Even Stalin's closest family.

Beria's face was a cast-iron mask, but his gut burned with acid at the memory of *that* discovery. What a dark day that had been, discovering Natalya's "memoirs." What an ocean of blood had been spilled to cover them over.

Malenkov, he noted with bleak satisfaction, appeared to be no more comfortable than he. The fat faggot looked even more like a weeping wheel of cheese than normal. Like an old woman with her rosaries, he fingered that stupid little notebook that was labeled *Comrade Stalin's Instructions.* Beria cracked open an icy smile for him, and was rewarded amply when Malenkov blanched.

It was getting late, which meant that Stalin would soon arrive at the Little Corner to begin work. He lived nocturnally, and had done so for years. It didn't bother Beria. As a secret policeman, he preferred the darkness. He considered opening his flexipad and doing some file work, but neither he nor Malenkov had moved since they'd arrived, and it seemed as if to do so now would be to give away an important advantage. So Lavrenty Beria sat in the funereal waiting room, with its shoulder-high dark wood panels, its polished floors and dreary drapes, its worn red and green carpets and, of course, its guardian, the unchanging Poskrebyshev, sitting at his immaculate desk, scratching at papers with his fountain pen.

Beria wondered if it was significant that Stalin's secretary did not have a flexipad. They were precious instruments, rare and valued, not just for their near magical powers, but for the status they conferred on those chosen few who were authorized to possess them.

Stalin had three, but he almost never used them. He still carried his most important documents around wrapped up in newspaper, and filled his pockets with scraps of paper covered in crayon scrawl—everything from the number of T-34s produced last month to the latest results of the never-ending search for traitors, and they pored through the enormous library of the British warship.

At last, Stalin appeared and bade them both enter his sanctum. The Soviet leader's office was a long, rectangular space, lined with heavy drapes but well ventilated, which it had to be because of the ornate Russian stoves that lined the walls. As winter closed in, the *Vozhd* was often found leaning up against one of the heaters, trying to unknot the muscles of his aching legs. For now, however, he strode right past them, making for the huge desk in the far right corner. Beria slid in behind him like a python. Malenkov, who was cursed with a pair of breeding hips like some enormous Georgian *baba*, waddled along like a goose, trying to keep up.

"You tested Khrushchev?" Stalin asked without preemption. "He confessed?"

Beria knew the question was directed at him. "Another miracle, comrade. He would have signed a statement saying he was Hitler's mistress, if I'd asked. And we were right to imagine that the drug protected him from feeling even the harshest interrogation. Again, I believe I could have shot him in the genitals and he would not have flinched. At least not much."

Stalin turned his flat, Asiatic glare on Beria. "A pity we did not discover this earlier. When we still had some of them to question."

Malenkov grinned maliciously, but Beria was ready for the attack.

"We still have the woman. She is being transferred to a special hospital where her 'inserts' will be removed."

"And she will survive?"

"I hope so."

"Make sure she does," growled Stalin, "or I will allow Malenkov here to fulfill his destiny. At least as it relates to you."

Malenkov did not react for a full second, standing as he was, as still as a corpse. Then, just like a reanimated dead man, he brought up his little notebook and jotted down an entry in *Comrade Stalin's Instructions* before closing it just as slowly.

Stalin managed a lopsided grin at the charade.

Beria fumed silently to himself. *Your time will come, Melanya . . .*

5

DEMIDENKO CENTRE, UKRAINE

It was revealing to see how well the SS and the NKVD worked together. Colonel Paul Brasch supposed he should not be surprised. They were cut from the same cloth. But still, four months earlier, you could not have found more implacable enemies. The hatred had been visceral, as though each existed simply to pursue the annihilation of the other.

Now, as he passed through the increasingly stringent subterranean checkpoints on his way to the mission control center, he was vetted by combined teams of German and Soviet security men. It wasn't that they were friendly with one another. He knew that under different circumstances, each would draw his weapon and gun down his opposite number without a second thought. But having served in the vast slaughterhouse of the Eastern Front, and having seen the inhuman cruelty of that conflict up close, he was amazed at the passionless and efficient way in which the machinery of the two states could knit together so quickly. The *Führerprinzip* in action, or whatever they called it in Russia.

The unfinished complex was being hastily constructed with a massive workforce of slave labor. Again, the SS and the NKVD had cooperated well, each organization providing hundreds of thousands of bodies from their networks of prison camps. Both the scale of the project and the speed with which it had progressed impressed Brasch, an engineer with professional qualms about using slave labor for any kind of skilled work. Whatever his own misgivings, he had to admit that the twenty square miles of half-built factories, proving grounds, test labs, and barracks that made up the Demidenko Center were a marvel. It was as though Satan himself had passed a hand over the barren earth and simply conjured it up.

"We must hurry, Herr Colonel, or we will miss the rocket launch."

Brasch smiled inwardly. His current SS shadow, *Untersturmführer* Gelder, was every bit as humorless and constipated on matters of military formality as his last minder, Herr Steckel, had been. However, he displayed none of Steckel's awe concerning the Iron Cross that Brasch had won at the front, perhaps because Gelder carried his own scars and medals from that same nightmare, and was not so easily impressed.

They picked up their pace, the fall of their boot heels echoing down the long cinder-block corridor. The paint on the walls was still so fresh that Brasch thought it was probably wet. The work crews had not completed the job, an indication of how rushed everything had been. About two hundred meters from the solid steel door that led into the control room, the paint job ended abruptly, revealing naked concrete blocks. Brasch could see bloody handprints on some of them.

Four guards stood at the doorway: two Germans, two Soviets. The latter had the primitive features of Mongols, causing Brasch an uncomfortable, momentary flashback. He had been all but overrun by a human wave of such men near Belgorod. Pins and needles ran up his back and neck as they checked his pass.

He noted with some amusement that two pink spots of high color had come out on Gelder's Aryan features at having to submit to inspection by the subhumans.

"What a world we live in these days, eh, Gelder?" he said, smiling conspiratorially.

The SS lieutenant took Brasch's comment as an indication of sympathy and shook his head. "Best not to speak of it," he cautioned, nodding at the Communist pair.

The check complete, the senior SS guard, a slab-shouldered *Unterschar-führer*, or sergeant, clicked his jackboots together and snapped out a Nazi salute. Brasch's reply was as enthusiastic as Gelder's, although for a very different reason. He was merely enjoying the discomfort that appeared now on the faces of the Mongol warriors. *You have to take your fun where you can find it in the Demidenko Center,* he mused.

The sergeant spun a large iron wheel mounted at the center of the blast door, reminding Brasch of the hatches on the submarine that had brought him back from Hashirajima. The two officers stepped through into a much shorter concrete passageway, also unpainted, which veered off at right angles after a few meters. They could hear the voices of the technicians bouncing off bare walls. The door closed behind them with a solid crash, and they continued on without delay, marching through a series of switchbacks before emerging into the main chamber of the blockhouse.

They were in a large room staffed by nearly fifty men and even a few women. All of the females were Soviet scientists. The German rocket program was not such an equal-opportunity employer. The bustle and excitement, the lack of interest in their arrival, and the countdown that appeared on a large alphanumeric clock all pointed to an imminent launch.

Brasch watched Gelder stiffen noticeably as he caught sight of the official party that stood in the far corner of the room. Three NKVD generals and a handful of SS officers were gathered around the diminutive figure of *Reichsführer* Heinrich Himmler. Even Brasch tightened up somewhat. Before the Emergence, Himmler had been an almost mythical figure. With the terrible purges of the last few months, that aura had grown even more powerful. Indeed, *he* was the führer's most frightening weapon: a one-man *Vergeltungswaffe*, protecting Hitler from those thousands of enemies who had been unmasked through information contained within the files of the future-ships.

Since June, it had seemed as though every night was given over to the Long Knives, as the SS raked at the heart of the Third Reich to see what treachery might be hidden there. For a while, Brasch had even stopped worrying about his son. Having been born with a cleft palate, little Manny was almost certain to go into a camp. But Himmler's minions were so busy purging the State of traitors such as Rommel and Canaris that for just a few weeks it seemed as though the pressure was eased on less significant "undesirables." Nearly a month had gone by without Gelder inquiring as to Manny's health.

But then, a fortnight ago, he had brought it up again. Brasch had responded noncommittally, knowing that the SS was, for the moment, content to simply remind him of his vulnerability. But that night he had not slept, as he was tormented by waking visions of his son choking to death on Zyklon B.

Seeing Himmler now, he was tempted by a rush of madness to draw his Luger and kill the man. Of course, that would condemn his entire family. So he forced himself to assume a neutral expression, the face of the perfect functionary. But while he threaded through the banks of control panels to join the delegation of high-ranking officers, a small part of his mind worked furiously, as it had been ever since he'd read about the Holocaust in the Fleetnet archive on the *Sutanto*.

It had been a long, unpleasant trip for the *Reichsführer*, clanking through Poland and into the Ukraine. The rail line carried them only as far as Sobibor before they had to transfer to an armored convoy. The cease-fire was holding, but the war had ravaged this part of the world, and bandits were everywhere. Plus, one could not be entirely certain of the Wehrmacht nowadays. Two outright mutinies had already been put down, and Heinrich Himmler was certain that they were acute eruptions of a deeper, chronic malaise. Treachery was everywhere.

His current duplicity was of no consequence. The Bolsheviks were not comrades. The arrangements with them were a fleeting matter, to be put aside after the Reich had dealt with the disruptions caused by this accursed Emergence. Unlike the Nipponese, Germany had not suffered directly from the appearance of the *Wunderwaffen* in the Pacific, but the implications of their arrival—well, that was entirely different. The revelations they had occasioned necessitated the boldest of gambits and the most ruthless winnowing out of criminal elements within the state.

An image of Field Marshal Witzleben thrashing about like a dumb beast on a meat hook arose unbidden before the *Reichsführer*'s eyes. The former commander of Army West was one of more than twenty thousand conspirators who had been dispatched, but he was one of the few whose demise Himmler had personally observed. It was necessary work, but quite upsetting, and he had left the scene of the execution shaking and white.

He had authorized two weeks' leave for all members of the *Einsatzgruppen* who were personally involved in the countersubversion operations. Unfortunately, the pace of their work was such that nobody had managed to take as much as one hour's break since their vital mission began with the translation of the so-called Web files.

A PA system announced the ten-minute countdown in both German and Russian.

Himmler noticed the arrival of Brasch and his SS chaperone. While many had been sucked down in the recent turbulence, others had flourished, and Brasch was one of them. The führer had personally promoted him to the rank of *Oberst*, thanking the engineer for his work in the Orient. Himmler, however, wasn't so sure of the man. The murder of Steckel remained unsolved and unsettling, but then Brasch could hardly be blamed for that. He'd been hundreds of miles away in Hashirajima when the intelligence officer was killed. And as a lieutenant in the *Ausland-SD*, Steckel had doubtless accumulated many foes. That circle of perverts from the Foreign Ministry were much more likely to have been responsible.

Still, Brasch had enjoyed unrestricted access to the historical documents for many weeks. It gave one pause to imagine how he might have been affected by them.

"Reichsführer!" Both men snapped out perfect salutes.

Himmler nodded at their arrival and flicked back a restrained salute. The NKVD generals remained impassive. The junior officers shuffled around to allow them to join the circle.

Himmler put his doubts about Brasch to one side. The man had been more than effective in carrying out the special tasks they had assigned him here, and Gelder, one of Himmler's better lieutenants, had found nothing ill to report of him, as yet.

The Demidenko operation was proceeding in excellent order.

"I am hopeful that your test will prove to be successful, Herr *Oberst*," said Himmler.

Brasch, to his credit, did not blanch at being directly addressed by the head of the SS. Nor did he dissemble. "We all hope for success, sir. But as I'm sure you know, I cannot guarantee it. The rockets and technical data we took off the *Sutanto* and her sister ship in New Guinea have been most helpful. The computers are like magic boxes. Even so, I don't anticipate a perfect trial. But we shall see."

Silence fell over the group, and the Germans waited on Himmler's response. When he acknowledged Brasch's short speech with a curt nod, they all relaxed slightly. The Soviets did not.

"We are more than hopeful of success, Colonel Brasch," said Orlov, the senior Russian general, in his heavily accented German. "Much effort has been poured into this project. We are not a rich country, and every kopeck spent here is lost to the reconstruction and repair necessitated by the aggression of your own."

"That is your problem, General." Brasch shrugged.

The Bolshevik flared at the insult, and Himmler found himself in the unfamiliar role of peacemaker. "Orlov, this project is a concrete symbol of our cooperation against the common enemy. We do not need to rake over scorched earth. Colonel Brasch, you will apologize."

"Of course," said Brasch with easy equanimity. "I am sorry, Herr General. In the drive to complete our work, I forget myself."

The PA announced, "Launch minus five."

The Soviets seemed mollified, and Brasch remained completely unruffled. Himmler found himself privately amused at the engineer's cheek. Nobody was happy with this new rapprochement, but needs must out when the devil drives. And the führer's plans were most definitely being driven by the devilish complications of the Emergence.

Himmler polished the lens of the specially tinted goggles they'd given him and turned to the foot-thick blast window. The striking sight of the prototype V-2 rocket, poised on its launchpad, was heavily distorted through the armored glass, but he preferred to watch the test as it happened rather than on the even fuzzier televiewing screen in the control room.

In truth, Brasch knew what would happen long before it transpired. The missile stood forty-eight feet high and measured five and a half feet in diameter. It weighed thirteen tons, most of which was liquid alcohol and liquid oxygen, to provide thrust to the 600,000-horsepower rocket engine. It was designed to carry a ton of high explosives, but did not do so for today's test. Theoretically it could reach a speed of 3,500 miles per hour, with a ceiling of 116 miles. Unlike the aborted V-1, a fast fighter could not intercept it.

All of which was irrelevant. This missile was never meant to fly.

As the metallic voice of the PA counted down toward zero, Brasch felt his heartbeat quicken. He had to will himself not to flinch. Himmler had retreated behind the tinted goggles. The Russians, in their excitement, had forgotten to put theirs on.

Stillness descended on the control room.

". . . five, four, three, two, one . . . *ignition*."

Even through the concrete walls and thick blast window, they could hear the roar of the engine. The wavy, green tinted armor glass distorted the view, but Brasch fancied that he could see the fatal tilt within a second of the giant lance taking off. Smoke and flame blasted away from the gantry at high speed. The missile shuddered and lurched skyward, and the small boy within him ached for it to keep going.

But it didn't. He had sabotaged the launch most effectively, and the room filled with intense yellow light as the V-2 tipped over, sending a long spear of superheated exhaust in their direction. *Now* he flinched, like everyone else, as the flames seemed to lick at the window. A gigantic, muffled explosion sounded as nine tons of rocket fuel detonated a few hundred meters away. Some of the technicians cursed; some cried out in panic. He heard somebody swearing in German and, from the tone, somebody doing the same thing in Russian.

After a few seconds, the thunder subsided and everyone unclenched themselves. There was never any chance of the bunker being breached. Orlov and his men looked shaken. Himmler was paler and more thin-lipped than usual. He turned on Brasch with an evil look. "Well, Herr *Oberst*?"

"An initial failure," he replied flatly. "As I said, it was always a possibility. We know that the original tests, as documented in the computer records, were also problematic."

"But we are supposed to have *learned* from those mistakes," hissed the *Reichsführer*. "The Soviets are not the only ones spending vast sums of money out here, Brasch. The Reich is engaged in a death struggle with the democracies, and we cannot afford this sort of thing."

Brasch could tell that the NKVD men, in spite of their shock at the explosion, were enjoying the spectacle of their exchange, though it meant nothing to him.

"I shall prepare a report on the failure by the end of the day, *Reichsführer*."

It seemed as if every pair of eyes in the room was on them. A siren sounded very faintly from outside as fire trucks rushed to the pad.

"See to it that you do, Herr *Oberst*, and I shall wish to discuss this in private . . . later," he added ominously, before dismissing them both with a flick of the hand.

"An unfortunate accident," Gelder muttered as they slunk out of the blockhouse.

Brasch sighed with exasperation. "It is science, my friend. Trial *and* error. We are years ahead of schedule, but this is not a magic wand," said Brasch, waving his flexipad. "There will be more days like this one—believe me."

"You'd want to hope not," said Gelder, with what sounded like genuine sympathy. "The *Reichsführer* does not like to be disappointed."

They walked in silence the rest of the way through the long, half-painted corridor, passing no other human beings. Just bloodied handprints.

"Excellent work, Brasch, just excellent. Those idiots were completely taken in."

"Thank you, *Reichsführer*. It was simply a matter of not doing my job."

Himmler smiled at the weak joke.

They met in a secure room, in the German section of the command compound. It was swept for listening devices every two hours, but none had ever been found. The Russians weren't all that sophisticated. Their own command buildings, however, were thoroughly covered by German surveillance. Listening devices built into the very fabric of the Soviets' command center had never been detected, and provided a wealth of intelligence for the SS to rake through.

The room in which Himmler and Brasch met was small and bare, just a few hard wooden chairs, a table, and a notice board on which was pinned a single yellow piece of paper, displaying the times at which the room had been cleared by the technical services section of the SS. They had been through ten minutes before Brasch was ushered in. The two men drank real coffee and nibbled at Dutch honey biscuits.

"You've done good work out here, Colonel. I shudder to think of the resources we've put into this place. But we must show our willingness, yes?"

"The Russians still don't trust us," said Brasch.

"No reason why they should," Himmler replied. "We will destroy them in good time, and they know it. I doubt this is the only investment they've made as a hedge against the future. But as long as we control their access to the technology, they remain beholden to us. We took our boot from Stalin's throat when we could have crushed the life out of him."

Brasch said nothing. Both of them knew that as awful as were the Red Army's losses in 1942, it had been the beginning of the end for the German conquest.

Before the silence could become uncomfortable, though, Brasch filled the void. "The führer is well? We do not have much news out here. Just rumors."

Himmler arched one eyebrow. "Really? And what might those be?"

"Terrible rumors, Herr *Reichsführer*," said Brasch. "I have heard of treachery at the highest levels of the Wehrmacht and the *Kreigsmarine*. Not so much with the Luftwaffe. I'm not sure why. And of course, not at all with the SS. At any rate, if even a fraction of the talk is true, it is a crime how some have abandoned their duty to the Fatherland."

Himmler appeared to regard him as a teacher might size up a dim pupil who had just said something profound, but quite by accident. Brasch worked hard at maintaining a slightly worried, somewhat bovine look on his face. Eventually Himmler took off his glasses and polished them with a handkerchief. Brasch recognized the gesture as a sign that the man had relaxed just a little.

"We have had a terrible time of it," Himmler admitted. "It has been a shock to us all, but naturally the greatest burden has fallen upon the führer himself. I have done what I can to protect him, but . . ."

He trailed off for a moment.

"A regiment of the Afrika Korps revolted when Rommel was recalled. Actually turned their guns on the men sent to collect him."

"The whole regiment!" Brasch gasped. "How?"

"No, not the entire regiment," said Himmler, somewhat exasperated. "Just a few men in a headquarters company at first. But then it spread through the ranks. The defense of El Alamein was thrown into chaos, and that pervert Montgomery took advantage—it was a disaster, Herr *Oberst*. Not at all like the spirit of Belgorod, eh?"

Brasch allowed himself a confused shake of the head. "No, not at all like Belgorod."

"There was a similar uprising when Canaris was exposed. Rebellion in both the *Abwehr* and the *Kreigsmarine*. An entire Waffen SS Division was required to put that one down."

"Good God!" said Brasch, who was genuinely surprised that the rumors he'd heard turned out to be true.

Himmler finished polishing his glasses and replaced them on his small, ratlike nose. "You understand these are state secrets, Brasch. They are not matters for idle chitchat."

"Indeed Herr *Reichsführer*. Of course, but why . . ." He trailed off.

"Why do I tell you? Because you need to know, Brasch. The Fatherland needs men it can trust. I am afraid the counterattacks on the criminal gangs who would undermine our leader have rather drastically thinned out our upper ranks. They have not weakened us, mind you!" he hastened to add. "But some of those swine held important positions. They must be replaced."

The room seemed to become hotter, and closer. Brasch tried not to let his hopes get the better of him. "I'm afraid I don't understand. Am I to be transferred? My work here—"

Himmler held up one, thin, pallid hand to cut him off. "Your work here is done. Stalin is convinced that our cooperation is sincere, at least in the short term. And your efforts here have played a large part in that. He knows there must come a final settlement between us, and we know he is frantically building his forces in the Far East, where he thinks himself beyond our gaze. It doesn't matter. When we have dealt with the immediate threat of the Allies, we shall turn on him with weapons he has never dreamed of. The trinkets we let him play with here will not save him, nor will those fleets of antique tanks he is building."

"I understand that, Herr *Reichsführer*. My mission briefing was quite specific. But what now?"

"Now," said Himmler, leaning forward. "You are going home. These idiots will think you have been transferred in disgrace, after today's failure. But you have proved yourself adept at working under extreme pressure, and there are projects that require your attention back in the civilized world.

"We are going to take the British Isles, Colonel Brasch. And you are going to help us."

6

SOUTHWEST PACIFIC AREA, CORAL SEA

It was as if they were counting her shots. Captain Jane Willet knew Yamamoto was lurking off to the north of New Guinea, well beyond the range of her Nemesis arrays. The *Havoc* had been out on point duty, hundreds of miles ahead of Admiral Spruance's diminished Task Force for nearly six weeks now. No Japanese ships had made it past them. Spruance may have had just the *Enterprise* and USS *Wasp* to call on for carrier-borne strike missions, but with the submarine's advanced sensor suites and battle management systems to act as a force multiplier, he could deploy his precious aircraft to devastating effect. Yamamoto, meanwhile, could not move directly against him, for fear of losing his capital ships to the *Havoc*.

The Japanese grand admiral seemed to be waiting her out. Sending a long line of tempting targets her way, hoping she would run down her stocks of torpedoes and cruise missiles. Willet assumed he knew what she was packing. Some of the basic specs for the *Havoc* were available online, and the Indonesian tubs had been linked into Fleetnet. God only knew how many pages they had cached before the Transition, but it would be prudent to assume that the Japanese were somewhere with an abacus, or a flexipad, ticking off every kill she made.

"Five contacts, Captain," reported her intel chief, Lieutenant Lohrey. "Good returns from the drone. We can have visual in ten if you want me to reposition."

The commander of HMAS *Havoc* leaned over her shipmate's shoulder to check out the data for herself. "You make them out to be transports, Amanda?"

"At least three, with a couple of destroyers for escort. No air screen, again."

Willet chewed her lower lip, but in the end the decision was easy. "Well, I'm not wasting any taxpayers' money on this. Especially as the taxpayers haven't even been born yet. Squirt a position fix to Spruance, see if they can vector a couple of those American subs on them."

Lohrey turned in her chair. "Begging your pardon, Captain, but the 'temps still haven't completed the changeover of their torpedoes. If they're packing Type Fourteens, they might as well shoot spitballs at 'em."

Willet nodded ruefully. The sub-launched torpedoes carried by American boats from this time had major problems with their running depth and warheads. Depression-era budgets hadn't allowed for proper testing, and the training shots ran with significantly lighter dummy warheads. This meant that in a real shoot-out, the torpedoes tended to "sink" a little, and could actually run right under the keel of their targets. The magnetic exploders that might have compensated for this didn't work properly, because they were designed to function in far northern latitudes, and they went a little haywire south of the equator.

Even if, by some chance, the captain got lucky and actually hit his target, the contact detonator often failed because they'd been designed for an earlier, slower type of fish. The 'temps' Mark 14 hit with enough speed that the firing pin often missed the exploder cap altogether. It was logical to assume that once this had been pointed out, it would have been attended to with all dispatch. But no, she'd just read an e-mail that morning from Kolhammer complaining that the civilian manufacturer, NTS Newport and the responsible navy office, ComSubSWPac, were still resisting a total refit.

"You're right," sighed Willet. "They could shoot their whole wad and still not hit anything."

"What about these guys here?" She tapped the screen with a light pen, instantly drawing a box around two blue contacts floating within a sheltered cove on the mainland, less than a hundred klicks to her east and 250 south of the advancing Japanese reinforcements. Lieutenant Lohrey worked her station quickly; a window opened and began scrolling text.

"That's a couple of PT boats, ma'am. Fifty-nine and One-oh-one. They're tasked for harassment and interdiction of Japanese supply barges coming down through the Whitsundays. If they're carrying the old Mark Thirteen's, they'd have a better chance than the subs."

Willet stood back from the screen and thought it over. She couldn't risk a radio transmission, and the PT boats didn't have the equipment to receive a compressed data burst. But she didn't want to use up any more of her precious store of weapons taking out a troop ship. She had worthier targets.

"Okay," she concluded. "Let's make some new friends. Helm, I want a fast run across to those torpedo boats. I'll talk to the skippers myself. Leave the drones up; we'll grab the take from them on the way."

She ordered the comms boss to send a compressed encrypted burst back to Spruance, explaining why they were moving off station.

Turning back to the flatscreen, she tapped her pursed lips with the light pen.

"The One-oh-one?" she said softly. "Do you think he's still driving it, Amanda?"

The intel boss shrugged. "Could be, Skipper. Who can tell, nowadays?"

SOUTHWEST PACIFIC AREA, NORTH QUEENSLAND COAST

Riding at anchor, the pair of contemporary American torpedo boats were invisible from the main shipping channels, and nestled in under a thick, tropical mangrove canopy, they had reasonably good topside cover as well. His men thought it would have been nice if they'd had a beach to relax on, and maybe some sweet-lookin' dolls to while away the long, hot afternoons, but you couldn't have everything.

Unless you were on one of those superships, of course. They came with their own dolls, and chilled air, and movies like you wouldn't believe. Word was they had comfier bunks than the swishiest hotels.

Lieutenant John F. Kennedy had stayed in a few swish joints before he'd signed up for the navy, but he hadn't had the pleasure of a visit to the *Clinton* or the *Kandahar*, or even the British or Aussie ships, which were rumored to have heads where the toilet water swirled down the opposite way. At least that's what Leading Seaman Molloy said, and he'd been on the *Astoria* at Midway, so he was the closest they had to an expert on all things related to the time travelers.

Kennedy mopped the sweat from his forehead and neck with an old gray cloth and tried to tune out the drone of the crew's voices. It was only late spring in this part of the world, but the days were already oppressively hot under the canvas shade they'd rigged up. He was working through an attack plan with Lieutenant George "Barney" Ross, and although he could appreciate the crew's endless conversation about the sexual practices of women in the twenty-first century U.S. Navy, it was becoming distracting.

"They've been slipping small barges through the passage, here and here, usually after midnight," Ross said, roughly circling an area on the map that lay between the two officers on the flying bridge. "We're going to have to move on from here tonight, anyhow. So why not try our luck where the reefs get nice and tight for them?"

Kennedy slapped idly at a mosquito that was buzzing around his ear. "Our turn to lead off, Barney?"

His friend smiled. "Sure you won't get run over in the dark?"

"Eyes like a cat, my friend. Like a cat!"

"The morals, too," Ross replied, grinning. "Okay, you take us out. We'll—"

Kennedy could never be sure, but he thought the crew reacted even before the alarm sounded. They'd been training so hard that their ability to anticipate one another was almost spooky. Before he consciously understood what was happening, men were charging to their battle stations. The ship's twin 50s were manned and ready, all the canons were tracking, including the 40 mm Bofors mounted aft, and a 37 mm antitank gun way up on the bow, flanked by a set of 30 cal machine guns and a deck-mounted mortar. The boat's supercharged V-12 engine, a Packard 4M-2500, was snarling furiously even before Kennedy got his helmet on, which was about the same time the boat's chief came stomping up, yelling at everybody to calm down and stow their peckers away.

"Over there, Mr. Kennedy," said Chief Rollins, pointing to a low, black shape that was heading toward them like a speedboat. It was flying an outsized Australian ensign.

Kennedy grabbed a pair of binoculars. Through the glasses, his first impression firmed up. It was about the size of a speedboat and powered by an outboard, but a very quiet one. He still couldn't hear it, in fact. There were five figures seated inboard, two of them women, for sure, and all of them carrying rifles of some kind—although he'd be damned if he knew what type. They looked big enough to stop an elephant.

"Goddamn," he muttered. "Chief, better tell the men to put their pants back on. Looks like we have polite company for a change."

George Ross was nearly dancing from foot to foot beside him. "Are they—?"

"Yup," said Kennedy, "they are."

The sound of the outboard reached them only when the boat was about twenty-five feet away. Chief Rollins whistled in admiration as it bumped up against the side of the torpedo boat. "She's a beauty," he said.

"Thank you, Chief," one of the women said as she effortlessly hauled herself up over the side. "I take it you mean the boat, right?"

Rollins hardly knew where to look, and Kennedy could see why. The woman was handsome, even striking, and her eyes sparked with a mischievous humor. She was dressed in some sort of dark blue coverall that did cover all, but still gave the men of both PT boats plenty to think about.

"Captain Jane Willet, commanding HMAS *Havoc*," she declared, and snapped a salute directly at Kennedy without having to enquire which of them was the captain. Even without a shirt, and with his eyes hidden behind dark sunglasses, she seemed to recognize him—*But of course she would*, he thought. Kennedy felt the strangeness of the moment, meeting someone

who seemed to know all about him—who probably knew more about him than he did himself, in some ways. He'd been able to avoid some of the personal ramifications of the Transition hiding away and fighting down here in the mangroves inside the Great Barrier Reef. After Midway, and the attacks on New Guinea and Australia, there'd been no time to indulge in undergrad fantasies of "what-if." He'd been promoted; then his boat and his men had been thrown into the firestorm and ordered to make the best of it. Now, he felt like his mind was stretching and twisting in a completely unnatural fashion. He hadn't felt it so strongly in months.

"I'm Lieutenant Kennedy," he said, returning the woman's salute. "And this is Lieutenant Ross, the skipper of the other boat." Kennedy searched his memories of the chaos after the Transition. "The *Havoc*, eh?" he said. "I guess you'd be the ones launched those rockets at Yamamoto's home base? Sank two carriers and a bunch of cruisers?"

"We are," said Willet, squinting in the fierce tropical sun. Kennedy had noticed that most Australians seemed to walk around with a permanent squint.

Lieutenant Ross stepped forward eagerly, cutting his friend off. "It's an honor, Captain Willet. And a privilege."

"Thank you, Lieutenant," replied the submariner. She appeared somewhat taken aback by his earnestness. Kennedy smiled to himself. He doubted there was a man anywhere in the navy who believed in this war as much as his friend.

Ropes dropped down to secure Willet's launch as another pair of her shipmates came over the side of the 101: a second woman, smaller and a few years younger than Willet, and an old salt who wouldn't have looked out of place on Kennedy's boat. The captain introduced the woman as her "intel boss," Lieutenant Lohrey, and the guy as her own chief, Chief Petty Officer Roy Flemming. He was grinning hugely, and paying almost no attention to Kennedy or Ross. He only had eyes for the boat.

"If you'll excuse me, this doesn't look like a standard early-series Elco, Lieutenant. You got a lot of mods here."

Kennedy smiled again. "You mean the armaments? Yeah, well, the welds on some of them are still warm."

Willet's boat chief walked over to the nearest cannon, the forward-mounted 37 mm can opener, and stroked it with a loving air that Kennedy recognized only too well. His own chief had been inordinately proud of the refit, which the squadron had done on their own initiative back in Pearl, using a bare minimum of information cribbed from a copy of *Jane's Fighting Ships of World War II* that had arrived with Kolhammer's Taskforce. They didn't have any superrockets or death beams to play with, but every man on the 101 was certain they'd turned the old girl into a really formidable fighting ship.

"You didn't really see this sort of configuration until late forty-three, forty-four," said Chief Flemming. "You know, pound for pound, the old PT boats were just about the heaviest hitters of the war."

"You'll have to excuse, Roy," said Willet. "He's an enthusiast."

Kennedy had climbed down from the flying bridge to the deck, where the last two Australian sailors had come aboard. Their coveralls were much thicker than the other three and seemed heavily padded. They wore some sort of protection at their knees and elbows, which reminded him of athletic cups, of all things. Each carried a pair of mysterious black tubes slung across his back. Their headgear resembled German helmets, and their eyes were hidden behind goggles that reflected his image like a mirror. They never stopped moving their heads, scanning the tree line and the mangroves like hunting dogs. They didn't smile much either.

Willet saw him checking them out. "Sorry, we don't mean to be rude, Lieutenant. But you're way behind enemy lines here. And good manners are always the first casualty of war."

Kennedy shrugged it off. He was acutely aware of being caught half-naked, but neither of the women seemed at all interested. Perhaps the rumors were true after all. "Well, Captain," he said, "visitors are always welcome. But I assume you're here on business."

"We are." She nodded. "How would you like to do me a big favor?"

"Anything for a lady."

Willet gave him a lopsided grin. "That's what I hear."

Kennedy wasn't sure which was louder, the laughter from his shipmates or the rush of blood in his ears as he flushed with embarrassment.

The four officers repaired to the now very cramped flying bridge, while Chief Petty Officer Flemming disappeared on a tour of the boat with Collins. Willet's security detail took up positions fore and aft and politely refused to talk to anyone. Sneaking a look at them occasionally, Kennedy wondered why they didn't faint from heat exhaustion. They were entirely cocooned within their strange battle dress.

Willet caught him looking once as he wiped at the sweat from his own neck.

"The suits are thermopliable, Lieutenant. They're much more comfortable than you or I at the moment."

Kennedy nodded absently, then turned back to the amazing devices that Lohrey had produced from a backpack. The data slates, as she called them, were about the size of a large book, and not much thicker than a packet of cigarettes. One of them displayed about a dozen graphs and readouts that made no sense at all to Kennedy and Ross. Willet explained that this was a live link back to her sub, feeding her updated intelligence. The pictures in the other data slate made a lot more sense, but were hard to believe.

"This is a real-time feed from a Big Eye drone we've got shadowing this Japanese convoy," Lohrey explained. "It's sitting way above the ceiling of any air cover, but as you can see, there's none to speak of anyway."

The two torpedo boat officers had been briefed on the capabilities of the Multinational Force, and when he'd joined the ship's complement, Leading Seaman Molloy had kept everyone entranced for days with stories about the *Leyte Gulf* and the *Astoria*. But to experience the future firsthand, that was something else altogether.

The slate taking the feed from the surveillance craft—Lohrey called it a drone—was full of movies, obviously shot from somewhere above the Japs. One large frame, showing all five ships, dominated the screen. Surrounding it, five smaller "windows" carried live images of each individual ship. Lohrey played with another device, a flexipad, and the images danced around, the focus zooming in until it was like they were floating just above the deck of one of the ships. Kennedy could see hundreds of uniformed men there. It looked to be seriously overcrowded, perhaps a sign that the Japs were having transport problems. On one of the destroyers he thought he recognized the signs of an antiair drill in progress.

"These are good kills, gentlemen," said Willet. "But not good enough to justify burning up a couple of my combat maces. We can lead you guys right onto them, though. You can hit them tonight. There wouldn't be much moonlight anyway, but our weather radar says the cloud cover is going to be thickening up, too. You up for it?"

"Hell, yeah!" said George Ross.

Kennedy was just as eager, but he didn't leap in as quickly. "Captain Willet. These, uh, slates are amazing, but we don't know how to use them. Are you planning on leaving anybody with us?"

"I'll be staying," said Lohrey. "And I've brought some night-vision gear in the launch. We've got holomaps of this whole coast, and we've already planted beacons to take a solid position fix, so the lack of GPS won't be an issue."

The Americans stared at her with blank incomprehension.

"Trust me," she said. "It'll be cool."

SOUTHWEST PACIFIC AREA COMMAND, BRISBANE, AUSTRALIA

Hundreds of kilometers away, Lieutenant Commander Rachel Nguyen sat in a small, fourth-floor office of a colonial-era sandstone building, the headquarters of General Douglas MacArthur's Southwest Pacific Area Command. There was no air-conditioning, and her workstation pumped out enough heat to make the room extremely uncomfortable, even with the windows thrown open and a couple of old wooden fans spinning at top speed. Indeed, she suspected that their tiny motors probably dumped more heat into the room than the fans took out. Mold had discolored the walls and ceiling, and the smell of uncollected garbage drifted up from the alley below.

She was oblivious to it all, though, her attention focused only on the three Bang & Olufsen flatscreens arrayed across the huge desk at which she sat. Two officers from MacArthur's Intelligence Division sat in with her, an American major and an army captain from New Zealand. They were both 'temps, and although they outranked her, they deferred to her technical expertise, which meant that neither of them was comfortable using a wireless mouse. Or any kind of mouse, for that matter.

The screens ran video coverage and data dumps received from 21C assets positioned all over the local theater—vision recorded by a marine recon squad probing the Japanese garrison at Mackay, transcripts of signal intercepts sucked up by the AWACS birds, drone coverage of the frontline battles north of the city, even media packages from embedded journalists like Julia Duffy. Rachel hadn't spoken to the reporter since they'd briefly worked together on the *Clinton* after the Transition, but she followed Julia's stories whenever she could, and had privately cheered her on as she elbowed her way into the front rank of local war correspondents. She was as big a name as Ernie Pyle now. Somewhere behind the dozens of open windows, Julia's footage of the 'temp marine sergeant who'd turned the ambush earlier that day was running in a silent loop. Rachel had downloaded the feed from the local net as soon as a digital spyder alerted her that the reporter had filed. Nobody was watching now, however.

Instead, all three officers were concentrating on a data burst from the *Havoc*. The submarine was patrolling just south of the Whitsunday passage, blocking all attempts by the Japanese to land reinforcements closer to Homma. The small convoy of troopships and destroyers was cautiously beating south in a large window on the central flatscreen.

Rachel pulled in close on the largest of the transports, a captured tourist liner by the look of her. "It still doesn't seem right to me," she said. "There's something, I dunno . . . It just doesn't *feel* right. C'mon, you guys are the spooks. Do something spooky."

Major Brennan, the amiable American, just shrugged. "None of it makes much sense, Commander. The whole campaign is like the charge of the Light Brigade. They shouldn't have done it. They took New Guinea by balls, and surprise, and sheer weight of numbers. And even then, it cost them badly. They needed at least twenty divisions to take Australia, not the seven they sent. They needed air dominance, which they don't have. They needed secure supply lines, which they don't have. They can't move without you guys spotting them. They can't reinforce the forces they did get ashore. It's not rational. *None* of it looks right."

Captain Taylor, the Kiwi, leaned forward to squint at the screen. "I would have said it was a diversion. Like the Aleutians were supposed to be for Midway. But they've been here for weeks, and nothing else has happened. They're just running their heads into a brick wall."

Rachel still wasn't satisfied. She pulled the keyboard over and typed quickly for a few seconds. "I'm going to ask for a tighter frame on the big troop transport," she said. Her request flickered along fiber-optic cables scavenged from her old ship, the *Moreton Bay*, up to a dish on the roof of the building, which pulsed the signal into the ether. It was picked up by an AWACS flight, which relayed it to a communications drone. From there it traveled to the *Havoc*.

A few seconds later, a new control panel opened up, and Nguyen tapped out another set of commands. A Big Eye surveillance drone, keeping station at seventy thousand feet above the Whitsunday passage, began its descent to ten thousand feet. Even at that height, it remained invisible to the ships below. Tiny motors whirred, lenses refocused, and new data streamed back via the relay links to Brisbane.

Nguyen pulled in tight on the deck of the ship, where hundreds of men performed an exercise routine. But despite the activity, they appeared listless. "Not exactly ripping it up, are they?" she said.

"It's probably hot," offered Brennan.

"What about these guys?" Nguyen asked, pointing at four clusters of Japanese soldiers who weren't doing anything. They just seemed to be watching over the other men.

She refocused again, bringing them to a height of fifty meters virtual above the deck of the ship. "They look like guards to me. They're carrying rifles with bayonets fixed. They never take their eyes off the men exercising on deck, so they can't be lookouts. Take a look at the prisoners, if that's what they are. They look Chinese to you?"

She didn't insult the men by making the obvious joke about them thinking all Asians looked alike. Brennan and Taylor had both spent years working in the Far East before the war, and in the time that she'd worked with them, they'd never once given her reason to think of them as anything other than the most broad-minded of souls. It made her sort of ashamed of her own assumptions. She'd wrongly figured that everyone she met here would be dumb-arse bigots. It turned out her biggest problem with Brennan was her not sharing his encyclopedic knowledge of the puppet emperors of French Indochina. It had been his specialty as a visiting fellow at Poitiers University before the war.

The two male officers leaned forward and gave the scene their undivided attention. Taylor seemed just about to speak when something strange happened. One of the men exercising on the boat broke away from the others and made a run at the gunnels. He leapt over the side and dropped out of sight. Everyone on the deck froze for a second, but then two armed soldiers suddenly ran to the same side and raised their rifles.

Nguyen quickly refocused directly on them, pulling in to twenty meters virtual. "They're shooting at him," she said. "That's it. I'd bet my much-reduced pay packet that he's Chinese, not Japanese."

There was no sound, but they could all see the puffs of smoke and the impact of recoil.

"I think so," Taylor agreed.

The American major tapped at the screen with his index finger. "You know, these things are just marvelous, but I think we're going to need to grab some of these characters for a little—what do you guys call it—face time?"

Nguyen nodded. Almost to herself. "That's a bit beyond my reach, sir. But if you're willing to take it up the line, I'll cut you together a briefing stick from the take."

Brennan agreed as they watched the shooters on the deck of the ship slap each other on the back.

"I guess that one didn't get away," said Lieutenant Commander Nguyen.

7

NEW YORK

She wasn't Rita Hayworth, and it wasn't the Ritz, but Slim Jim wasn't about to write to his congressman, either. He'd never had his dick sucked so often or so well by a movie star. In fact, he'd never had his dick sucked by a movie star. Or by anyone he hadn't paid, really.

Not that Norma was a movie star just yet, but she *would* be. He'd already seen most of her films, and she was gonna turn into a seriously hot piece of ass.

And if his apartment wasn't the Ritz, it was nearly as classy. So classy, in fact, that all his dough nearly hadn't been enough to get him in. *Ms.* O'Brien had been forced to twist a few arms before the board had consented. And old Walt Winchell had helped out some, too.

He was a good fuckin' egg, old Walt was.

In fact, lying in his big bed overlooking Central Park, recalling every detail of the previous night, Slim Jim Davidson figured himself to be just about the happiest guy in the world. He wondered whether he ought to call Norma at the little studio apartment he'd bought for her, just to get her to come over and give his pipes a really good cleaning before he got up and seized the day. After all, it never hurt to remind a girl like that who held the purse strings.

But in the end, he didn't reach for the phone. His hand was stayed by something he'd never once experienced in his short and—up until now—reasonably shitty life. He was overcome by a small, warm feeling he vaguely recognized as a sense of . . .

Generosity.

A smile tugged at the corner of his lips, and a great rich, rolling laugh burst forth. Yeah, that was it, all right. He felt like just about the most generous motherfucker in the whole wide world. His mother would have been shocked, even appalled, since she was one of the worst fucking grifters he'd ever met. At least she had been, until she was beaten to death by that bum she'd hooked up with down in Tallahasee way back in—what, '35 or '36? Still, she'd a been proud that at least one of her boys had amounted to something. Then she woulda cheated him of at least half of what he was worth.

And he was worth plenty.

"Top o' the mornin', Ma!" he crowed to his empty bedroom. *"Top o' the fuckin' morning!"*

He reached around under the covers, enjoying the slippery feel of the silk sheets, taking his time to find what he wanted. His remote for the sound system had got itself kicked down near the foot of the bed. He snagged it up with his foot and thumbed the button to fill the apartment with music. The neighbors had complained about him playing AC/DC before breakfast, and he didn't want to get kicked out. So he'd dialed it back a little, programmed some Elvis, some Benny Goodman, a little Herb Alpert and Garth Brooks, to mix in with his favorite bits of Metallica, Sacre Coeur, and the Beach Boys. He had what Ms. O'Brien called "eclectic" tastes, but then, he had eighty years to catch up on, so she could just go fuck herself—a thought that brought on a slow smile.

So he was about to reach for the phone to call Norma after all, when his good humor was ruined by a hammering at the door.

Shit.

Only cops banged away like that, like they had a perfect right to go hassling guys in their jammies with half a woody on. He spat out a few curses, wrapped himself in a thick white robe—which he *had* actually bought from the Ritz, just for the effect—and stalked out of his bedroom, snatching up his flexipad from a low marble coffee table that was littered with cold food. He powered up, dropped the volume, and triggered the apartment's security system without even having to watch what he was doing. Slim Jim spent hours practicing with his flexipad. He loved it more than he loved any human being he'd ever known.

The hammering sounded again, and he yelled that he was coming.

His head had cleared remarkably quickly, considering all the champagne he and Norma had enjoyed last night. He swung open the door and barked at the two cops who stood there to get the hell inside, and stop disturbing his neighbors. He needn't have bothered, though, since they were inside before he even finished. A cursory glance told him right away they were feds.

Bureau men.

Ah shit.

He didn't piss his pants the way he might have ten years earlier. He had too many miles on the clock for that, but he could feel a shit-eating grin freezing in place on his dial. He turned away a touch too quickly, hoping they didn't catch it, and praying that his voice didn't waver too much.

"Sorry, boys," he called out as he headed into the kitchen to make himself a coffee. "My girlfriend don't sleep over, and she keeps all her best frocks at her place. I'm afraid Mr. Hoover will just have to call her himself if he wants to borrow a little something for the—"

Without warning, a blinding pain exploded inside his head. He was distantly, stupidly aware of it being on the left side as he toppled to the hardwood floor and down into darkness. Somehow it seemed important, that he'd been whacked from the left.

. . .

. . .

. . .

Garth Brooks was singing a cover.

When a man loves a woman.

Slim Jim was still in darkness. Then he was in . . . a sort of red fog. Like he was looking at the world from the inside of a bottle of wine. Then a jagged spike of fire shot through his head—the left side—and he needed to vomit.

He was lying facedown in a broken plate of cold linguine, and his beautiful bathrobe from the Ritz Hotel was all gathered up in the small of his back, leaving his butt exposed to the breeze. He thought about rolling over, but gagged on a mouthful of bile, then groaned as somebody grabbed his robe, yanked him up, and threw him into a lounge chair. The robe came open. His nuts were slapping around. It was all very undignified, and a million miles removed from his new life as a respected businessman and registered Democrat.

"Jesus Christ," he coughed. "I was only joking, fellas. He can *have* the dresses. She left 'em in the other room."

"Shut up, you cocksucker."

"Ha! That's good, coming from one of J. Edgar's boys," he said, even though he knew he was risking another whack upside the head. When none came, he blinked away some of the blurred vision that turned his attackers into dark blobs of attitude and body odor. They came into focus. Two feds, just as he recalled. Dark suits, white shirts, red ties. Everything buttoned down to within an inch of its life. Just as Mr. Hoover liked it.

"Okay, so I'll be shutting up now. But you *are* gonna want me to talk, aren't you? Ain't that the way it works? You beat the crap outta me, so I'll tell you what you want to hear?"

"Not really."

That surprised him, so he decided to shut up for real.

The room was quiet for a moment, save for Garth Brooks. As his stomach settled, Slim Jim decided that he really wanted that coffee now, perhaps with a shot of bourbon. But he decided it wasn't the brightest idea, giving these fuckin' apes another chance to beat on him, so he just kept quiet.

They both stared at him a little while longer, at least one of them with eyes that looked like hard little pellets of hatred. He spoke first. "Think you're pretty fucking smart, don't you, Davidson?"

"Dunno about that, man. Never finished high school." He shrugged.

Then the other one spoke up in a much friendlier, even cheerier tone. "Take a smart guy to end up here, wouldn't it, Jimbo? You couldn't buy most of this stuff on a special agent's salary. Definitely not on a seaman's wage."

Jesus Christ, they were gonna tag-team him. Good cop, bad cop. He would have laughed, if his head weren't pounding so much. "I do what I can," he croaked.

Bad Cop was back. "If you keep smart-mouthing us like that, asshole, the only thing you'll be doing is playing pick up the soap at Leavenworth. You got a house full of contraband here."

Slim Jim almost opened his mouth to protest. The apartment was the registered business address of at least half a dozen of his investment companies, and those companies all had valid permits authorizing them to obtain and use twenty-first-century technology. But the memory of his fearsome lawyer, Ms. O'Brien, arose to shut his trap before he starting babbling.

Bad Cop plowed on regardless. "I wonder how much the IRS would enjoy going through your books? That's how they got Capone, remember? And for that matter, what would the navy make of your new billet? You're supposed to be on active duty, aren't you, Davidson?"

"I do special services for the USO now," he said. And it was true, sort of.

"Does that mean banging that factory worker's wife? The actress nobody knows? Norma or Marilyn or whatever her name is now."

"She left that guy!" he blurted out, and instantly regretted it.

"And I'll bet he'd love to know where she's been these last few weeks," the agent continued with a palpably evil grin. "And what she's been doing. Or *who* she's been doing."

Slim Jim felt about half the blood in his body rush into his head, then just as quickly drain out again, leaving him giddy. He took in a long slow breath to settle himself and waited for the squeeze to come. He wasn't much surprised when it came from his new chum, the kindly special agent with the altogether friendlier line of patter.

"Yeah, you've got yourself a sweet setup, here, Mr. Davidson. Be a terrible shame if it all went sour and you ended up back on that chain gang. We could probably help you with that, you know. If you could see yourself clear to helping us out with a little problem . . ."

"Is that so?" Slim Jim replied without bothering to keep the bitter sarcasm out of his voice this time.

"Yes, it is," said Good Cop. "You see, we're a little worried about these characters you've been doing business with, out in California. Not all of them, you understand. Just a few bad eggs, here and there. We hear things about some of them. Disturbing things, really, that'd make a red-blooded man feel a little sick."

The agent seemed to falter over his next line. Slim Jim couldn't help but be impressed with his acting ability. He was very good.

"Sexual things," the agent said with a little choke in his voice.

Slim Jim was tempted to make another crack about Hoover, but that would only get him beaten again, so he rearranged his bathrobe to cover himself and buy some time to think. Some of the racier scandal sheets he liked to read had published big chunks of a couple of books written about the maximum cop after he'd died, or would have died, a few decades from now. Of course, you rarely saw that kind of gossip in the "quality" press, not straight up, anyhow. But Slim Jim understood there'd been a couple of slanting references to it. He'd been all fired up to publish the fucking books himself and sell them on the black market. But Ms. O'Brien had talked him out of it. Said he didn't need the headache of a fight with a vicious old fag like Hoover. That's what she called him, too, "a vicious old fag." Anyway, word was, J. Edgar was going berserk over the things people were saying about him back in the Zone. So maybe this was something to do with it.

Or maybe they were just busting his chops because he was—let's face it—a career criminal. Reformed or not.

Whatever.

His confidence was coming back now. If these guys had something on him, they'd a frog-marched him out of the place already. For the umpteenth time he found himself pathetically grateful to Ms. O'Brien and her ramrod-straight, pain-in-the-ass, do-it-by-the-fucking-book ways. She had insisted that *everything* he do be completely aboveboard—legally, if not morally. He even paid his taxes now. More than he had to, if truth be known. It was almost as if she'd expected this to happen.

He was gonna have to step lightly around Norma's old man, though. You could never tell what a pissed-off husband was gonna do. But the rest of the feebs' routine was all bullshit and bluster.

His silence seemed to convince Bad Cop to ham it up even further. The guy put his foot against the heavy coffee table that sat between them and gave it a vicious push, slamming the edge into Slim Jim's unprotected shins. He yelped in pain as tears welled up in his eyes.

"We know you're in thick with these time-traveling assholes, Davidson. We know some of these companies of yours have picked up contracts from them. You mix with them, and you got the inside track. You're gonna start working for your country again. Keeping us informed about them."

Two painful lumps were already coming up on his shins. He rubbed at them and complained in his whiniest voice. "I don't know what the hell you're talkin' about, or what you need me for. They don't make any secret of it, all the shit goes on there. They got nightclubs and bars for queers and lemons. They got all the races sleeping together. They don't give a fuck *what* you think about them. And neither does Congress, or weren't you paying attention. They're in *the Zone*, man. That's their world now."

At that, the friendly one looked disappointed.

His unpleasant partner leaned forward and bared his fangs. "For now, smartass. Just for now."

Bad Cop placed his foot on the edge of the coffee table again, causing Slim Jim to wince in expectation. But the agent just gave the apartment a good looking-over, and he didn't appear to like what he saw. Again, Ms. O'Brien was responsible for much of the decoration.

She'd flipped the first time she saw how Slim Jim had decked the place out, with moose heads and porn and ratty old furniture. "This isn't the image we're trying to create, Mr. Davidson," she'd said in that quiet, level tone that frightened him a little. "We are trying to establish you as a serious if somewhat rakish businessman, and this looks like the waiting room of a Chechen bordello."

And so, instead of seeing hunting trophies and a pair of billiards tables, the still-nameless agents got to appreciate his taste in fine Italian furniture, restricted technology, and modern art. *Lots and lots* of modern art, which had cost him nearly three hundred thousand dollars. That had made no sense to Slim Jim, until O'Brien told him that in eighty years, all this art crap would be worth tens of millions of dollars.

"What the hell is that shit, anyway?" asked Bad Cop.

Slim Jim smiled. O'Brien had made him memorize the schtick for when that Hersey guy came around to write about him for the *New Yorker*.

"Those ones over there are by a guy called Pollock. He went nuts in '38, and he started painting like that. It's like he was cribbing from that Picasso guy over there, don't you reckon? The three by the piano are called *Bird*, *Male and Female*, and *Guardians of the Secret*. My lawyer tells me they're full of seething imagery."

"Jesus H. Christ," muttered Good Cop, falling out of character for a second. "My little girl draws better than that."

"Yeah, looks like something a fruit would hang on his wall."

Slim Jim just deadpanned them. "Well, at least I'm banging the welder's wife, and not Assistant Director Tolson."

Both men colored visibly, and Slim Jim actually wished he could take it back. What the hell was up with him, making fun of Hoover and his boyfriend in front of a couple of hired gorillas like this? He had to stop watching those wise-guy movies.

The roughneck leaned forward again, his face bright red and shoulders like bowling balls moving around under his suit. "Listen, you little pissant. You might think you're a big man now. But you're a fucking bug, and you're gonna get squashed if you don't cooperate. You'll do as we say, or it's gonna go hard on you. That fucking lawyers of yours, we've got her number. You're going to start recording every conversation you have with her, every crooked fucking deal you put together. She's about *this* close to being disbarred, anyway. Her papers mean nothing here. All those bullshit laws she goes on about that nobody here even heard of. If you're smart, you'll dump her and give this guy a call."

A small slip of paper appeared in his hand.

"He's Bureau approved. He'll set you straight, and when you've done that, you're going back to California, and you're taking this with you." He held out a small black disk, about half the size of a garden pea. Slim Jim recognized it instantly. A microcam. Commercial, not mil-grade. The sort of thing that'd be picked up by an elint sweep in less than half a second.

What a pair of fucking bozos, he thought. *Probably don't know what an elint sweep is.* His expression, however, gave nothing away. "Okay, fellas," he said, showing them his open, honest palms. "You got yourself a narc."

"That's great, Mr. Davidson." Good Cop beamed at him. "You won't regret it, and your country will be grateful."

Slim Jim nodded and smiled nervously, as he figured he was expected to.

He never once looked at any of the eight microcams that had recorded everything in the apartment from the moment he'd opened the door. And those microcams *were* mil-grade.

HONOLULU, HAWAII

Detective Sergeant Lou "Buster" Cherry didn't so much wake up as find himself more conscious than unconscious, a state in which he slowly became aware of how much he felt like a bag of shit. It wasn't an unfamiliar feeling. There were the usual sorrows of an elephant-sized hangover, the headache like a meat ax to the brain, the nausea, the burning throat, the taste of bile, and the sour stench of his own sweat and unwashed bedclothes.

Then there was a growing list of unrelated woes. The chronic pain of a bullet wound he'd received on the job what seemed like a hundred years ago. The hateful longing for his first shot of the day. A dreadful suspicion that there was no booze left in the apartment anyway. A fading twitch of resentment at the bitch he'd once called his wife—a woman he hadn't heard from in well over a year.

There was something else this morning, too, as he lay on the fold-up cot in his studio apartment, under a pile of dirty laundry. He couldn't quite put his finger on it but . . .

"You're a disgrace, Detective."

He would have sat bolt upright, but that would've hurt too much. So he groped about for his revolver, knowing in the back of his mind that it was futile.

"Don't bother. We moved it out of reach, just to make sure you didn't hurt yourself."

"Who the fuck—?" The raspy voice was almost unrecognizable as his. He suddenly realized how long it had been since he'd spoken to another person.

He rubbed his eyes and lifted his head, taking in the two figures who stood in the center of his room. They looked as if they didn't want to move, for fear of stepping in something nasty.

"We're from the Bureau, Detective."

At first he had no idea what they were talking about, but then some very rusty memories of his former life began to creak back into place. "Hoover men?"

"Yeah. Special agents."

As they spoke, he became increasingly aware of just how much worse this headache was than normal.

"You got names?"

"Not today, Detective."

Cherry could feel a small storm building inside his head, but he tried to ignore it. "I'm not a detective anymore," he said. "They suspended me. Six years in uniform. Nine in plainclothes, and they fucking shit-canned me because that asshole Jewish kraut pulls some strings." He pushed himself up in his cot and saw a half-empty fifth of *Old Granddad* lying on the floor. *Hell, what's half-empty is half-full, too.* He was about to reach for it—thinking it'd make a fine breakfast, right about now—when one of them spoke again, and he froze in place.

"You think Admiral Kolhammer caused you to be suspended?"

"I don't think. I know. I got my owns strings I can pull."

The feeb grunted. "Maybe so. Because you're back on the job."

Then something—two things, in fact—landed in his lap: his badge and his gun.

A squall of confusion blew through his head, and there was no way to ignore it now. He'd been drinking something like a bottle of bourbon every day since they'd ass-fucked him.

He'd never been much for your actual *detecting*, in the past. Mostly he just knew whom to shake down. But the mystery of this resurrection, of the badge and gun that were lying between his legs . . . well, it was beyond him.

So he stared at the two men who called themselves special agents. They were dressed identically. Dark suits, white shirts, red ties.

The taller one shrugged. "Everyone knows you shot that guy during the riot in Honolulu. But not everyone cares. Get up, Detective, and pull yourself together. You've got work to do."

A tangle of emotions—relief, dread, indignation, and self-loathing—all boiled toward the surface. "I'm back on the same case? That dyke from the future got whacked with the Jap?"

"No. That won't be possible. You're going back to your old office, but you're going to be working for us—on the side."

"The Bureau?" he asked.

The tall agent just smiled.

8

He still used the wheelchair, although the treatment had restored his mobility to an amazing degree. Eleanor said he looked twenty years younger, but Franklin Roosevelt still felt uncomfortable.

He knew he wasn't long for the world, even with the treatments devised by Kolhammer's doctors. He might have given himself an additional three or four years at best, but you could never tell. There was so much to do, and he wasn't sure he could see it through to the end. The Transition had proved to be as hideously complicated as he'd expected. Creating the Special Administrative Zone where companies like Douglas and Boeing and Ford could fully exploit the patents they already had on future technologies meant that the market drove the pace of innovation as fast as it possibly could, without sending a shockwave through the "old" economy. But of course, it had also meant establishing an enclave within the body politic of the Republic, which many saw as being a protected reserve for the worst sort of subversive elements. It had cost him enormous amounts of political capital to ram the thing through Congress, even with a sunset clause, and he just knew that his enemies would play merry hell with it at every opportunity. Indeed, they were already doing so. The damnable House Un-American Activities Committee of Congressman Dies had suddenly stopped investigating the Ku Klux Klan and the German American Bund and announced hearings into the Zone that very morning.

Roosevelt had to wonder whether it was significant that Dies had met with Hoover and Tolson for dinner last night.

He really needed a smoke.

Giving up had been remarkably easy after receiving the implant, and it was a wonder how clear-headed he'd become. His mind ran at twice the speed, and he seemed to retain much more of what he read and heard. The physical craving for a cigarette was only a fleeting twinge nowadays, and even that bothered him less and less frequently. But at times like this, he still suffered a powerful need for the soothing familiarity of the habit.

It made him ponder what to do about the cigarette companies when the war was over.

For the moment, however, the war was a long way from being over. In fact, from many angles, the situation looked significantly worse. From the point of view of Lord Halifax, the British ambassador, who sat in the armchair directly across from him in the Oval Office, the course of events must have looked very grim, indeed. A long Roman nose and a high domed forehead conspired to give the ambassador a mournful countenance at the best of times. These last few months, his naturally forlorn expression had grown longer and more strained.

Admiral King wasn't helping.

"Ambassador," King rumbled, "you've got the *Trident* blocking the Channel. And you still have one of the most powerful fleets in the world anyway. If and when Hitler is fool enough to send his pissant little navy against you, it will be destroyed."

Halifax, who had been born without a hand at the end of his withered left arm, managed to balance a bone china cup of tea on his knee, and take a sip without any apparent effort. "Admiral King," he replied calmly, "the *Trident* is indeed a powerful deterrent. But she cannot be rearmed. She wasted a good many of her rockets on the Singapore raid."

King raised an eyebrow. "Wasted, you say?"

"You know what I mean, Admiral. It was a marvelous achievement, rescuing so many of our POWs—and yours, I suppose. It played very well with the press, and the Parliament. A second Dunkirk, and all that. But in so many ways, it was *irresponsible*."

Roosevelt felt the need to break in before this old argument flared up again. There were no representatives of the Multinational Force present, just the president, his three joint chiefs, and the British ambassador. But he'd found, time and again, that whenever two or more people gathered together, they could quickly and easily find themselves coming to blows on this particular topic. Indeed, it had joined religion and politics as a third great social taboo, never to be discussed in bars or at dinner. He knew, as well, that King privately agreed with Halifax, but he could see the navy chief squaring off for an argument.

"Gentlemen," he interjected, "there's no point raking over these coals again. The choice was not ours. It belonged to Kolhammer and his people, and they knew exactly what they were doing. Let's just move on, and deal with the present, shall we?"

It was midmorning in Washington, with an autumn chill lying hard against the windows of his office. Gusting, uncertain winds blew drifts of fallen leaves across the manicured lawns of the White House. The newly formed joint chiefs had gathered to give Halifax some unwelcome news. The U.S. Army simply did not have enough combat-ready divisions to bolster Great Britain's defenses against a renewed threat of invasion. The navy, heavily engaged in the South Pacific and still reeling from Midway and the seizure of convoy PQ 17 by the Soviet Union, could not secure the Atlantic or offer much more than token assistance in the event of a lunge across the channel by the Third Reich. And the army air force was still training pilots and building up its squadrons.

Of all the joints chiefs, Admiral King was the most dedicated to the idea of defeating Japan first. He was a constant critic of the accepted Europe First strategy, and the recent events had only hardened his resolve. "We are already heavily engaged in repelling an invasion, Mr. Ambassador," he said with customary bluntness. "Unless you had forgotten about abandoning your former colony. Remember? Australia? We have nearly a quarter million men down there right now because your Royal Navy built its guns facing the wrong way in Singapore, letting the Japs run wild."

Roosevelt closed his eyes and counted to five, but Halifax was a practiced diplomat and refused to rise to the bait. As brilliant an officer as King was, Roosevelt wished he could curb his tongue sometimes. He was without a doubt the most deeply loathed admiral in the U.S. Navy.

"Do I need to remind you, Mr. Ambassador, that if we lose Australia, we will find it virtually impossible to fight our way back into Asia? Tojo will control the East. He'll also have seized a significant manufacturing base and all the continent's natural resources, including *massive* uranium deposits."

When King sat down, the other joint chiefs started up, and Halifax listened to all the arguments, sipping from his precariously placed cup of tea, waiting until the last man, General Henry H. Arnold, finished explaining why precious resources were being diverted from building B-17s to B-29s, and even a prototype test squadron of B-52s.

Then the ambassador placed his teacup on the table in front of him and spoke quietly, but with great force. "Do you not see, gentleman, that this is *exactly* what Hitler is gambling on? That he can strike, and make up for his blunders, while we are still reeling from the aftermath of the Transition. It is *exactly* what the Japanese have done in the Pacific, withdrawing from China and moving their forces south to block any advance on the Home Islands. You may think yourself safe, protected by two oceans as you are, but we all know they are rushing to develop their own atomic weapons, and the means of delivering them onto your cities. If we give them time—even a little time—they will succeed."

Admiral King had developed the habit of playing devil's advocate in any discussion with the British, and much to Roosevelt's chagrin, he did so again now. "Mr. Ambassador, it's inevitable that Hitler will *attempt* a Channel crossing. We all agree with that. He shut down the Eastern Front when he had Stalin on the executioner's block. He would only have done that because he discovered what was about to happen out there. And no doubt, Stalin agreed to cease hostilities when records from the future confirmed us as his ultimate foe.

"But Hitler doesn't have it all his own way. I don't believe he can cross the Channel in the face of your air and naval forces. And from what we can gather, he and Stalin have agreed to a cease-fire, *not* an alliance. We're not facing two enemies. In fact, it's most likely that Stalin is using the breather to build his forces up for an assault into Western Europe."

Halifax pursed his lips, showing his annoyance. "And how, exactly, is that reassuring? Do you imagine that exchanging one tyranny for another is any sort of comfort?" He turned to face Roosevelt. "The British Isles remains the keystone, Mr. President. For the foreseeable future, American security is ultimately to be found in Europe, and you cannot secure Europe without first securing Great Britain.

"I understand the temptation to avoid every crisis and entanglement that might just befall you over the next hundred years. Nobody wants to see their mistakes repeated *before* they even happen. But the next six months might render all of that null and void. If Hitler controls Britain, you will be trapped inside your continental fortress, forever . . . or at least until he develops a missile capable of reaching you. You know he's mad enough to start an atomic war. He's most likely planning one against Russia, before he even completes his first bomb."

Roosevelt regarded the ambassador, then considered the faces of his joint chiefs, King, Arnold, and General George C. Marshall. Each man wore the same gloomy expression. It had been an increasingly common sight in Washington, ever since Stalin had pulled out of the war and the Japanese had turned away from China to launch what looked increasingly like a strategic kamikaze raid into the South Pacific.

The president realized he was playing with an imaginary cigarette, and he was irritated with himself for showing the weakness. The subdermal patches had ended his addiction to nicotine, but they could not eradicate the *habits* of a lifetime.

"General Marshall," he said to the Chairman of the Joint Chiefs. "The ambassador is essentially correct. Hitler is going to invade, or try to anyway, and he's going to do it very soon. He's building up forces just like he did after Dunkirk. He's moved two entire army groups from Russia into France. He's stopped bombing the cities and returned to attacking airfields. We have to assume, given his rapprochement with Moscow, that he is going to receive some sort of help from them, although God only knows what. And if he takes the British Isles, we may find it impossible to take them back.

"I need to know what we can do about it. We are looking at a new Dark Age, General. If these maniacs do develop atomic bombs, we may even be looking at the end of the world."

Marshall shifted uncomfortably in his chair, then spoke. "We've just sent the First Marine and the Americal Division down to MacArthur in Australia, Mr. President. They should have been on Guadalcanal by now, but after Midway we didn't have the Fleet assets to contest the island, and the Japs took it when they swarmed south out of China. It will be months before any more of our divisions come online. Even with the revised training techniques coming out of California—"

Roosevelt noticed that all three of his military advisers glanced awkwardly at the floor at mention of California.

"—we just can't push them any further."

"Can we move some of the trainees to the British Isles, to continue their training there, just as the Canadians have done?"

Marshall didn't look happy at the suggestion. "We could, sir. But in the event of an invasion, you would have unprepared troops fighting battle-hardened Nazis."

The comment hung in the air, unaddressed, for an uncomfortably long time. Roosevelt stared at the painting of George Washington that hung on his office wall. The first American president had also led poorly prepared forces against a formidable enemy. Ironically, that enemy now sat across from him, pleading for help.

"Nevertheless, please do it, General," he said at last. "If a nation of shopkeepers can stand against the Nazis, I don't see why our armed forces can't do the same. Prepare for the redeployment."

The office was immaculate, as always. Unlike many of the other seats of power in Washington, it did not boast any newfangled technology, such as computating machines or flexible pads.

Director Hoover had certainly secured a goodly number of those for the Bureau, to be certain, but they were located elsewhere, in the Records Department, in the laboratories, and in Assistant Director Tolson's office. Hoover liked to boast that steely nerve, a good aim, and unquestionable moral rectitude were still the primary weapons of any FBI agent. These new gizmos were really just better filing cabinets, and he, for one, didn't need them cluttering up his desk. He was perfectly capable of running the best counterintelligence service in the world without having to rely on some *electronic brain*.

When he used that line with the press, as he had at least six times this week, he always managed to put such a mocking emphasis on the last phrase that he never failed to gain an appreciative laugh from his audience of Bureau-approved reporters.

There was no laughter in the director's office this morning, however. Indeed, J. Edgar Hoover was incandescent with rage. His double-breasted suit squeezed around him like a straitjacket. Sweat prickled in his hair and ran down his neck. It hurt to breathe, and it was all he could do to stop himself from taking the sheaf of paper he was holding, ripping it into tiny little bits, and throwing them back in the face of the trembling agent who stood in front of him.

Normally, Hoover spoke in a high-pitched, rapid-fire staccato. It could be hundreds of words a minute when he was particularly upset. However, he'd sat white and shaking and utterly silent for ten minutes while he read the agent's summary report, over and over again. Sometimes, when he reached an especially odious passage, he was tempted to skim, but he forced himself to read those parts twice.

When he was finished, he put the paper down and said nothing. His small mouth puckered once or twice, but mostly his lips remained pressed tightly together. Assistant Director Tolson sat nearby and stared at the carpet. Agent Clayton, the bearer of bad news, waited for the hammer to fall.

"Despicable, filthy, gutter talk," Hoover managed to squeak out at last.

Clayton's mouth worked like that of a fish that had been snatched out of its bowl.

"I'm sorry, sir," was all he could say.

"Filthy!" Hoover roared now. "Get out of my office, and *never* set foot in this building again."

Clayton gaped and blubbed some more, but finally he had no choice but to bow and exit at high speed, with the director's red-rimmed eyes boring into his back as he fled.

"Is it as bad as people have been saying?" Tolson asked when the other man was gone.

Hoover turned on him like a spitting cobra, but as Tolson flinched, the director got a hold of his temper. It wasn't Clyde's fault, after all. As best anyone could tell, it was some egghead named Pope who was ultimately responsible, and he was dead. Hoover had briefly contemplated assigning a team of agents to track down this Pope fellow's parents or grandparents, just to ensure they never met, but he'd been told such efforts would be futile. This accursed time travel didn't work like that. Even if Pope was never born, it wouldn't return any semblance of sanity or balance to the world.

No, he was stuck with things the way they were, with a colony of perverts and half-castes spreading the most terrible lies about him, and poisoning America with their toxic philosophies and practices.

He again read the first page of Clayton's report, gripping the papers so tightly, his hands were trembling. Twenty-two subversive bookstores had been caught stocking copies of these awful books about him. They were cheap, pulpy copies, and there was no publisher's imprint on the spine, but the booksellers were all known Communists or fellow travelers, so there was no doubt the reds were behind it. He could hardly bring himself to look at Clayton's description of the latest "biography" that had surfaced out of California. *American Tyrant* by this so-called Professor Forstchen. A dime-store novelist of some sort, according to Special Agent Clayton. A purveyor of filth and fiction, even when he was writing alleged history like *American Tyrant: The Biography of J. Edgar Hoover.*

Again, if only he could stop this Forstchen's parents from meeting . . .

The director read Clayton's summary of the book.

It claimed that he was a blackmailer. That he befriended criminals and that he had suppressed evidence about the assassination of a President John F. Kennedy—the son of that bootlegging villain in London, no less! It said he was corrupt, and a liar, and had nothing at all to do with the killing of Dillinger or the capture of the Lindbergh baby's kidnapper, two of the greatest triumphs of his career so far.

There was even one claim that his mother had twisted his mind, and that he was a . . . a homosexual, and a pervert who dressed in women's clothing.

His head reeled. It was practically unbearable.

"Eddie, people have always gossiped," said Tolson, who looked worried even when he wasn't. "You can't let it get to you. It's just words."

Hoover's eyes were nearly brimming with tears as he regarded his constant companion. For once he spoke slowly. "Junior, words . . . they are . . . grossly insufficient to express the thoughts in my mind and the feelings in my heart for you. But mark me well, words can be weapons, too, every bit as deadly as a knife or a gun.

"Look at this, just *look at it*, would you. They're saying I knew about Pearl Harbor before it happened. That little weasel Popov is behind that, or that bastard Stephenson, or both of them, believe you me. And that Jewish rat Kolhammer is pulling their strings, and . . ."

He was beginning to heat up again, accusations and insults spilling out of him in a cascade of high-pitched, verbal machine-gun fire.

Tolson rubbed his eyes and shook his head from side to side. It was unusual for him to play an assertive role in their relationship. He was loyal, but very much the subordinate partner, two steps behind and one to the side. "Eddie, Eddie, *please*, you'll kill yourself. Come on, now, we've faced worse than this before. And besides, these people are vulnerable. They're a rabble. There's not a genuine hero amongst them, not like you and me. You know what it's like in California now. Those sort of degenerate shenanigans might play well with the Hollywood set, but decent Americans won't stand for it. You need to rally the people against this menace. You know Roosevelt won't do it. Why, he's half a red himself, what with that awful wife of his. The New Deal was naked socialism, no less. And then there's this desegregation garbage."

Tolson had actually climbed to his feet, and was stalking around the office now. He slammed the door closed and turned on the startled director. When he spoke, it was with unusual intensity.

"The *real* people aren't happy at all with that gang of perverts out there. They want things put right again. And we can do it, Eddie. They'd *expect* us to do it, to protect them the same way we protected them from the mobsters and kidnappers. They expect *you* to do it."

J. Edgar Hoover blinked away a tear. It fell to his desk, smudging a line of Special Agent Clayton's report, a horrid passage alleging that the director had worn—or would wear—a red dress and a black feather boa to some sort of homosexual orgy in a hotel in the 1950s. It was all lies and filth, carefully crafted to break his will.

But Clyde, that wonderful, dear, dear man, had led him through the darkness that threatened to envelop them both.

"You are my sword and my shield, Junior," he croaked as he stood and hurried around his desk to embrace the only human being, besides his sainted mother, whom he had ever really known and loved.

Clyde was right. Kolhammer and his kind would have to be fought. And J. Edgar Hoover, American patriot, would lead that fight.

As he pressed up against the familiar, reassuring bulk of Clyde Tolson's body, he was already plotting his counterattack. "I think I need to see Congressman Dies again," he said.

SPECIAL ADMINISTRATIVE ZONE, CALIFORNIA

A long time ago, in a universe far, far way, a much younger Phillip Kolhammer had read a book, *A Man Called Intrepid.* William Stephenson, the Canadian adventurer who was Winston Churchill's personal representative in the United States, was every bit as impressive in real life as he had been in the pages of that book. An infantryman and later a fighter ace flying Sopwith Camels in the First World War, he became a very successful businessman after the armistice—so successful, in fact, that he performed his current duties, as the head of Britain's intelligence operations in the western hemisphere, without being paid.

According to his biography, he was a believer, and for that reason, Churchill had placed him in his position above the objections of the old guard within British Intelligence. Stephenson had used his extensive business contacts to funnel information about the Nazis to Churchill during the latter's wilderness years, and when the old warhorse had finally made it to Downing Street, the Canadian had offered to personally assassinate Hitler. That plan was quashed by Lord Halifax, who was then foreign secretary.

For once, Kolhammer allowed himself a wry smile concerning the tangled threads of fortune within which he'd become trapped. He'd bet big money that Halifax regretted his decision now.

"Is something funny, Admiral?" asked Stephenson.

"Not really," Kolhammer said. "Idle thoughts, that's all. It's late."

And it was. They met in his office, which was swept every few hours for bugs. It was a bare space, particleboard walls and government-issue furniture. Kolhammer had softened the raw fit-out with some personal photographs, a rug he'd bought many years ago in Cairo, and a couple of armchairs, where he and Stephenson now sat, nursing mugs of coffee with rum shots. The office might have looked unimpressive, but it was a central node of the distributed infotech system he was building in the Valley. There was more network capacity in this one small room than in all of Washington. Not all of the equipment was authorized, however.

"You wouldn't believe the number of these things we keep finding all over the Zone," Kolhammer commented, holding up a bulky, primitive listening device. It was most likely an FBI plant. His counterintelligence people had swept it out of a bar down on Ventura that was popular with his officers.

"Actually, I would," Stephenson replied. "Hoover's more trouble than the *Abwehr* and the NKVD put together, at least as far as my work goes. You know, we gave that guy one of our best double agents—"

"Popov," said Kolhammer, who'd downloaded *Intrepid* for a skim-through before he'd first met Stephenson.

The Canadian rolled his eyes. "Yeah, Popov. You know, I can never get used to the idea that the world is full of people who know all my secrets now. Anyway, Popov was sent to New York by his *Abwehr* controller, this guy Auenrode. This is *before* Pearl Harbor, right? The Japs wanted to know all sorts of things about the defenses in Hawaii. The exact location of ammo and fuel dumps, which hangars are where, what ships and subs anchor at what piers.

"Hoover did *nothing*. He let this guy cool his heels for two weeks while he took off on a holiday with his boyfriend, with the mob probably picking up the tab. When he finally does get back, Hoover explodes, screeching at Popov to get out of his office."

Kolhammer knew the story. He even vaguely recalled that Popov had described Hoover as looking like "a sledgehammer in search of an anvil," although he hadn't seen that phrase when he quickly reread the book about Stephenson. He thought it was apt.

"Well, this is a pain, but I can live with it," Kolhammer said, twirling the antique listening device around his finger.

"I don't think you can, actually," Stephenson countered.

Kolhammer took a sip on his cold cup of coffee. It needed more rum. He was tired, and looking forward to a few hours' sleep on the cot he kept in the room next door. But he'd come to respect Churchill's spymaster as much as anyone he'd ever met, and if Stephenson was concerned enough to fly all the way out to California, it probably meant he had some real concerns.

"How so?" he asked.

Stephenson leaned forward as if to impart a secret, an unconscious gesture, given that this room was probably one of the most secure places on Earth.

"You know he's got agents crawling all over the Zone," he said. "And he's probably paying more for informants here than he is throughout the rest of the United States, and probably even in South America, too."

Kolhammer shrugged. "There's no secrets for him to dig up out here. The Zone operates under twenty-first century U.S. law and custom. He could set up a love shack with Tolson and start selling medical marijuana tomorrow, if he wanted to. No one would stop him. And likewise, he can't interfere with or stop what goes on out here. It's not his turf anymore."

"No, it's not," conceded Stephenson. "But underestimate him at your peril. Bill Donovan has OSS keeping very close tabs on Hoover, and he says the strain of the last few months is eating the man up. If he lashes out when he goes down, it's you he'll be aiming at and believe me, for a fairy, he hits hard. It's a laydown that he's behind this Un-American Activities bullshit. Donovan says a Bureau car picked up Dies and ferried him to dinner with Hoover and Tolson the night before the committee announced its new investigations. They've been all over one another like cheap Chinese suits for weeks, and remember, not everybody wants to publicly snuggle with Hoover nowadays."

Kolhammer snorted at the image and put his empty mug aside. A shaded lamp threw a small circle of light onto his desk. He peered into the gloom that lay just beyond. He could just make out a picture of his wife hung on the wall in the shadows on the far side of the room. She was lost to him now. He knew that, and the pain of their separation was never-ending.

"Bill," he said, "I don't doubt that you're right, and I'll give some thought to whatever precautions might be necessary. But my own comfort is a tenth-order issue right now. I have *real* enemies trying to kill my people, even as we speak.

"If I have to deal with Hoover, I will. Trust me."

Stephenson was not convinced. "You want to follow this HUAC thing very closely, Admiral. Every dollar you spend out here is raised in Washington. And they can cut you off, just like that. Dies isn't the only person Hoover is talking to, and the director is not the only one who wants to jam you back into your wormhole, or whatever it was."

Kolhammer made a rueful face at that. "Believe me, Bill, there are days I'd love nothing more. But the reality is, we're here. We fucked things up royally by coming here, and now it's my job to set them as right as I can. I know enough politics to watch my back, and if I have to kick someone's head, it'll get kicked. But I'm not going to pick fights for the sake of it. You're right. Our position here is tenuous. Bringing home those POWs generated a lot of goodwill. I get a couple of hundred letters a week thanking me for bringing home somebody's son or husband or brother. But in the end, we don't belong here. Not yet. Not for a fucking long time. And muscling up to somebody like Hoover, who enjoys genuine support—well, that's just dumb."

Stephenson poured another tot of rum into his empty coffee cup. "That day is coming, Admiral, whether you want it or not."

"I know. But a smart man chooses his battles. And he doesn't lash out at a strong enemy."

"Hoover's not as strong as he once was. None of the quality press have moved on him yet, but those pulpy biographies keep turning up like bad pennies, and the yellow press have been running with them. It's hurting him."

Kolhammer was as still and quiet as a bronze Buddha.

Stephenson smiled. "But you wouldn't know anything about that, would you?"

"I think," replied Kolhammer, "that it would be a mistake to personalize everything in terms of Hoover. Not all politics are personal."

Stephenson nodded, before changing the topic. "So, how are you settling in here, Admiral? I see you're still sleeping in that damned army cot. Couldn't you at least have requisitioned some kind of inflatable superbed from your own stores?"

Kolhammer smiled sadly and rubbed at his eyes. "I don't mind. A big bed would just remind me how empty it is every night."

"Excuse me, I'm sorry," said Stephenson, glancing at the picture of Marie Kolhammer on the desk. "It must be very difficult for you."

"And millions of others," said Kolhammer. "There's nothing special about me. Listen, Bill," he said suddenly, "would you like the grand tour? I normally can't get to sleep right away anyhow. I like to take a drive before turning in. I could show you the manor, as the Brits say, and drop you into town afterwards."

"Sure," said Stephenson, finishing his drink. "If you don't mind the drive."

Kolhammer called through to his PA to lock down the office and tell security he'd be sleeping at home for a change.

"You'll need your coat," he told Stephenson. "It gets chilly this time of year."

A female sailor was waiting by his Humvee out in front of the building. "It's been swept, sir. No bugs."

"Thank you, Paterson."

"I didn't think Admirals drove themselves anywhere," the Canadian quipped as he swung himself into the front passenger seat. "Or is this just another example of creeping socialism from the future."

Kolhammer shrugged. "It's like I said. I like to drive. It helps me wind down."

The campus was laid out around winding roads that had once been sheep and cattle tracks, when the land was owned by a grazing company. It was one of the few areas in the whole Valley not laid out on a grid system. The complex was still small, although large areas of land had been set aside for later expansion. They drove out through the checkpoint at the front gates within two minutes of Kolhammer starting the engine.

"I thought we'd run over to Sun Valley first," he said. "A lot of the aerospace companies are setting up there. It's close to Glendale airport, and there are good rail links."

"Fine by me," said his passenger.

There was almost no traffic on the way. A major change from his own time. They swung north toward the Verdugo Hills and around onto the old San Fernando Road. The temperature had dropped as the night deepened, and without the light pollution or smog of a megacity to block them out, the stars shone down hard and brilliant.

"Do you mind if I ask you something?" Kolhammer called out over the engine noise and the roar of their passage through the clean, autumn air.

"Not at all."

"Why do you care what happens out here? A lot of what you see here in the Zone must make you uncomfortable."

Stephenson didn't spend long mulling over an answer. "I'm here under orders. Mr. Churchill believes it's imperative that we speed up our research and development. The Nazis are doing so, and their engineers are very good. Better than ours in some fields. He thinks—we both think—that reinventing the wheel would be a criminal waste of time, given the circumstances. The real strength you brought with you was the knowledge and technical skills of your people. Concentrated here they form a—what do you call it?—a critical mass that the enemy can't hope to match. It's important that nothing interfere with what's going on here."

"So you don't care about the . . . ah . . . social . . . ramifications."

"Mr. Churchill feels that it's really none of our business," Stephenson replied.

"No," said Kolhammer. "But of course, Mr. Churchill doesn't have the complication of up to ten thousand time travelers setting up shop in one of his villages, does he? He's just got Halabi and her crew on the *Trident*, and maybe a hundred others scattered around—most of them the right sort of chaps who'd have no trouble at all getting membership at a good club in London."

"Admiral," Stephenson said around a smirk, "you wound me with such sarcasm."

They turned onto Sunland Boulevard, where North American Aviation was building a massive factory to produce F-86 Saber jet fighters. Work continued around the clock, with the sounds of construction loud enough to hear over the growl of the Humvee. Giant lights illuminated the complex like a sports ground in high summer.

"How many people do you have working there?" asked Stephenson, all business again.

"None yet, but there's about thirty aeronautical engineers off the *Clinton* attached to North American in Dallas and Kansas City. They'll move out here in a few weeks. Mike Judge is going to run the program from our side."

"There you go, then," said Stephenson. "I'll bet it's the same story all over the Valley. The war is going to be won here, Admiral."

"I thought I was the tour guide tonight."

"Well then, drive on, MacDuff."

They motored away from the island of light back into the dark bowl of the Valley, heading toward the glow of Sepulveda and Ventura. No blackout covered the L.A. Basin, which lay under the protection of an all-seeing Nemesis array. Traffic along Ventura was heavier, with a lot of cars from the city having hauled themselves over Cahuenga Pass and down into the Valley for a look-see. The neon signs of burger joints and all-night bars were strung along the side of the road like cheap Christmas lights. A dusty coupe sped past, full of teenagers who cheered and waved at the Humvee before powering into the night.

"Probably going to park outside a strip club for a couple of hours," said Kolhammer. "Trying to work up the courage to talk their way in."

"I saw my share of strippers in Paris during the Great War," said Stephenson. "I doubt there's much would surprise me here."

"Yeah?" said Kolhammer, who knew he was wrong.

The strip fell behind as he pointed the car at the foothills below the Hollywood ridgeline. The edge of the Zone was up there, at the boundary with L.A. A few lonesome lights winked at them from behind trees hiding the mansions of movie stars and producers. More of his loyal subjects.

For a while he'd had to assign two lieutenants to the job of screening him from the depredations of studio executives who thought the most important thing about the Transition was the access it gave them to a vast library of their own product they hadn't had to spend a dollar actually making. As frustrating as it was—and he'd come *this* close to shooting Sam Goldwyn—it had led him to make a decision that would probably alter the course of history as profoundly as the disaster at Midway had. It just wouldn't be as obvious or spectacular.

He agreed with everything that Stephenson had said earlier. But he'd also been speaking true when he said he was no position to get into a public brawl with Hoover, or any of the forces behind him. If his arrival here was going to mean anything beyond chaos and madness, Admiral Phillip Kolhammer would have to be willing to reach out and shape events with his own hands. But he could not be seen to be doing so.

He'd given a lot of thought to the problem, and in the end he could see no way around it.

He had carefully drawn up his plans, selected the right personnel, and put them to work in the Quiet Room.

9

PT 101, CORAL SEA, SOUTHWEST PACIFIC AREA

The tropical night was inky black, but out on deck, the wraparound goggles, which seemed to mold themselves onto the face, turned everything a bright emerald green. Everybody tried them at least once, and the worst anyone could say was that you lost a little depth perception, but it was a hell of a lot better than groping around in the dark.

"I'll bet somebody back home is making a packet, building these things," Chief Rollins said as they bumped over a slight swell on their way out.

"Not these, Chief," Lohrey replied. "That's a sixth-generation set of Oakleys you got there. The gelform seal alone is about seven decades beyond what you could manufacture here. But you're still right. At least two British and three U.S. companies are working on prototypes of a basic NVG. Of course, the Germans will be doing the same."

"What about the Japs, ma'am?" asked a young seaman.

"Doubt it. Not if they're smart, anyway. German optics are much more advanced. Tokyo would be better off leaving it to them, and not duplicating the effort."

Peering at the screen, Kennedy checked his position against Ross's boat. They were both booming along at top speed, following directions given by Lohrey and Chief Flemming, who talked to each other as though they stood just a few feet apart, rather than riding on separate boats. The night was particularly warm, and the blast of air across the decks was refreshing after having hidden out in the stillness of the mangroves all day.

The pilothouse was lit by Lohrey's glowing data slates, but they had covered the boat's windows with heavy black plastic. To steer, the helmsmen on both PTs were using the feed from a couple of dinky little "battle-cams." Lohrey and Flemming had rigged them up that afternoon, before spending a couple of hours acquainting the crewmen with the most basic functions of the equipment they'd brought on board. "Just in case we get killed," Lohrey had said in an offhand manner that had unsettled Kennedy.

New orders had come through from MacArthur's office via an encrypted data burst, requiring them to secure a number of survivors after the attack. That meant rewriting the plan, because Lohrey had originally designated the warships as secondary targets. Now they had to make certain the destroyers were sunk first. Some little Asian woman called Lieutenant Commander Nguyen (it sounded like *Noo-win* to him) had appeared in a recorded movie to brief them about it. The boats they had thought were troopships apparently looked more like prison transports now. They were still supposed to sink them, but now they had to grab a bunch of survivors for interrogation, too. That order came all the way down from MacArthur's office, but Kennedy suspected that Captain Willet was somewhere in back of it.

The PT boat skipper thought it very cold-blooded, and not at all the sort of thing he'd expect from a woman, although looking at Willet's intel boss, Lieutenant Lohrey, he'd bet his bottom dollar that she'd killed many more times than he had. When the revised orders came through, she'd been largely unconcerned, quickly redesigning the attack plan to knock out the destroyers first. Then they could nail the transports and pluck a few prisoners out of the wreckage without having to worry about any interference.

"Are they all like that, Moose?" he'd whispered to Leading Seaman Molloy at one point.

The survivor of the *Astoria*, a huge slow-witted fellow, had nodded sagely. "Aye, Skipper. I wrote my old man about them—you know he's on the Chicago PD—and he said they sounded a lot like gangsters' molls. Just as soon cut a man's throat as look at him."

But the thought hadn't put Kennedy off at all. Now, as they approached the point where they would wait for the Japanese, in the lee of a small, uninhabited island, the skipper of PT 101 found himself drawn to this female officer again. He couldn't help but admire the hourglass curves of the visiting lieutenant as she bent over a slate, jotting notes on the much smaller flexipad that she held in one hand. There was a two-foot swell running, but she had no trouble keeping her balance, and she moved around the cramped confines of the wheelhouse as though she'd spent her life there.

He wondered if she had a boyfriend or—even more exciting—a girlfriend somewhere. Possibly away up in the twenty-first century, when—

"We have contact," she announced. "Six thousand meters out and tracking south-southeast. Mr. Kennedy, you might want to have your men come to general quarters."

"I might at that," he agreed. "Chief, let's have at them, shall we?"

Chief Petty Officer Dave Rollins nodded once. "Aye, sir." Then he slipped through the blackout curtain, adjusting his borrowed night-vision goggles as he left.

Kennedy nudged the engines up so that the gurgle of the supercharged V-12s increased to a moderate growl. He could feel the power surge coming up through the deck as he grabbed his helmet and checked the straps of his Mae West. The Australian submariner donned her own helmet, the one that looked like SS headgear, and then fitted a pair of outsized reflective goggles over her eyes. She tugged at the straps on her body armor and fit the flexipad into a clear plastic pocket on her forearm. In doing so, it seemed to Kennedy, she transformed herself, losing even more of her individuality. Becoming less of a living, breathing thing than the creaky, roach-infested boat on which they sailed.

She looked like a killer, and nothing less.

It was an effect emphasized by the toneless voice in which she communicated with her comrade on the other PT boat. They exchanged information in a language that Kennedy recognized as English, but which was so heavy with jargon as to be impenetrable.

Lohrey turned her bug-eyed goggles on him and said, "*Havoc* confirms that Big Eye has designated five kills. Mr. Kennedy, on screen you'll see five thin beams. They're being directed onto the Japanese ships from the surveillance drone we've got keeping station above them. They're invisible to the enemy. They'll flash in sequence to mark the priority targets. So the first blinking line, there, is designating the lead destroyer. When she's taken out, the beam marking her sister ship will begin to strobe."

They'd been through this before, but Kennedy didn't mind being led through the mission again. Truth was, he felt more than a little unsure of himself. They were mashing together some very different fighting techniques, but he put away his misgivings and simply concentrated on not fucking things up.

"All ahead, full," he ordered, and the growl of the boat's engines became a roar as they leapt toward the enemy.

In the Combat Center of the *Havoc*, Captain Jane Willet watched the attack on-screen. Kennedy's boat was the first contemporary vessel she'd set foot on, and it had left a strong impression. Standing in the slightly antiseptic chilled air of her own submarine, she couldn't help but remember the raw sense of displacement she'd experienced as they climbed aboard the 101, to be greeted by its famous skipper.

He was the first celebrity she'd ever met. The runner-up in the fourth and final *Australian Idol* competition didn't really count, even if a much younger Jane Willet had once upon a time waited for three hours outside the Sydney Hilton to get his autograph.

"So, Captain, were you swept away by the famous Kennedy charm?" asked her executive officer, Commander Conrad Grey, as they waited for the attack to unfold.

"Did I let him shag me, you mean, Mr. Grey?" she smirked.

"Oh, Captain, please, what will the junior ranks think?"

Willet snorted in amusement. "Well, he was a very handsome man, Commander. The image files don't do him justice. But, no. Future president or not, he didn't get a leg over. Didn't even try. He seemed—I don't know—very well mannered and quite normal."

On the twenty-three-inch Siemens flatscreen, the two torpedo boats appeared in the opalescent green of low-light amplification, their wakes spreading and overlapping as they raced toward their prey. Part of her mind was out there with them. She recalled the faint stench of the boat's Copperoid bottom paint, the smell of *atabrine* tablets on the crew's breath, the abrasive feel of the saltwater soap in the officers' head, and the taste of the powdered eggs and Spam covered in chutney that they'd eaten for lunch.

The strongest memory she took away, however, was of the crew's grim black humor. They were a ratty-looking bunch, all half-naked except for the cut-off shorts and greasy baseball caps. They were unwashed and unshaved and had the resigned look in their eyes of men who didn't really think they'd make it back home. But they adored their captain, who would obviously do anything for them. And the only nod he'd made in the direction of the bizarre fate that might await him was the hand-painted sign on the outside of the boat's flying bridge.

It read, THE GRASSY KNOLL.

SOUTHWEST PACIFIC AREA HEADQUARTERS, BRISBANE

The small office in which Lieutenant Commander Nguyen now worked was crowded with men, all of them 'temps. There must have been fifteen or more squeezed in there, none of them sporting as much as a drop of deodorant. She was glad for the small circle of inviolate personal space around her that was guaranteed by the presence at her elbow of General Douglas MacArthur.

Nguyen had seen him around the building enough not to be completely freaked out. She'd even been part of a briefing team that had reported directly to him on one occasion. Nonetheless, it was quite an experience having such a legendary figure sit down next to her, so that she could talk him through the PT boat attack.

Interest in the convoy had metastasized since the incident captured by the drone earlier that day. More surveillance time had been allotted to the troopships, and additional analysts had been drafted in.

"It's like they *want* to be seen," Nguyen mused. "They have to be decoys."

MacArthur removed the unlit pipe from his mouth—she had told him the smoke would degrade the computer's circuitry. It was simpler than explaining the dangers of secondary smoke.

"How so, Commander?" he asked.

"Their blackout is seriously half-arsed, if you'll excuse my French, sir. Ditto their emcon—emissions control, you know, radio silence and so on. They know from experience that if we can see them, we can kill them, but it's like they're not even trying to hide."

"So you agree with Major Brennan that they're a lure of some sort?"

"I think so—very much so, in fact—but I don't have enough data to say for certain, General. If I had to take a punt, I'd say they've been sent down as sacrificial goats. Not to lure the *Havoc* into a fight, exactly. More to soak up whatever she fires at them."

"Let's hope we can get you some data, then," MacArthur grunted as the torpedo boats began to churn up a lot of water. It showed on the display panel as an explosion of lime-green fairy floss on a dark emerald sea surface.

Everyone in the room with a view of the monitor could clearly see individual figures moving to their stations on the deck.

"They're accelerating for the run in."

"Which one's Kennedy?" somebody behind her asked.

"The lead vessel," said Nguyen.

"Ha, that figures."

She couldn't tell whether the speaker meant well or not. She ignored him to concentrate on the feed from the drone. In contrast to the Japanese ships, the Americans weren't giving anything away. They maintained radio silence, and no telltale jewels of light sparkled from within their blacked-out cabins. They were shut up nice and tight.

Great fans of seawater began to spray back from their bows as they sliced through the swell. None of the small jade figures on deck moved now. They would be coiled and waiting. Nguyen wondered how loud their engines would be, and whether any lookouts on the Japanese ships had managed to obtain night-vision equipment of their own. Some had certainly fallen into enemy hands.

SOUTHWEST PACIFIC AREA, CORAL SEA

Ensign Shinoda, on the bridge of the *Wakatake*-class destroyer *Asagao*, did not have any night-vision goggles. Nobody on any of these ships did. In fact, the junior officers joked that the only new piece of equipment they'd taken south was a giant bull's-eye painted on the hull.

But Shinoda, who had graduated near the bottom of his class, did not question the wisdom of their orders. He had no doubt there was some good reason why they were nursing three ships full of Chinese and Korean prisoners through some of the most dangerous waters in the world. He was equally certain the captain would have been told why this most difficult task was assigned to two of the oldest, least capable ships in His Majesty's fleet.

So the young man pressed the Tsushima vintage binoculars to his eyes and scanned the obsidian blackness that lay beyond the windows, with the zealous devotion of a true believer. Even without the glasses that saw in the dark, or the ghost planes that floated just over the mast and took pictures that could see right through a man's uniform, even without the death beams and super-rockets of the gaijin, he still would bring honor to his ancestors. He would—

"*Shimatta!*"

The clouds parted for a second and let through a shaft of moonlight as bright and clear as a searchlight. And roaring toward him through the small oblong of illuminated ocean were two enemy vessels.

PT boats!

Shinoda screamed out a warning to the officer of the watch, turned his head away for just a second, and lost sight of them completely as the broken clouds knitted back together again. Chaos erupted on the bridge as Klaxons sounded to bring the crew to general quarters. Someone was yelling at him to explain, someone else was stabbing a finger at the skies, insisting that super-rockets were flying toward them. Curses and shouts reached him from the open decks, where men hurried to the ship's sad little battery of 4.7-inch guns.

The floor began to tilt as they came around to bear down on the heading where he'd last seen the boats.

"We've been spotted," Kennedy said with such detachment that he surprised himself.

"Pity," Lohrey said, staring into the pearly glow of her data slate. A dense mosaic of data and images was quickly filling all the available space. "Helm, bring us around on two-two-five," she said. He heard her voice through the strange cushioned pads that covered his ears, as though she were talking on the phone.

"We'll see if they got a lock on us, or just a sneaky peek," she added.

Kennedy spun the wheel, and on the slate in front of him caught a glimpse of the other boat biting into the swell on a new heading, just as the rush of the first shells screamed overhead. He felt and heard them explode behind them. His men held their fire, not wanting to give away their new position.

"He's changing course, but blind," said Lohrey. "He got lucky, that's all, and it won't last. Follow the strobe in, Skipper, and let 'em have it."

Star shells burst in the air behind them with a muffled *whump*, and suddenly the sea was alight with a fierce white blaze of light. The pictures from the battle-cams disappeared momentarily, until Lohrey adjusted the filters. Kennedy bored in toward the target, heedless of the new danger. It was a straight shoot-out, and whoever got off the first good hit would win.

The engines howled at the outer limits of their power, driving the boat across the light choppy waves in a series of long, loping jumps from one wave crest to the next. The sound of the hull as it smacked down was massive and hollow, a series of booms that threatened to shake them apart before the Japs could land a blow.

On screen he saw the first two fish leap from the tubes on the other boat and go racing away, just a second before the word LAUNCH flashed up in front of him.

"Fire!" he called out, hoping that the funny little headset he wore was turned on and working.

His own torpedoes launched. The long finger of a searchlight swept over them as all his machine guns opened up to put it out. He swung the boat around in a viciously tight arc as shells exploded in the seas around them, raising plumes of salt water that fell on his decks like heavy monsoon rain. Lohrey was braced in a corner of the wheelhouse, her head tilted at a strange angle, as though she were daydreaming. She could have been staring off into space, but with her eyes hidden behind the goggles, he couldn't tell.

"Hit!" she called out a split second before he felt the double crump of two torpedoes detonating about a thousand yards away. A few seconds later, the same sound, even closer, as two more struck home. The panel display split, showing two images of crippled ships. While he watched, secondary explosions tore along the aft section of one of them like a string of giant firecrackers. Then one volcanic eruption of fire and light blew the entire ship apart, whiting out one half of the split window. The supersonic blast wave reached them within a heartbeat.

It was like hitting a wall. Everyone was thrown off their feet. The boat slewed around, uncontrolled for a moment while Kennedy wrestled with the wheel.

"New targets, Lieutenant," Lohrey called out in a strangled voice. She was nursing an arm that dangled lifelessly.

"Got them," he called back as the navigation screen reappeared on the panel in front of him. He spun the wheel until he'd lined up the flashing blue arrowhead, which designated the bow of the 101, with the red line, along which the battlespace arrays of the HMAS *Havoc* wanted him to launch his next attack. *Or something like that.* The details were beyond him now. All he knew was that he had to follow the red line at top speed and trust in some glorified box of nuts and bolts about two hundred nautical miles away, which apparently knew more about these things than he did.

He desperately wanted to snatch aside the blackout curtains and have a good long look at things with his own two eyes, rather than relying on the battle-cams. As long as he didn't think about what he was doing, it was simple enough to follow the schematics on the screen, but if he gave even a moment's consideration to the situation, it all got very scary—driving a boat at top speed through a burning formation of enemy ships, with torpedoes and cannon fire filling both the air and the water.

LAUNCH.

The word flashed up, and he relayed the order again.

"Fire!"

The aft tubes spat their loads into the water, and he wrenched them around on a new heading that appeared on the panel. All his guns were firing now, the big twin 50s thrashing away like jackhammers over the ripping snarl of the 30-caliber turrets. The 37 mm antitank gun barked, and the Bofors mount thundered. The uproar was so great, he wondered how anyone heard his orders, even with the little wire microphone sitting so close to his lips.

A distant *boom*, like the cracking of a mountain.

Lohrey's voice, strained but not shouting. "We just lost a transport. It must have been carrying ammunition or something."

ALL TARGETS SERVICED.

Kennedy eased back on their speed and asked Lohrey if she knew where Ross's boat was. She propped herself against the bulkhead, reached across her body, and used her good hand to pull the injured arm over to where it could rest on a raised knee.

"Broken elbow," she explained before he could ask. "I've medicated myself."

The flexipad was sheathed in a clear plastic pouch on the bad arm. She used a pencil of some sort to input the query and nodded to his panel. Kennedy looked back and realized that now he had a top-down view of the whole area. Three ships were ablaze and going down, with hundreds of tiny figures streaming over their sides. A small box of text floated next to each of them, marking them as the two destroyers and a troopship. A couple of large floating pools of wreckage and smoke and burning oil marked the points where the other ships had been completely destroyed. They were tagged as FLOATING DATUM POINT 1 & 2.

PT 59 was surrounded by a flashing blue box as it described a long elliptical course around the nearest FLOATING DATUM POINT. Kennedy reached over to tear down the blackout curtains, so he could see where he was going at last.

"You may find it easier to leave them up," said Lohrey. "*Havoc* is sending a burst downline now, nav data to grab us up some prisoners."

As the words left her mouth, the skipper's slate reformatted into another top-down perspective, with an inset window magnifying a small group of survivors swimming away from one of the sinking troopships. A red line plotted the suggested course to pick them up. It avoided the danger of sailing too close to the crippled vessels, which might yet explode, but seemed to run right through masses of struggling swimmers.

"Can that be right?" he asked.

Lohrey considered the image for a second, before nodding. "You'll think me unladylike, Lieutenant, but you should just get on with it. We want to clear this area as quickly as possible. *Havoc* says there are hostile aircraft within the threat bubble. They'll see the fires."

Jack Kennedy struggled to keep the distaste off his face. She was suggesting he open the throttles and ride over the top of dozens, if not hundreds, of survivors. Most of whom might not even be Japs, if that Nguyen lady was right.

"Can you patch me through to Barney Ross on this thing? It's secure, right?" he asked, tapping the headset.

She played with the flexipad and nodded.

"Barney, you there? It's Jack."

"I can hear you, buddy. That was great driving before. And good shooting, too."

His friend's voice was so clear, he might as well have been standing right next to him in a quiet bar.

"Barney, I've got to pick up the prisoners now. You want to get going, and we'll catch up. There's bogeys about."

A short, hard laugh told him that PT 59 wouldn't be going anywhere until her sister ship was ready to cut out, as well.

Kennedy signed off. This time he did pull down the blackout curtains, and he looked out onto the burning oil slicks with abhorrence distorting his features. The screams of dying and injured men reached him faintly over the industrial noise of buckling metal and exploding munitions. He could see the flashing navigation schematics at the lower periphery of his vision, but he kept his eyes fixed on the waters in front of his boat.

"What the hell's he doing?"

"He's threading his way through the survivors," said Willet, watching the minor drama on the Intelligence Division's monitor. "Mr. Grey, bring all of the Nemesis arrays online, and keep Lieutenant Lohrey updated on the threat boards via the live link."

"Aye, ma'am," replied her exec.

Willet had been crouching over the display for the last twenty minutes, and now she stood up. She stretched her back muscles but never once took her eyes off the feed from the Big Eye drone.

She'd wondered whether Kennedy might do this, endanger himself and his crew rather than run down a few men he'd been trying to kill just minutes earlier. It said something about the 'temps, or maybe just about him, that the war hadn't yet coarsened their spirits completely.

She envied him, in a way. She'd lost almost any feeling she might have had for her enemies when her sister was beheaded on camera by Moro

Front guerrillas in the Philippines, ten of her years ago. Corina had been a field-worker with the Save the Children Fund when she was kidnapped from a village she was assessing for a new water treatment program and a microcredit loan scheme. The guerrillas had murdered her and two doctors from Médecins Sans Frontiéres, doing so "live" on the Web.

When Filipino and U.S. Special Forces arrived at the village, they discovered another atrocity that hadn't been broadcast. Everyone in the hamlet who'd been tended to by the "infidels" had been executed, including children who had been treated for cataracts. They'd had their eyes put out with burning sticks. It was the only time in her life that Willet regretted joining the submarine service. For weeks, she'd been tortured by a violent desire to sink her fingers into the throat of the man who'd killed her baby sister. "Captain?"

The *Havoc*'s commander drove away the haunted memories. It'd been a long time since she'd thought of her sister in anything but the most positive terms. Years of therapy had taught her how, but now the defenses she'd erected seemed to be creaking—and threatening to collapse.

"I'm sorry, Mr. Grey. Go on," she said.

Her exec didn't embarrass her by asking if she was all right. He simply relayed the update. "Lieutenant Lohrey reports that they're picking up the prisoners now, Captain. There are two aircraft, probably Japanese flying boats, inbound for their position. ETA nineteen minutes."

Willet nodded, an old melancholy pain settling around her heart. "Tell them to get a move on."

It was just about the worst thing Moose had seen since that night on the *Astoria*, when the other ship had suddenly "appeared" right inside his own.

Lieutenant Kennedy was stomping up and down the decks, a machine gun in his hand, cursing like Moose had never known him to before. He'd had to shoot a Jap who tried to fire a flare pistol into his face when they pulled alongside him, although to Moose's way of thinking, he should have known that was going to happen. The Japs, they'd sooner swim into the mouth of a shark than surrender. You could tell which ones they were, too. Anybody trying not to be rescued was a fair bet to be working for their rat-fuck little Emperor.

These other guys though, Chinese and Koreans according to the lady officer, they were a mystery to everyone. They couldn't swim over to the boat fast enough, and now there was maybe a hundred or more of them jammed up against the hull, all thrashing and yelling and carrying on like Charlie Chan gone loco.

Lieutenant Kennedy said they were only supposed to get six of them, but they'd all been crying out "America number one!" and "Japan bad, USA good!" And what with them clawing at each other to get up over the sides, there had to be nearly twenty on board already, and soon there'd be almost no room to move. Moose had spent all his time on cruisers before he got moved to the little mosquito boats after Midway, and he was sort of worried they might capsize at any minute, given how much extra weight they had to be carrying.

Chief Rollins was yelling at him to get the prisoners' hands tied up. Mr. Kennedy was yelling at Miss Lohrey that this was the dumbest fucking idea anyone ever had. Some dripping-wet Chinese guy was trying to hug Moose as he tried to cuff some Japanese guy who'd had all the fight shot out of him. And then someone else was calling out that the planes would be here any minute, and then one of the ships they'd torpedoed went up in this gigantic fucking bang that lit up the whole ocean and guys were screaming and crying and the next thing he knew there was a *real* long burst of machine-gun fire and then a long, long second of quiet, before someone said, "Holy shit."

And Moose looked over and saw Miss Lohrey standing at the edge of the boat with one arm in a sling. In the other, she had an old tommy gun, with a drum mag just like the ones his dad said Capone's men used to have, and goddamn if she hadn't just emptied the whole fucking thing over the edge of the boat and into the guys swimming below. Well, maybe she hadn't. Maybe she'd shot it into the air or something. But then maybe not, because the Chinese were swimming away from the boat now, 'cept for a whole bunch of bodies that just bobbed up and down on the water leaking blood everywhere in the warm orange light of the oil fires.

SOUTHWEST PACIFIC AREA HEADQUARTERS

"Jesus Christ. She killed them."

Rachel Nguyen's stuffy little room had become unbearably hot and close. They'd watched the relayed vision of the pickup with mounting concern as more and more survivors crowded around the PT boat. As they formed a thick carpet of thrashing limbs and bobbing heads, the men around her murmured that it was all going wrong, that they couldn't possibly get away before the planes turned up and spotted them. MacArthur himself had just told everyone to pipe down when the female officer from Willet's submarine grabbed a gun off a sailor, walked over to the edge, and opened up on the densely packed mass of floating men.

On the screen, the 101 was now moving again, motoring slowly through the disbursed survivors, but nobody said anything until MacArthur spoke up.

"What the hell just happened, Commander?" he asked, turning away from the screen to offer Rachel his full, glowering visage.

She looked at him quizzically. "From what I could see, the mission was in danger of failing, General," she said. "Lieutenant Lohrey acted to regain the initiative."

MacArthur's face was a dead mask. He gave away nothing of what he was thinking. But the men around him weren't so well controlled. Rachel caught some of them staring at her like she had suddenly grown a second head.

"I can see," she said quietly, "that you disapprove."

10

PEARL HARBOR, HAWAII

The old girl was a ghost ship, or she felt that way to her new skipper.

Captain Mike Judge squinted against the glare of the midday sun and tried to feel the heartbeat of the USS *Hillary Clinton*. Dozens of screens functioned around him, constantly updating the reports on the state of the great warship. But Judge had spent nigh on six years of his life aboard this vessel, in one role or another, and he fancied that he could still feel something that the circuits and plasma screens couldn't tell him.

His darlin' was lonesome.

She'd lost a quarter of her complement to the tragedy at Midway. Another two thousand had transferred Stateside, into the research and training facilities that Kolhammer was building in the Zone and at Fleet in San Diego. Pilots without planes to fly now found that their engineering studies were a national asset of such value that they were banned from frontline combat. Systems operators and engineers, programmers and flight technicians had ceased to perform any duties at the sharp end of conflict. They, too, had been reclassified out of harm's way and into hundreds of lecture rooms and laboratories.

The *Clinton* echoed to their absence.

She ran on a skeleton crew now. Her fuel–air explosive catapults were beyond patching up again. With no spare parts left, and no prospect of manufacturing them in the near future, she couldn't hurl her few surviving warplanes into battle. A pickup squadron of eleven SeaRaptors constituted her entire strike arm, and half of those had been rebuilt from parts scavenged off fighters wrecked beyond all hope of repair. Most of her AWACS wing had been attached to the Eighty-second MEU in the South Pacific. The rest were stationed on shore with the F-22s and a couple of in-flight refuelers. The heavy lift choppers, the search-and-rescue birds, the Seahawk troop transport, and Apache ground-attack squadrons had been split up and repositioned all across this part of the globe. Some were here in Hawaii; others were in California, being reverse-engineered as part of a hundred or more programs to accelerate contemporary weapons systems and technology. The bulk had gone to MacArthur down in Australia. It said a lot about the weakened state of the *Clinton* that she was effectively running away from that fight, which was the main game in the Pacific theater for the moment.

"Let's get you home, Hillary," Judge said to himself. The much-reduced bridge crew didn't hear him. Maybe a quarter of the number of men and women who normally staffed this station were posted at the remaining consoles today. So many screens and panels had been removed from the bridge that it felt like a half-completed house.

A mile away, the diminutive form of a couple of contemporary cruisers rode proudly at anchor by the *Siranui*, a dozen tenders fussing around them as they prepared to escort the *Clinton* back to the U.S. mainland.

And hadn't he taken some bullshit over that—not all of it good-natured, either. Here she was, the most powerful warship in the world, trailing along on the apron strings of a couple of old tin cans. There'd been more than one barroom brawl over it down in Honolulu, although nothing as bad as the riot that had burned down half of Hotel Street just after they'd first arrived at Pearl.

An ASW Seahawk was fueling down on the flight deck, one of the few aircraft they'd be ferrying home. Even with her teeth pulled, the *Clinton* remained the highest priority target for Axis forces in the Pacific theater. She still represented the single greatest collection of twenty-first-century technology, and there would inevitably be Japanese submarines willing to risk it all just for a shot at her. British Intelligence was even warning that the Germans had uncrated a prototype long-range U-boat specifically to go hunting for her. It was said to be heading their way via the south Atlantic and southern circumpolar latitudes. Not that Judge was likely to lose much sleep over it.

Now, if they'd grabbed a 21C Chinese Warbow submarine through Manning Pope's wormhole, then sure, that'd be worth staying up late for. But if the Nazis had just dusted off the old *Walther* blueprints, then there were going to be a bunch of German submariners dying a long way from home sometime soon.

A female lieutenant appeared on a screen to his left. "Captain Judge.

We'll have the vidlink to Admiral Kolhammer established in five minutes, if you're ready, sir?"

"Thank you, Brooks. I'll take it in my ready room."

He stood up and prepared to hand the ship over to his Exec, Commander Takeshi Morgan, as a flight of Hellcats buzzed overhead. They'd be just out of the plant in L.A. As he left the bridge, he tried to imagine the *Clinton* with F-86 Sabres, or even a squadron of supercharged Corsairs spotted on her decks after the upcoming refit, but it was just too weird. Even four months after the Transition.

SPECIAL ADMINISTRATIVE ZONE, CALIFORNIA

Kolhammer was always glad to see Mike Judge. They were able to vidlink only once every couple of weeks, when a relay became possible via a series of AWACS planes or Multinational vessels or both.

Jeez, what I wouldn't give for just one lousy fucking satellite.

Sometimes he thought it was like waiting for the stars to align, a concept that would have amused his wife, an enthusiastic consumer of astrological forecasts and a self-proclaimed skeptic. He never understood how she managed to be both. *It's a chick thing,* he supposed.

"Happy trails, Admiral? I don't believe I've seen you smile since we got here." The stars had, indeed, aligned, and Mike Judge was on-screen, speaking from the ready room next to the *Clinton*'s flag bridge, where Kolhammer himself had once worked.

The admiral sent another, slightly sadder look down the encrypted link to Hawaii. More a gesture of resignation than a smile. "You caught me out, Mike. I was thinking about Marie."

"You meet her folks like you were planning to, sir?"

Kolhammer admitted that he had. "It was good, too, Mike. They were wonderful people. Marie used to speak so fondly of her grandpa and her nana, I figured it was because her own parents were away so much with work, and she spent so much more time with them. But they were good people, Mike. The best, like she always said."

He let go a long breath that he hadn't even realized he was holding in.

A dialog box opened up in the corner of the screen: LINKS VERIFIED SECURE. The sysops at each point in the communications chain had just confirmed that no Elint sensors were attempting to crack open the link between the two men.

It was time for business.

"We'll be ready to leave in four hours, Admiral," Judge reported. "I've already got antisub patrols out. All the approaches are clear. You have any word on that phantom Nazi boat?"

"Hysteria and bullshit, as best anyone can make out," Kolhammer replied. "Having said that, though, I want you to proceed on the basis of a worst-case scenario. After the *Nuku* and *Sutanto* landed in Japanese hands, we can't assume anything. We don't know for sure that the *Dessaix* or the *Vanguard* didn't make it through as well. One of them might have materialized in Hitler's bathtub, we just can't tell."

"We've been running active scans here, sir. Haven't had a ghost of a return yet."

"I know. They're probably back home right now. But they were both stealth ships. And even though I can't imagine the crews cooperating if they were captured, we have to plan for it anyway. What is it that Lonesome is always saying? Prepare for the worst, and dare the good Lord to disappoint you."

"Well the worst would be the nukes falling into the wrong hands," Judge pointed out. "We haven't heard from our subs since the Transition, either."

"Yeah, but we would have," said Kolhammer. "If Yamamoto or the Nazis had got their paws on a boomer, half the world would already be glow-in-the-dark. I'm less worried about them, Mike. But I really want you to sneak back as though you *do* have a rogue Nemesis cruiser on your case."

"I promise we'll sneak out of here like a preacher slipping away from a Reno whorehouse, sir."

Kolhammer allowed himself another small grin. He did miss Mike Judge's Texan charm. "Okay. Just don't fuck around with half-measures, Mike. If you get even a hint that you're being stalked, I want the *Siranui* to go wild. How's Colin Steele doing, by the way. He happy with the way the ship's running now?"

Kolhammer had promoted the *Leyte Gulf*'s executive officer to command the *Siranui* as soon as Steele had gotten out of hospital after Midway. He'd been shot early in the brief battle belowdecks between the crews of the *Gulf* and the *Astoria*, the contemporary cruiser in which the late Captain Anderson's ship had partly materialized. The images still gave Kolhammer the creeps.

"Yeah, he's pretty much got the cobwebs shook out," said Judge. "All the software's been converted. There's a few differences between the Japanese Nemesis boats and ours, but Steele has had most of those systems taken offline, so his guys don't have to worry about them. It'll be cool. Anderson and Miyazaki did most of the hard work before, you know . . ." He trailed off.

Kolhammer didn't reply, beyond a brief grunt. The investigation into the killing of his two officers on Honolulu had gone exactly nowhere in the past four months. To his own shame, he'd let the matter slip off his radar, too. There was just so much to do. He made a note to e-mail Admiral Nimitz about the case in the morning. He hadn't been close to Anderson, but she'd been a fine officer, and he'd been very impressed by Miyazaki, the *Siranui*'s surviving senior officer, in the short time he'd had to deal with him. From all reports, the two of them had worked well together, quickly getting an American crew settled onto the Japanese Self-Defense Force vessel. They deserved better.

Kolhammer returned to his discussion list. "Halabi's been bouncing her sigint take across to me every twelve hours. Things are grimmer than hell in the U.K., but she doesn't think the *Kriegsmarine* would try a sortie while she's still packing. She's down to six antiship missiles now, though, with four antisub, and her air defense stocks are at fifteen percent. Pretty soon she'll be like you, Mike. A floating Radio Shack. But Raeder can't be sure of that. So he's bottled up for now."

"How are the natives treating her, sir? If you don't mind me asking."

Kolhammer frowned. "That guy the Brits had as liaison in Pearl, Sir Leslie, he's been supportive. And Churchill has backed her. I think Prince Harry has been twisting arms at the Palace on her behalf as well. But I suspect she's doing it tough, Mike."

"She *is* tough, Admiral."

Kolhammer thought he detected something more than professional respect in Judge's voice, but he let it pass. The new captain of the USS *Hillary Clinton* wasn't married. He hadn't even been seriously hooked up before they arrived here.

"She is, indeed, Commander. Now, see that you get yourself back in one piece," he continued, changing tack. "I know it's breaking your heart, but we need to clean out the Big Hill. She's a lot more valuable to us stripped down to bare bones. The retrofit's going to take a good eight or nine months, and even then she's not going to need more than a fraction of the systems she's still carrying. Meantime, I got Leslie fucking Groves turning up here every second day with empty deuce-and-a-halves, telling me to fill 'em up with everything from Nemesis processors to espresso machines."

"Well, he is building a better A-bomb, sir," Judge teased.

"Yeah, I know," said Kolhammer, rolling his eyes. "And he gets only about a tenth of what he wants, but it plays hell with the project management for everyone else. Even with all our processing muscle, and some of our people holding his hand, that bomb isn't going to be ready until late '43, early '44 at best. It's not like we brought any centrifuges or fast breeders through with us. Meantime, I've got immediate need for processing time on about a hundred and forty different design and production lines, damn few of which I would have chosen as priorities, but what are you gonna do?

"We're trapped by the politics, Mike. Roosevelt got the Zone bill through Congress by the skin of his teeth and the grace of that goddamn sunset clause. You've never seen anything like it, the scaremongering and bullshitting that went down. You'd think we were setting up the fucking Fourth Reich here in the Valley."

"Or the USSA, if you listen to Hoover," Judge added, causing Kolhammer to throw up his hands.

"Oh, jeez, let's not get into *that*. We just don't have time. Listen, Mike, I'm sending data in this transmission. It's the specs for the project I want you to take over when you get here. I want to ramp up production of the F-86 by the end of winter, but I also want to be ready to jump through another generation, up to a prototype F-5 by the end of next year. You're going to get that ready for me. Study up on the package while you're en route, and choose your division heads from the guys you've got with you. You can prep them along the way. I want you to tie up and come running down that gangway, raring to go."

Kolhammer wasn't really expecting Judge to object, even though he was effectively taking the *Clinton* away from him. He'd been out to Hawaii a month earlier, and the ship had a lost feeling about her, like an unfinished story that would now never be written. Everyone he spoke to wanted to move on to their next assignment. It was a sorry way for the old girl to end up, but he told himself—they all told themselves—that she'd be back one day, kicking butt and taking names, just like her namesake.

The two men had a few more minutes before they lost the link.

"What's the latest with Jones?" asked Kolhammer. "I haven't had an update today."

"I've sent along his last four data bursts, Admiral. The latest came an hour ago. They pretty much blocked Homma's advance before it really got going. Lonesome wants to pull his armor and close air support out of the line, link up with 2 Cav, and hit the Japanese flanks. They can't get reinforcements past Willet and Spruance. They've tried air supply out of Moresby, but it's just not their gig. They're well and truly fucked.

"Jones should have it wrapped up pretty soon, which'll be a boost for the Aussies. Truth is, they were shitting themselves."

Kolhammer shrugged. "Fair enough. They had good reason, too, after New Guinea. The whole thing was developing a very unpleasant momentum. So you think we can get the Eighty-second back here soon?"

A lopsided grin spread over Captain Judge's tanned face. "I don't believe

General MacArthur will let Colonel Jones or a single one of his marines out of sight before VJ Day. He knows possession is nine tenths of the law."

"Tough shit," said Kolhammer. "I need him here to work up the land warfare programs. The training cadre we put together is good, but it doesn't have the critical mass I need. MacArthur can make do. You'll see—I've also included a package for Jones in the transmission. Make sure it gets out to him before you leave."

"Will do, Admiral."

Kolhammer looked at the handwritten list on his desk. There was one last item he need to discuss. "I really don't like the look of the reports coming out of Europe, Mike," he began. "When did you get your last update from Halabi?"

Judge frowned on-screen. "We received an encrypted burst via relay yesterday. Why, has something else happened? The Soviets haven't moved, have they?"

Kolhammer shook his head. "No. Nobody's sure which way they're going to jump, or when. Only that they will, when they think they can. No. I'm just worried about the pace of the German buildup. I have our sigint and imaging people on them twenty-four–seven, and we all think it looks like the surge is coming very soon."

Judge pursed his lips. "You really think they'll try a crossing in autumn?"

"I doubt they'll wait until next year. First of all, they've killed thousands of their best officers in the purges, post-Transition. The survivors are the sort of yes-men and buttheads who'll tell Hitler what he wants to hear—that the Channel's just a glorified river crossing."

Kolhammer leaned back in his chair and ticked the next points off on his fingers.

"And of course, Hitler—fuckin' nutjob or not—doesn't think he can afford to wait. And he's right. There's already a shitload of 'temp forces training in the U.K., and more men and matériel flooding in by convoy every day. Young Harry's set up his regimental HQ in Scotland, and the Brits are working hard to leapfrog some of their key technologies. Our new weapons system will start coming online early to mid next year, and of course, Groves is going to deliver the bomb a hell of a lot quicker than he would have before we arrived. So Hitler knows he has to go now or never."

Judge nodded and shrugged fatalistically. "That's why the Luftwaffe's been hammering at the RAF and the *Trident* so hard."

"Yeah," said Kolhammer. "It's really costing the Germans, but the attacks *are* degrading the air defense net, and eating up Halabi's own antiair stocks. There's going to come a day soon when her Metal Storm pods run dry, and the only thing protecting her then will be the 'temps themselves."

Judge nodded. "You want me to fly some of our Triple-A stocks over ahead of us?" he asked. "Our laser packs are good, and Metal Storm's at forty-eight percent. We can still spare some."

Kolhammer thought it over. He didn't want the most valuable ship in the world left defenseless. Even without her catapults and squadrons, the *Clinton* was still a prize worth risking a whole fleet for. He'd sleep a lot easier when she was safely back in San Diego and being stripped for her retrofit.

"Hold off on that for now, Mike," he said. "But when you get closer to home and I can cover you with shore-based CAP, we might rush a few pallets of MS reloads across to Halabi. She's going to need them."

A time hack in the corner of Kolhammer's screen began a one-minute countdown, indicating the end of the comm-link. He let himself relax a little. "It'll be good to have you folks back, Captain. Even if the old tub is down at San Diego, I could use a few more friendly faces out here."

Judge took his lead from the senior officer. He dropped out of character, as well. "From what I understand, you've got too many new best friends there. Every longhair and hippie in America is making tracks for the Valley, if you believe the press."

"This is nineteen forty-two, Mike. Hippies and long hair haven't been invented yet. But you're still right, after a fashion. American population's about a hundred fifty million right now, and some days it feels as if about fifty million of them are moving here. They've all got their reasons, I guess. Some personal. Some political. But you know, we could do without it. I even had a delegation of African-American labor unions in here begging me to run for president after Roosevelt—"

Judge grunted. Knowledge of the president's impending demise had sent the country into a tailspin until Roosevelt had promised to submit to an intensive course of therapy, supervised by Kolhammer's senior medical officer, Major Margie Francois.

"I think they see me signing the new millennium into law on my first day in office," Kolhammer grumbled.

Mike Judge smiled at the admiral's obvious discomfort. "You gotta wonder how Ike and Harry S. feel about that," he said. "Or Kennedy, speaking of which, there's an intelligence package came through on the last relay from Brisbane. Young Jack features prominently. Jones wants to forward it to your intel people. I've got mine working it now. We didn't have it long enough to brief you."

"Understood. We're about to lose the link. Take care, Mike."

"Will do, sir."

The picture dropped out instantly.

Of all the artifacts they'd left behind, instant global communications, and the feelings of omnipotence they engendered were perhaps the hardest to let go. He had a lot of technical and human capital devoted to reinventing them, even though it would be many years before they showed any real results.

His usual policy was to invest massively for the short-term gain. This war wasn't going to be won by the side that launched the first orbital rocket. More prosaic advances like a good grenade launcher, a better tank with a more powerful gun, penicillin, and smarter human resource management were the paths to victory. Even so, 4CI—command, control, communications, computers, and intelligence—were still the key to dominating the battlespace of the future, and he was not going to let anyone get a march on the U.S. in these fields.

Kolhammer couldn't shake his frustration at the makeshift data links that forced them to patch together relays and jerry-built networks like the one he'd just used to talk to Mike Judge. It was annoying as hell. Although he still had Fleetnet access on his desktop, it was restricted to material that had been archived in the lattice memory of the Task Force ships when they were ripped out of their own time. Not only did they have to deal with the comm-links, but they had lost access to the almost infinite resources of the Web, as well.

He supposed he shouldn't really complain. He was old enough to remember life before quantum computing. Hell, he could even recall his old man setting up the family's first TRS 80, with a magnificent 4K of RAM and a tape cassette for permanent file storage. But having grown used to what now felt like infinite bandwidth and processing capacity, it was maddening to have to deal with scarcity again.

As he reviewed the discussion with Judge, the admiral felt a nagging sense of having forgotten something. He flicked an eye over his handwritten notes. *Nothing there.*

He was about to shut down his computer for the night when it came to him. Judge had asked him about the Soviets. They were the great unknown. Would they sit out the whole war, conserving their strength? Would they attack Hitler when he was fully engaged in Western Europe? Or would they turn on their former allies, the liberal democracies, which seemed fated to consign them to the garbage dump of history? Apart from signing a separate cease-fire with Hitler, and impounding the ships of Convoy PQ 17 when they arrived in port at Murmansk, the Kremlin had given no indication of which way it might lean in the future. The intelligence services of the West were devoting enormous resources to the riddle of Soviet intentions, but so far to no avail.

Kolhammer rubbed at a headache building in his temples as he contemplated the problem. Without the satellite capabilities he'd left behind on the other side of the wormhole, there didn't seem to be much he could contribute. He'd largely been left out of discussions on the issue in Washington.

But that didn't mean he was content to leave the matter in the hands of the 'temps. In some ways it suited him to be out of the loop. The KGB had so many moles in the West at this time that Kolhammer was happier to work on his own. In the twenty years he'd been fighting a holy war, there'd been some staggering advances in electronic intelligence gathering. But there had also been a return to the basics. Spy cameras in low Earth orbit were great for some things. But there was nothing like having a real pair of eyes on the target.

Kolhammer leaned forward and cut the power to his computer. As secure as it was, it held no files of any relevance. The covert team he had sent into the Soviet Union were from the Quiet Room.

They didn't exist.

YAKUTSK, SIBERIA, USSR

Without GPS, they would have been lost, were it not for the guide. Major Pavel Ivanov had seen a great deal of his homeland during the long wars of the twenty-first century. His duties as a Spetsnaz officer had taken him to a dozen different former Soviet republics, to fight enemies as diverse as death-obsessed Muslim jihadi and private mercenary forces serving the Motherland's oligarchic supercapitalists. He had seen the slaughter at Beslan, taken part in the even bloodier siege of the Cathedral of the Resurrection in Saint Petersburg, and fought all over the Central Siberian Plateau during the Chinese incursions. He knew Chechnya and Kazakhstan and Georgia better than he knew his family home in Saratov. But he had never been to Yakutsk.

The old Korean who had agreed to lead them had spent eight years in a labor camp on the Lena River and was convinced that Ivanov and his team were White Russian grandees, or maybe Cossacks. For Mr. Kim that was enough to explain why they would be fighting the Bolsheviks. He had not heard of the Transition, and had goggled at Ivanov as though confronted by an escaped lunatic when the Special Forces officer tried to explain.

They had decided, in the end, that Mr. Kim should just think of them any way that suited him.

The guide was sleeping now in the back room of the cabin, cocooned in a thick Polarguard sleeping bag, snoring loudly, his belly full of self-heating MREs. He was in heaven. Ivanov was not.

The woodcutter's lodge had been abandoned many years ago, when this tract of forest was logged out. It offered the benefit of isolation, but had needed three days of repairs to make it vaguely habitable. The six-man team had replaced half the roof and most of the floorboards, rebuilt the fireplace, braced a partly collapsed rear wall and shovelled about half a ton of bear shit out of the front door. There was no furniture. It had probably been looted, according to Kim, so they had fashioned their own tables and benches from the almost petrified limbs of cedar and birch lying on the floor of the denuded forest. Solar sheeting covered the roof, recharging the batteries of the slates and flexipads that added their glow to the smoky, pungent oil lamps. Five slates cycled through the feed from their Sentinel Systems, watching for any human incursion into the area around their camp. There had been none, but two of the team were out checking on the defenses anyway.

They took turns to work the perimeter every four hours. The only vehicular approach to the little valley was along an overgrown logging road, two klicks to the south. Surveillance cams covered the track, beaming images back to the lodge via laser-link relay. Command-detonated mines could turn long stretches of the approach into killing boxes.

The Sentinel Position Denial Systems, or PODS, which had been the very first item of kit unpacked when they arrived, were now buried on five surrounding hilltops, ready to deploy against any serious ground or air attacks.

The team was good to go. They were taut and straining, like a bow drawn for too long. But Ivanov was waiting. He would not move against the targets until the first snow flurry touched his nose. Then he could be reasonably certain of their isolation and relative safety from reprisals.

For the moment he checked his watch. Two hours until nightfall.

"Mikhail," he called out to the stocky, brown-haired man who was watching the Sentinel feeds like a hungry cat watching a mouse. "It's time to swap with Vendulka. You need to rest before we head out."

"Okay, boss."

Mikhail spoke with a guttural New York accent, but could drop into good Russian, the language of his migrant parents. Sergeant Michael Fedin, from the Eighty-second, was one of two marines who had been assigned to Ivanov, both of them first-generation Americans from Russian émigré families.

The other, Corporal Joe Pilnyak was out in the woods with a British SAS Lieutenant, Pete Hamilton. The Englishman had picked up his workmanlike grasp of Russian at Eton, where he'd played rugby with Prince Harry. He later polished it at the Foreign Office language school and on a posting to Moscow as a junior military attaché.

Fedin called out to Lieutenant Zamyatin that it was time to get up. Vendulka, or Vennie, Zamyatin was a Russian Navy medical officer who'd been on secondment aboard HMS *Fearless*, the British helicopter carrier, when it was destroyed by the Transition. Now she was one of only eighteen survivors. She emerged from the small room where they'd built three sets of primitive bunk beds, rubbing her eyes and yawning.

The last member of Ivanov's squad, a Turkic-speaking Russian Navy diver, came off the Australian Light Littoral Assault Ship *Ipswich*. Petty Officer Victor Abizad was still sleeping in the bunkroom, adding his snores to those of Mr. Kim.

As Fedin disappeared into the bunkroom for a quick nap, Zamyatin poured a coffee from the pot atop the camp stove and took his place in front of the displays.

"Josep and Peter are just passing the fourth POD," she announced.

Ivanov grunted in acknowledgement. He busied himself with packing the supplies he and Fedin would need for the thirty-mile hike to the nearest camp just outside Ust Maisk, on the river Aldan. They would lie up and observe the camp for three days before returning. Mr. Kim said that at least a thousand prisoners were being held there under the control of the Ministries of Coal Production and Forests. Many were lowly draftees, caught up in the purge of their units by the NKVD. At least eighty to a hundred, however, were officers. They were being held in a separate compound just outside the main camp. Signal intercepts indicated that they came from a division that had openly rebelled when the NKVD had arrived with orders to detain three quarters of the staff officers on the charge of crimes against the state.

The men were doing punishing physical work in the coal mines of the Lena Basin, living in the most primitive accommodation, on starvation rations, with no medical care. They would not survive the winter. Ivanov's team had traveled to the ends of the earth to find these men, and to liberate them. He and Admiral Kolhammer hoped they would form the nucleus of a Russian resistance.

11

SOUTHWEST PACIFIC AREA, THE BRISBANE LINE

While Julia Duffy was growing up, having received a good deal of her education from popular media, she assumed that the Mobile Army Surgical Hospital, or MASH, was born in the Korean War.

In fact, the idea of a self-contained medical unit, performing surgery and providing postoperative care immediately behind the front line, was a child of the Second World War. The first MASH units were established in August 1945. Or they would have been.

Duffy drove into the 8066th Mobile Army Surgical Hospital in early October 1942, not in Korea, but about a hundred kilometers north of Brisbane, Australia. It looked just as she expected from all those years of watching syndicated reruns on TV: the khaki tents and ramshackle huts made of corrugated iron and ply board, the odd assortment of harried-looking medicos, the sense of barely controlled chaos as waves of casualties arrived on litters. It even boasted a helipad, on a hill cleared of vegetation, just up from a big open area that served as a triage point. The seasons were turning to summer in the southern hemisphere, drying everything out, so that some days she felt as if the air itself might just catch alight. The MASH unit was caked in a fine red dust, stirred up by passing choppers.

There were only nine dedicated medevac choppers in this theater, however, so they tended to fly in only the most critical cases. Marine Sergeant Arthur Snider definitely wasn't critical. He might yet lose his leg, but his life wasn't in grave danger.

His company CO had shoved him onto a Blackhawk that was dusting off five of his comrades who *did* need to get onto an operating table, and inside of fifteen minutes if they were going to pull through. Those who did survive would do so thanks to Snider, who was the toast of his unit for rallying the counterambush back on Hill 178.

Julia Duffy arrived about an hour and half after Snider, determined to get an interview. She had a shit-hot story to relay back to New York, via Rosanna in Hawaii, if she could just find this guy for an interview.

Her jeep slewed to a halt in a cloud of red dust in front of the hospital's postop ward. She thanked the driver and hopped down, heaving her backpack, Sonycam rig, and machine pistol. She waved away an Australian nurse who came running at her with a horrified look on her lumpy 1940s face. Julia was still matted with gore and filth from the fight back on the line. Her reactive-matrix armor was so heavily caked with blood and mud that she could feel it stiffening up in the warm spring sunlight.

The nurse kept coming. "Are you okay, young man?" she cried out.

Julia eased off her helmet, shaking her hair free.

"Oh!" said the nurse. "I see. You're one of them."

The reporter couldn't help but smile. It was a thin, wan shadow of a smile that peeked out from under the adrenaline backwash and deep body revulsion with which she was so familiar—but a smile nonetheless.

"That's right," she said. "My name's Duffy. I'm looking for a marine corps sergeant, a 'temp, would have come in about ninety minutes ago. Leg wound. Got clipped up on One-seventy-eight in that big ambush this morning."

The woman brightened up considerably. "Oh, you mean Sergeant Snider!" She beamed. "He's still waiting to go into surgery. They say he saved his whole company. There's a Movietone cameraman coming to film him tonight."

"Is there?" Julia said. "Well, I was up on One-seventy-eight myself, this morning, Nurse . . . Halligan," she continued, reading the woman's name tag. "Do you think I could talk to him?"

Nurse Halligan seemed to consider Julia in a new light now. She took in the befouled armor and the futuristic machine gun; the fighting knife that was still covered in dried, blackened blood; the bandaged hand and the field sutures that had reattached a flap of bruised skin on her left cheek. "Are you one of those special soldiers, Miss Duffy?"

"Actually, I'm a reporter, ma'am. For the *New York Times*. Normally embedded with the Eighty-second MEU." She hoisted the Sonycam. "But I was on assignment filming the sergeant's platoon this morning. I'd very much like to talk to him now, if I could."

Not for the first time was Julia interested to see the wonder, and even a touch of dread, that so often came over contemporary women when they met their counterparts from the next century. More important, this one displayed no hint of the guarded response that might have characterized a more media-aware individual from her own time.

"Well, it's not usual, but I suppose, if you were with him this morning . . . of course, of course, just follow me."

For just a moment, Julia allowed herself to enjoy the warmth of the sun on her face, even if that face presented a savage mask to this other woman. She threw the backpack over one shoulder, her MP-5 over the other, and hung the powered-down helmet from an eyehook on her web belt. She then detached the little Sonycam, checked the battery and lattice memory, and slipped her fingers through the hand strap as she followed Nurse Halligan to one of the big preop centers. The Sonycam was little bigger than a pack of cigarettes, and sat quite comfortably in her palm. She wet a fingertip to wipe away a bloody smear that was obscuring part of the lens.

Turned out, the 8066 was a big facility. It looked like it could handle a lot of death and trauma. Julia estimated that they could probably deal with a surge of a thousand or more cases—say, a couple of shattered battalions. She made a mental note to grab a few stats and some background on the unit before she left. There might even be a good feature in it, especially if nobody else had thought to cover the premature birth of the MASH concept.

The censors would go for it, for sure, because they loved stories that made the folks back home think their boys were getting the best treatment in the world.

The coppery smells of blood and horror hung over everything, blotting out the mentholated scent of the eucalyptus trees, the smoke of battle, and even the stink of so many unwashed bodies. Trucks rumbled in and out constantly, disgorging litters weighed down with unconscious men, taking away freshly patched-up marines and soldiers. American uniforms dominated, most of them 'temps, but she heard British and Australian accents. Even some French. Three soldiers walked by who could only have been from the New Zealand Maori Battalion, their faces dense maps of native tattoos.

Just when she was beginning to sink into the period detail, a flight of Super Harriers off the *Kandahar* screamed overhead, thousands of pounds of locally made dumb bombs slung under their hard-points. Nobody even looked up anymore.

Nurse Halligan threaded around a couple of stretcher-bearers who were grabbing a few z's. She threw a look back over her shoulder to make sure Julia was keeping up, and pushed through a set of swinging doors into a large building that seemed to have been stapled together out of materials scavenged from an abandoned building site.

As she pushed through the doors behind Halligan, Julia caught the reek of disinfectant and dying flesh. It rose up to unlock memories of other casualty wards, some military, some civilian. In the end, she decided, they were all the same, just mounds of broken bodies and the glazed-over, uncomprehending eyes that all asked the same question. *Why me?*

The men in here still wore the bloodied uniforms in which they'd come off the line. Nonetheless, Duffy's entrance drew a few stares. She was an alien, almost barbarous vision, even among these men who presented a facade of martial savagery. Not everyone followed her path through the gurneys and canvas cots, though. Most in fact did not, either because they were insensible with pain or medication, or because battle had numbed them to a state of existential collapse. However, enough of them struggled up, and pointed, and whispered to qualify as a minor commotion.

Snider saw her, even before she could find him. "Hey, Miss Duffy. Over here!"

He was propped up on a folding chair in a far corner, his injured leg resting on a wooden crate and enclosed in a bright orange inflatable tube that could only have come from a twenty-first unit. They must have fitted him on the dust-off. Five or six men were gathered around him, clearly hanging on his every word. They all turned to check her out. Some were completely taken aback at the sight of her, their eyes going wide in surprise. One whom she recognized from Hill 178 nodded and waved. Snider beckoned her over as Nurse Halligan said good-bye and wished her well.

"This is her, boys. The reporter I told y'all about. She's from the future!" Then without warning, his excitement and gladness to see her turned to uncomfortable solemnity. "Miss Duffy, I didn't get to thank you for what you did this morning. Some of the boys told me you shot them Japs was fixing to stick me after I got hit. Said you drilled 'em like fucking paper targets on the range, if you'll pardon my language. They also said you got the Jap who killed poor Smitty."

They all peered at her fighting knife then. Some staring openly, some just flicking a nervous glance at it.

"And Miss Duffy, I'm sorry if I was out of line with you, you know . . . when things was turning to shit up there."

Julia raised a bandaged hand and demurred. "It was a busy day at the office, Sarge. I've had worse. But how are you doing? I see they got you a gel sleeve on the chopper. That's good. You'll probably keep the leg."

Snider perked up at the news. "Better than that, Miss Duffy. It's a fuckin' million-dollar wound. I'm going home. Won't be dancing too many foxtrots from now on, but who really gives a fuck, eh?"

Julia pulled up an empty ammo crate and insinuated herself into the circle of wounded men. She slipped off her backpack and leaned the MP-5 up against the wall. Snider gave her a quick introduction to all of them, bar one, whose name he didn't know. The man introduced himself as Corporal Robert Payne, a Canadian artilleryman who had been standing near a howitzer when a shell exploded in the tube.

"You know, Sergeant," said Duffy, "You might just dance the foxtrot again after all. It'll take a while, but knee reconstruction wasn't a big deal up in my day. And most of the senior Task Force medical staff have been pulled off active duty and put into teaching hospitals. Of course, I gotta tell you, the fuckin' foxtrot is never coming back."

Duffy waited until the men's laughter and ribbing died down before speaking again.

"Sarge, do you think you could see your way clear to an interview? There's already a lot of talk about what you did this morning. You want my opinion, they're going to turn you into a hero and send you out on the road back home, selling war bonds with John Wayne and Hedy Lamarr."

Sergeant Snider was openly surprised to hear that. "Hedy Lamarr, you say. That's a classy dame. You think she'd want to hang out with the likes of me?"

"Buddy, when I'm finished, you'll be beating her off with a stick. Matter of fact, you'll be able to walk into a room full of Hollywood starlets and know there won't be a dry seat in the house."

Snider's friends all broke out into catcalls and cheers, and Julia made certain to grab a few lines from each of them about what they thought of his efforts on the hill.

When she was finished she checked to make sure that the lattice memory had stored the interview, and she copied it to a spare stick, just in case.

"There's one other thing you could do for me, Sarge, which I'd really appreciate."

Snider pulled himself a little higher in the fold-up canvas chair, wincing as he did so. "You name it, Miss Duffy. I figure there's no way I can repay you for drilling those guys."

"Well, in fact, there is, Sergeant. There's some guys from Movietone who are going to be looking for you later. Could you possibly tell 'em to fuck off?"

Snider winked theatrically. "Consider them fucked, ma'am."

The University of Queensland sat within a great bow of the Brisbane River about seven miles from the city center. There wasn't much to it, thought Robertson, just hundreds of acres of open fields. The area had previously been given over to the cultivation of sugar, arrowroot, cotton, maize, and pineapples. Only one building had been completed before the outbreak of war, a grand colonnaded sandstone structure with two wings, divided by a massive clock tower that also housed an imposing atrium. Before any students or teachers had had the opportunity to move in, the Commonwealth Government had requisitioned it for the advanced headquarters of all Allied Land Forces in the Southwest Pacific.

In August of 1942, it had changed hands again, becoming the theater HQ of the Multinational Force ground combat elements, which was to say, the U.S. Marine Corps' Eighty-second MEU, and the Second Cavalry Regiment of the Australian Army.

The Abrams tanks and LAVs, Bushpigs and attack helicopters assigned to those two forces did not spend much time at the HQ, having been thrown into crucial blocking positions to secure General Douglas Mac-Arthur's much-vaunted Brisbane Line. The line was less a natural stronghold than a strategic concession that he didn't have the forces he needed to hold ground any farther north. It conceded about two thousand kilometers of coastline to the Japanese. To be sure, there were significant Allied forces intact and operating to the north out of Cairns and Townsville, but they were cut off from resupply and reinforcement. They were surrounded, but the Japanese in turn hadn't managed to land enough men and matériel to snuff them out. So the forces there were effectively under siege.

The press made great play on "the new Tobruk," and "the new Bastogne," even though the latter hadn't happened yet. But that was just propaganda—what Colonel Jones called "spin." Small teams of Special Forces were operating up and down the coast, disrupting the Japanese rear areas with great effect, and the reports they sent back of atrocities against the civilian population were enough to reduce the prime minister to tears in his private moments.

The PM was staring at a map in the briefing room—a lecture theater that had yet to hold its first class. Paul Robertson, his principal private secretary, wondered what the other men and women in the room saw in that map. MacArthur seemed fixated on his great defensive line, the arc of Allied Forces blocking the Japanese drive south. Jones and the senior 2 Cav officer, Brigadier Barnes and his SAS colleague, Major Horan, undoubtedly saw hundreds of miles of exposed Japanese flank, just begging to be ripped open. He knew that General Blamey, the contemporary Australian land force commander saw twenty thousand miles of largely indefensible coastline. New Zealand's senior representative General Freyburg probably saw the distance that remained between the leading edge of Japanese expansion and his homeland across the Tasman Sea.

As for the others, about a dozen staff officers, two of them women from the Multinational Force, the former banker had no idea.

"We are attriting the enemy into defeat," MacArthur insisted, repeatedly flicking the screen that one of Brigadier Barnes's young ladies had set up. Robertson wondered where he'd picked up that terrible word—*attriting*. "He's bleeding out, I tell you, gentlemen. He cannot sustain these losses and he cannot be reinforced. We don't want to risk upsetting this excellent arrangement by letting Colonel Jones and Brigadier Barnes go gallivanting across the countryside. Their remote-sensor coverage and fire support are in large part responsible for denying Homma the city. Every time he moves, we hit him. Soon there will be nothing left to hit."

Barnes remained silent and unmoving, but Jones bowed his head and rubbed wearily at his eyes. "General," he rumbled in a deep bass voice. "We are not going to remove all of the surveillance assets from the line, nor the Crusader guns. They will remain in place and be staffed by our specialists to make sure you retain full coverage. But we can roll up the Japanese in a *fraction* of the time if we get our armor on the move, and around into their rear."

MacArthur's thinly compressed lips warned of an explosive retort, but Prime Minister Curtin calmed him down with a gesture. "General, you've had my full support at every point in this campaign, but I must tell you I am not willing to allow these animals an extra day's grace. While we sit here jawboning, they are torturing and raping and murdering with impunity, up and down the coast."

MacArthur was becoming visibly angry, but he maintained a better working relationship with Curtin than he had with anyone in the Roosevelt administration. "Prime Minister, I can understand that," he said in a placatory tone. "But it won't be that much longer. We can—"

"If I might, Mr. Curtin."

Everyone turned to face Brigadier Michael Barnes. High spots of color flared on MacArthur's cheeks at being interrupted so abruptly, but the Australian continued in his flat nasal accent.

"This morning we received an encrypted burst from a long-range SAS patrol around Bundaberg. You need to see this."

Barnes thumbed a control wand, and the theater map disappeared, replaced by a movie, quite obviously shot in stealth. The cameraman—or woman, Robertson supposed—was lying in scrub, on a raised position overlooking what appeared to be a schoolyard. A number of civilians, maybe three dozen of them, were being bruted into a rough circle by a platoon of Japanese soldiers.

Major Horan provided a commentary. "This vision was taken by a four-man patrol. The Japanese have established a major garrison and staging post at Bundaberg, which had a prewar population of approximately thirteen thousand people."

As the officer spoke, seemingly without emotion, two soldiers in the movie clubbed an old man to death in front of the other prisoners. Robertson felt ill just watching it. The PM's face twisted with revulsion. Most of the time travelers, he noted, did not react with anything like the same intensity, although Brigadier Barnes's jaw muscles were moving slowly, as though he was grinding his teeth.

"The civilian population have been separated from the small contingent of Allied personnel who were based in the town, all of whom, as best we can tell, have been executed. The civilians are being held in a large open area on the banks of the Burnett River. During the day they are employed building earthwork defenses. There is very little food or water, and casualties are estimated at thirty percent to date."

"Good God," breathed the prime minister. "Are they giving any succor to the women and children, Major?"

"None whatsoever," replied Horan. Brigadier Barnes handed him the video control, and the officer brought up a new window within the main display. Hundreds of children, some of them little more than toddlers, were shown working in a large excavation. The focus zoomed in on two small boys scraping away at the dirt with toy shovels. Their arms were engulfed in spasms. When one stopped digging, the other appeared to encourage him, but to no avail. The picture began to shake a little, but steadied itself again. The lower half of a Japanese soldier appeared and kicked the child who had stopped working in the head. Audible gasps filled the briefing room, followed by several groans and protests when the other boy attacked the soldier, only to be run through with a bayonet.

Robertson heard a strangled sob somewhere nearby, but he couldn't identify the source. It may well have been Curtin. The fight seemed to have gone out of MacArthur. He was standing, his shoulders slumped, his face a picture of pure horror. Robertson recalled that the general had a son of about the same age as the boys in the video.

Horan closed the pop-up window, returning them to the scene at the schoolyard, where Robertson was mortified to see that many of the prisoners had been killed. An untidy scattering of headless bodies lay in front of the survivors, mostly women, who were silently screaming as a boy—who couldn't have been more than ten years old—was forced to his knees in front of a Japanese officer wielding a long sword.

Curtin's voice boomed out. "I think we've seen enough, Major Horan."

The screen went blank, for which Robertson would be forever grateful.

"Was there nothing your men could do, Major?"

The PM's adviser was surprised to find that he himself had asked the question.

"It's a four-man patrol, sir, under orders to remain undetected. They have endeavoured to collect enough identifying material so that the responsible enemy combatants may be sanctioned when the opportunity arises."

"We're still a long way from war-crimes tribunals," said Freyburg, the New Zealander.

Brigadier Barnes replied before Horan could speak. "Actually, sir, under ADF Standing Rules of Engagement, enemy combatants apprehended in the course of, or after the commission of, crimes against humanity are to be summarily executed without recourse to appeal."

The statement fell into empty space, the implications tumbling over and over in everyone's minds.

Nobody spoke for what felt a long time, until MacArthur broke the spell. "Colonel Jones, do American forces operate under the same rules?"

The giant marine nodded his shaven head. "Something like them, General. The effect is the same. President Clinton signed an executive order in two thousand nine. Congress passed its own legislation a year later."

Robertson could see from the faces that the contemporary personnel and their civilian counterparts, many of whom had thought themselves well adapted to the disturbingly predatory culture of their grandchildren, were given pause to think again.

Major Horan interrupted their thoughts. "Prime Minister, as you know, all Multinational Force elements still operate under their original rules of engagement. The guilty parties in this instance have been identified. They could be sanctioned immediately, if you wish. But it would inevitably lead to reprisals against the surviving population."

"Inevitably," breathed Curtin in a very soft voice. He sighed heavily, coming to a decision. "I'm sorry, Mac, but I can't have this. We need to act now. Colonel Jones, Brigadier Barnes, pull whatever forces you need out of the line and shut these bastards down."

"We're on our way," said Barnes.

The glory of a subtropical spring day was a jarring contrast with the darkness of the footage they had witnessed in the briefing room. Jones and his Australian colleagues lingered under a stand of jacaranda trees, their foliage a riot of bright pink blossoms. Jones stood with his foot propped up in the doorway of his Humvee while the Australians leaned against their smaller Land Rover.

"That was quite an ambush, Major Horan," the big marine growled, but not disapprovingly.

Horan shrugged. "Strategy, policy, it's all a fucking wank. Bottom line, it's always some poor prick trying to outrun a bullet."

"Uh-huh. Speaking of which, how're your war stocks?"

Barnes waggled his hands in a so-so gesture. "Fuel's not a problem. We've got enough JP-Eight off the *Clinton* to last another two months, by which time the locals will have the blend right. At least that's what they assure me."

Both men rolled their eyes.

"Be nice if we had some more bladders to move it around in," he continued. "And some heavy lift choppers to do the moving. Ammo *is* getting to be a worry. We're going to have to gear down after this op. I spoke to that Robertson bloke this morning. They've got an arms plant at Lithgow retooling to produce a simple AK-Forty-seven clone, but using thirty-aught-six cartridges. Should have a pretty good underslung launcher, too. He's promising a full production run by Christmas. The prototypes are ready now, if you'd like a look."

Jones sucked air in through his teeth. "I just wish things were that simple at home. Kolhammer's banging his head against a brick wall, trying to get an assault rifle into general production."

Horan used the toe of his combat boot to dig a well in the thick carpet of jacaranda blossoms that lay at their feet. The air was almost sickeningly sweet with the scent of their decomposition. "He's equipping the guys you've got to train with one, isn't he?"

Jones nodded. "With a Forty-seven knock-off, just like you. Weapon of choice for the third world, and that's the comparative level of industrial sophistication we're dealing with, even in the U.S. I think it's going to be a long time before we see caseless ceramic again."

"Or GPS," added Barnes.

"Or VR porn." Horan grinned.

Jones grunted. "Colonial riffraff."

The dull thud of rotor blades reached them through the warm, moist air, but the sound trailed off before they were able to spot the helicopter.

"Well, gentlemen, I suggest we get our staff together ASAP and sign off the plan for this party."

Brigadier Barnes fetched a data stick out of his shirt pocket and handed it over.

"Holomaps of the route I'd suggest we take. We've got rail transport for about a hundred and twenty klicks. Robertson has already requisitioned the rolling stock. It'll save on the fuel bill."

Jones slotted the stick into his flexipad and thanked the tank officer for the maps. "Just one thing, Mick," he said. "How in hell do they fit you into a tank, anyway? You're what, six-three?"

"Six-four." Barnes smiled. "I crouch."

12

PACIFIC THEATER OF OPERATIONS

It was a cruel trick of the gods, allowing a magnificent warship like this to fall into the hands of a barbarian such as Le Roux.

Commander Hidaka was an educated, well-traveled man, and he knew at an intellectual level that the gaijin were not all hairy brutes, *as such*. Their technical accomplishments, for one thing, had to be acknowledged. But Le Roux actually did look like a barbarian. He did not shave regularly. He stank of some ditch weed called garlic. And the uniform he wore was stained!

Hidaka wondered how he retained the confidence of his men. But of course, these weren't "his men" in any formal sense. They were mutineers, effectively. Little better than pirates. But for now, they held the key to Admiral Yamamoto's grand design.

"I think the *Clinton*, she is leaving now," said Le Roux in his heavy accented English.

"Why do you think that?" asked Hidaka, barely able to conceal his scorn.

The Frenchman tilted his head to one side and pushed out a fat lower lip as he crossed his arms over an ample belly and examined the giant screen in front of them. "Well, this is not my specialty, you understand. The men who ran this station, they would not cooperate. But the ship's Combat Intelligence, she tells us that a great deal of radar and energy waves they are passing over us right now."

Hidaka's heart gave a sudden lurch. "We are being scanned!"

"Yes, well, no. She is scanning for a general threat, not to locate a specific target. So she does not know we are here. The ship you tell me they lost at Midway—the *Leyte Gulf*—she was their Nemesis cruiser, a protector. Her sensors were more capable, *much* more capable. But even so, the *Dessaix*, she is a stealth ship, too. The Americans do not have—how do you say?—a monopoly.

"So no, the *Clinton* will not see us."

Hidaka regarded the hairy lout with an expression of open disbelief. "And the *Siranui*?" he asked.

"*Oui*. She is there, too." He pointed at a window in which a colorful set of lines pulsed and undulated. "These are her sensors. They are not operating at full power. They have not, for as long as we have been observing them, and we must assume they were damaged at the Emergence."

The Japanese commander considered that for a moment. His orders were specific. The *Clinton* was not his target. But he could not help asking. "So we could strike at her?"

Le Roux snorted in amusement, colored by a contempt that he didn't bother to conceal. "Oh, well, yes, we could. But there would be no promise of success. The missiles would be detected, and targeted for countermeasures. The launch would be detected. *We* would be detected. And so on . . . you understand."

Hidaka didn't bother replying. He would no more disobey Yamamoto's precise instructions than he would piss in the goldfish pond at the Imperial Palace. His warrior spirit was simply piqued by the idea that such an enemy was being allowed to slip away. That, too, however, was an integral part of the grand admiral's plan.

Even so, he found it difficult to contain his frustration. Not with Yamamoto's strategy, but with the unrealized potential of this ship, the *Robert*

Dessaix. From the first moment he had seen her, deep in the wastes of the Great Southern Ocean, he recognized her as a vastly more powerful weapon than the *Sutanto* or the *Nuku.* She was larger, for a start, at least three times their size. But more important, she was obviously a generation or more advanced. He had come to understand that the most capable ships from the future did not necessarily proclaim their strength in massed tiers of gun mounts. Indeed, the sleeker the lines, the less there was for the eye to linger over, the deadlier she was likely to be.

The decks of the *Robert Dessaix* were almost bare. From the outside, the raked-back silhouette of her "teardrop" bridge, in which they now stood, barely rose to the height of a man. It had thrown Hidaka at first, until he realized that the floor must have been sunk below the line of the deck outside.

Everything about her suggested stealth and danger.

What a pity she hardly had a crew to sail her.

Le Roux was an enthusiastic buffoon, but it was more than apparent that he lacked the technical skills to pilot such a sophisticated vessel. It wasn't surprising, really, since his original duties had been confined to the servicing of the ship's two helicopters, neither of which was on board now.

The pilots, too, had "refused to cooperate."

Commander Hidaka let his eyes drift away from the panel that was displaying the radar pulses originating aboard the American and turncoat Nipponese ships. The Pacific was calm, and quite beautiful beneath an unseasonably warm autumn sun. The boy he had once been wished for nothing more than to take this ship under his control, and to charge at the Americans under full power, with every rocket on board blasting up out of their silos and roaring away on columns of white fire.

But the adult he was today knew they'd be lucky to successfully complete their much more limited mission.

There were two other French sailors on the bridge. One of them—a junior officer, and little more than a boy himself—said something to Le Roux. Hidaka waited for the translation. The two men took their time about it, babbling on in their incomprehensible native tongue. The boy, an ensign named Danton, actually outranked Le Roux, who was merely a *premier maître,* a warrant officer, but the older man enjoyed a clear advantage over his comrade. The boy seemed almost terrified of him.

They were an unconvincing pair of allies—if allies indeed they were. Hidaka had trouble understanding their motivations. To his great surprise, he found himself feeling much more at ease with the thirteen Indonesian crew members who had come aboard with him at the rendezvous. It wasn't that he was a believer in Pan-Asian solidarity. In his opinion, the Indonesians were monkey men. But he had grown accustomed to them in the months since the Emergence, and when he wasn't working with the handful of French or the *Kriegsmarine* officers who were on board, he actually preferred the company of the apes.

Le Roux finally deigned to speak to him. "*Enseigne* Danton believes an airborne radar plane is aloft, and probing north of the *Clinton's* battle group," the Frenchman said. "It is best that we should retire, now we have learned what we needed to."

This time Hidaka did not question. They had achieved the first relatively simple task allotted them. So he nodded his consent.

Le Roux spoke to the third Frenchman, a leading seaman, who at least had an appearance that fit his role as helmsman. A tall, shaven-headed brute whose arms were covered in tattoos that reminded Hidaka of the markings of South Sea islanders, he responded to Le Roux's gruff burst of instruction with a Gallic roll of the shoulders. Sitting at a "workstation" rather than standing at a wheel, the giant sailor consulted with the navigator, a German commander, and began to type out instructions with the casual air of somebody doing exactly what he'd been trained for.

It was a pleasant change.

It was the second time the Combined Fleet had set out like this, and the first time since the Emergence that he had dared concentrate his forces in this way. They were still vulnerable, but the noble sacrifices of Homma and Nagumo in the South had done much to draw the attention of their new foe.

Grand Admiral Isoroku Yamamoto stood proud and ramrod straight on the bridge of his flagship the *Yamato* as it plowed into a heavy southeasterly swell. But he had lost all of the intuitive confidence that had characterized his opening moves in this game. Midway had all but destroyed his sense of certainty.

Nearly sixty ships covered the gray, wind-scored seas, stretching out to the horizon. The sight would once have filled him with pride and an unshakeable belief in destiny. Now, however, he could not help worrying that a British drone might be watching him from above. Or that damnable Willet woman from below. A flight of American rockets might be screaming toward his fleet at an inconceivable velocity.

A small grunt escaped from deep within his chest.

It was infuriating, but it was war, and he had started this war knowing that his enemies possessed much greater resources than he. Nothing had changed, in that sense.

What *had* changed was that he now enjoyed the advantage of surprise, and technological superiority of a sort. His heart beat rapidly, as it had in the few hours since Hidaka's encrypted message had been received.

The *Clinton* had sailed with the remnants of her battle group, and a window had opened through which they might steal a victory. *Or the makings of a victory.*

Yamamoto's eyes traversed the scene around his great battleship. He had two carriers with him, three other battleships, half a dozen cruisers, two-dozen destroyers, and a host of tenders, oilers, and transports. It still felt like the greatest fleet that ever put to sea, and if it weren't for Kolhammer's untimely arrival, that would have been true.

True, his losses had been heavy at Hashirajima, thanks to the *Havoc's* missile swarm, but they were still light compared with the disaster that befell Spruance at Midway. That had given Yamamoto just enough breathing space to try a radically different line of attack.

And then the divine gift of the *Dessaix* had arrived.

In all the world, there were still only a handful of people who knew of its fate, and he was the only one within the Combined Fleet. The emperor and Prime Minister Tojo knew, naturally. Hitler, Himmler, and their closest surviving cohorts were aware of its existence and its mission. None of the Soviets had been informed.

There were forty-eight crewmembers of the German submarine U-96 who had learned of the *Dessaix's* inexplicable arrival, weeks *after* the Emergence at Midway, and sixty miles south of the Spanish Canary Islands. They had acquired the information by virtue of nearly running into her, shortly after she had materialized.

Yamamoto wondered what had become of those men. The Germans had assured him that there would be no chance of the secret leaking out. Thus, he presumed they were all dead.

Both the Reich and the Soviet Union had become vast charnel houses since their rulers had gained the deadly power of foresight. It was confirmation—as if any were needed—that power was wielded by ill-bred savages, almost everywhere but on the Home Islands. And it meant that, even if he was able to avoid defeat in this particular war against the Anglophone democracies, an era of ceaseless conflict stretched away in front of them all.

It was enough to make him question the wisdom of the course on which he was now embarked.

He wondered about his enemy. The archives—the Web files—that had been retrieved from the *Sutanto*, and now from the *Dessaix*, told of a prosperous Japan, living in peace after having been conquered by MacArthur and Nimitz. Nothing he had learned about the *Siranui* and her curious crew gave him cause to think of them as anything other than men of *giri*.

The Nazis, on the other hand . . .

They gave barbarians a bad name. And the Soviets were even worse. There could be no doubt that they would turn on each other again at the first opportunity. They were both preparing for just such an eventuality, even as they pretended to fashion a new and congenial relationship. Could there be any reason to imagine that they would hesitate to wage war on the Japanese Empire, as well? He knew the Nazis regarded all Asians as barely human.

"Hmmph!"

"Admiral, is everything all right?"

Yamamoto was annoyed that a lack of control had betrayed his thoughts. "Captain," he grunted, "what on earth could be wrong?"

The *Yamato*'s skipper seemed confused by the question. "Why, nothing, Admiral. We sail to victory, of course."

"Of course," Yamamoto echoed, nodding abruptly.

Le Roux thought himself handy in the galley, but he still missed the ship's head chef. Petty Officer Dupleix had grown up in a family bistro outside Auxerre and was, in Le Roux's opinion, the best pastry chef in the entire French Navy. He had begged the Germans to spare the man's life, but to no avail, so they had been reduced to eating frozen croissants and brioche ever since.

Still Dupleix had been an idiot, like most of the crew. The *Dessaix* hadn't been like his posting on the frigate *Masson*. There he'd been amongst like-minded men. The *Masson*'s captain had had a brother-in-law who was a deputy minister in the new government, and the captain had shared his sibling's enthusiasm for the policies of the National Front.

That was only natural, after the Paris intifada and the atrocity of Marseilles. How anyone could think otherwise—well, it was beyond Le Roux's understanding.

Yet he had been on board the *Dessaix* for only two weeks when the ship's executive officer, Lieutenant Underzo, had frog-marched him into the *capitaine*'s quarters to receive a terrible dressing down. *Capitaine* Goscinny did not think it appropriate for a senior member of his crew to be actively politicking belowdecks, whether it was in behalf of the government or against. The old fool had insisted that Le Roux cease all political activity forthwith, or face charges when they returned from their Indonesian deployment to the Pacific Fleet base in Noumea.

It was all he could do not to laugh in the man's face.

This was exactly the sort of thinking that had so very nearly led France into ruin under the socialists. Old farts like Goscinny had given the country over to illiterate migrants and jihadi scum, and it was only when the streets were finally running with blood that they admitted they might have been wrong.

Still, when Goscinny had upbraided him, Le Roux had bolted a mask onto his face, saluted, and barked "Yessir!" But in his mind he was already composing the letter to his old *capitaine*, asking him to forward a complaint to the navy's political investigators and outlining Goscinny's antipatriotic tendencies. Perhaps, if the *capitaine* could speak with his brother-in-law, the deputy minister, things might be resolved even more quickly.

The microwave pinged now, bringing him back to the present, and he removed a steaming hot Sara Lee brioche—God help him. As he carefully tore open the pastry and watched the chocolate sauce spill out, he had to smile at the memory of the last time he had seen Goscinny, naked and beaten to a purple pulp in the Gestapo cells at Lyon.

True to form, the dumb bastard had failed to see what a gift the Emergence had been. It had put them in a place where they could ensure that *Frenchmen* would determine the future of France, not a cabal of mad mullahs and bearded nuts. And perhaps just as important, it meant that with bold action they could also check the rise of America, the nation most to blame for the ills of the world.

After all, who had created bin Laden, the first of so many Islamist heroes? And whose appetite for oil had funded the Saudis, who in turn funded the madrassas of so many of the Wahhabi lunatics who had overrun the slums of Paris? It was the United States, Le Roux mused, who had turned the Middle East into a sinkhole of violence and Islamist revolt thanks to its support of Israel, its occupation of Iraq, its bombing of Iran, and its wars against Syria and Yemen.

Le Roux ate the brioche slowly, enjoying it in spite of himself, and enjoying also the prospect that lay before him. The prospect of rewriting history.

It mattered little that most of the men on board the *Dessaix* had gone into the cells at Lyon rather than serve the Republic by seizing a chance to wipe out eighty years of mistakes and perfidy. Some of them were those traitorous bastards who'd only *pretended* to agree with him. But they'd got theirs, in the end.

Yes, it was *his* ship now. The *Boche* needed him.

He washed down his snack with a mouthful of black coffee and stared in distaste at the two Indonesians eating some foul-smelling rice dish across the room from him. They had no language in common, but even if they did, he would not have spoken to them. He knew from the wailing that filled the ship five times a day that they were Islamists. Not jihadi, to be sure—he would never have allowed *them* on the ship, no matter what the Germans said.

He dreamed of a day when he could go about his business as a Frenchman and not be assailed by some illiterate ditchdigger droning on about the

Koran. The sooner they trained some of his countrymen to operate this ship, the better.

"Warrant Officer, your colleague, Danton, tells us we have moved beyond the range of the enemy's sensors, and that we may soon use our own arrays. Do you agree?"

Le Roux almost choked on the last piece of brioche. He hadn't noticed Hidaka approaching. He nodded and hastily stood up, brushing crumbs from his shirt, smearing it with a dollop of hot chocolate sauce in the process. *"Oui,"* he coughed. "But let us be safe and say another hour before Danton can turn on the arrays. He can set them to look forward, so that there is less chance of their being detected. Then we make the rendezvous, *non*?"

The Asian shot him an irritated look, but nodded curtly.

Le Roux would be happy to see the back of him, too. Perhaps when the war was over he might return to the Pacific, as governor of all French Polynesia or something. But for now he would be glad to get away from it, and from madmen like Hidaka. He had that same blankness in his eyes as one of Mullah Zaheer's Horror Brigades. *Fanatics, all of them.*

"We shall be refueling soon, when we meet with the oiler," Hidaka continued.

Le Roux shrugged. "Assuming you have got the mix right, at last. If not, well then . . . the game is over, yes?"

The Japanese glowered in reply. "We have followed your instructions precisely. You had better hope *you* got it right."

"Oh, my instructions were precise," countered Le Roux. "But I cannot know whether you primitives were able to follow them at all. You never developed jet engines, did you? So it is safe to assume that a basic jet fuel mix is also beyond your abilities. Still, we shall see."

Hidaka looked as if he was about ready to pop a vein, which very much tickled the Frenchman's sense of humor. He smothered a snigger and turned away, calling back over his shoulder. "I shall be in my quarters. Wake me when I am needed."

He didn't bother to wait for Hidaka's reaction. The fucking savage didn't seem to understand what an achievement it was, just getting the heads to work on a complex ship like this, what with most of her crew locked up on the other side of the world. The Germans who'd come on board were good. He got on famously with them. Even the Indonesians, he could admit, were well trained. But really, if it weren't for Le Roux himself, they would all be completely fucked. The *Dessaix* would still be back in the Atlantic, floating around like an astronomically expensive bathtub toy. The Germans would certainly not have been able to remove all the equipment and weaponry they'd insisted on, before allowing Yamamoto access to her.

He pushed into the commander's quarters—which he had appropriated as his own—and fetched himself a cognac. Then he sat down at *Capitaine* Goscinny's desk. A giant Siemens display ran constant updates on ship status and mission progress, all controlled by the vessel's Combat Intelligence. Le Roux checked his watch. Soon it would be time to verify command ID again.

There was a DNA reader on the desktop, and he wiped it down with a cloth doused in methylated spirits. Then he powered it up.

In the corner of the cabin stood a small bar refrigerator from which he withdrew a sealed specimen jar. There were many more like it in there. He carefully unscrewed the lid and, using an eyedropper, extracted a few mils of the precious liquid. Then he squeezed a drop or two of the *capitaine*'s blood onto the sensor. Carefully, but without showing too much concern.

After all, he still had plenty left in the fridge.

Le Roux wondered how the Gestapo were doing, trying to get the rest of the *Dessaix*'s crew to cooperate.

Not very well, he imagined.

Apart from the six original crewmen still on this ship, and another twelve who were helping the Germans with the missile facility at Dozenac, the entire complement of the *Dessaix* had proved themselves to be quite fatally stupid and shortsighted.

13

AUSCHWITZ, POLAND

The special-purposes camp lay a few kilometers away from the I. G. Farben Monovitz facilties, but Brasch fancied that he could still smell the scent of depravity that blanketed the place. Some nights he imagined that the three main camps and thirty-nine subcamps gave off a poisonous mist, a concentrated essence of the suffering and evil that took place here. It was invisible, but you could smell it as it sank into the pores of your skin, and eventually into your soul.

Nothing he had witnessed on the Russian Front had prepared him for it. Even Himmler seemed more subdued than usual when they were forced to attend one of Hess's demonstrations. Everybody knew the *Reichsführer* was squeamish. He had vomited the first time he'd personally witnessed an execution, and that had been a good clean head shot: the Reich's version of merciful release.

Today Brasch kept the contempt from his face as he watched Himmler dab at his lips with a perfumed handkerchief while the subjects were led in.

"Oh, my," Skorzeny roared in mock amusement. "They are only stick men. I'm a good shot, Herr *Reichsführer*, but I cannot promise to hit them for you first time. If they turn sideways, they will disappear!"

Himmler allowed a wan but dutiful grin at the large man's brutal jokes. Brasch suspected he'd rather not be there.

They were in a long subterranean bunker. The sweating cinder blocks receded at least two hundred meters away from them to a thick revetment of sandbags, in front of which stood three scarred wooden poles. The prisoners were actually much less skeletal than most of their fellow inmates. They were *Sonderkommando*, or Kapos, selected prisoners who acted as guards and enforcers in the death camp at Birkenau. They received special privileges: extra rations, the pick of the females, and so on. But eventually they, like all the others, went into the ovens.

These three, however, were to complete their service to the Reich as experimental subjects. Over their gray striped camp uniform each wore a bulky vest of a slightly differing size. The project director, whose name Brasch had forgotten, spoke excitedly of the leaps in development they'd achieved since being given access to a calculating machine and a trained operator.

"What we have now are three options," he enthused. "Each is a trade-off, in its own way, Herr *Reichsführer*. More protection still means greater bulk and weight, unfortunately, but the Farben engineers have made great strides the last two months. The material samples you delivered us have proved invaluable in answering a number of . . ."

Brasch was hardly listening. He was focused on the three men being tied to the poles at the other end of the bunker. Not one of them was struggling. He fancied he saw one of them sob, but that was about the extent of their reaction. As a man who had spent the better part of the last three years involved in mortal combat, often against the most overwhelming odds, he found it depressing that these men could go to their doom so meekly. Even more depressing, however, was the path his life had taken to deliver him to this place as a witness to their deaths. Since he'd arrived at Monovitz, the black wolf of his depression was stalking him again. He felt again as he had during the battles at Belgorod, like a bug about to be crushed under the tracks of a tiger tank.

"A good rifle, this Garand, yes?" Skorzeny said, interrupting his train of thought. The giant Nazi was turning a captured weapon over in his hands.

"Better than the Tommy's Lee Enfield piece of shit. Semiautomatic, gas actuated. A good tool, although I do not like the way it makes so much noise when the clip ejects. That will get a few cowboys killed, I think."

"It may not be in use for much longer," said Brasch in a flat monotone. "I believe they may be moving in the direction of an assault rifle."

Himmler took the hankie away from his thin lips. "Don't be so glum, Herr Colonel. The SD tells me that is not yet a foregone conclusion. There is open disagreement in America over whether to retool for mass production of that weapon. At least outside of the Californian Zone."

"So Kolhammer is going to build these Russian guns for his mud people, then?" Skorzeny said. "I hear they are a good weapon, too. But in the hands of half-castes and fairies, what would it matter?"

"The bullet would kill you just as dead, no matter who fired it," Brasch replied. "I lost many comrades to rounds fired by untrained *Untermenschen* in Russia, Herr Colonel."

"Well, let's see if we can do something about that," bellowed the SS man, refusing to be cast out of his usual high spirits. "You are ready for us now?" he asked the research director.

The civilian checked with an aide, who confirmed that the prisoners were firmly secured. A horn blared harshly, and behind them a red lightbulb shut off while a green one lit up.

"We are ready for the test," he confirmed.

Brasch screwed in a pair of earplugs and hardened his heart to what was about to happen. He had personally killed dozens of men, some of them in hand-to-hand combat, but he had never murdered anybody in cold blood. And he was about to become complicit in three murders at once. It made him sick.

Skorzeny looked to Himmler, who had just finished fitting his own earplugs. The *Reichsführer* nodded, and Skorzeny hefted the American rifle as smoothly as if he'd been practicing since childhood. He sighted down the barrel and squeezed off three shots. All three prisoners jumped. Skorzeny then picked up a British Lee Enfield 303 rifle and performed the same action, this time taking a little longer, as he was forced to work the bolt after each shot.

Again, the prisoners jumped, but their heads whipped back in a way that told Brasch they were already dead or unconscious.

Skorzeny was much less impressed with the English weapon. "Pah! You could not get great accuracy with this. The chamber is too loose, and the two-part stock and these rear-locking lugs on the bolt are all very poor design . . . And now for my old friend."

He scooped up a K98 Mauser and squeezed off three shots from the bolt-action weapon with as little thought as he would give to scratching his nose. Three dark puffs indicated where the 7.92 mm rounds hit.

"Shall we?" asked the director.

"They don't look very well, Herr Director," Himmler said as the small group made its way down the firing range. "Are you sure these vests are bulletproof?"

"Not as such, Herr *Reichsführer*," the man said quickly. "The vests will stop a small-caliber handgun round, and all manner of shrapnel and flak, but we are not using what the Allies call nanotube technology. What we have done is to synthesize a lightweight but very strong polymer from alternating monomers of para-phenylenediamine and terephthalic acid. The resulting aromatic amide alternates benzene rings and amide groups. In a planar sheet structure, which is like a silk protein and—"

"But why do you call them 'bulletproof vests' if they do not stop bullets?" Himmler asked testily.

The researcher paled, and he hadn't had much coloring to begin with. "The vests by themselves could not stop a high-velocity round," he explained. "But we have augmented them with differing types of ballistic plate, and together they are enough to provide excellent protection."

They reached the three men, each of whom looked quite dead to Brasch, until he saw that they were breathing. But only just. The director hurried on, lest Himmler decide the whole exercise was a waste of his time. A good idea—people had died for less.

"Now, Herr *Reichsführer*, these subjects were not in very good physical condition to begin with, certainly not as good as one of your storm troopers. And they have been hit three times with high-velocity rounds. It would still be an enormously traumatic event for the body. But I think you will be pleasantly surprised at the results."

Paul Brasch often felt as if his capacity to feel anything had been burned away during his time in the Soviet Union. Now as the project director's aides roughly stripped the bulky black vests away from the men's bodies, he found himself thankful for the crust of scar tissue that had formed around his feelings. It allowed him to appear as inhuman as his colleagues.

The director was babbling on to Himmler about some production-line issue that would involve the use of concentrated sulfuric acid. Skorzeny was boasting of his marksmanship to another SS officer, who was laughing at the way one of the prisoners' eyeballs had popped out onto his cheek. Brasch breathed in slowly and fought down the urge to draw his pistol and kill them all. Instead he watched with apparent detachment as SS orderlies finished removing the body armor and the men's prison camp shirts.

Their torsos were massively bruised, and one man had a large concave

depression just under his heart. But none of the rounds had actually penetrated. Their guide was holding one of the jackets, pointing out features
such as the pivoting shoulder pads, grenade hangers, and rifle butt patches.
Himmler wanted to know how many of the vests would be ready in time for
Operation Sea Dragon, and he was unhappy to be told that four hundred
was the limit of current production capacity.

As the director kept babbling about sulfuric acid, Himmler tuned him
out and turned to face Brasch instead. "Well, Herr Colonel, another miracle for you to work in our behalf, yes? I don't expect to be able to outfit
every Waffen-SS Division, but I need at least two thousand of these vests by
the time we are ready to go. Can you guarantee me that?"

Brasch shook his head emphatically. "No, Herr *Reichsführer*; but I shall
increase production by whatever amount is possible. Based on my experience at Demidenko, I imagine we can get you at least fifty percent more
than the director believes possible."

Himmler, he had discovered, preferred realistic assessments from his
underlings. He asked for superhuman efforts, but did not actually expect the
impossible. "Good enough, then." Himmler nodded. You shall stay here another week, supervising the operation, then join me back in the Fatherland.
Göring wishes to discuss the jet project with you."

Brasch did not roll his eyes, but he did not meekly accede to the order,
either. "With all due respect to the *Reichsmarshall*, there is almost no chance
of getting his fighters aloft in time for Sea Dragon. I would very much
like to return home to see my family, but I would not wish to waste time in
doing so."

A smile played across Himmler's rodentlike features. The Luftwaffe
chief had already lost a great deal of influence after failing to destroy the
RAF in 1941. The bombing of Germany's cites by the Allies and the poor
performance of the air force in the Russian campaigns had left him a much-
reduced figure. Only his unquestionable loyalty to the führer was thought
to have saved him in the bloodletting that had followed the Emergence.

"I agree that the *Reichsmarshall* is probably being overambitious," purred
Himmler. "But he is a *Reichsmarshall*, and you are not. Indulge him, Colonel.
There is important work for you at home. And the führer himself would like
to personally thank you for your efforts at Demidenko."

Brasch snapped his heels together and saluted like a machine.

Himmler returned the salute crisply but without any flourish. He even
managed a wry smile. "My word, these Wehrmacht types do know how to
salute well, don't they Skorzeny?" he said.

Brasch felt a meaty paw thunder into his shoulder as Skorzeny slapped
him on the back. The report was almost as loud as the rifle shots of a few

minutes earlier. "He's a grand fellow, all right! Not *Totenkopf* material, but pretty damn good anyway."

Brasch faked a hearty laugh as the three Jews were cut down and dragged away. He wondered if anyone would bother to finish them off before they were reduced to ashes and hot wax. He had never felt like less of a man in his whole life.

He took a train from Monovitz a week later and tried to relax on the journey, but every time they passed carriages heading in the other direction, it jolted him awake, or out of whatever semiconscious state he'd managed to drift into.

The trains were running east with much greater frequency now. Partly it had to do to with the shift of many heavy and special engineering projects into Poland and the Ukraine, beyond the easy reach of the Lancaster bombers and B-17s. But also he suspected, it had to do with a greatly accelerated program at Auschwitz.

Unlike most Germans, Brasch could not pretend he knew nothing of the massive series of camps that made up the Auschwitz facility. Some of them were labor camps, some were specialist research facilities—now hosting small teams of Japanese doctors—and some were simply designed for mass extermination.

As he stretched out in the first-class carriage and tried to rest, he was haunted by the idea that one day his son would be tossed into one of those fetid cattle cars that so frequently roared past rattling the windows of his train.

At times he tried to work. He was one of the few men in all of Europe who had been allocated not only a flexipad, but a much larger data slate, as well. As a war hero, and the principal consulting engineer to so many high-priority projects, he was trusted—a rare thing these days. But even so, he noted that his drives and data sticks had been purged of a great deal of material he had been able to access freely back in Hashirajima, aboard the *Sutanto*. There was no trace of the Holocaust in his Web archive. No mention of a country called Israel. And only sketchy material relating to Germany after the year 1944.

He wondered that the vandals had left anything.

But there were still extensive technical files, and he was adding to the store all the time.

As the train shuddered to a halt at a siding in Poland, Brasch tried to concentrate on the file he'd created to contain all the material he had concerning Göring's new pet project, the ME 262 jet fighter. The fat fool wanted hundreds of them in the air over Britain, slicing through Spitfires and Hurricanes like screaming hawks. The impossibility of doing so, and more seriously the waste of resources in even trying, meant nothing to Göring. He was determined to regain his former prominence in the führer's affections, and he had become obsessed with this new fighter as the answer to his dilemma.

It was night, and as Brasch peered out the windows he could see nothing in the darkness. The reflection of his cabin in the cold frosted glass, and the steam drifting back from the engines, blocked his view entirely. He could hear shouting, vehicle traffic, a whistle, and even, he fancied, some distant gunfire. *Partisans, perhaps?* Many of them had turned against Stalin. There were the Poles, of course. And small, scattered renegade units of both the Red Army and the Wehrmacht, which had been caught up in the internecine warfare of the post-Emergence period.

Again he found himself wishing for a quiet life, perhaps in a villa somewhere in the East Indies, where Ali Moertopo could help out. He marveled at how the little Indonesian sailor had managed not just to save his own hide, but also to arrange the governorship of a Javanese province for himself. The man was a survivor. There could be no doubt of that. Nor of the debt which Brasch now owed him.

He shook his head and returned to the file. It was his job to convince Göring to stop wasting time and money on a project that was never going to be ready in time for Operation Sea Dragon. Brasch had worked with engineers at Messerschmitt on CAD/CAM programs that employed early twenty-first-century propeller designs, to extend the range of an ME 109 and give it forty-five minutes over England, rather than twenty. He had dozens of minor suggestions for improving the "ergonomics" of current fighters and bombers—simple things like recessed switches that wouldn't puncture a man's skull in a crash, or quick-disconnect throat microphones so that a crewman desperate to get out of a doomed plane wouldn't die trapped in a cord he forgot to unplug.

These were all simple changes with potentially massive effects, but Göring's eyes glazed over whenever he raised them, and if Brasch persisted in arguing, those same porcine eyes would eventually cloud over with rage, and the *Reichsmarshall* would start to pound on the table screaming, *"Nein, nein, nein!"*

Brasch brought up the file in which he had compiled a list of all the 262's problems in what he referred to as "original time." The Junkers Jumo 004 engines were unreliable, being constructed of inferior alloys due to materials shortages. At any given time, the majority of those fighters could expect to be grounded. They were unstable, and generated less thrust at low speeds than prop-driven fighters. But worst of all, there would never be enough of them.

Brasch had read of a mission by thirty-seven of the jets on March 18, 1945, during which they had attacked an Allied force of 1,221 bombers and 632 escorting fighters. Using long, level approaches to compensate for their lack of dogfighting agility, they simply blurred in past the fighter screen and tore apart a dozen bombers and one escort with their 30 mm cannons, all for the loss of only three 262s—a four-to-one kill ratio.

But the important figure was the gargantuan size of the Allied raid. Nearly two thousand planes, against thirty-seven German jets. You would think that spoke volumes for the need to concentrate efforts on achievable goals. The productive capacities of the English-speaking world were simply beyond imagining.

But no. Göring had only last week authorized tens of millions of reichsmarks to be spent on changes to the 262's swept wings, low drag canopy, and engine placement. And all this on his own initiative. Brasch would have been furious if it weren't for one thing.

He himself was working to wreck the Nazi war machine.

Brasch hadn't told anybody, of course. Not even his wife. He knew that he could trust Willie with his life, but he also knew that the SS regarded him with reserve at best. Now that he was away from Demidenko, he didn't have Gelder shadowing his every move, but the specter of the SS was a constant. His son's disorder—easily fixed in the future—would be more than enough to see the boy fed into the camps under the Nazis' T-4 program, to ensure the purity of the race.

No, Colonel Paul Brasch understood the nature of the regime he served. Like most of his countrymen, he had *always* understood it. Unlike most of them, he had witnessed the evidence firsthand, and he had decided to resist.

The irony of his current position was that he hadn't been snatched up in the post-Emergence sweeps of "future and prospective traitors" that had gutted the Reich, and yet he was probably one of most dangerous men in Germany. Fate had thrust him into the center of events as they spun out of control. His character determined that he would not allow himself simply to coast along in the wake of that turbulence.

As his train lurched into motion again, and began to pick up speed for the long run home, he worked on the 262 file—*multitasking*, as the phrase had it, a series of files on automatic assault rifles, rocket-propelled grenades, and prototype helicopters for the newly formed SS Special Forces. He was the very model of a loyal and tireless worker laboring in the service of his führer. In a small, very private part of his mind, however, Brasch, turned over the problem of how best to strike a fatal blow against the Nazis.

14

KINLOCHMOIDART HOUSE, SCOTLAND

The Special Air Service began life as a deception. It had very little to do with airborne raids. It was a small, somewhat irregular unit of the British Army in the North African campaign, established in late 1941 by a mere Lieutenant, David Stirling. He put together a group of irredeemably unusual soldiers—specialists, loners, virtual pirates of the desert. He threw them in with the New Zealanders of the Long Range Desert Group and set them loose behind Rommel's lines, attacking fuel and ammo dumps, destroying aircraft on the ground, and generally spreading mayhem and confusion.

Breaking things and hurting people, thought Harry as he marched across the gravel. *A cracking fuckin' way for a bloke to earn a quid. Better than being chased around by those paparazzi cunts, at any rate.*

He clamped down on the surge of rage that always threatened to get the better of him when he thought of the misery those vultures had made of his life. Killed his mother. Ruined his father. And wrecked any chance he had of getting a bit of innocent leg-over without having to explain himself to the whole fucking world. He'd only worn that stupid swastika armband because the silly twit he was dating got all lathered up when she saw it. And how was he to know that Paris bloody Hilton wasn't wearing any knickers when he took her to Royal Ascot? That's not the sort of thing a bloke would find out until after cocktail hour. In many ways, he was happier here. Fewer twits and no tabloids. Now all he had to do was stop the Nazis from taking over the place. He forced his thoughts back onto the task at hand.

The SAS in this period had become such a thorn in the side of the Afrika Korps that they were partly responsible for Hitler's infamous *"Kommandobefehl"* order, stating that all captured Allied commandos were to be summarily executed. That order would have been issued on October 18, 1942. After the Transition—or "Emergence," as it became known in the Axis states—Hitler issued the *Kommandobefehl* in the first week of October. British Signals Intelligence picked up the order as it was transmitted quite openly around the Reich, without the use of quantum encryption, and passed news of it on to the relevant parties: the Commando Regiment; the Special Operations Executive; the American Office of Strategic Services; and the SAS, both in Africa and at Kinlochmoidart House, the new Regimental HQ in Scotland, an hour outside of Fort William.

Prince Harry, with freshly minted major's pips still gleaming on his shoulders, called the regiment to parade on the lawn in front of the manor to tell them the good news. Kinlochmoidart was a baronial mansion set within two thousand acres of private gardens and woodland, which had been given over to the Special Air Service for the duration of the war. Having an heir to the throne make the request had smoothed the process considerably. The secluded location was perfect, with easy access to Loch Shiel and Loch Sunart for the boat troop, and to the highlands and the Grampians for the mountain troop. Parachute training could be done out of Fort William, where Harry's celebrated ancestor General Lord Lovett of the commandos was ready to provide every assistance. The forests of the estate were also well suited to honing the field craft of the trainees.

And there was a really excellent pub, just a four-mile run down the road.

The Palace had Harry placed on the Civil List as soon as it became known that he had arrived with Kolhammer, providing him with a handsome income. This he used to open a personal account at the Glenuig Inn so that any man who was able to run the four miles to the pub in full kit in twenty-four minutes could drink his fill on the royal tick—as long as he could make the return run in thirty.

"Harry's Little Marathon," as it became known, wasn't *officially* listed as a prerequisite for graduating from the selection course, but no one who failed to make the run was ever seen wearing the sandy beret of the regiment.

It was a cold, autumn afternoon when he called the men together. One hundred and twenty of them jogged onto the makeshift parade ground in woodland camouflage battle dress, having come in from an orienteering exercise in the hills around the manor. They were supervised by fourteen of his own, members of the sixteen-man troop that had come through the Transition. One of his officers—Lieutenant Peter Hamilton—was on assignment God only knew where.

The prince was dressed like the others, in a twenty-first-century British camouflage pattern. He climbed on top of a wooden ammo crate to address the men. They were the first training cohort to come through, but they already looked very different from the general run of squaddies and conscripts found in the contemporary British Army.

For starters, they were all combat veterans who had served at least four years in the Regular Army before applying to attempt the six-week selection course. Having completed that course only a fortnight ago, they were now looking forward to twelve months of training that would turn them into "basic" SAS troopers. *Or they would be,* Harry thought darkly, *except they'd probably be thrown into action very soon, when the Germans invade.*

There had been no break between the end of the brutal selection course and the start of their "basic" training, but Harry was about to give them one.

A towering "Jamaican" with a thick East End accent, Sergeant Major Vivian Richards St. Clair, roared at the men, instructing them to stand at ease.

Harry held aloft a piece of paper, which he let everyone see, flapping in the breeze. "I have here an order from Adolf Hitler," he called out.

The men were too disciplined to react overtly, but he did note a ripple of surprise as it passed through the ranks.

"I wasn't expecting it for a little while longer, actually, but it's come in a bit early," he continued, raising his voice to project over a blustery nor'easter that had sprung up. "Shall I read it?"

Some wag couldn't help himself. *"If it's from Adolf, you could wipe your arse with it, sir!"*

Harry smiled as laughter broke out. He damped it down with a wave of his hand. When he spoke again, it was in an exaggerated Prussian accent. Sadly, none of the 'temps recognized it as his best Schwarzenegger. "For some time, our enemies have been using, in their warfare, methods which are outside the International Geneva Conventions. Especially brutal and treacherous is the behavior of the so-called Commandos . . ."

A great cheer went up at that point, and Harry let it subside before he continued, switching to his own voice.

". . . who, as is established, are partially recruited from freed criminals in enemy countries."

An even louder roar of approval greeted that.

"I believe they may be talking about the Australian SAS, Sergeant Major," he said in a voluble aside to St. Clair. "Convict stock and all that, I suppose."

Peals of laughter rolled over him, almost, but not quite, drowning out the protests of the three or four Australians in the ranks.

"From captured orders," Harry continued, "it is divulged that they are directed not only to shackle prisoners—"

A cheer.

"—but also to kill defenseless prisoners."

A bigger cheer.

"Naughty fucking commandos!" somebody called out.

He let the commotion die down completely before he read on.

"I therefore order that from now on, all enemies on so-called Commando missions in Europe or Africa, challenged by German troops, even if they are to all appearances soldiers in uniform or demolition troops, whether armed or unarmed, in battle or in flight, are to be slaughtered *to the last man*. It does not make any difference whether they are dropped by parachute. Even if these individuals, when found, should apparently be prepared to give themselves up, no pardon is to be granted them on principle."

A few of the bolder types tried to raise a few *hoorays* at that, but the effort fell somewhat flat. Harry let his gaze slowly traverse over every man watching him. He grinned wickedly.

"Well, you lads are new to the regiment, and we don't expect you to be familiar with all of our traditions just yet. But let me assure you, where we come from, this is very old news. Where we come from, our enemies don't just pop a bullet into the back of your head if you're foolish enough to let yourself be captured. Where we have come from, *they cut off your fucking head and make a movie of it for the whole world to watch!*" he yelled.

Silence was the only reply. The faces of the new men, he saw, were decidedly uneasy. His own troopers, however, were grinning wickedly.

"And what, Sergeant Major, is regimental policy in the face of such piss-poor hospitality?" he asked St. Clair.

"*A bloody good drink, sir,*" the gigantic black noncom roared back.

"*Right then,*" yelled Harry, "*to the pub!*"

"Smashing spread, Major Windsor!" said a young trooper juggling a southern-fried chicken leg and a pint of ale. "Me old mum doesn't cook half as good as this nosh."

Harry clapped him on the shoulder. "Well, eat up, son. We'll be busing it back to barracks tonight."

"Yes, sir!"

The tables of the Glenuig Inn were groaning under the weight of the feast Harry had organized. Kitchen staff from Balmoral castle had been driven in two days earlier to prepare the food in secret. A banner hung across the bar congratulating the troops for passing the selection course, the first official acknowledgment that they had achieved something even remotely noteworthy. The day they'd actually graduated, the training cadre simply tapped those who had made it, and sent them on a twenty-mile forced march in full kit, followed by two hours of jujitsu training, and a night-maneuver exercise.

"Nice one, gov," St. Clair said as he leaned against the bar with a glass of Highland Park almost hidden in one enormous paw. "The lads was beginning to suspect you were a bit of a tyrant."

Harry took a long draw on a pint of Wee Heavy. "I am," he said, licking away some froth. "Sibling issues."

The small whitewashed alehouse couldn't contain all the soldiers and invited locals who'd crowded in for the celebration. Despite the chill of approaching dark at high latitude, they spilled out of the building and onto the grounds, where they tended to cluster around large braziers of burning peat. Quite a few wandered across the road to take their drinks onto the white-sand beach that fronted a small bay letting onto the Sound of Arisaig.

"You think these lads will be ready?" asked St. Clair.

"Not a chance," Harry replied quietly. "Not what *we'd* call ready, in any case. But I can't see Hitler waiting until next spring to have a go. He knows he's got to get in and finish us before the U.S. can build up enough combat-ready divisions and matériel. He'll try it on well before Christmas, Viv. I've got an old-fashioned fiver says we won't even see out the month."

"Sorry, guv, can't take that bet. Reckon I'd do me dough cold."

Harry watched as the crowd swarmed around tables laden with venison and boar from his newly acquired estates. Piles of fresh vegetables, roasted taters, and Yorkshire pudding nearly buried dozens of smokehouse hams and chickens. It was a bacchanalian feast, given the wartime restrictions. Mutton pie and carrot pudding were the staples of the local diet. The sweets jars in the village shops were all empty, and the chocolate bars in the windows were made of wood. Only the wrapping was real. For Harry, the highlight of this evening promised to be the Hitler-shaped piñata stuffed full of real chocolates and toffees and boiled sweets that he had organized for the village children. When he lay in his bunk at night, he prayed that they, and his own men, would survive what was coming.

"You really put the wind up 'em, with that *Kommandobefehl* stuff," St. Clair mumbled around a Thai chicken stick he had lifted from a table of "modern" foods. The curries and rice dishes were popular with the small twenty-first crew, but mostly provoked curiosity and a little fear among the locals. Harry had restricted himself to a small bowl of lamb korma. He scooped up a last mouthful with a piece of garlic naan, washed it all down with a slug of ale, and shrugged off St. Clair's concern.

"Best they know, Viv. Should fire them up. Like that time we nearly got caught in Surabaya by old Ibn Abbas and his mob. *A damn close run thing, what!*" he mugged, dropping into a parody of an upper-class twit.

As the night wore on, Harry let himself bathe in the atmosphere of the room, both its actual warmth as the mercury dropped outside, and the balm of close companionship with decent people. He'd known very few moments like this since his college days. None since he'd returned to the regiment at the reduced rank of captain after a four-year spell in civvies. When the government had reintroduced conscription after the intifada, his brother, King William, had called all the royals together and made it clear that he would not have his subjects forced to endure dangers and hardships that the principals of the firm were unwilling to face alongside them.

Harry had actually been intending to return to uniform anyway, but as so often happened when Wills made one of his pronouncements, Harry ended up feeling as if his own decisions were being presented to him as a fait accompli. It was incredibly galling, but such was the fate of the second heir to the throne. Still, he missed his brother.

"You all right, guv?"

Harry let go a long breath he'd been holding. "Sorry, Viv. Miles away."

"Years, you mean."

"Yeah."

"Your Highness, Your Highness!"

Harry's spirits dropped at the sound of the voice, but his face somehow managed to light up with a credible imitation of surprise and pleasure, another benefit of royal training. Miss Deborah Jones, the schoolmistress, was bearing down on him with a couple of heifers in tow.

He'd paid a visit to the school one afternoon, to give a talk to the kiddies. Besides the village and estate children, a hundred evacuees from London had been relocated locally and were in attendance. He'd thrilled them with tales of the future, most of which were true, and it had been an altogether pleasant diversion for a couple of hours. But Miss Jones had been pestering him ever since, trying to set him up with one of the many dumpy red-haired lasses who were so common hereabouts.

Jones herself was a thin, painfully angular woman with a mouth like a puckered cat's anus, and whenever excitement got the better of her—as it had at the moment—the anus would pucker all the more violently.

"Your Highness, Your Highness!"

"Please, Ms. Jones. It's just Major Windsor."

Viv, he could see, was grinning like a big black Cheshire cat.

"And who are these lovely young ladies, Ms. Jones?" asked the sergeant major, not so much as flinching when Harry dug a callused thumb into a very sensitive pressure point on his upper arm.

"This is Miss Lang, and this is Miss Biggins," she trilled.

On closer observation, Miss Lang was what he and Wills used to call a bit of a six-pack, which was to say, if he threw down that much beer in a short space of time, he might just well have a crack at her on general principles. She wasn't even afflicted with red hair. Perhaps . . .

"Major Windsor, sir?"

In his panic at being fronted by Miss Jones, he hadn't noticed the dispatch rider who appeared through the crush of the room.

"Yes, Corporal."

The rider was dressed for the road, in heavy oilskins, crash helmet, and goggles. He pulled an envelope from his satchel and handed it over, probably wondering why the woman with the cat's butt for a mouth was glaring at him so fiercely.

Harry thanked him and then made his apologies, assuring the three women that Sergeant Major St. Clair would keep them entertained for the rest of the evening. He moved around the bar and into the relative calm of the pub manager's office. Closing the heavy oak door behind him cut the sound of the party down to a muted roar. He broke the seal on the envelope, which came from Downing Street.

The prime minister had ordered that he proceed to London with all dispatch.

THE SOLENT, SOUTHERN ENGLAND

As a child, Captain Karen Halabi had retreated from a deeply unpleasant family life by hiding herself in books, specifically by seeking refuge in the lore and mythology of English seafaring. From her preteen years, when her school friends were plastering their bedroom walls with garish posters of pop stars, she dreamed only of running away to sea and escaping the prison of her father's house. Her obsession was a mystery to all.

Not in its origin—because anybody who had endured the misfortune to deal with Khalil Halabi was soon possessed of the same desire to flee—but because Karen had no seafaring blood in her at all. Even on her English side, her late mother's family ran back through an entirely unimpressive lineage of slum-dwelling lumpen proles. There was no reason why she should have been drawn to the sea, other than the obvious one: it was so much more pleasant than going home.

And it was still the place she chose as her home, she realized as the lighter carried her across the waters of the Solent, which separated the Isle of Wight from England, back to her ship and crew. Still the one constant in her painfully conflicted life.

The sea spray was cold and stinging on her coffee-colored skin as they motored into the chop. The sailors, 'temps, were used to her by now. They'd made the trip from Portsmouth to the *Trident* dozens of times, ferrying across crew and all manner of visitors. She had even organized a brief tour for them. After that, their initial reserve—which sometimes bordered on hostility—had gradually morphed into tolerance, if not outright acceptance.

She wondered if it would always be that way here. If she would forever be allowed to serve her function, grudgingly valued, but never appreciated for herself.

Halabi huddled deeper into the thick jacket and woolen scarf she wore against the stinging spray and sharp, biting wind. She could feel winter's teeth in the chill of the sea air, and wondered idly whether she was just imagining that the autumn seemed colder here. The air was certainly cleaner, when you got away from the war. If only everything could be cleaner and simpler, but the longer she was here, the more conflicted she became.

She'd promised herself she would not become emotional over the snub she'd received in London, and for most of the return trip to her ship, she had managed to maintain an admirable detachment. But as the little motor-boat thumped and beat against the confused swell of the Solent's meeting waters, she found it increasingly difficult to contain her anger and distress. After all, the insult had been as much directed at her crew as at her.

She'd been in the capital only a short time. She had a briefing to deliver to the Combined Chiefs of Staff at the War Room and a meeting with Professor Barnes Wallis, the head of the government's new Advanced Research Council.

The journey up had been uneventful, if more than a little interesting. As was the case with most of her crew, Halabi had duties that kept her on station almost permanently. She rarely left the *Trident*. On the few occasions she did get away, the trip to London was always fascinating. Not just for the opportunity to examine the historic city and its surrounds firsthand, but also to see the human face of a war that had featured so prominently in her studies at Staff College. There were almost no private cars on the roads, and those very few she did see were gas conversions—preposterous contraptions with a small barrage balloon on the roof or trailing a gas burner in a sort of chariot arrangement. Cyclists were numerous and just as hazardous to life and limb as bicycle couriers in her day. Teams of horses drew post office vans. What few taxis were available tended to be monopolized by GIs with a lot more money than the locals. The open wounds of zigzag trenches defaced parks and playing fields. Women cooked over open fires in bomb sites and hauled buckets of water from who knew where. Occasionally she would spy somebody trying to pee in private behind a bush, often enough to suggest that the Nazis had some mad plan to destroy British morale by bombing all the country's public conveniences out of existence. It was a feast for someone like her, with a first in social history from Oxford, and Halabi had allowed herself to become lost in her observations as she motored toward the War Room meeting.

That had gone well enough. Churchill was there, and she'd come to appreciate his presence when dealing with the contemporary military hierarchy. The PM was a famous curmudgeon with absolutely no tolerance for any nonsense that might interfere with the important business of making war on the enemies of the realm. The Defense Committee had reviewed the contingency plans for whatever Hitler might throw at them in the coming weeks. Halabi had explained, yet again, the capabilities and limitations of her ship, and brought everyone up to date on the latest intel take from her drones and ship sensors. The meeting had concluded on a somber note, with all agreeing that the storm was about to break over the island. But there was also some confidence that the Allies would weather it, however savage it might be. England was not defenseless, as she very nearly had been in 1941. Huge numbers of troops from the U.S. and the British Commonwealth were already in country, preparing to repel the assault. The *Trident* provided them with nearly total coverage of the enemy's movements. And although the Advanced Weapons programs of Professor Wallis would not begin to deliver in strength for a few months, they still had a few unpleasant surprises in store for the Germans right now.

Halabi had left the meeting satisfied, and even a little more optimistic than when she'd arrived. The battle was unavoidable, but by no means unwinnable. There would be a terrible bloodletting, perhaps every bit as bad as the horrors of the First World War. But she thought the opposition had the bigger task. For all the firepower Hitler was bringing to bear, he was still faced with having to leap the Channel in less than perfect conditions, against a well-prepared opponent. It was not just a river crossing, whatever his loopier generals said.

Perhaps if she had been a little less sanguine, she wouldn't have been so badly upset by what had happened next. Halabi was climbing the stairwell back up to King Charles Street. It was a long climb, the Cabinet War Rooms being buried so deeply underground. She was juggling her briefcase and flexipad, attempting to link back to the *Trident* for a situation report, when she suddenly made out her own name in the low burble of voices ahead of her on the stairwell.

Some part of her said, *stop.* She could just wait and let whoever it was get farther ahead of her. But her feet kept climbing, and she found herself unable to tune out the conversation.

". . . unbelievable, really. That Winston would allow everything to turn on someone like that."

"Well, he's been hitting the bottle rather more enthusiastically of late."

"Well, who hasn't? It's no excuse. A bloody darky and a woman. It's a wonder the RAF lads haven't jacked up, the losses they've taken saving her arse time and again."

As she climbed the steps, Halabi was wrenched back to the tortures of her childhood. She suddenly felt, without having to distinctly recall each and every incident, the accumulated torment of a thousand cruel, unthinking petty insults. She felt the rising heat of free-floating shame and a prickle of panic sweat under her thick, hot clothing.

"I tell you what, if I had that ship of hers, old Raeder would know he'd been in a fight. There wouldn't even be a bloody *Kriegsmarine* to worry about beyond a few e-boats. But she just sits there on the Motherbank doing her bloody knitting."

"Wretched woman."

"Well, we'll see what happens when the real fighting starts, won't we."

Back on the Solent as the small boat swung around an old *Halcyon*-class minesweeper, her flexipad buzzed on her hip, jolting Halabi out of her reverie. She lifted the hem of her oilskin coat, unhooked the device, and powered up in one fluid movement, despite the rough conditions.

Her XO, a severe looking Scot named McTeale, appeared on screen. "We've got another big raid coming, Skipper," he said. "About a hundred and thirty. All for us again, by the look of things."

As McTeale spoke, she looked around and, sure enough, the ships of her antiair screen were coming to life. Thick smoke began pouring from the funnels, water churned as they maneuvered to best place themselves between the Luftwaffe's attack and their priceless charge, the *Trident*.

The irony had long since faded, of her futuristic supership being guarded by a pack of creaking antiques. Three 'temp destroyers had already gone to the bottom protecting her.

As the ships picked up the pace, positioning themselves to counter the approaching enemy aircraft, McTeale continued to bring her up to speed. "They won't be here for thirty-five minutes yet, ma'am. And two of Mallory's big wings have already scrambled to meet them. They'll be considerably thinned out even before they reach us."

As he finished, Halabi thanked him and signed off, slapping the lighter's helmsman on the back and shouting over the engine noise and brisk wind. "Get a move on, Bumpy. Company's calling. Tie up, and cross deck with me. You'll want to be out of the way if any of Göring's boys get through."

"Aye, ma'am," the sailor called back, opening up the throttles and making the ride even more challenging. Halabi scanned the gray, dismal skies, but she already knew she'd be unlikely to catch sight of the RAF as it headed out to do battle. Her own CIC would vector the Spitfires and Hurricanes onto the incoming raid well before it reached the Channel. The *Trident*'s Nemesis arrays would provide a detailed picture of three-dimensional battlespace out to five hundred kilometers. It made the country's contemporary air defense radar network—which had done so well in the Battle of Britain—utterly formidable. By the time the stealth destroyer had deployed its small fleet of drones, the UK had real-time surveillance cover deep into Germany itself.

It still doesn't stop them coming, though, she thought.

The Luftwaffe was sending hundreds of German airmen to their deaths every day, attempting to destroy the RAF. And despite the losses, it was having an effect. The strain on the Royal Air Force was beginning to tell. If they cracked, invasion was inevitable.

It certainly appeared imminent. The buildup of Axis forces across the Channel had nearly reached critical mass, despite the best efforts of Bomber Command to disrupt Nazi preparations. Halabi's best guess was that they had another fortnight to prepare, although if any of the continuous Luftwaffe raids actually broke through and took out the *Trident*, the attack would begin almost immediately. Because even with all her ground-attack cruise missiles gone, and her antiair missiles too precious to launch against flying crates like Stukas and Heinkel 110s, she remained the keystone of Britain's defense.

Admiral Raeder couldn't be sure how many ship killers remained in her vertical launch tubes—in fact, there were six. But he *could* be certain that her sensors kept London aware of every move made by anything bigger than a *kübelwagen* on his side of the Channel. Meanwhile, the ship's combat intelligence and human sysops could coordinate Britain's defensive efforts in a way that was far more effective than pushing wooden blocks around on a big table.

Yet still they were coming.

As the lighter moved to within a hundred meters of the *Trident*, Halabi linked her flexipad to the ship's CIC and brought up a display of the dogfight that was unfolding to the south. The screen wasn't big enough to show a real-time video feed from the high-altitude drones on station above the Channel, but the CGI schematic showed her enough. The raid had formed out of three airfields near Lille, St. Lo, and Rouen. Fighter cover, which was just peeling away to engage the RAF defenders, accounted for thirty hostiles. The rest were the bombers.

She doubted many would get through. Radar-controlled triple-A on the Isle of Wight and the destroyer screen would most likely deal with any planes that evaded the interceptors.

Halabi felt her biochip implants link to the ship as the lighter bumped against the *Trident*'s composite skin.

With a chime, McTeale reappeared on the pad's display. "CI has analyzed the attack profile, Captain. It's a new one. There's an eighty percent chance they'll come in low, to try and get under the guns we've got positioned on the island. The destroyer screen is moving into position, as recommended by Posh."

Halabi couldn't entirely suppress a smirk at that. Posh was an AI with the voice of an unborn pop star, and every time they got bossed around by the "glorified abacus," as they called her, the Royal Navy captains couldn't help getting their knickers in a twist.

Deck crew helped secure the lighter and get the 'temps on board as she compressed the formalities of her return into a quick salute and a brisk recommendation that everyone get below ASAP.

She moved quickly but without apparent haste. It just wasn't appropriate for one of His Majesty's stealth destroyer captains to be seen rushing about like a giddy schoolgirl, and she felt the keen responsibility of setting a good example.

"Chief Waddington, escort our guests to the mess for a cuppa. They'll be with us for the next little while."

Her senior enlisted man ushered them toward a hatch at the rear of the teardrop bridge as the Metal Storm pods deployed from their recessed containment cells with a whirr. "This way, Bumpy, Freddie," he said. "Keep out of the captain's way now. She's got Nazis to be killing."

The 'temps were obviously torn between fascination and the feeling that they were hopelessly out of place. They'd both been through a tour of the ship, but they'd never seen her in action before.

"Not, today, I think, Chief," Halabi said as she pushed past them on her way to the CIC. "I've got a pound says we don't fire a volley."

Waddington gave it a second or two before nodding brusquely. "Done then, ma'am. For a quid. Right you two, follow me." The chief left with his guests in tow, and Halabi hurried on.

A leading seawoman announced the captain's arrival, but she bade everyone to keep working. It was always reassuring to get back into the CIC, even with the ship's offensive capability so drastically diminished. On the forward bulkhead of the hexagonal shaped center, six giant flat panels had been linked into one theater-wide display.

Four of the panels were presently devoted to the attack on the *Trident*. Two remained fixed on schematics of Axis deployments on the mainland. She could see as soon as she entered the soothing blue light of the center that even more units had been moved toward the French coast. Another Waffen-SS division had been billeted at Brugge in Belgium. Two regiments of Panzer Grenadiers had moved north from Amiens to Douai. And more radar-controlled antiair units had appeared around the ports of Le Havre, Dieppe, and Calais.

"Looks like they're warming up for the Cup, Mr. McTeale."

"Aye, ma'am," said her executive officer. "It's beginning to look like a right fucking teddy bears' picnic. The RAF is chopping into those wee beasties right proper, though." He nodded at the screen where multiple windows of cascading data clearly indicated that a substantial toll had already been levied on the attackers.

Before Halabi could concentrate on the readouts, however, her chief defensive sysop called out. "Captain, we have a development. Three hostiles approaching at low altitude, from one-forty-three relative, airspeed of eight hundred eighty kilometers per hour."

A low-grade jolt ran through the combat center—nothing that a stranger would notice, but enough for Halabi to pick up.

"Jets," she said without showing her surprise. "Ms. Burchill, reassign Drone Zero Three to the new contact."

A new window opened up on the four screens feeding coverage of the air battle. A real-time feed appeared, from a Big Eye that was keeping station at 110,000 feet.

"They're Two-sixty-twos," said Halabi. "A little premature, I would have thought. Intel, quickly, give me the *E! News* version."

A young lieutenant worked his keyboard, calmly but quickly. "In the Original Timeframe, first jet flight July eighteenth, nineteen forty-two, ma'am. Tests proved engines to be unreliable. They mostly remained so. Used as a bomber rather than a fighter. Not very maneuverable. Long, straight-line attacks with cannon when engaging Allied bombers."

"Posh indicates a ninety-eight percent probability that we are the target, ma'am," said Lieutenant Burchill.

"What does she say about the air screen's chances of knocking them down?"

"Less than thirty percent, Captain. She recommends that we designate for Metal Storm."

The big screen showed the three prototype jets slashing across the Channel at nearly twice the speed of the Hurricanes fighting it out thousands of feet above them.

"Designate them," said Halabi, "but let the destroyers and the shore batteries have a go first. They might have been able to jump-start these jets, but I doubt they've been able to build a decent Exocet yet. It might be another dummy run. A ploy to trick us into using up more of our war stocks."

"Posh is resetting the air screen, ma'am, based on probable attack vectors."

"Thank you, Ms. Burchill."

Halabi watched intently as the thirteen corvettes and destroyers emerged from the mouth of the Solent and spread out in a formation determined by the *Trident*'s Combat Intelligence to provide the most effective interlocking fields of fire.

"The Daleks are locked and tracking, Captain," reported her defensive sysop.

Halabi threw a quick glance at a feed from the deck-cams, showing three Metal Storm pods that were deployed and making micro-adjustments as they awaited the order to fire. She wondered who had first nicknamed them Daleks. *A Brit, probably.* The name had never really caught on in the U.S.

Her comm boss appeared at her side. "Flash traffic from London, ma'am. A movement order, for you, from Downing Street."

"It can wait," she replied curtly. "I'm about to lose a bet with Chief Waddington. Comm, send a message to Fighter Command. Warn them about the Two-sixty-twos. Tell them they can counter for the jets' increased speed by using their superior maneuverability. I don't think it's going to be an issue today. But you never know."

"Aye, ma'am."

The distant thunder of old-fashioned ack-ack reached them through the composite ram-skin and monobonded-carbon armor of the *Trident*'s hull. The air screen had opened up. She watched a top-down view of the ships as flame and smoke poured from Bofors and small-bore cannons and .50-caliber machine-gun mounts. Two armored motorboats appeared from the northwest quarter to lend their efforts, as well, although they weren't plugged into the air-defense grid that controlled the fire of the other ships and the shore emplacements.

"Splash one!"

A German jet erupted into a bright yellow ball of flame and oily smoke. A small cheer went up, but quickly subsided as the two remaining jets pressed on.

"Captain, Nemesis telemetry data indicates that a five-inch shell from HMS *Obdurate* took out the hostile."

"My compliments to Commander Amis," she said.

"Splash two!"

A second jet fighter disappeared inside a boiling cloud of burning debris.

There was no applause this time. The third plane continued on its course, ripping past the destroyers in a matter of seconds. On screen, the sparkling lines of white fire danced along the opposite sides of the defending ships.

"HMS *Obedient* got number two, Skipper."

"Thank you, Mr. Evans. My compliments to Commander Welsh."

Halabi took her seat in the center of the CIC and slowly rubbed her lips with one finger as she watched the last plane cross into her fire-zone.

"Intel, ma'am. Analysis indicates air-launched missile capability. Possibly prototype R-Four-M rockets, with a PB-Two warhead."

"Thank you, Ms. Burchill. Estimated time to release of hostile weapons package?"

"One minute, plus or minus ten seconds, ma'am."

"Service the target if it's still viable in twenty seconds."

They watched and waited as their defensive screen continued to hammer away at the bogy. Fixed antiair defenses on the Isle of Wight commenced firing, as well.

"Brave man," McTeale said as the 262 bored in at high speed on a long, straight line of attack.

"He's a dead man, now," Halabi replied. The blue-lit space momentarily shook due to the short bark of a Metal Storm pod that was unleashing a minimal burst. Forty-three rounds of hypervelocity ceramic slugs intercepted the fragile airframe at a combined speed of Mach 6, tearing it into metal confetti.

"Stand down the Daleks."

"Threat boards are green."

"Screen deploying to original intercept path."

Halabi continued to stare at the flat panel, where she had just watched a man die. "Was it worth it, Mr. McTeale? Three men and their planes to make us fire off another few dozen rounds?"

The *Trident*'s XO pondered the question by examining his highly polished shoes. "I suppose, ma'am, that come the day we have nothing left in the cupboard, then yes, it will have been worth it. But not today."

"Captain, the initial attack appears to be breaking up and returning to base. RAF is pursuing."

"Thank you, Ms. Burchill. Let's keep an eye on them for now."

She remembered at last that her comm officer had given her a message from Downing Street. The piece of paper was crumpled in her hand. She unfurled the printout and read it while the tempo around her wound down a few notches.

"Mr. McTeale," she said somewhat irritably. "Have the air division warm up a chopper. Apparently I'm needed at high tea."

15

He hadn't been back East since lighting out of Grantville in the worst part of the Depression. The little mining town had done it hard—harder than most—and when he'd won a union scholarship to State, his old man had virtually run him out of the house, saying he ate too much to have around anyway.

Dan Black had never seen either of his parents again.

His dad died in a coal gas explosion in August of '34, and his ma had passed away a week later. Died of a broken heart, they said, although Julia insisted that it was more likely to have been a stress-related myocardial infarction. Dan preferred the romantic explanation.

He'd been on the Roosevelt program in California by then, and hadn't been able to get back in time for his dad's funeral, or his mother's broken heart. No matter how sensible and level-headed Julia was about it, he still felt that if he'd just been able to afford a train ticket, he might have saved her from dying of her grief.

Those memories hadn't afflicted him in two or three years, but they came rushing back as the big Lockheed Constellation banked over the San Fernando Valley and turned its nose toward home.

Well, not home, exactly. Grantville didn't boast an airport of any kind, and he wouldn't be visiting his old stomping grounds. But to Commander Dan Black, heading East still meant heading home even if he'd be spending all his time in Washington and New York.

He had two days of briefings ahead of him in the capital, and three days' leave in the Big Apple. He'd made a play of refusing the leave when Kolhammer had first suggested it. But the admiral had been all the more insistent when he found out that Julia would be back from Down Under and working out of the *Times* office while Dan was there. He hadn't kicked *too* hard, though. He really needed to see her.

On his lap he had yesterday's edition of the paper, folded over to obscure her last piece off the Brisbane Line, a pen portrait of some jarhead who was lined up for a medal after routing a Japanese ambush. He wouldn't read it until they'd leveled off. Julia's stories were always a waking nightmare for Dan. She wrote very differently from Ernie Pyle or any of those guys. Her pieces were like war novels. He often wondered how they got past the censors. They were always vivid and incredibly violent, and she was always right there in the middle of the action.

Her voice was always there, too, though, and that's why he never missed one, no matter how much they gave him the heebie-jeebies. He could always hear her speaking as he read.

The Connie's four shining Wright R3350 engines strained for maximum power as they sought altitude, the brand-new computer-designed propellers biting into the hot dry air of the L.A. Basin with an extra 20 percent efficiency. He'd led a group of Army Air Force generals through the factory two days earlier, and had told them all about the redesign. Below him, in the western reaches of the San Fernando Valley, he could see the huge complex of half-finished buildings and bare excavation sites that formed Andersonville and Area 51, the dormitory and production centers for the Special Administrative Zone. He was sitting on the wrong side of the plane to catch sight of the military camps that had sprung up to house the expanding Auxiliary Forces, but he spent most of his workday shuttling among them, and knew they were almost as big.

From this height, however, he was surprised by how much ground the new developments covered, and he wondered how long it would be before the entire valley floor was carpeted with asphalt, tract homes, and factories. About twelve months, he guessed, if they kept expanding at this rate.

The ground glistened, as though they flew over thousands of lakes and ponds, but he knew that it was just metal and glass. You couldn't hope to defeat—or even contain—the sort of energy that had been unleashed down there, he mused. The plane he sat in had come out of a massive new plant, right over there near the Verdugo Hills. Squinting his eyes against the glare of reflected sunlight, he thought he could pick out another three or four new aero plants, all of them working with some element of twenty-first-century technology, even if it was just a single computer.

Of course, there had to be places like this in Japan and Germany, as well. Or Poland, if the intelligence was right. They knew the krauts and the Japs had access to some of the same gear they did, computers and such, and even if they weren't as powerful as the stuff they'd taken off the *Clinton* and the *Leyte Gulf*, there was no denying the fact that the enemy had some great engineers working for them.

Admiral Kolhammer said that a big chunk of America's rocket program back in his time had been built with the help of Nazi scientists snatched right out of their laboratories at the end of the war. It didn't bear thinking about, what those guys were doing with flexipads and computing machines.

And even if the Nazis weren't sharing with the Commies, you had to figure old Joe Stalin would do what he could to steal anything he needed to catch up.

He had to know that if and when Hitler knocked out Great Britain, it'd be his turn again. Made you wonder—

Dan was knocked out of his thoughts by an elbow to his ribs. "Hey, Mac, you got a light?"

"Don't smoke," he said to the burly, short-haired man who sat in the seat next to him.

"Ah, not you, too? You don't look like one a them. What's a matter, Mac? You ain't buying all that hooey about a smoke being bad for a man, are you?"

"Nope. Just don't smoke."

Dan turned his shoulder away from the guy, letting him know that he didn't really want to chat, but the big palooka wouldn't take a hint.

"You gonna read that paper, Mac?"

"I am," said Dan. "My girl works for them. She's a reporter."

The man's face lit up. "You don't say. What's her name? What's she do? She work on the ladies' page?"

Despite himself, Dan couldn't help it. He was proud of Julia. "No, she's an embed. You know, a war correspondent. She's been down in Australia with MacArthur and Jones."

His companion's eyes went a little wider, as the plane leveled off and the copilot announced that they could undo their belts.

"No kidding? So she's from the future, eh? You lucky dog. I hear those dames, they're insatiable. Am I right, or am I right?"

Dan didn't answer right away—he was half-embarrassed, and half-pleased. He knew Julia hated him bullshitting with other guys about this stuff, but really, he couldn't see the harm. "Well, that'd be none of your business, buddy," he said. "But . . . well, yeah, you ain't a million miles from the truth."

The news seemed to please the guy. "*Goddamn.* I knew it. All those things you read, some of them had to be true. What is she—?"

Dan held up his hand. "Sorry. I meant it. It's really none of your beeswax."

Lucky for him the guy didn't seem put out at all. "Sure, sure thing, Mac. Listen, my name's Hurley, Dave Hurley. I'm in sheet metal. What about you?" he asked, pointing at Dan's uniform. "Why'd you make the jump? You want to fly rocket planes? You political? Or you just wanted to make out like a bandit with those dames?"

Black snorted. "I was at Midway. I was one of the first guys onto their ships. Went across to the *Clinton* in a helicopter with a youngster by the name of Curtis. An ensign—"

"Yeah, I read about him," Hurley said, nodding vigorously. "Ernie Pyle says he knew what the rockets and the death beams were before anyone else, didn't he? And he was the guy told Spruance how it all worked."

Dan nodded, recalling the night on the bridge of the *Enterprise*, when they'd watched helplessly while the Pacific Fleet was destroyed around them.

"Yeah, I read about that kid," Hurley continued. "Were you there, too, with Spruance?"

"Yeah, I was a planning officer. Curtis and I volunteered to check out their story, but things moved a little quicker than we did, and we became sort of irrelevant. I was on the *Clinton* for a while, ended up falling into a liaison role. I'm still doing that. So no, to answer your question, I'm not officially AF. But I'm on secondment for the duration."

Hurley took that in and readjusted his sizable frame. The seats were generous, but he was a big man. He took up all the space they had to offer, and then some.

"What about you?" asked Dan. "You look a bit like a cop, maybe even ex-navy. But you're in metal, you say?"

"Yeah. I used to be a cop, a sheriff actually," Hurley said. "But I was pensioned off about five years back. Crashed my patrol car during a chase. Busted my back. This flight's gonna be hell on me before it's done. I went into my uncle's sheet-metal business, since he was getting ready to retire. Turns out I had a nose for a dollar. Got me a few contracts with you guys, in fact, running up warehouses out Burbank way. Hell's bells but things are hot out there, aren't they? I've got crews working around the clock. In fact," he said, leaning over conspiratorially, "I've been trying to get my hands on a computer, to help run things even better. But I'm not that important."

"Don't be so hard on yourself," Dan advised. "Warehouses are important. We're growing so fast, storage and distribution is one of our real problems."

"Yeah? You think you could get me a computer, then? It'd be worth your while, if you know what I mean."

"Nope. Sorry."

Hurley gave him another elbow, playfully this time. "Can't blame a guy for trying though, can you?"

"Guess not," said Dan.

And he wasn't offended, really. In fact, he couldn't help but like the guy. If he had to be trapped on a transcontinental flight, he could do worse, he supposed.

Hurley didn't even light up a cigarette until they were about an hour into the trip. By that time they were deep into a discussion about the war, and the Zone, and the politics of both. Dave Hurley proved to be more of a broadminded character than Dan would have given him credit for. He wasn't at all concerned about women trying to "liberate" themselves. He said that as a businessman, he'd be doing himself out of a dollar if he didn't use all the skills his employees had to offer, whether they were women or blacks or Latinos or whatever. He didn't even seem to mind the fact that fairies and lemons, as he called them, felt free to live openly within the boundaries of the Zone, although he *did* wish they'd keep it private.

"After all, it's not like I go around groping my wife in public, is it?" he said.

No, Dan agreed. It wasn't.

In fact, Dan Black didn't have to share his trip with Dave Hurley all the way across America. The former sheriff left the flight in Denver, where he said he had a new branch office to visit. There was an element of truth to it, too.

Special Agent David Hurley drove to the Bureau's field office in Denver, where he grabbed a spare secretary and a teleprinter, to immediately file a report with Washington.

He had made contact with Commander Daniel Black, he wrote, but did not think he would be willing to act as an operative, or even an informant. The commander had formed an immoral sexual relationship with a reporter from 21C, a Miss Julia Duffy (file no. 010162820). He was planning to travel across state lines with Duffy for the purposes of said immoral sexual conduct, in violation of the Mann Act, and openly admitted to having done so before.

Black seemed to share many of the subversive and Communistic leanings espoused by Duffy in particular, and the wider population of the Multinational Force in general. During their discussion, he expressed approval of many sexual perversions, including mixed race and homosexual activities. His family background may have led him to embrace socialistic tendencies, since his father had been a unionized mine worker. Black himself confessed to having been a union member, before joining the navy.

Commander Black spoke openly, without regard to security, about his duties and about developments taking place in the Special Administrative Zone, although he declined the opportunity to enter into a corrupt relationship when it was proffered.

Special Agent Hurley did not consider him to be a good American, or a friend of the Bureau. However, he did not seem to be a particularly guileful individual, and might well be cultivated as an unwitting source of information, given his lack of sophistication and his access to the highest levels of command within the Zone.

For this reason, Hurley recommended that contact be maintained.

NY MUNICIPAL AIRPORT, NEW YORK

She was never going to get used to these fucking flying coffins. It took forever to get from Brisbane to Honolulu, and then to Frisco, and New York. She traveled in a Catalina Flying Boat, and a Boeing Stratoliner, all of it supposedly first class, paid for by the *Times*, but Julia Duffy still got out at the other end feeling like she'd spent four days on the roof of a Pakistani goods train with about a hundred unwashed peasants and their livestock.

The period piece aesthetics of the Stratoliner had been amusing at first. The wicker chairs, the cigarette girls, the cocktails, and waiter service were all great fun if you were into historical slumming. But really, droning around the world in unpressurized tin cans that couldn't even match the speed of a Q-class Beemer—like the one sitting back in her garage in 2021—well, *that* was her idea of hell.

As she waited for a porter to appear with her luggage at a very primitive LaGuardia Field, she swayed on her feet and fought to keep her eyes open. She could feel people looking at her. In her Armani jeans, Redback boots, and HotBodz thermopliable rain jacket, she was obviously Twenty-first. *But then* she thought, *these guys are very obviously 'temp.* They dressed differently, they looked different, they even moved differently. Part of it was obvious; sitting more primly, for example. Although she suspected that was partly a class thing. *We must slouch around like a bunch of vulgar low-lifes by the standards of anyone with enough money to afford private air travel in 1942,* she thought. But there was some subtle stuff, as well, a sort of stiffness and "blockiness," and a way of swinging the arms and legs that was different from her time—perhaps the movement equivalent of saying *cannot* rather than *can't.* She'd noted that even the basics set them apart, like how they got into a car. People here sat and then swung their legs in, rather than climbing in with their asses hanging out.

And of course, women moved in a more distinctly "feminine" way. They sometimes reminded her of the stylized way a drag queen of her time would move his hands and hold his head. To Julia, the handful of women disembarking from her flight or waiting for someone in the arrivals lounge all seemed artificial and blatantly coy. To them, she supposed, she must look like some sort of bull dyke from hell.

Man, she was too fucking tired. She patted the personal flexipad peeking out from under the bright yellow slicker. There was no local net for it to link to in New York, but Julia had been working on story files during the flight, so she hadn't wanted to pack it away.

Plus, she thought, it was a lot safer on her hip than in her luggage. The black-market price of an Ericsson T4245 Flexipad was probably upward of two or three million bucks.

That's why the first piece of hand luggage she'd unpacked was her trusty SIG Sauer, which she'd made a great play of openly fitting into her shoulder holster. That was at least one good thing about the 1940s. No airport security, or none that she recognized as such, anyway.

The terminal at LaGuardia—still known as New York Municipal Airport—was relatively quiet for an early evening. Her flight had disembarked, and its passengers were awaiting their baggage. A flight to the Bahamas was due out in forty minutes and one from Toronto was due in. But the place felt like a ghost town.

She was contemplating a limo run to her apartment, which was a little exciting because the interior designers should have finished the renovations by now, when her arms were pinned to her side from behind, and a sandpaper rough face pressed up against her cheek.

"Guess who!" Dan Black whispered into her ear. "Don't hit me!" he added quickly, hopping away, just in case her reflexes got the better of her.

She jumped when he grabbed her. Her heart skipped forward a few beats, but she didn't grab his nuts and try to rip them off, as she had last time. They were both learning. Dan, she noticed, had turned his body a little to the side, in order to avoid just such an attack.

"Hiya, sexy," she said, beaming, her lethargy falling right away with a hot surge that started somewhere down in her thighs and ran right up through her stomach until she was sure her face was flushed bright red.

"Hello, darling," Dan said, a tad more demurely.

Julia, however, grabbed him by the belt and wrenched him into her, keeping hold of the buckle while she slipped her other hand around to grab a butt cheek. She gave it a good squeeze as they kissed. "God, it's good to see you," she said.

As they parted slowly, both of her legs now firmly clamped around one of his, Dan patted her jacket where it covered the handgun. "You expecting trouble from your editor?"

"Girl can't be too careful," she said, smiling. "Get me home quickly, and you can take it off. Or you could leave it on, if you think you'd like that."

"*Julia.* People could be listening."

"Really? Well, that's a little kinky, but if you want it that way . . ."

A porter appeared, carrying her bags. Two Antler suitcases, with retractable wheels and a telescoping handle, which he clearly thought of as the greatest invention he'd ever seen. And one medium-sized backpack in jungle camouflage, still carrying one large, faded bloodstain—about which he seemed less enthused.

She tipped him what felt like a ridiculously small amount and shouldered a smaller backpack full of electronic equipment: her carry-on luggage. Then he followed them out to the limo pool.

"I didn't expect to see you at all, Dan," she said. "It's so *nice* of you to surprise me like this."

He slipped an arm around her slim waist as they passed into the cold night air, drawing more looks—some offended, some envious. "I didn't want to get your hopes up, telling you I'd be here before I knew I had the leave. And then you were out of reach anyway. So I figured, what the hell? It's no fun arriving in town when there's nobody to meet you."

"Man, you can say that again. This city still freaks me out. I keep expecting to turn around and see my friends on every corner, but, you know . . ."

She trailed off, the weariness and jet lag—or prop lag, she corrected herself—catching up again.

"I know," he said, kissing the top of her head.

Then they went home and fucked for three hours without a break.

"This place looks amazing, Jules!"

"It is cool, isn't it?"

Yes, it was. Dan had never seen anything like it. Not that he'd ever thought much about design and architecture before he met Julia. Even so, he'd never imagined that an apartment could look this way. His idea of how rich folk lived was informed entirely by Hollywood. Their homes were larger; the furniture was plush. But an armchair was an armchair, whether it was a hand-me-down from the welfare, or a big leather chesterfield in the Vanderbilt drawing room.

The stuff in Julia's apartment, however . . . even the way the rooms were laid out . . . it was . . . Well, words failed him.

He hadn't noticed it at first, when they'd spilled in through the door, hands all over each other, clothing already half-undone. They'd made love standing up, half-undressed, right inside the entry hall; then she'd hauled him straight into a bedroom and onto the mattress, which hadn't left for a long time.

Jules had disappeared to get a bottle of champagne at one point, but otherwise neither of them had ventured out of the room until much later in the evening.

After the third time, when it was going to take him a little while to re-cover, he'd begun to notice the bedroom in the light of the candles she'd lit.

The bed looked Japanese, like a *futon*, they called it, if he remembered right. It had no headboard to speak of. A big rectangle of padded leather seemed to be fixed to the wall behind the pillows.

And the wall itself was inset at random places with boxes or something, in which Julia had set up books or little pieces of art. He noticed that some of them were faintly backlit, adding a soft glow to the light of candles that were burning on tiny white shelves that protruded from the other walls just as randomly as the insets. There was no other furniture to speak of, just two fuzzy cubes, covered in what looked like polar bear pelt. He wondered where she kept her clothes.

"They did a great job, don't you think?" she said as they stood in the liv-ing room—or what he assumed was the living room—just before midnight.

"Where'd all the space come from?" he asked. "I've never seen such a big parlor before."

Julia smiled at him with that almost-pitying look she got sometimes. He suspected it was because he'd used the word *parlor*.

"Well, this used to be a three-bedroom apartment," she explained. "But I had them knock out a bunch of walls, and now it's one bedroom with a massive open living area which flows from the kitchen down there, through the dining and entertainment space, into my chill-out zone, here."

Dan sort of understood what she meant, but only because they were standing in the "chill-out zone," a strange, sunken, carpeted half-moon heaped with piles of weird Arabian-looking cushions. It seemed like the sort of place Fatty Arbuckle could get himself into a lot of trouble.

A data slate hung on the wall like a picture, and he guessed the area would serve as a sort of mini movie theater. Thirty or more data sticks sat in tiny slots, on top of another small white ledge that grew straight out of the wall by the slate.

"I thought nobody was allowed to own that sort of technology without a government permit," said Dan.

"Settle down, Eliot Ness," she said. "That's my personal slate. Only government-issue property is covered by the legislation. We were deploy-ing for three months, so I brought quite a few personal items with me."

She moved through the sunken lounge to pluck a data stick off the tiny shelf.

"Twenty-five years of *The Simpsons*," she said, clearly thrilled with what-ever that meant. "Every episode of *Sex in the City* and *Desperate Housewives*. Before I left the *Clinton*, I downloaded terabytes of shit from the library. I've got movies, TV, music, games, books, magazines, *the whole nine yards*. I'm telling you, Dan, I can *live* here now. It's just like my place at home. I even had the library run me up a couple of print-on-demand books for the shelf, some old favorites, just so I can see them when I come through the door. I can't tell you how much that means to me."

Those must have been the books he saw in her bedroom earlier. He noticed others now, tucked in recesses spotted around the massive room.

The long, rectangular "space," as she referred to it, seemed to get harder and colder as it receded toward the kitchen at the far end of the apartment. That space was arranged around a long central bench that appeared to have been fashioned out of railway sleepers and stainless steel. He couldn't be sure until he got down there, but it looked as if she'd had all her carpet and linoleum removed and left bare wooden boards and concrete in their place.

"It's polished concrete," she said enthusiastically when he asked. "Fucking cool, isn't it? And it's well within the very limited abilities of your local builders, thank God."

"It's, uh . . . I've never . . ."

"I know. You've never seen anything like it. You wouldn't have. I had a hell of a time finding a designer who could understand what I wanted," she said, beginning to pace around and whip herself into a frenzy. It made Dan wonder if she'd found a new supply of combat drugs. She spoke faster and faster, but with an enthusiasm he'd never seen her display for anything before.

It was actually kind of cute. She was like a teenager, for a change.

"I had a couple of copies of *Monument* and *Wallpaper*," she said, picking up a magazine from what was probably a coffee table and passing it to him. "I bought them at the airport in Bangkok, back in my time, before I flew down to Darwin to join the *Clinton*. And that was all I had to work with. But I read about this totally outrageous gay guy in *The New Yorker*, you know, your *New Yorker*, and this graphic designer—he was just about to pack his bags and head out your way, to the Zone—but I grabbed him before I flew out last time, showed him the magazines and he, like, *totally* got it. He agreed to manage the renovation. We were using these Italian builders who got run out of Florence by the fascists. And anyway, I'm *stoked*. It's just like being home."

She threw her arms around him, and Dan could tell she was as happy as he'd ever known her to be. She was almost jumping with pleasure.

"It's a great-looking pad, Jules—Is that the right word?"

"If this was nineteen sixty-two, and I was Gidget, then yeah. But go on, keep telling me how great it is."

Dan made a show of flicking through the *Wallpaper* magazine, which wasn't about wallpaper at all, as far as he could tell. He could see where the designer had picked up some ideas and recreated them in Julia's apartment.

"That's like what you've got, right?" he said, pointing out a review of a restaurant, which seemed to have only one table, a long bench, like in a mess hall.

"Close enough," she said, squeezing him again. "Do you like it?"

"I think so," he said. "It looks, I dunno, like a house at the World's Fair. The view looks good."

"It's got a *great* fucking view!" she cried, grabbing him by the arm and dragging him over to the window. They were at least nine floors up in a corner apartment, and when he looked out, ribbons of light and moving traffic stretched away beneath them. He hadn't been paying attention in the limo, but the building had to be somewhere on the extreme eastern side of Manhattan, overlooking the river, which cut through the scenery outside like a black ribbon of negative space. He'd been to New York a couple of times before and was pretty sure he could see Brooklyn and Queens and Long Island. From the corner window, a wide sliver of Manhattan proper was visible, including a small dark wedge of Central Park, then the West Side and what he guessed was the Hudson River.

"This must have cost a mint, baby," Dan said, and he regretted it instantly. Had he broken some weird twenty-first-century taboo, implying that she couldn't afford to pay for her own home?

But Julia was surprisingly matter-of-fact in her answer. "Well, I sold some of my stuff. You know, silly little things like an old calculator, and a digital translator, and this ancient fucking iPod that'd been in my backpack for a decade. And I got a fucking packet for them."

As she explained how she'd cashed in, Julia grew increasingly animated again, leaving Dan confused. He'd always thought of her as an adventurer, someone for whom ties and commitments were nothing more than dead weight.

But as she spoke, her voice became faster and her hands began to fly around like birds released from a cage. "The *Times* had just deposited some hazard money into an account for me," she said, "back up in twenty-one, which I could access through the *Clinton*, and the office here agreed to pay that out dollar for dollar, in order to get me on staff. Which meant I got another big fucking payday right away. And then I had a lawyer do my contract negotiations for me, this chick named Maria O'Brien. Actually, she was the one helped me set up my garage sale. I would never have thought to charge anyone fifty grand local for an iPod with a flat battery. She used to be with the Eighty-second, but she finished her hitch about five days after the Transition. She's gone into business for herself here, providing legal services for anyone wanting to do business in the Zone. I tell you, Dan, she's going to be as rich as a fucking astronaut."

"A what?"

"It's an in-joke. Forget it. Anyway, she got the *Times* to honor my pay and bonuses, and to pay me what she called a temporally adjusted salary—which, bottom line, is a shitload more than a reporter gets here, and she squeezed a great big fucking on-signing bonus out of them, as well. It was all more than enough to pay for this, and make some strategic investments with the leftovers. I've got another place, even bigger than this, over in Gramercy Park. I bought it with Rosanna, and we're going to redo it together.

"Maria's formed a partnership with a local brokerage house, and I'm having about half of my salary invested by them. You could get in on it if you wanted, Dan. You should think about it. This war's not going to last forever, and when it's done, you're looking at compressing eighty years of growth into a decade or two. It's going to be fucking crazy. It's *already* crazy."

He didn't know quite what to say. He'd never been on the receiving end of a spiel quite like it. The closest he could recall was opening his door to a Fuller Brush salesman once. That guy had made him feel like he'd be on the road to hell if he didn't finish the day owning a complete set of Mr. Fuller's brushes.

Julia made him look tame.

"Uh, well, I guess I could," he said. "I don't have much to do with my pay, except buy you presents."

"Well, forget about that, buddy. Get yourself a portfolio. You're in town for, what, three days? We'll set up a coffee with Maria and . . . Hell, fuck that . . . Let's go see her right now. She *never* sleeps."

As so often happened around Julia, Dan Black felt himself swept along in her wake. She disappeared into her bedroom and reappeared with her flexipad.

"There's no net here," he said.

"I know. But Maria's got a mil-grade unit that'll pick up a point-to-point message within five klicks, if it's on . . . Hah! And it is!"

Julia ran her fingers through her hair and looked into the flexipad as though it were a makeup compact.

"Hey, Maria. It's Jules. Dan's in town and my head's in a different time zone. You up for a drink? Zap me." She tossed the unit onto a cushion in the chill-out zone and took his hand. "Come on, baby. Let's have a shower and get ready."

As she led him through into the bathroom, which looked like something out of the later Roman Empire, he heard the pad chime behind him.

Music and the sound of a party followed them into the shower.

"Hey, Jules!" he heard a woman call out. "Great to hear from you. Bring your big boy out. I'm with the famous Slim Jim down at the Bayswater. And get this, Frank Sinatra's here!"

16

SPECIAL ADMINISTRATIVE ZONE, CALIFORNIA

Having been born in 1969, Admiral Phillip Kolhammer wasn't a true child of the digital age. He grew up with rotary telephones, cassette recorders, black-and-white TV, pinball machines, one type of Coke, and the unfortunate musical legacy of the 1980s. The most secure personal files on his flexipad were a collection of bootleg tracks by a long-forgotten country rock band called Lone Justice, and the first two seasons of *Miami Vice*.

He'd never really mastered text messaging by thumb, but like everyone who grew up after the rise of digital entertainment, he had learned to split his attention along multiple tracks. Given the immense flows of data that streamed in from a properly monitored battlespace, he was often required to concentrate on a surprising variety of information from competing sources.

Even so, chairing the R & D committee was a real pain in the ass.

Six full-time members came to each meeting, but anywhere up to eighteen or twenty part-timers, consultants, or guests might also attend. The sessions were held every Friday afternoon, between 1400 and 1600 hours, in the largest briefing room of the nondescript, two-story prefab offices that were the power center of the Special Administrative Zone.

The building sat in a tight cluster of similarly unimposing structures, at the western edge of the Valley, in a huge agglomeration of half-built factories, empty warehouses, and unfinished offices known collectively as Area 51.

Kolhammer couldn't recall which of his underlings had first coined the name for the facility, but it had stuck, largely because it appealed to his own quietly mordant sense of humor. Half the country seemed to imagine that dark conspiracies were carried out there as a matter of daily routine. In truth, most of his time was taken up with land development, transport, housing, and industrial project management.

He had effectively become the mayor of the greatest boomtown in U.S. history, and he spent a good deal of his down time wishing he was still a junior officer, so the Zone would have been somebody else's headache. Then he'd be free to go off and fly jets. Or even build them, which was one of the things the R & D group met to thrash out every Friday morning.

On this particular Friday, with the formal part of the meeting over, everyone had broken down into smaller discussion groups scattered at tables throughout the room, to knock heads over things that should have been easily resolved. The main problem, Kolhammer had found, was the seemingly infinite bounty of knowledge the Multinational Force had brought through the wormhole. This seemed to induce a state he'd once heard described as "option paralysis."

He could feel his patience running out as he moved through the briefing room, on the way back to his own office.

"We should just forget the torpedo problem," one of his officers was arguing, "and concentrate on mines instead. Those babies sank more tonnage than any other weapon, and in fact—if I recall correctly—more than all the other weapon types combined in the Pacific theater."

At the next table, a marine, one of Lonesome's people, was counting off points on his fingers as he tried to make his pitch for the projects *he* thought should get priority. "We need to begin immediate mass production of the Vought F-Four-U-One Corsair," he said emphatically. "It was a tough, reliable ground-attack fighter which saw constant active service through to the end of the Korean War. It'll make a *huge* difference in the Pacific, in places like Iwo Jima and Guadalcanal, when we finally get there."

A 'temp, an army captain, made another point. "I agree that we have to keep on building the Sherman, to make the best of a bad situation. But what would even the odds against the Axis tanks—and the Soviets, if that became necessary—would be upgunning it straight away to the E-Eight Super Sherman. Those were originally produced in late '44, as the result of two years' hard combat experience, and the technical data is available immediately, in the goddamn Fleetnet lattice."

Another captain put down the flexipad he'd been waving around and held up a finger. "We ought to be spending a helluva lot more time on psyops. The Sovs and the Nazis are absolutely *goring* themselves, because Stalin and Hitler can't trust anyone, now that they've found out what's gonna happen—"

A contemporary navy officer interrupted him. "With all due respect, that's an interesting sociological point, but it's not a technical one . . ."

Kolhammer heard a civilian contractor arguing that it would take too long to build a jet fighter, and that it wouldn't give the Allies much of an advantage, anyway.

"From what I've read, all the early jets were fuel hogs, with a short range. If we want to quickly build a fighter for air superiority, I'd be marrying the P-Fifty-one with the Rolls-Royce Merlin engine. We had plans to do this before you guys turned up. You get a P-Fifty-one-D in squadron service by February next year, and you've got a reliable long-range fighter which can outperform anything the Luftwaffe or Japs can throw at it."

Kolhammer guessed the man was working for the division of North American Aviation, who were hoping to get the P-Fifty-one into the air before the F-86 made it redundant.

A group of army officers, all of them 'temps, were arguing energetically just a few feet away from him, about the Australian government's decision to ram through production of a variant AK-47.

A Lieutenant Hunt was in the throes of delight discussing the unrealistic prospect of building large numbers of FN Minimi squad machine guns.

A Captain Ken Young, an English Guardsman, cut across him, as if he had never spoken. "You know, if you Yanks had been serious about replacing the BAR, there were plenty of alternative designs available from the Lewis to the Bren, or even the Johnson."

"The Lewis?" spluttered an American. "You can't be serious? The BAR might be flawed, but the Lewis is a piece of *crap*. Haven't you read these briefing papers? There are something like fifty different types of jams just waiting to screw up that gun, and the pan magazine is an abortion."

Kolhammer sighed, and wondered where that turn of phrase had come from.

Dan Black would normally have handled this meeting, but he was still in New York on leave with his girlfriend, the reporter.

"You're a lucky man, Commander Black," he muttered to himself as he reached the exit, where his PA was waiting for him. And then he grinned, because it wasn't so long ago that the idea of spending three days in the company of Julia Duffy would have filled him with creeping horror. He supposed everything was relative.

"Turboprops. Those are really worth the effort," someone called out across the room in a strident voice.

"God help us," Kolhammer said to himself as Lieutenant Willy Liao fell in beside him.

Kolhammer put his head down and hurried on out of the room. The briefing notes from the meeting would be on his system by that afternoon, and some of them might even be useful, but only insofar as they supported the decisions he'd already made. It was important to give everyone a say, especially with the "old" armed forces being in a state of high anxiety about their collective futures. In the end, however, Phillip Kolhammer firmly believed in the old saying that a cow was a racehorse designed by committee.

And he'd be damned if he was going to sit around waiting for this committee to decide on how best to scratch its own ass.

Liao handed him a flexipad with about a hundred documents to be signed. He scribbled out one electronic signature which the document manager then affixed to each file. The young officer was ferociously competent, and Kolhammer knew there was no point wasting his own time checking each paper individually.

"Am I still on for that meet later today?" asked the admiral.

"In one hour twenty minutes," Liao answered. "You have a video link to General Groves booked in five minutes, sir. Then you are scheduled to inspect the new Boeing plant and progress on the new lots at Andersonville."

"How many people are under canvas out there?" he asked as they hurried down the stairs and out into the surprisingly warm late afternoon sunshine.

"Eighteen thousand in tents. Another fifteen thousand are moving into the Quonset huts, which went up last week. And they're just the workers. Most haven't brought their families with them yet."

Kolhammer sucked air in through his teeth. It was an unconscious gesture he'd picked up from his old man. Whenever Dave Kolhammer popped the lid of the family car to tinker with the recalcitrant engine, he'd suck air in through his gritted teeth just like that. "Do we have any better estimates of population growth over the next six months?" the admiral quizzed his PA again.

"Nine percent a month, at present rates. But of course, the new factories will start coming online very soon, and that will pull even more manpower in."

Kolhammer nodded silently as they reached his Humvee.

This was not what he expected to be doing when he joined the navy.

As the heat leaked out of the day, he drove himself up to Mulholland Drive, pulling off the road and into a culvert just before the Hollywood Hills. The teleconference with Leslie Groves had gone as expected. The director of the Manhattan Project had huffed and puffed and demanded more resources and staff from Kolhammer. The admiral blocked and dodged and had given up about one tenth of what he'd been asked for. But that was it, he'd decided. The well was dry. There was nothing and nobody else he could send to Oak Ridge or Los Alamos that was going to appreciably speed up the process. Groves and Oppenheimer already had hundreds of his best officers and technical specialists. Indeed, the *Clinton*'s fusion reactors were being run by a skeleton staff because so many had been transferred to the A-bomb project. And Groves had grabbed up more than his fair share of the IT systems that had been salvaged and stripped from all over the Multinational Force. His work was definitely of prime importance, given the Nazi's own accelerated nuclear programs, but it wasn't the only game in town.

That thought led naturally to his next meeting, an altogether more informal affair. He'd driven across the San Fernando Valley, with an escort, a Navy SEAL, ghosting him in a black Packard, watching for tails. Hoover's men were everywhere, but their field-craft hadn't been honed in a vicious twenty-year holy war. Chief Petty Officer Vincente Rogas was more than capable of seeing them off.

It hadn't been necessary, however. Kolhammer had driven through the flatlands north of Ventura, through remnant beet fields and walnut groves, past vast tracts of dry, coarse grassland and abandoned orchards, all staked out and fenced off for housing development in the coming months. He'd swung through the established settlements of Encino and Woodland Hills, tracked the whole time by both Rogas and a high-altitude surveillance drone that scanned for patterns in the thin traffic on the valley floor that might indicate he picked up a tail.

There was nothing.

They drove up through the foothills, weaving in and out of wild oaks and patches of sycamore and eucalyptus. He couldn't be sure, but Kolhammer felt that as they climbed the range he could taste clean air coming off the Pacific. He felt strung out and a little stale from overwork and lack of sleep. Even the hint of an ocean breeze was enough to revive him, although it fired memories of his wife and left him feeling sad and a little bewildered, an echo of the wild confusion he remembered from the first hours after the Transition.

He heard Rogas in the small earbud speaker he wore. "We weren't followed," the man reported. "But I'll keep an eye out, just in case."

"Thanks, Chief," replied Kolhammer.

They pulled off the main road into a canyon where millionaires did not yet tread. The road jinked back and forth a few times, overlooked by steep, crumbling hills that seemed to be held together with nothing but sagebrush and manzanita. The road curved left one last time and died at the base of a small, hard cliff.

His contact was waiting there. With blueprints spread out on the bonnet of his car, he looked more like an architect than a builder.

Kolhammer strode up to him. "You Donovan's man?" the admiral asked, referring to the Office of Strategic Services Chief.

"Uh-huh. Mitch Taverner's the name."

"Okay, why are we here, Mr. Taverner?"

The man picked up a roll of blueprints and waved it back up the canyon.

"You guys have a lien over this land. You're going to build a signal relay station here, in time. But you've got problems with L.A. over it. Or specifically, with the local rich folks. So it gives you a reason to come up here for a meeting with your builder." He tapped himself on the chest. "And the long drive gives your man Rogas over there a lot of visible ground, to check whether or not you've been followed."

Kolhammer suppressed his irritation and forced himself to speak slowly, in a reasonable tone. "Okay, so you've proved to me that Wild Bill has almost as many feelers inside the Zone as Hoover. Is there any other reason for you to be dragging me up here?"

Taverner, a barrel-chested man with what sounded like a Texas accent, grinned broadly. "Admiral Kolhammer, Mr. Donovan is a friend. He's not like the others."

"Wonderful. Imagine my relief. But I still don't see the need for subterfuge. If you're as good as you think you are, Mr. Taverner, you'll know that I don't much care for spooks, and I definitely don't have time for this sort of bullshit. So tell me, exactly what are we doing here?"

But the Texan refused to be bullied out of his role. He reminded Kolhammer of somebody. *The guy from that* Walking Tall *movie . . .*

"Mr. Donovan wanted you to have this, but he had no reliable way of getting it to you. It's a list of all Hoover's agents, informants, and sources within your area, as best as we can tell."

Taverner handed over a couple sheets of paper. They seemed to be full of typing. A freshening breeze stirred the leaves of the Cyprus pine and eucalyptus that bordered the road.

Kolhammer took the list and pocketed it with barely a glance. "You tell Wild Bill I'm much obliged, but if he and Mr. Stephenson think I'm going to crank up a war against J. Edgar Hoover, then I'm afraid they should prepare themselves for disappointment. He's simply not my concern," Kolhammer said firmly.

Taverner pushed himself off the door of the Packard. Kolhammer saw Rogas start moving toward him in the reflection of the car's windscreen. He waved the SEAL back.

Taverner moved in close. The man smelled of cheap soap and breath mints. "He should be your concern," said the OSS agent. "That asshole has a lot of congressmen in his pocket. Roosevelt got the bill through, setting you up here, but he had to twist a lot of arms harder than he'd ever had to before. You know why? Because there was a little fairy flitting around, pouring poison into the ears of our honorable legislators. And he's still doing it.

"You got your Zone, Kolhammer, but the money to pay for it still comes out of Washington, and you do *not* have a lot of friends over there. You got enemies to spare, though. And you'll want to start paying attention to them, or else you're gonna get yourself cornholed in the town square, my friend."

Taverner didn't wait for a reply. He turned around and opened his car door, then looked back over his shoulder.

"Oh, and personally, I think the P-Fifty-one is a *damn* fine piece of fightin' technology." He winked, climbed in behind the wheel, and drove off, forcing the admiral to step aside.

Kolhammer watched the car disappear around the bend.

Rogas wandered over, his eyes scanning the area. "You know, boss," he said. "I've never known happy news to come out of these sorts of meetings."

Kolhammer essayed a tired grin. "Would you feel happy about a trip East, Chief?"

Rogas turned his palms out in a "whatever" gesture.

"Then pack your bags. And put together a team: two men, two women. Covert entry and prolonged surveillance. Full-spectrum coverage. Draw whatever kit you need from the Quiet Room. I'll authorize it when we get back to Fifty-one."

"Aye, aye, sir. Mission brief tonight?"

"When you've chosen your team, bring them over to my office. I'll be working late."

They both turned and walked back to the cars.

Kolhammer decided to wait until he was alone, but he was itching to open the papers Taverner had given him.

He was certain he'd spotted Dan Black's name on the first page.

WASHINGTON, D.C.

Five nights a week, without fail, J. Edgar Hoover and Clyde Tolson dined at Harvey's Restaurant on the 1100 block of Connecticut Avenue. A little dais, which raised them slightly above the other patrons, was blocked off for their private use. Hoover always sat with his back to the wall, while Tolson always faced the door.

They paid two bucks fifty for all they could eat. They were supposed to cover their own tab at the bar, but a local businessman took care of that unpleasantness in their behalf. It was a healthy tab, too. Pooch Miller, the maître d', poured six shot glasses of Old Granddad and club soda every night as soon as the director arrived.

Hoover nearly always had a medium rare steak, but would occasionally go wild and order green turtle soup. He was a demon in the restaurant's oyster-eating competitions, too, rarely failing to win. Every night when they left, the manager would provide him with a bag of ham and turkey for his pet dogs.

J. Edgar Hoover was a creature of habit.

On this night, however, things were different. They had two guests joining them for dinner. Two somewhat reluctant guests: Congressmen Gentry and Summers.

Very few newspapers or magazines had published a word of the rumors that were flying around Washington about the director. Certainly none dared do so openly, preferring instead to play up Hoover's love of delicate china, the expensive cologne, and his fastidious dressing. No tittle-tattle had ever been aired on the wireless by the likes of Walter Winchell and his peers. But that didn't mean the city wasn't alive with venemous gossip.

Congressman Summers had been to three dinners and two cocktail parties over the last week, and in each case the hors d'oeuvre had barely arrived before somebody was making merry with the latest breathless revelation from the future—courtesy of a friend of a friend of an acquaintance in California. They concerned the president, some future president, the president's wife, a movie star, an entertainer, or—increasingly—director Hoover and his longtime companion.

That was what they were calling Clyde Tolson nowadays, "The director's longtime companion." Tolson, who was sitting opposite, was nursing a grudge against his fourth martini. A senator's intern had told Summers that Tolson had exploded in the foyer of the Bureau earlier that afternoon, when he'd arrived downstairs from a meeting with Hoover and found a delivery had just arrived for him.

A bunch of pansies.

Oh, Hoover still had his allies. Some who refused to believe or even listen to the whispers. Others, like Gentry and Summers, who couldn't afford to cross him. Tame reporters still turned out anodyne puff pieces and glowing testimonials concerning "the man who stood on America's front line against subversion."

But Washington was a town acutely attuned to the merest hint of a shift in the wind, and there was a silent gale howling around J. Edgar Hoover. He still held power, but the perception that it might ebb away was enough to start the collapse, and he was the sort of man who would take half the city down with him when he went. As a rule, it was always best to distance oneself from such spitefulness. Unfortunately, it wasn't always possible.

Congressman Summers, like every politician who arrived in Washington, had an FBI file with his name on it. He assumed that Gentry did, too. Otherwise why would he be here? The existence of these files was an open secret. They were probably illegal. They were certainly dynamite. A complete file would allegedly document entire family backgrounds. Education and employment history, whether or not they'd played sports, whom they had socialized with, slept with, feuded with, cheated, betrayed, and so on. Of most interest to the director, however, was whom they had slept with.

That's why Summers was at dinner with Hoover, despite his best efforts to be somewhere else. He had made a few mistakes, and they had been discovered. He'd taken the call at home, lying in bed beside his wife for a change. Just two months after he'd been elected Hoover had called him personally— at one in the morning to say that one of his agents had come across the most *awful* photographs of the congressman. It was clearly the congressman: he was easily identifiable. But he didn't need to worry, because the director understood that he was a friend of the Bureau, and the Bureau looked after its friends. There would be no chance of this scandal ever seeing the light of day.

And then he had hung up, without waiting for a reply.

Summers could only wonder what awful indiscretion Gentry had committed.

"Would you like some butter with that bread roll, Congressman?" Hoover asked in his squeaky voice. "You haven't touched your plate or had a sip of wine all night."

"I'm sorry, Mr. Hoover," Summers replied. "I'm simply very tired. The war, you know."

"I know, I know," said Hoover. "We all work like Trojans, don't we? Not like some of those union sluggards in California, I'll bet, what with their mandated hours and legislated undutifulness. I swear, Congressmen, that if this tergiversating Herr Kolhammer had his way, the national defense would be subject to veto by the Wobblies and the Comintern."

For one horrid moment, Summers wasn't sure if Hoover was making a joke, and he remained suspended in an agony of indecision. Should he laugh, and risk enraging the vindictive faggot? Or should he nod vigorously and pound the table with an open palm and exclaim something like "Exactly!" thereby looking like a fool who couldn't appreciate Hoover's mordant wit? He could feel his fellow congressman stiffen with tension beside him.

Tolson saved them by snickering cruelly, providing him with a cue to chuckle. Hoover joined in the happy moment, his braying laugh sailing over the heads of the other diners.

Surely this was hell.

Summers was actually grateful when the deal came down at the end of the main course, and Hoover leaned forward to turn the screws. "Congressmen, this week your committee will be reviewing significant expenditures allocated for the Special Zone, if I'm right."

"We will," said Gentry, trying to appear eager to please. "We're looking at an appropriation measure to pay for emergency housing, for all the workers flooding in there."

Hoover stared at him for a long, long time without speaking. His pouchy, bulldog eyes burned fiercely. Air whistled between his crooked teeth. He wouldn't even let the congressman drop his gaze. Summers was glad he wasn't on the receiving end. It felt like staring down the barrel of a gun.

"I am sure," the FBI director said at last, "that you will take as long as is absolutely necessary . . . to give full and proper consideration . . . to the best interests of the country . . . and all of its servants."

"Of course," agreed Gentry after a slight delay.

Summers just nodded. His throat was so dry, he could hardly form the words.

"Excellent," said Hoover. "You can pay your bill on the way out."

17

IN TRANSIT TO LONDON

The *Trident*'s Eurocopter hammered across the green patchwork of the southern counties at top speed. Villages, woods, cricket grounds, lakes, and farms all slipped by in a blur as Karen Halabi wondered what might be waiting for her at the other end.

Before taking off, she'd downloaded the latest compressed burst from California. Admiral Kolhammer had fought hard to keep his command in one piece, but strategic surprise had made that impossible. The destruction of the contemporary Pacific Fleet, the invasion of Australia, and the threat hanging over Britain meant that any Allied resources had to be sent where they would be most effective in forestalling an enemy that was lashing out in all directions.

To some extent, they'd done well. The Japanese thrust into Australia seemed to be doomed, as the ground combat elements of the Multinational Force moved to directly engage Homma's forces. Reports of atrocities had aroused outrage in the press and Parliament, and led to another round of accusations that Britain had abandoned her former colony in its hour of need. But really, it was nothing out of the ordinary.

The Japanese continued to reinforce their holdings in the southwest Pacific, using the divisions they had stripped from China. The *Clinton* and the

Siranui had left Honolulu for San Diego, but some of the carrier's surviving air wing remained on the island as a guarantor against misadventure by Yamamoto.

There was the usual level of witless hysteria on the mainland United States. The encrypted briefing from Kolhammer, for her eyes only, covered the rather tense political situation of the Special Administrative Zone.

The Soviet–German cease-fire remained intact, for now. Stalin was still refusing to return any of the Allied ships or personnel that had been trapped at Murmansk when he unilaterally withdrew from hostilities against the Reich. The German buildup continued, but there had been no obvious surge to indicate that an attempted channel crossing was likely to being immediately.

There was nothing, really, that justified dragging her away from Portsmouth and the *Trident* without notice.

She heard the pilot's voice through her earpiece. "ETA twelve minutes, Skipper. We'll be setting down at Biggin Hill. There's a car waiting there for you."

"Thanks, Andy," she said. "Don't hang around if there's a raid inbound while I'm gone. I wouldn't trust that hardened shelter to stand up in a sun shower."

"Righto, Skipper."

They passed over a convoy of American trucks on a road heading south. The line of vehicles stretched out for well over a mile, and at least half of them seemed to be towing artillery pieces. Troops in the open trucks waved as they roared over.

A thunderhead far away to the west dropped sheets of gray rain on rolling farmland, while beneath them she could see dozens of schoolboys in uniform, digging with spades to widen a stream into a makeshift antitank ditch. Fields and pasture were marred by the sprouting spikes of sharpened stakes to prevent gliders landing. The sight reminded her of Branagh's *Henry V,* which was immensely popular in the movie theaters at the moment. The BBC had telerecorded a master copy to film from her own ship's video library. Here and there, crossroads were marked by barrel-like blocks of concrete, or piles of wrecked cars, rusty plows and mounds of rubble, ready to be pushed on the road surface to form another small obstacle to any possible German advance. Sometimes she saw trees that had been cut down by the roadside, ready to be dragged across as further obstacles.

The open countryside gave way to more roads and buildings. As they swooped over a village, her pilot pointed out the firing slits that had been knocked into the upper floors of two whitewashed houses that had probably been built when Shakespeare was a boy. Concrete cubes lay scattered around a radar station, even though it had been made entirely redundant by her ship's Nemesis arrays. It made sense to keep the contemporary facilities active. They'd be needed if the *Trident* was ever successfully attacked and disabled.

The airfield at Biggin Hill drew closer, a broad area of clear ground, criss-crossed with tarmac, dotted with hangars, protected by bristling nests of antiaircraft artillery, some of it now radar controlled. The pockmarks of previous Luftwaffe bombing raids were clearly visible as discolored patches of grass and runway, damaged buildings, and piles of wreckage.

They set down alongside a specially constructed hangar, which was supposedly designed to withstand a direct bomb strike. The chopper settled onto its wheels a hundred meters from the bunker as ground crew made ready to run in and secure the propeller blades against any gusts coming from the storms to the west.

Halabi jumped out, crouching, and hurried over to a waiting jeep.

"Putting her in under cover, Captain?" asked the ground crew chief with a hopeful tone. Judging from the look on his face, he'd never had the chance to get a really good look at the exotic warcraft.

"Only if that storm comes over, Sergeant. And if we get a head's-up that Jerry is on his way, my lads are out of here. Sorry."

"Right you are, ma'am," he said, disappointment echoing in his voice.

With the omniscient arrays of the *Trident* on hand to warn of developing air attacks long before they could even form up over France, a curious dissonance had come over the British high command. They lived under the sword of Damocles, knowing that it must fall. An attempt at invasion was imminent. Yet the power of those early-warning systems meant that a degree of relaxation now existed in London, even as preparations to meet the Nazi blitzkrieg accelerated. Halabi saw no street signs as she drove through the city, no locale indications of any kind. Even war memorials had been defaced to remove the names of local boroughs. There were no milestones to be seen. They had all been pulled up.

The devastation of London, whole blocks demolished by blast damage and fire, never failed to stun her with a fractured sense of the familiar. It wasn't just the city. It was the echoes of other cities. In every street, drums of oil-soaked rags stood ready to be lit to provide a smoke screen, just as in the Baghdad and Damascus of her youth. Then of course, there was the unfamiliar. In this London, like hers, military uniforms were everywhere, but here, apart from an occasional African-American soldier, there was nobody like her. No darkies, as the locals would have it. There were no curry houses or Indian spice shops. And it seemed that every spare patch of grass had been given over to growing carrots, potatoes, and cabbage. Flyers outside theaters advertised the new Agatha Christie play, *Ten Little Niggers*, while official posters promised that YOUR COURAGE, YOUR CHEERFULNESS, YOUR RESOLUTION WILL BRING US VICTORY.

Halabi found herself charmed and a little amused by the clunky, pompous slogan. It wasn't a patch on the free-market propaganda from her day, like the swimsuit posters for the French Connection (United Kingdom) fashion label, which featured an Iranian "dignity officer" waving a copy of the Koran at smirking, lower-case supermodel, caitlin lye, who was clearly thinking of the advert's tagline.

"Fcuk Off."

Oh well, thought Halabi, *to each their own*.

Reaching their destination, Halabi climbed out of the jeep, thanked the driver, and checked in with the single bobby who was guarding the approach to the PM's office and residence. It was nothing like the Downing Street of her day. For starters, the iron fence railings had been removed and melted down for scrap. They were probably enjoying a new life as Spitfire parts, or a destroyer's armor plating.

An attendant met her at the front door, which *did* look just the same as always, painted black, with a lion's-head knocker, lamp, brass numbers, and letterbox inscribed FIRST LORD OF THE TREASURY. The man ushered her into the entry hall.

The windows were sandbagged, and long heavy drapes the color of port had been drawn, but it remained a large bright room, the floor mostly covered in black-and-white marble tiles—except for two surprisingly tacky pieces of brown carpet on either side of the front door. Five desk lamps added a golden glow to the light provided by the small chandelier in the center of the ceiling.

"The Prime Minster will see you immediately," whispered the attendant, a gaunt fellow in dark civilian clothes who wouldn't have been out of place in Boswell's *London Diaries*. "You will find him and his party in the Blue Drawing Room."

She followed him through into another room, this one lit mainly with lamps and chandeliers, and cluttered with Chippendale chairs and card tables. Again, the windows were all blast-proofed, although the drapes remained open, exposing old-fashioned window seats. Blue silk wallpaper lent the room a brooding atmosphere, unleavened by the portraits of Nelson and Wellington glowering down from above the doors.

Winston Leonard Spencer Churchill was standing beside the mantelpiece over a hearth in which three logs burned amid a large pile of embers. Talking with him were Major Windsor, a woman, and another man, she didn't recognize.

"Excuse me, Prime Minister," said Halabi. "I'm sorry to be late. We had a little trouble, which delayed me unavoidably."

The PM waved her over. She was struck by how much he resembled the caricaturists' pictures of him as a British bulldog. When he spoke, however, his voice sounded much stronger and even richer in tone than she remembered from the famous BBC recordings of his wartime speeches. "Not to worry, Captain. Do come in, and please join us. I've already heard about the jet plane attack. I understand you're going back to the Admiralty later to brief them."

"I am, sir. It was hard to tell from the vision we took, but the Germans appeared to have fitted primitive missiles of a sort that wouldn't have come into use for quite a while yet. It's an unsettling development, I'm afraid."

"Well, I'm sure they'll keep you busy with that this evening. For now, well, you know the dashing prince, of course. This is Lieutenant Jens Poulsson, and Miss Vera Atkins."

"Oh! Of the Special Operations Executive? I saw Cate Blanchette play you in the movie," said Halabi, shaking each hand in turn. She hadn't been expecting to meet such interesting characters as these. The SOE was famous, or perhaps *infamous* would be a better description, as the Western world's first state sponsored "terrorist" organization. Tasked by Churchill with "setting Europe ablaze" after Dunkirk, they had gone about the mission with a passion.

Atkins looked slightly discomfited. "Yes. And I must say, it's rather a bother when the whole world suddenly knows all about your secret life."

"I am sorry, Ms. Atkins," said Halabi. "I didn't mean to come across as a smart arse. I'm sure it must be very difficult."

"No more so than your own situation."

"Lieutenant Poulsson is from Norway," Harry told her.

The light suddenly went on for her. "Ah. I see. The heavy water plant."

"Yes, Captain," said Poulsson. "It is still there. We know it. And they know that we know. It's a most unfortunate situation. What you would call a sticky wicket, I believe."

Halabi understood now that she'd been summoned to London to receive orders concerning one of the key facilities in the Reich's atomic program. Most likely, they wanted her to destroy it. Norwegian commandos had originally attacked it in 1943, after an earlier raid by British forces had failed abysmally. In this world, however, that first raid had yet to take place. And there was every chance that the Nazis knew all about the way things were supposed to play out.

They may even have had access to a copy of the Hollywood movie, or the BBC miniseries that told the story of the "the heroes of Telemark."

"Unfortunately, we have no land attack missiles left," Halabi said. "But surely the *Havoc* does? Or one of the Task Force surface ships? They could take it out without any fuss at all."

Churchill grunted in exasperation. "Indeed they could, Captain. But Prime Minister Curtin will not release any of the forces currently assigned to the defense of Australia. And the *Clinton*'s battle group, or what remains of it, is still in the Pacific en route to San Diego. It will be some time before they're in any position to help. Assuming, of course, that they would. Admiral Kolhammer seems to think of himself as something akin to a Chinese warlord, and he reacts to direct orders as if they were nothing more than gentle suggestions."

The destroyer captain said nothing.

When it was obvious she wouldn't take the bait, Churchill waved the issue away with another irritated mumble. "Well, we're not here to discuss your colleagues, or their continued refusal to accept the new realities. I need you and His Highness to undertake a mission of the utmost importance. The destruction, as you certainly must have surmised, of the heavy water factory in Telemark."

"Is there some reason it has to happen immediately?" Halabi asked.

Jens Poulsson spoke up. "We maintain contact with some of our sources at the plant. The Germans are about to move ten thousand gallons of heavy water. We do not know where, but regardless, they cannot be allowed to do so. They must have learned of the original raids that took place in your history. So they have decided to act quickly."

"But if your source is still alive and in touch," she reasoned, "the Germans obviously cannot possess perfect knowledge of the plant's history. Otherwise, they'd know about him. They must have picked up scraps here and there from the lattice cache on the *Sutanto*. But not the whole story."

"It hardly matters," countered Churchill. "The point is, they must be stopped. And the plant must be taken out of action—permanently. If they succeed with their atomic program, we will be utterly defenseless. And if Britain falls, it will make it just that much harder for the U.S. to strike, particularly at such a great distance.

"I fear, Captain Halabi, that the Axis powers are now less interested in global conquest than they are in holding their current gains, and they hope to do so by getting access to these 'weapons of mass destruction,' as you call them. They want Britain and, I suppose, Australia, largely to deny America any base usable for a counterattack."

"I see," said Halabi before addressing the Norwegian. "And you have some plan in mind, I suppose."

"We *do*," replied Poulsson, "but it requires your help, and the prince's, for it to have any chance of success, particularly at such short notice."

"No notice, really," said Harry.

"Indeed," the SOE man conceded.

Halabi looked down and realized she was standing next to William Pitt's writing desk. Somehow, it seemed very small. "You'll need the *Trident* to move Major Windsor's men, and Lieutenant Poulsson's, too, I imagine. Into Norwegian waters, for the assault."

"Exactly," confirmed Harry. "I'll be taking two squads. Poulsson and two others will come with us. We're to rendezvous on the ground with local resistance fighters who will get us to the plant. We'll need to chopper in and out."

"Can you do it?" asked Miss Atkins.

Halabi did not reply immediately. She took a few moments to consider the variables as best she could: the need to sneak past the *Kriegsmarine*; the chance that, with forewarning, the Nazis would simply be waiting for them in the fjords or at the plant itself; the odds of making it back after the strike alerted the Germans to their presence; the possible cost of losing the *Trident*, balanced against the risk of Hitler getting his hands on a nuclear weapon. This last one was the most important consideration of course.

The Nemesis battlespace arrays of her ship gave the British high command virtually total awareness of the tactical situation in the local theater. The Luftwaffe could not launch raids of any size on the nation's capital— or anywhere else in the southern half of the United Kingdom, for that matter—without the Allies knowing of it almost immediately. Admiral Raeder could not put his relatively weak naval forces to sea to protect any invasion fleet while he faced certain destruction at her hands.

The Germans knew that the *Trident* was the linchpin of England's defense, and they had spent enormous amounts of blood and treasure trying to take her out. The Allies, on the other hand, could not afford to lose her, which was why she had never sortied to directly engage the German capital ships, and why so many fighters that should have been protecting British airfields against bombing raids were instead assigned to covering her arse.

If the *Trident* appeared in hostile waters, Göring would probably send his entire air force against her. But if she remained here and Poulsson and Atkins were right about the atomic plant, the question of the *Trident*'s survival would become moot anyway.

Halabi shrugged and looked at Churchill. "I don't know if we can do it sir. But we can give it a damn good shake."

Churchill nodded. "England expects that every man, and woman, will do their best."

. . .

As the two SOE agents left, the PM asked Halabi and Harry to stay for a moment. The attendant who had shown her in appeared with a trolley that rattled with a collection of teapots and china cups. The prime minister shooed him away, offering to pour the tea himself.

"White and one sugar," said Halabi as the attendant fled.

"Black, with a squeeze of lemon," Harry added.

When the doors had closed and they were left alone, Churchill bade them sit in the nearest armchairs.

He produced a cigar from his waistcoat and lit up without bothering to ask whether they would mind. Harry seemed to find it amusing, but it annoyed Halabi, though she held her tongue. Everyone in this era seemed to live in a dense cloud of carcinogenic smoke, and it was one of the things she found hardest to accept. They thought you mad if you asked them not to smoke in your presence, or even to avoid blowing their smoke in your face.

She put her aggravation aside as best she could.

"I have not had a chance to thank you both for the work you have put in here," Churchill said without preamble. He held his hand up when Halabi made to protest. "No, Captain. I am the prime minister, and that means you have to sit and listen, whether you want to or not. I imagine the rules are not much different from your day."

The two officers admitted that they were not.

"I know you wished very much to keep your Task Force together, and I can understand that, politically as well as militarily," the PM continued. "This is a very hostile world you have found yourselves in. And I don't refer only to Herr Hitler and his little friends in the East. I understand that you, in particular, Halabi, have not had the sort of welcome in Portsmouth that might be thought of as appropriate for a returning Royal Navy captain. Young Harry here has excellent family connections to smooth his way. You, on the other hand, do not."

"My crew are my family, Prime Minister, and we're in this together."

"Stuff and nonsense," he barked. "Sir Leslie Murray speaks very highly of your crew and the way you handle them. After being one of your fiercest critics, I might add. But you cannot spend the rest of your life on the *Trident*, Halabi."

He must have seen the panic that registered on her face.

"Oh, don't worry," he hurried to add. "I'm not going to attempt to hijack your ship. God knows there are more than enough rum-sodden fools at the Admiralty who are dedicated to that goal. Rest assured, as long as I am prime minister, that will not come to pass.

"Your work with the Ministry, on the modernization programs, has been exemplary. I only hope Providence will bless us with a chance to see some of your projects come to fruition. However," he admitted, dunking a short-bread biscuit into his tea, "you are of greatest value to the realm on the bridge of your vessel."

Halabi found herself unable to reply. Her throat had locked up with emotion. After leaving home, and the dark presence of her father, she had very deliberately constructed a new life and family for herself within the embrace of the senior service, consciously drawing on the heritage of her adopted clan to gather the strength and purpose she'd always felt was missing as the abused daughter of a faithless drunkard.

Standing in front of her country's greatest statesman, however, she felt her legs shaking with uncharacteristic gratitude for the compliment he had just paid her.

"Why, thank you, Prime Minister," she said when she had regained a measure of control. "That means a lot to me."

"I'm sure it does," he said with surprising tenderness. "I have not been unaware of the blackguarding of your name, Captain. But I judge my captains by results. When Stalin betrayed us, I thought we'd have the barbarians at the gates of London within the week. Your fast arrival here, and your actions since that time, have given us a chance to save ourselves. I asked Major Windsor to stay, so that this conversation, while private, would not be secret."

Churchill turned his ample frame so he could face the prince.

"I would appreciate it if you would apprise your family of my feelings in this matter. It will be most important, particularly if I do not survive the coming weeks."

Harry didn't bother with any melodramatic objections. He simply agreed. "Of course, Prime Minister."

On the surface, Halabi was a picture of professional restraint, but she reeled within. Ever since she had set herself on course for a life in the Royal Navy, she'd felt the constant weight of judgment upon her, as though a long, foreboding line of ancient mariners and warriors were all watching to see if she was worthy of them. Yet here she was, almost in tears that this old man—who was the antithesis of her wretched father—had made that judgment in her favor.

"There is one final matter I would like to discuss," said Churchill. "There are contingency plans, outlining how to evacuate the king and his family, myself, and the War Cabinet to Canada in the event that the situation here becomes hopeless. The *Trident* plays an important role in those contingencies, as well. Whatever happens, she is *not* to fall into the hands of the enemy."

Halabi nodded firmly. She reviewed her own operational plans for the coming battle every day.

"But even if those plans are activated, I will not be going with you," said Churchill. "I cannot declare to the world that we will never surrender, then go scarpering off to leave the common people to their fate. I will be staying here in England, no matter what."

Captain Halabi nodded again. This time a single tear tracked down her cheek, to fall to the carpet.

18

NEW YORK

The Bayswater was actually nowhere near water. It was located in a hotel on Broadway, near Washington Heights in northern Manhattan. The crowd was fantastically eclectic. Jewish refugees fleeing Germany and Austria in the late thirties and early forties had colonized the area, and quite a few of their more bohemian number were likely to be found in the Bayswater at any time of night.

It was a determinedly open establishment. A sign on the door read, NO DOGS OR BIGOTS. Jazz and bluesmen like Muddy Waters and Charlie Parker were regular guests. The city's boho art scene had adopted it as a second home. Magazine editors met with senior contributors there. Even Albert Einstein had dropped in one evening.

"I know the guys who run this place," Julia said as they stepped from the town car when it pulled up at the hotel portico. "They were reporters, not embeds, though. Jakey worked for PBS, and Joybelle was over at Fox. You wouldn't have thought they'd have worked together so well."

A line three or four deep stretched down to the corner, hopefuls waiting to see if they could get in. Dan moved to join the end of the line, a gesture that caused Julia to roll her eyes.

"Oh, puh-*lease!*"

She took his arm and strolled on up to the velvet rope. A one-armed colossus bowed as they approached. He wore a white dinner jacket, and a lapel pin that Dan was almost certain read DOORBITCH.

"Ms. Duffy," he said, unhitching the rope and waving them through. He sounded as though he took voice coaching from grizzly bears. "That was a great piece you wrote the other day."

"Thanks, Max," she said, throwing a kiss as she swept past, carrying a bemused Commander Black along in her wake. She was wearing one of her magic dresses, a little black thing that came out of a bag not much bigger than his fist, then slid over her body like oil. The hopefuls in the line were all rugged up for a cruel wait in the cold, but her only warmth came from a thin wrap of some sort of material Dan couldn't identify.

They moved into the Bayswater via French doors that were policed by another wounded giant, this time a man with only one eye. The short hallway opened up into a restaurant and a bar, depending on which way you stepped. The bar was roaring and packed so tightly that Dan wondered how anyone could raise a hand to actually take a drink. After the chill of the night air outside, it was almost uncomfortably heavy with the steamy heat of confined humanity.

A band was playing back in there somewhere, a tune he didn't recognize, but at least it was a tune, unlike so much of the music from Julia's world.

The place was full of her type of people, though. Twenty-first and their friends. He was getting quite good at spotting the uptimers, and he could see a few of them in the bar, and at the restaurant tables. Julia held his hand and cut through the crush like a salmon swimming upstream in a series of leaps. They found themselves at a lectern, where a smart young woman with her blond hair tied back in a ponytail asked them if they had a reservation. But Julia was already waving and calling out to someone. Without missing a beat, the girl smiled, produced a couple of menus, and asked them to follow her.

Again, Dan was dumbfounded. The restaurant—Julia called it a brasserie—was obviously a high-tone affair. The wine and white linen, the cutlery, and the food all looked expensive, at least to his untrained eye. And yet the atmosphere had none of the heavy, leaden feeling he recalled from his own very limited and generally disastrous forays into the world of fine dining—all of them in pursuit of various women over the years.

The crowd seemed to be much younger than he would have expected, and none of them was dressed for dinner. He couldn't see a lounge suit anywhere. Some of the men sat in rolled-up shirtsleeves, their ties undone. Others wore no ties at all! And some, who must have been artists, surely, even wore T-shirts. He felt very much out of place in his dress whites, but there were a number of other AF uniforms there, too, and even a scattering of 'temps. It was as though the whole world had come to the table just as they damn well pleased.

"Dan. Hey, Earth to Dan! Over here, baby. It's Maria. Come say hello." Julia had let go of his hand and got away. Now she was shouting at him, over the din of the bar and the slightly less deafening clamor of the dining room. It was the most extraordinary thing he'd seen since Midway. Although, now that he thought about it, he might have to qualify that, having seen her apartment.

She was already seating herself at a small round table with a woman who was very obviously twenty-first. He noticed the woman's looks right away, but he then noticed how well conditioned she appeared: the width of her shoulders, which were bare; the strength of her arms; the crushing power of her handshake. She wasn't long out of the service—probably the Marine Corps.

"Hey, Dan," she said, without any further introduction.

"Ms. O'Brien."

"No, please. Call me Maria."

"Okay," he agreed. "Maria."

"Jules tells me you've just come out of the Zone for a couple of days."

"It's my first long spell of liberty since we got back from Midway," he said. "I thought I'd surprise her."

"Ah, that's great to see." She smiled. "She's got you well trained already."

"So where's Sinatra?" Julia asked, leaning forward and openly scoping out the other tables.

"Oh, he's in the back with Slim Jim and the local Mafia," said O'Brien. "He's going to do a few numbers later on. D'you want to come backstage later and meet them?"

"Shit, yeah. Are the mob guys going to be there?"

"Probably," replied the lawyer. "But don't worry about them. Davidson is a silent partner in the club, and he's *way* too big for them now. Plus I let them know the first time they came that they were welcome to have a drink and enjoy themselves, but they definitely had no *business* here, if you understand what I'm saying."

Dan watched Julia's eyebrows climb halfway up her forehead. He had no idea what they were talking about, but she'd obviously been taken by surprise, which he found astonishing.

"Shit," she said. "How'd *that* go down?"

O'Brien shrugged. "I played some footage taken off a couple of microcams we planted on them. They had no idea what we'd done or how we did it. But they know we're totally out of their league. So they won't fuck around. They're just here because it's the hottest fucking joint in town. Oh, and the food, of course. They love the food."

"I can imagine," said Julia. "Dan, darling, you've got to try *everything* on the menu. Joybelle used to produce Sir James Oliver's show on Fox, before she moved over to the news."

Dan's blank look was eloquent.

"He's a chef, sweetie. Modern Italian, by way of Cool Britannia."

He was still floundering.

Julia sighed. "She had all his books and shows on stick. Not just recipes, but the actual chef demonstrating how to put them together. Then she grabbed a crew of young guys out of kitchens all over town. Of course they're going to *kill* for the chance to jump their own cooking up to warp speed—you know, eighty years ahead of the game. And it's like . . . honest to God . . . it's like eating in New York the week we left."

"Well, not exactly," O'Brien corrected her. "Try getting a decent plate of *wagyu* in this town."

The young waitress reappeared. In the rush of the arrival, he hadn't noticed before, but she was dressed like a man. In a white shirt and a business tie. "So, have you made any decisions?"

The two women didn't even bother checking the menu. O'Brien ordered her usual, whatever that was.

"I'll have the flash-fried spanner crab omelet, to start," said Julia, "with a glass of that thirty-eight pinot grigio, if you still have it. And a bowl of spaghetti *alla vongole* for main. Now, Dan, I know you'll want to order the T-bone, but how about letting me do you a favor?"

"Okay," he conceded, but with no sense of confidence.

"Good. The big guy here will have the truffled mushrooms on olive toast with Reggiano and *rugetta* as an appetizer, and the seared pork belly with scallops to follow. Bring him a beer to settle his nerves, and a very light, peppery red to have with the meal. The sommelier can choose."

"Excellent." The girl's head bobbed once as she finished the order.

Dan shifted on his chair. "Don't you feel a little, uh, odd eating you know—"

"Enemy food?" said O'Brien.

"Well, yeah."

"*No,*" they both answered at once.

Without missing a beat, O'Brien plowed on. "Now, Dan, Jules tells me you need to look at an investment portfolio. Because of your position in the Zone, we'd have to establish it as a blind trust so there could be no question of your having profited from inside knowledge."

The former Marine Corps captain reminded Black of a hundred other women he'd met in the Multinational Force. As soon as they switched to work, they became almost robotic. Even though she was no longer dealing in war Maria O'Brien gave him the impression she would have briefed a team of fighter pilots or navy divers in the same tone of voice she was using now to review his investment options.

Truth be told, he had no real interest in his investment options. He'd only agreed to come because of Julia.

". . . are no-brainers," she was saying. "Burroughs. And IBM, unless the Holocaust connection bothers you. Aerospace. GM. Ford. All of them easy picks for both wartime and postwar expansion. Then there are the less obvious, longer-term options, like pharmaceuticals, especially corporations that will be registering patents in drugs for heart disease, obesity, diabetes, and so on.

"No matter what happens with the baby Bells, you'll want a lot of exposure to telecoms. That area is going to go ballistic. I wouldn't advise putting anything into the content providers for now, though. The copyright issue is going to be twenty years getting itself sorted out, especially with so many German, Japanese, and Chinese firms holding the rights to stuff like Disney and Warners. A better bet would be intellectual properties developed by firms with no parentage in this era, especially if the IP was generated in jurisdictions which don't exist yet, and may *never* exist, for all we know."

Julia, he noticed, was nodding as the lawyer delivered her pitch, dropping in the occasional comment of her own. He was really surprised—by both of them, actually. They spoke like Wall Street veterans, but neither of them were what he thought of as capitalists. *A reporter and a marine.* You didn't think of those sort of people as having these sort of concerns. It opened another window onto the world they had come from, but even so, he wasn't sure what he was seeing. Grantville hadn't prepared him at all for this. They were talking like the mine bosses his daddy hated so much.

"Here you go." The waitress was back, delivering their first course.

Dan's plate held one large, flat black mushroom, drizzled with some kind of oil and sprinkled with spiky green leaves and shavings of a dry, pungent cheese. Julia's omelet looked just like an omelet, for which he was unexpectedly glad.

"What are you having, Maria?" he asked, glad of an opportunity to change topics. He just didn't feel comfortable talking about money. It wasn't a proper topic for the dinner table. He figured he'd agree to some sort of investment, just to keep Jules happy, and also, he thought, because they'd need a little nest egg to start a life together after the war.

"I always go for the vegetarian option," she said, clicking out of her professional personality. "It's nothing philosophical, really. I don't mind meat stocks or sauces. But when you've exhumed as many mass graves as I have, you lose your taste for T-bones."

He was sorry he asked, but she didn't seem to mind.

"And they do the most exquisite minty peas here," she added.

So that's what she was having. A big bowl of minted peas.

"Wow," said Dan. "My ma would have died a happy woman if she thought I was eating a whole bowl of peas for my dinner. She used to have to stand over me with a wooden spoon to make sure I didn't flick mine out the window."

"Try your own dish, Dan," said Julia. "It's not meat, but you'll love it. Trust me."

In fact, he *didn't* mind it. It was warm, and felt a bit like steak in his mouth, which, O'Brien explained, was why she didn't order it. If he thought there would be a respite from the financial conversation, though, he was wrong.

Julia had no sooner swallowed a mouthful of omelet before she started up again. "Maria, you were warning us off content providers, but I know you've got Davidson and some of your other clients hooked into that market."

The lawyer shook her head. "No. We've signed them up to an agency agreement, you know, guys like Elvis and Sinatra. And we're taking the industry-standard commission off their royalties, but where there's an extant commercial entity that could claim ownership of say, the words and music to 'Blue Suede Shoes,' we've actually sought them out, provided the product, and offered the right of first refusal. Nine times out of ten, they jump at it, and we negotiate a much better deal for the client than was the case originally, back in our world. So everyone's a winner."

"Really?" said Dan, who was only following a fraction of what she was saying.

"Well, no, not really," she admitted. "The recording companies are getting screwed, because their original contracts were so onerous. But they know a guaranteed income stream when they see it. They don't want to lose it to a competing company, which they could do, because their legal claim is tenuous at best. Nobody likes arguing jurisdictional issues, and there is no case law in Multiverse Theory. So most of the time they just sign up. And the artists *do* get a much better deal.

"For example, we got Sinatra out of Tommy Dorsey's band and right into his solo career. He's so grateful that he's playing four nights a week here, for free."

O'Brien spooned up a mouthful of peas, drew a breath, and started talking at a mile a minute again.

Julia looked fascinated.

Dan decided to concentrate on his dinner. He wasn't sure why he didn't like the sound of this, but it all made him feel decidedly uneasy. It seemed as if this woman was making a fortune out of thin air, but she wasn't *producing* anything. She was just making people pay for things that, to his way of thinking, belonged to them anyway.

"It's a lot easier when you have a single artist involved," she continued. "But it gets nightmarish very quickly when you get into things like movies, and you have hundreds of people who lay claim to be being responsible for some part of the production. And of course, you have a lot of the parent companies like MGM or Paramount operating right now. I advise my clients to stay well clear of them. There are *hundreds* of cases working their way through the lower bowels of the court system, and you can tell that nobody has a fucking clue about where to even begin untangling the mess. Anyway," she said, scooping up another mouthful of peas, "I always saw the entertainment industry as a sunrise initiative. Most of the opportunity has come and gone there. We're looking at medium- to long-term strategies now. Like what's going to happen in the Middle East when the war is done. I don't imagine we're going to bend over and invite the Saudis to buttfuck us again, for the next eighty years."

"So what, you're looking at alternative energy sources already, back here in nineteen forty-two?" Julia asked.

O'Brien shrugged. "I like to think of it as foresight." Then she leaned forward. "I hear there's OSS teams in Vietnam already, talking to Ho Chi Minh."

"So what are they doing there?" asked Julia in a voice Dan recognized immediately. She was at work again.

O'Brien smiled. "Well, I don't know. If they *are* there, I didn't send them. But I imagine they're telling Uncle Ho that he can have the fucking place, and as many surplus Springfield rifles as he wants, as long as he uses them to shoot Japanese soldiers. I mean, what's Lyndon Johnson doing now? He's off somewhere in the navy, but I'll bet he's spending every minute boning up on his presidency. He's not going to want to make the same mistakes, and he's already plugged into Roosevelt. He ran for Congress as a New Deal Democrat in 1937. He won and got himself straight onto the Naval Affairs Committee—as a freshman! FDR put him there. He's only in the navy now because he lost a race for the Senate last year. I don't imagine he's behind the OSS thing, but nor can I imagine him sitting around with his thumb up his ass when he knows what's coming."

Like millions of Americans, Dan Black had read a couple of the "future" histories published within weeks of the Transition. Julia's colleagues on the *Clinton* had written many of them, and she'd pointed him in the direction of some of the better ones. So he had a pretty good grasp of what they were talking about.

"So that's what you mean by foresight," he said.

"Exactly. Things aren't going to be the way they were in our time, Dan. That's what makes this business so exciting. If you were betting on a race that had been won already—"

"Like Slim Jim has," Julia added, grinning.

"No comment," O'Brien replied, her own smile just as wide. "But if you were betting on a done deal, sure, it's easy money. But where's the challenge? And of course, once people know the future, they immediately start fucking with it. So that's where the challenge comes in. That's why I love it."

"I thought you loved it for the money," Dan said, letting his offended sensibilities get the better of him. But neither of the women obliged him by taking offense.

"Sure," agreed O'Brien. "And there's the money, too."

"There's nothing wrong with the money, Dan," Julia chimed in. "Money's what makes the world go round."

Slim Jim loved this place. Of all the things O'Brien had hooked him into, the Bayswater was the best. He would never have thought he could get so jazzed about a club that not only let in your niggers and your Jews—but actually *invited* them to come.

He never would've thought you could make money on something like this, either, especially not with the top-shelf wages he was paying. But the money rolled in like a flash flood that never ended. And anyone who was *anyone* in this town was beating on the doors, trying to get in and throw their money around. It was one of the seven fucking wonders, was what it was.

And two or three of the other wonders were right in here with him, too.

That Sinatra kid, up on stage singing "Slow Boat to China" with Joybelle—you had to admit, that kid's voice was a wonder. And this piece of ass Slim Jim had here on his arm, the fabulous Norma—or Marilyn, as she was calling herself now that Ms. O'Brien had sorted out the business with the movie guys—this fantastic piece of ass was such a natural wonder of the world that he was sure every guy in the room would crawl a mile over cut glass just to jerk off in her shadow.

But the biggest wonder had to be that table of wise guys over there, mooning over Joybelle and Frankie's duet. Just six months ago, those guys wouldn't have crossed the road to piss on his heart if it'd caught fire. *Crazy fucking mobsters.* And now they were ringing him up, asking him if they could come to *his* club. And the hell of it was, they were really *asking*.

Oh, sure, they'd rolled in here like kings of the fucking hill that first time. He didn't know what O'Brien had done or said to them, but after that you couldn't have asked for a quieter, more well-behaved pack of wops. He'd been terrified, expecting them to muscle in on his action. But no, they came for the show and the food. They couldn't get enough of the fucking food.

They'd also liked staying behind after the place had closed, to watch *The Sopranos* and all of his Mafia movies on the big flatscreen. But Ms. O'Brien had put a stop to that pretty quickly. She said it was "inappropriate."

Well, a lot of people would look around this place, with its mixed races and nightly parties, and they'd swear on the Bible that the Bayswater redefined *inappropriate*. But Slim Jim Davidson called that "bull talk from a one-eyed fat man." That was his new favorite phrase, ever since he'd seen John Wayne in *True Grit*.

"Hey, darlin'!" he shouted to Marilyn over the noise of the band and the bar crowd. "You think John Wayne worries about turning into such an ugly, fat old prick?"

"Well," she said, sipping at a cocktail he didn't recognize, "at least he got to grow old."

Slim Jim rolled his eyes and gave her a squeeze. "Now you know we ain't lettin' that happen to you, sweetheart. You ain't marrying that drunken ball player. You ain't fucking those Kennedy boys. And you—"

A painful grip on his bicep tore his hand off Marilyn's ass. "Out in the back. You're with us, Romeo."

He recognized the voice, and his heart skipped a beat. It was the two bozos. The feebs who'd rousted him in his crib.

The unfriendly one—at least they'd kept their roles straight—had made some sort of Chinese burn on his elbow. It hurt like hell. Before he knew it, he was up on his tiptoes and being hustled away from Marilyn as fast as they could handle the move without attracting attention. Even so, there were plenty of patrons beginning to point and stare.

The Bureau men shoved him through a set of doors and into the first office on the left.

A push sent him into the desk, and he corked his thigh painfully. "*Ow!* You didn't have to—"

"Shut up, shit head. What the *fuck* are you doing here?"

Rubbing at his leg, his mind racing, Slim Jim played dumb. "I got an interest here. It's strictly legit. If you guys were as smart as—"

"You know what we mean. You're supposed to be in California. You're supposed to be working for us now. You were supposed to have ditched that bitch, and—"

"Why, gentlemen, I do believe my ears are burning."

The two bruisers spun to find Maria O'Brien standing in the doorway, flanked by Marilyn and some couple Slim Jim didn't know. They must have been the friends O'Brien said she was meeting for a late supper, he guessed.

"Agents Geraghty and Swinson, I presume." She smiled, but not in a friendly way. "You'd know them as Good Cop and Bad Cop, in that order, Mr. Davidson. Now, would you care to cease your criminal assault on my client?"

"We never touched him!" Swinson protested. "Did we?" he asked, turning a baleful eye on Slim Jim.

"The *hell* you didn't, you fucking assholes. You frog-marched me in here and then you threw me into the desk, and I'll bet I got a big bruise out of it. I could prove it, too." He started to undo his belt.

"That won't be necessary, Mr. Davidson," said his lawyer. "I'm sure we can find a doctor who'll testify in the civil suit."

"There won't be any suit," Swinson blustered. "A two-bit hustler like Davidson. Done time for chiseling somebody's grandmother. Good luck, sister."

Slim Jim winced uncomfortably. That goddamned rubber check was always bouncing back in his face.

It didn't seem to bother Ms. O'Brien, though. She still had that nasty smile on her face: the one that reminded him of feeding time at the zoo. "Well now, Agent Swinson, I don't believe Mr. Davidson has ever made a secret of his former life. In fact, it's very much public knowledge. Just as his efforts to reform himself, and to make amends for his past misdeeds, are also public knowledge. You may not be aware of it, but Mr. Davidson has made an ex gratia payment of five thousand dollars to Mrs. Durnford, the grandmother to whom you refer. A significant return on the twenty-four-dollar check he wrote to her grocery store, when he was unfortunately unaware of a shortfall of funds within his account.

"You may also be aware of—"

Swinson cut in over the top of her. "Hey, we know all about your client, *Miss* O'Brien. You might have earned a pretty penny turning him into the new fucking Santa Claus, but water still finds its own level, lady. And he's a crook. Always has been. Always will be."

"I guess we'll see about that," said O'Brien. "In the meantime, I'll be pursuing an order against you gentlemen, and any other agents of the Bureau who are sent to harass my client concerning anything other than legitimate government business."

"We're just doing our job," Swinson growled. "Some people still work for their country, O'Brien."

Slim Jim wondered how she'd take that. Ms. O'Brien was inordinately proud of her time in the Marine Corps—much more than he was of his hitch in the navy. If they meant to get under her skin, though, they failed. She simply raised an eyebrow and produced a large leather folder. It contained a data slate. She powered up, opened a file, and there was Slim Jim's apartment on screen.

There he was in his bathrobe.

And there were the two feebs, muscling him.

It was the surveillance footage from the microcams hidden all over his home. Geraghty was administering a savage, unprovoked blow to the back of his head.

"Hmm, not such a good cop after all, are we, Agent Geraghty?" Ms. O'Brien teased with a smile quirking the corner of her mouth. At that moment, Slim Jim thought he might just be in love with his scary lawyer.

The others had crowded into the small room and were also watching, which only added to the agents' awkwardness. The video made them look and sound like a couple of stupid thugs. Marilyn gasped when Swinson threatened to tell her ex-husband where he could find her.

"You bastards," she said. "That was just a marriage of convenience. If I hadn't hooked up with him, I would have been sent back to the orphanage. My guardian used to pay him to go out on dates with me!"

Slim Jim wasn't the only one who found himself caught out by that. Every man in the room, and even the other two women reacted with obvious surprise. Norma turned a cold, level stare on the feds. When she spoke, it didn't sound like her at all. There was nothing soft in her voice. It sounded like she was grinding up rocks with her teeth.

"Don't you imagine for a second that you can involve me in any of your grubby schemes," she went on. "You have no idea of the life I've just escaped. Or what I will do to avoid going back there. You can expect to hear from *my* lawyers."

Slim Jim began to wonder whether it was such a good idea dating someone like Norma. She apparently had hidden depths.

Hidden depths were not good. Not in his experience. He began to wonder if *she'd* been using *him* all the way along.

The man and woman who'd come in with her remained silent. But he could tell they were fascinated. The chick, in particular. Davidson didn't doubt she was twenty-first. Her clothes told him that much. But he began to wonder what angle she had. She didn't strike him as the soldierly type. Ms. O'Brien spoke up while he was wondering.

"According to the contemporary law specialists at my firm, there's evidence of seven separate indictable offenses on this stick alone. But of course, that's only if I file here. On the other hand, if I file in-zone, by my count there are sixty-two civil and criminal actions available to Mr. Davidson, should he wish to seek a remedy for the Bureau's actions."

Geraghty came out from behind his bland persona. A large vein was throbbing in his neck, and his knuckles were white with the effort of controlling himself. "You won't be filing anything anywhere, you bitch. You'll be lucky to come out of this without doing jail time yourself."

The agents hadn't noticed—they weren't as familiar with the technology—but Slim Jim distinctly saw the dark-haired woman press a hot key on the flexipad riding at her hip. She had to be recording this.

"Once again," O'Brien said, "I'll guess we'll see about that. But you gentlemen should inform your superiors at the earliest opportunity that I will be dragging you ass-backwards and buck-naked through the briar patch. You should also inform your superiors that I intend to call Director Hoover as a witness, and if he tries to blow me off the way he does with every inconvenient inquiry that comes his way, I'll ask the bench to issue a warrant for his arrest. And I *will* have him dragged kicking and screaming to the stand. So he might want to go out and buy himself a nice new dress for his big day in court."

O'Brien's voice didn't get louder or faster as she spoke. Quite the opposite, in fact. When she was finished, she leaned forward, almost close enough to kiss Agents Geraghty and Swinson on the tips of their noses, and Slim Jim had to strain himself to hear. The faces of the two men, however, told him that they'd understood everything.

They were—what was that thing Ms. O'Brien liked to say?—oh yeah. They were *toast*.

The agents sent a threatening glare in his direction as they slunk out of the room, but as a confidence man himself, Slim Jim knew they'd been rolled.

"You owe Ms. Monroe a steak dinner, Mr. Davidson," O'Brien told him once they'd left. "She came and got me as soon as they grabbed you."

"Thanks, sweetie," he said to Marilyn.

"What a pair of assholes," spat the soon-to-be starlet. "I can't believe the FBI would employ such people."

Both O'Brien and the other chick, the one with the flexipad, snorted in amusement.

"This is Ms. Julia Duffy, Mr. Davidson, and her escort, Commander Dan Black," O'Brien said. "Ms. Duffy works for the *New York Times*, and she had asked me if she could interview you about the harassment you've suffered at the hands of Mr. Hoover. As your attorney, I would advise you to agree to the request. Although I should mention that I act for Ms. Duffy in another capacity, and if—"

Slim Jim held up his hand. "That's enough. I'll talk to her. You wrote that fucking amazing bit about that guy called Snider, didn't you, Ms. Duffy. On the Brisbane Line. Walter Winchell reckons he's gonna get a Medal of Honor for that."

Julia Duffy shook his hand. She had a grip as firm and dry as O'Brien's, but he noticed with surprise that her hands were heavily callused, like a workman's.

"If he gets it, it won't be because I wrote a story. It'll be because he deserves a medal," she said. "He saved our lives, and at great risk to his own."

"Uh-huh," said Slim Jim. "Be a feather in your cap, too, though, wouldn't it?"

"Mr. Davidson," O'Brien cautioned him.

"It's okay." Duffy smiled. "Your client is a lot smarter than most people would give him credit for. Not by book learning, but with rat bastard cunning, if I'm not mistaken. Wouldn't that be right, Slim Jim?"

His eyes crinkled and a wide grin split his face. "Something like that," he said. "When would you like to do your interview, *Ms.* Duffy?"

19

BUNDABERG, 350 KM NORTH OF THE BRISBANE LINE, SOUTHWEST PACIFIC AREA

It wouldn't be long now. No supplies or reinforcements had made it through to them, although the navy hadn't really pressed the issue. The enemy's "special soldiers" moved at will behind the lines, destroying precious stockpiles and even murdering his officers in their bedrolls at night. His men died bravely, but for no good reason.

The ridiculously outmoded Brisbane Line still held, protected by the superweapons of the Emergence barbarians. And now, with his guns almost empty and his men unable even to forage enough food from the scorched earth, those barbarians had emerged once again, this time from their dugouts and revetments. His forward scouts, reporting by radio now that it no longer mattered, told of monstrous tanks and armored vehicles, cutting through any resistance like a *katana* through a single reed.

Masaharu Homma, the poet-general, adjusted his sword and cap and centered his *hara* with a deep breath as he prepared to address the divisional staff.

He stood in the office of the former mayor of this town, Bundaberg. It was a rather fine whitewashed edifice for such a small settlement, typical of British colonial architecture. He doubted it would survive another day. The dull, distant thunder was drawing close, becoming louder, sharper, and more significant. Barbarian artillery was no longer nibbling at the edge of the town. It chewed whole streets to pieces, smashing houses, shops, and schools, setting fire to the large swaths of bushland. His own artillery sounded in reply, once a monstrous rumble but now growing perceptibly weaker with each passing minute.

The barbarian guns were hellishly accurate. It seemed as if everything they hit was important to him in some way. A house where some of his officers were bivouacked. A parking lot full of trucks. This town hall must surely be marked, as well.

How many hours left? wondered Homma. Would this room still exist, the building still stand? He looked about dolefully. His staff hurried about, packing some files, destroying others. Hopefully there was some systemic method at work there. His adjutant waited by the door.

"I imagine it was all worth it, Admiral," he muttered to himself bitterly and to an absent Yamamoto. More bitterly than he would have thought possible even a year ago. A corrosive decay of the soul had settled upon him, and refused to lift.

"Excuse me, sir?"

Had he spoken aloud? He'd been prone to that recently, and the lieutenant was looking at him most strangely.

When he didn't respond, the young officer continued. "I have your papers, General. And we don't have much time. Enemy soldiers have secured the aerodrome. They came in helicopters after the garrison was overcome by a strange gas. Special soldiers, we think. They are animals, sir. They fight without honor."

Homma was both amused and a little touched by the young man's furious sincerity. Surely the empire would prosper with men like him to defend it, even if this particular one was fated to die in a benighted wasteland of red dust and savages.

He hoped the enemy would pay due respect to the spirits of his men, but he doubted it. These new barbarians were supposed to be even more advanced than the white men he had fought in the Philippines and New Guinea. But he couldn't see it. Why, many of them weren't even white men at all. They were not a race as he understood it—just a cabal of mercenaries, from what he could tell. For whom did they fight?

They did so effectively, though; that was undeniable. Their weapons were almost supernatural in their powers. But the men and even the women who used them could not claim to be the moral equal of the emperor's troops, or even MacArthur's. His scouts reported that they were executing their prisoners en masse.

They didn't have many prisoners to take, of course. No fighting man of Nippon would willingly allow himself to fall into the enemies clutches. Yet . . .

"General?"

"I am sorry, Lieutenant. I forget myself."

How long had he been standing there, daydreaming? The symphony seemed closer now. A large explosion, an aerial bombardment he guessed, rocked the ground nearby. He checked his watch. Five minutes? Yes, well, he could understand why his young aide would be keen to be off. The office seemed much emptier than it had been just a few moments ago. Fewer clerks were shuffling about. There was more paper on the ground. A chair had been turned over in the middle of the room.

Fancy that.

The lieutenant took his arm and gently maneuvered him out of the room, into the corridor, and down the stairs to a waiting car. A security detail of four soldiers stood by in a captured American jeep, manning a .50-caliber machine gun and watching the street as though MacArthur or Jones the giant black barbarian himself might just pop out of one of the boarded-up stores.

Garbage lay everywhere. Strewn between abandoned cars and the burnt-out shells of commercial buildings. A black dog trotted by with a charred bone in its jaws, snarling at one of the soldiers who made a lunge for it.

Chaos lurked on the edge of perception here. The blood-dimmed tide was close at hand. What was that English poem? The one seemingly written for these, the end of days? *Things fall apart, the center cannot hold. Mere anarchy is loosed upon the world.* Yes, he thought. The end was nigh. The rough beast approached.

He could see huge boiling towers of oily smoke climbing into the sky a few miles away. The leviathan murmur of the big guns was now underscored by the harsher, staccato rattle of small-arms fire. Two civilizations were grinding against each other like great mill wheels over there, and he feared that he had fed the lives of unknowable numbers of men into that demonic foundry for naught.

To what end would they perish? To buy another six or twelve months' respite?

He wondered if he should just turn away from this vehicle. Trust himself to the spirits of his ancestors and his *katana*. Join his men at the front and disappear into history. One small noble act that might perhaps be noted with approval by a scholar in the long distant future, when the dark age had passed.

The lieutenant must have read his mind, because Homma suddenly noticed the man's grip, forcing him into the jeep. "We have to get to the meeting, General. The staff are waiting for instructions. The counterattack—it *must* begin. There is no time."

But the poet-general had time to pause and survey the field of his last failure. There would be no counterattack. Masaharu Homma examined his inner landscape and found it as barren and desolate as the dying city.

Just as he cosigned the order to carry out the field punishment of the three captured Japanese officers, Jones remembered where he had seen that sergeant before. The one who'd turned back the ambush on the Brisbane Line. The memory brought forth a rich, rolling baritone laugh, which he had to clamp down on, quickly, lest somebody imagine he was enjoying himself as he signed the death warrants on the company clerk's flexipad.

The woman didn't look put out. She'd seen the mass graves in every town they rolled through.

But he explained anyway. "Something I just remembered, Corporal. Please excuse me. It was nothing to do with this," he said, handing her the pad.

"Thank you, Colonel. I'll zap this over to the Aussies via laser link. Wouldn't have bothered me none anyhow. I'd pull a cold trigger on those fuckers any day, sir."

Jones sent the clerk on her way and took a drink from his canteen. He parted the sunshades in the little wooden police station where he'd set up a temporary HQ as they prepared for the final assault. His Crusader guns and the Australians' smaller battery of 155s shook the frame of the building and raised small clouds of dust as they blasted away.

They were firing on the last Japanese strongpoint, a few thousand men dug into the city of Bundaberg. Circling drones brought the barrage down with such accuracy that individual foxholes could be targeted, if he so chose. But of course, they didn't have the luxury of unlimited ammunition, so his gun monkeys were tasked with reducing the major enemy concentrations. The Crusaders fired twelve shots in a volley, each individual shell screaming through an arc that covered eighteen thousand meters, to slam into a target selected by a combined fire control team in a command LAV.

The guns roared, and eighteen klicks away, a water tower disintegrated into fiery splinters, killing the Japanese forward observers who were sitting on top of it. A platoon dug into a deep trench was entombed; three mortar crews and their guns were atomized; a stand of eucalyptus trees, which had been hiding two light tanks, disappeared inside an explosive maelstrom. And a beautiful old white stone building in which the Japanese commanders were thought to be holed up suddenly blew apart.

But Colonel Jones's thoughts were elsewhere. Sergeant Snider, he recalled at last. That redneck asshole who'd fronted him on the *Enterprise* when he'd landed with Kolhammer and Halabi to meet Spruance for the first time. On top of everything else that went wrong that night, Snider simply hadn't been equipped to deal with an African-American Marine Corps colonel. Jones had bruted him into his place and pretty much forgotten about him ever since.

But that fellow who'd led the charge, and held Hill 178 back on the Brisbane Line—that had been him, for sure. He searched his memory for the name of the embed who'd filed the story.

Duffy. Julia Duffy.

She'd gone into Luzon and Cabanatuan with them shortly after the Transition. He'd heard good reports about her, too. She could handle herself in the thick of it. And she gave good copy, too.

Jones took another drink. Duffy must have gone out with the 'temps, looking for something different. And she'd turned old Snider into a hero while she was at it.

Actually, Jones mused, that was unfair of him, thinking that way. He'd seen the download of that firefight. It was pretty fucking willing. If they wanted to lay a bit of fruit salad on the sergeant's dress greens, well, fact was, he'd earned it. Jones doubted he'd ever see the prick again, but he'd make an effort to congratulate him, if he did.

The guns roared again, this time followed by the faintly ridiculous *pop-pop-pop* of three pistol shots.

Field punishment of the Japanese officers had been carried out.

His flexipad pinged. It was Sergeant Major Harrison. "We're getting buttoned up, Colonel. Ten minutes till the bottom of the ninth."

"Thanks, Aub. I'm coming now."

Jones strapped on his powered helmet, checked the load on his G4, and screwed the cap back onto his canteen. In his reactive matrix armor, he had to turn slightly sideways to get through the doorway and out onto the street.

His LAV sat about a hundred meters away, one of four parked on the main street. Well, the only street, really. As he adjusted his combat goggles and moved quickly to the vehicle, he tried not to think about the open pit in the town square, full of rotting bodies. Three more had been left at the edge: a Japanese captain and two lieutenants who had commanded the small garrison in this town.

Jones could see their corpses clearly in the harsh tropical light. A small group of enemy soldiers had been forced to watch the field punishment, and an Australian squad was leading them away to a truck. They would be taken to the rear and held, pending further investigation. If any were found to have been directly involved in the murder of the town's population, they would be trucked right back to the edge of the pit and shot in the head in exactly the same fashion as their superiors. Unless they were transferred into the custody of the contemporary forces, in which case, they'd probably be hanged in Brisbane in about six or seven months, after a court-martial.

As far as Jones was concerned, it made no difference, one way or the other.

He had a battle to get to.

Thankfully, thought Mitchell, none of the men in the squad had grown up in Bundaberg. It would have made navigating the town easier, of course. But that little bit of emotional distance helped when moving through the scene of a large-scale atrocity.

The SAS officer still found it maddening, having to sit still while he watched innocent civilians killed without reason. But he had a strictly covert brief for this stage of the operation. Their mission was to move around under the cover of darkness, marking targets for the big guns, plotting troop movements, and—wherever possible—identifying enemy combatants for Sanction 4 field punishment later. Unlike the first and third squads, his men had no order tasking them to directly interdict the enemy's higher command authorities.

So they retired to the layup point, a small hill with a clear view of the town, and watched as it was systematically reduced to ashes and rubble by the artillery they had called in. Most of the squad was busy adjusting fire and drone coverage, feeding new data back to the guns, and monitoring the direct approach to their small encampment. Pearce Mitchell and Sergeant Cameron McLeod, however, had dug into the hillside a short distance away, and were watching over the reverse slope, guarding against the possibility of an attack from the rear.

The only significant concentration of Japanese forces in that direction were the soldiers guarding the surviving townspeople in a rough, unsheltered barbed-wire enclosure that had been run up on a football field. The sun blazed down on the unprotected prisoners. Neither of the SAS men had seen any sign of a water supply, organized medical care, sewerage, or even a system for disposing of the increasing number of bodies.

The guards largely ignored their charges, who rarely moved. Scoping out the encampment with powered goggles, the men could see why. The prisoners were close to death. The smell of putrefaction was strong, even from this distance. Most telling, however, was their lack of reaction to the sounds of battle as it crept closer. They had no energy to react, and were simply waiting to die.

Mitchell and McLeod stayed silent. They occasionally tapped each other and pointed out some detail that had caught the eye: a pile of tiny bodies that had to be young children; a stick figure hanging from the wire; a solitary man moving about, apparently to tend to the sick and injured. A town doctor, perhaps?

The troopers had their flexipads out and were file-sharing a plan of the camp, which they added to as the time passed. Over on their hillside McLeod sketched out potential lines of approach, while Mitchell noted the position of the fixed gun emplacements, and plotted their fields of fire. They each counted the numbers of Japanese guards and checked each other's figures.

It helped not to have to think about the people who were dying down there.

SOUTHWEST PACIFIC AREA HEADQUARTERS

General Douglas MacArthur was getting mightily pissed off at being ambushed by these characters. He stalked back and forth across his office in Brisbane. He was already late for the press conference he'd called up on the Line, where he was going to take the reporters through his victory, step by step. He had half a mind to just go anyway, to leave the prime minister hanging. But he restrained himself, mainly because he wanted to know what fresh hell Jones was about to spring on him.

It had to be something to do with Bundaberg. Some crazy scheme they were cooking up to steal his thunder while—

"General, it's Prime Minister Curtin on the phone, sir."

"About time," he grumbled, before switching to a more appropriate tone as he picked up the heavy, old-fashioned handset. It was funny how quickly he'd become accustomed to the lightweight materials the twenty-first people used.

"Yes, Prime Minister."

The harsh, flat accent of the Australian PM crackled out of the earpiece. "General, I'd like you to hold off on that press conference you're planning."

MacArthur barely contained the outburst that instantly threatened to erupt past his lips. He drew in a quick breath and waited out the political leader.

"Jones is still some time away from taking Bundaberg, and we've had a request from Colonel Toohey, the Australian field commander, to alter the operational plan. They want to try to rescue the surviving townspeople. They're being held in an open field some distance from the town center, and Jones agrees that it's worth trying.

"In that light, I'd rather we didn't go trumpeting our success on the Line just yet. It should be only a few more hours."

MacArthur had to squeeze his eyes shut and fight the urge to bellow down the phone. "Prime Minister, with all due respect, I have to disagree. The Japanese have spent themselves in front of the Line. They've collapsed, and that part of our operation is effectively complete. I don't see how it can have any effect on what Jones or Toohey are planning. *However,* I am your servant, as always, in these matters. And if that is your wish, then so be it."

His rage was so great that he had passed beyond the point of mere anger and into a strange calm place, where everything was devoid of color and utterly flat. His voice didn't shake at all as he spoke.

Curtin probably understood him better than did his own commander in chief. At least the prime minister hadn't handed him a fait accompli. He was shrewd enough—or considerate enough—to present the matter as a choice, not an order.

"As I said, it's only a couple of hours, General. It simply means there'll be more for you to talk about with the press. And you'll want to familiarize yourself with the details of Bundaberg, so you can handle any questions arising from that, too."

"Yes, I suppose I will," MacArthur agreed.

"One other thing, General. We're keeping this business of the dummy convoys under our hat for the moment. Young Kennedy seems to have stumbled onto something that may be of much wider significance, and we'd like to question Homma about it, if at all possible."

MacArthur glowered just at the mention of the Kennedy clan. They were no allies of his. "As you wish, Prime Minister. Although I doubt General Homma will allow himself to be taken alive."

"Perhaps not, but let's wait and see. Colonel Jones says that if they can lay their hands on him, he *will* talk."

At this MacArthur turned to his office window, squinting into the late afternoon glare. The city of Brisbane seemed to doze in the heat of an early summer. It had been spared, for now, but he still wondered what plans Tojo might have for all the other divisions he'd withdrawn from China.

And MacArthur was irritated at all the attention that had been focused on Jones and Toohey's sideshow, rather than on the magnificent defensive effort he had organized to the north of the city. He couldn't help but indulge himself in a moment of spite. "I suppose you read Kennedy's entire report, Prime Minister. And Captain Willet's also?"

"Of course," the PM replied warily.

"Were you not disturbed by the actions of that young female officer?

The Australian? It seemed to me that she lost her head completely when she opened fire on those men in the water."

MacArthur could tell he'd scored a small victory when Curtin didn't reply immediately.

"Prime Minster?"

"I had an opportunity to speak to Captain Willet about that matter, General. She assured me that Lieutenant Lohrey's actions were in no way out of the ordinary. Not as far as *their* rule book is written, anyway."

The PM's voice carried a suggestion of sadness.

"It was an ugly business, General. Very ugly. But you're a soldier, and I don't doubt that you've seen just as bad, if not worse. I'm afraid that, given the emergency we face, I cannot find it in my heart to condemn either Lohrey or Willet. And of course, they still operate under their own rules of engagement, so no legal question will arise from the incident. But you are correct if you think me troubled by it. I've been kept up-to-date on the progress of the counteroffensive, and while I shed no tears for the Japanese, I wonder what became of our two countries that they evolved into such pitiless societies."

MacArthur hadn't been expecting that at all. He found himself caught flat-footed for a moment, unable to reply.

He had followed the debate at home, the pros and cons of allowing Kolhammer to run his little fiefdom as a separate country, if only for a limited time, but the hysteria surrounding that decision was largely a matter of Sunday school morals—an argument about the bedroom, not the battlefield. Still, Curtin must have taken his silence as an invitation to continue.

"The press is already running stories from those reporters who are embedded with Jones about the summary executions they're carrying out. It plays very well with the public, of course. They've got the blood up. But that's what worries me, General. We're supposedly fighting this war to secure ourselves *against* barbarism, not to embrace it. I accept the fact that those enemy officers who were responsible for the crimes against my people must die for what they have done. But this business of simply dragging them out into the street and shooting them in the head smacks of gangsterism, don't you think? It's a long way removed from what Lieutenant Lohrey did in the rush of battle, when she thought her mission and her comrades were imperiled."

MacArthur shooed away an aide who appeared at the door. Curtin had tapped into some of his own, very strong misgivings. Whilst he had welcomed the incredible power of Jones's MEU and Colonel Toohey's Armored Cavalry units, he had to admit that he found some of their procedures to be deeply disturbing.

"I don't know that we're in a position to judge them, Prime Minister. It's not simply a matter of supporting your allies. They've been at war for twenty years. Can you imagine what your people, what *mine* would be like, after fighting with the likes of Tojo and Hitler for that length of time? Not much different, I would assume."

A sigh came through the handset. "You're right, of course. I had just hoped that things might be different in the future."

"That's a pipe dream, Prime Minister, I'm afraid."

"Let's hope not," Curtin replied.

20

SOUTHWEST PACIFIC AREA, BUNDABERG, 350 KM NORTH OF THE BRISBANE LINE

The M1A3 Abrams was a man-killer.

Colonel J. "Lonesome" Jones thanked the good Lord that he had never had to face anything like it.

The models that preceded it, the A1 and A2, were primarily designed to engage huge fleets of Soviet tanks on the plains of Europe. They were magnificent tank busters, but proved to be less adept at the sort of close urban combat that was the bread and butter of the U.S. Army in the first two decades of the twenty-first century. In the alleyways of Damascus and Algiers, along the ancient cobbled lanes of Samara, Al Hudaydah, and Aden, the armored behemoths often found themselves penned in, unable to maneuver or even to see what they were supposed to kill. They fell victim to car bombs and Molotovs and homemade mines. Jones had won his Medal of Honor rescuing the crew of one that had been disabled by a jihadi suicide squad in the Syrian capital.

The A3 was developed in response to attacks just like that one, which had become increasingly more succesful. It was still capable of killing a Chinese battle tank, but it was fitted out with a very different enemy in mind.

Anyone, like Jones, who was familiar with the clean, classic lines of the earlier Abrams would have found the A3 less aesthetically pleasing. The low-profile turret now bristled with 40 mm grenade launchers, an M134 7.62 mm minigun, and either a small secondary turret for twin 50s, or a single Tenix-ADI 30 mm chain gun. The 120 mm canon remained, but it was now rifled like the British Challenger's gun.

But anyone, like Jones, who'd ever had to fight in a high-intensity urban scenario couldn't give a shit about the A3's aesthetics. They just said their prayers in thanks to the designers. The tanks typically loaded out with a heavy emphasis on high-impact, soft-kill ammunition such as the canistered "beehive" rounds, Improved Conventional Bomblets, White Phos', thermobaric, and flame-gel capsules. Reduced propellant charges meant that they could be fired near friendly troops without danger of having a gun blast disable or even kill them. An augmented long-range laser-guided kinetic spike could engage hard targets out to six thousand meters.

The A3 boasted dozens of tweaks, many of them suggested by crew members who had gained their knowledge the hard way. So the tank commander now enjoyed an independent thermal and LLAMPS viewer. Three-hundred-sixty-degree visibility came via a network of hardened battle-cams. A secondary fuel cell generator allowed the tank to idle without guzzling JP-8 jet fuel. Wafered armor incorporated monobonded carbon sheathing and reactive matrix skirts, as well as the traditional mix of depleted uranium and Chobam ceramics.

Unlike the tank crew that Jones had rescued from a screaming mob in a Damascus marketplace, the men and women inside the A3 could fight off hordes of foot soldiers armed with RPGs, satchel charges, and rusty knives—for the "finishing work" when the tank had been stopped and cracked open to give access to its occupants.

Lycombing gas turbines drove the seventy-five-ton brute a top speed of sixty kph, which was a touch slower than its forebears. But again, it was an unusual day when the driver got to put her into top gear and go wild. Mostly the A3 crawled through dense warrens of third world slums, pulverizing mud brick walls, smashing through the ground floors of low-rise buildings, crushing cars—and occasionally people—beneath its treads.

Not today, though.

Today the six Abrams of the Eighty-second MEU charged through light scrub, mowing down saplings and bursting through old wooden fences as they led an armored stampede toward the last line of Japanese defense. They led twelve older, reduced-capability M1A1-Cs of the Australian Second Cavalry, and twenty-six Light Armored Vehicles and "Bushpig" AASLAVs of the combined mobile forces.

It was a hell of a rough ride, but Jones was enjoying it thoroughly, watching the tanks on flatscreen while strapped into the battalion command LAV some three hundred meters behind the leading edge of the advance. Every vehicle was hooked into the Cooperative Battle Link and directed by a Distributed Combat Intelligence, working within operational parameters set by the U.S. and Australian commanders. The turret on one of his A3s swung thirty degrees to the left and fired a 120 mm round of XM1028 Canister at a platoon-sized group of the enemy, which emerged from the smoking ruins of a wooden cottage. More than a thousand tungsten balls, expelled from the container as the shot left the gun's muzzle, swept over the Japanese like an evil wind, reducing them to pink mist and bone fragments.

He saw a Japanese Type 94 "tankette" literally shredded into metal chips as four separate 30 mm chain guns took it under fire. It flew to pieces, the disintegrating steel plate perversely reminding him of leaves blown from a tree in a high wind.

His helmet banged into the padded ceiling as the LAV dipped and bumped and leapt up again with a series of grinding crunches. It wasn't firing any of its weapons, but the vehicles around it had begun to pop smoke and antipersonal munitions from their grenade launchers. Two Hellfire missiles streaked away from an Australian Bushpig, lancing out to destroy a couple of small field guns popping away on a hill just ahead of them.

Jones took in video and sensor feeds from dozens of sources. To the untrained observer, it was just violent chaos, but to him every image, every moment was another note in a deadly overture.

Even from his position, buttoned up tight in the LAV, the noise of the assault was colossal. The snarling of the command vehicle's engine, the crash and crunch of every impact as they smashed though the light bush and leapt over small gullies, the savage thunder of coaxial machine guns, auto-cannon, and mortar bursts.

A drone picked up a company-sized movement to the west, where a hundred or more men emerged from where they had hidden in a creek. The DCI alerted human sysops, who needed no warning. Two speeding A3's traversed their main guns and unloaded canister. The Japanese, however, were protected from the hypervelocity tungsten swarm by the fall of the creek bed. Their reprieve lasted all of one second.

While as they remained crouched where they couldn't be engaged by direct fire, the next two tanks in line brought their guns to bear as they bounced along at forty kilometers per hour. Simultaneous muzzle flashes preceded a massive distortion effect on the screen.

The tanks had fired high-impulse thermobaric shells.

Two blips flashed across nine hundred meters in the blink of an eye. The shells contained a slurry of propylene oxide mixed with a finely powdered explosive. As simple microchips in the warheads registered that they had reached the target, they cracked open and dispersed their contents over the heads of the enemy infantrymen. The soldiers had a split second to see the bright orange cloud, but no time to escape before small incendiary fuses sparked a titanic blast. At the epicenter, temperatures soared to 3,000 degrees Centigrade and overpressure reached 430 psi.

The men, the plant life—in fact, every living thing and most of the inanimate objects within the blast area—ceased to exist. Even the air was incinerated, creating a vacuum that pulled in more burning fuel and loose objects from a wide margin around the point of impact. Anyone who might have survived—even momentarily, by dint of having been entirely submerged—would have encountered the true meaning of hell, having been simultaneously flash-boiled, asphyxiated, and cooked from within as the blazing fuel–air mix penetrated all nonairtight objects.

As the first echelon approached the edge of the city, collapsing crude concrete bunkers with single-shot penetrators or the jackhammer effect of concentrated chain gun fire, attack helicopters roared overhead, autocannon and rocket pods working the increasingly target-poor environment. Rather than swooping and turning to rake at the enemy in their normal "bird of prey" routine, however, they swept right on over the town and out toward the open prison compound.

"Go! Go! Go!"

Mitchell and McLeod dashed forward, following the pathfinder beacons that overlay the real-world landscape in their powered goggles. Seventy thousand feet above them, a Big Eye drone tracked the SAS men via biolocator chips implanted in their necks, checking their progress against a hastily programmed software model of the killing ground around the prison camp.

The model had been adapted from a tourist holomap that the Distributed Combat Intelligence found within the personal files of a sailor on board HMAS *Ipswich*. Fleetnet was a treasure trove of such data—previously unremarkable, but now proving to be of tremendous tactical importance.

Neither Mitchell nor McLeod had time to waste thinking about such things. They were racing across open ground, sucking in great drafts of foul-smelling air, their legs pumping like pistons. Cascades of tac net overlay turned the world into a shifting mosaic of computer-generated imagery. Arrunta gunships whirled overhead, identified as friendlies by the bright blue rectangles that floated around them and turned green a second before long streaks of fire spat out of nose-mounted autocannon.

The stream of fire destroyed a small wooden cabin, which had been designated by a red flashing box, but which now turned gray and inert.

As they ran, this was their whole world, a mandala of electronic projections designed to make sense of the murderous insanity swirling around them. Both men knew that the other members of their section were very close, perhaps near enough to call out and be heard. But in reality, they were utterly alone, with one goal, to reach the bunker ahead, outlined in flashing red, before the time hack in the bottom left-hand corner of their goggles reached zero.

They had thirty-three seconds.

"Go! Go! Go!"

Mitchell's personal weapon coughed three times, killing a sentry who rose up without warning from a pile of dead bodies.

Thirty-one seconds.

They both leapt a tangle of barbed wire. As Mitchell sailed clear of the obstacle, the vision of a dead child passed over his eyes, like reflected text on a computer screen. The body bloated. Skin blackened and split. A filthy teddy bear clutched in the dark claw of a tiny hand.

Twenty-nine seconds.

The earth trembled underfoot as an immense explosion destroyed an ammunition dump two klicks away. Data flashed on their Heads-Up Displays and was gone before the aftershock had dissipated.

Twenty-six seconds.

They were almost at the bunker entrance. Another sentry.

McLeod fired first. Three hypervelocity caseless ceramic bullets smacked into the man, shattering his breastbone, releasing tendrils of nanonic razor teeth inside his chest, which in turn released an airborne wave of gore as the augmented rounds tore his upper torso to pieces.

Twenty-four seconds.

Mitchell fired into the yawning black entrance of the bunker. A flash-bang.

Their goggles briefly dimmed against the blinding light. Momentum and memory carried them forward until vision was restored. But just for a second, and then they were inside the bunker, and the small constricted space was rendered in the lime-green glow of low-light amplification.

Twenty-two seconds.

"Get down! Get Down!" Mitchell shouted.

Women and children screamed.

Howled.

Screeched and cried like trapped and dying animals.

Two Japanese soldiers flailed about with fists and clubs. One died as his head disintegrated. The other flew backwards into the sandbagged wall, a giant smoking hole where his heart had once beaten.

The SAS men switched to single shots now.

Twenty seconds.

"Get down on the fucking floor, *now!*"

Mitchell counted eight enemy soldiers. Still blind. He and McLeod picked them off, one by one.

Seventeen seconds left.

"Right. Get *up.* Get *out.* Run toward the light. Go-go-*go!*"

He had to push some of the women to get them started.

Two children, small girls of indeterminate age, had gone fetal in a corner. McLeod picked them both up as Mitchell put another round into an enemy soldier who tried to push himself up off the dirt floor.

Fifteen seconds.

Mitchell left first, weapon at the ready. Two other section members had joined them to hurry the civilians away.

"Move! Move! Over here!"

Fourteen seconds.

McLeod appeared. Somebody helped him with one little girl.

They all began to run through the firestorm and digital turmoil toward a slit trench.

Nine seconds.

McLeod dropped down in time to see another trooper cut the throat of a guard who had been hiding on the floor of the trench.

Eight seconds.

They made it with time to spare.

Seven.

Six.

Five.

Four.

Three . . .

Hellfire rockets destroyed the bunker three seconds early.

He was shaking. No matter how much he tried, he couldn't stop the deep body tremors that had seized him as the fury of the barbarian war machine fell upon his command.

General Masaharu Homma knew profound shame. He had failed his men and his emperor. He had expected to hold out for at least a week, but had lasted less than an hour.

Less than an hour.

He stood, trembling, in the open window on the second floor of the building where he had hoped to make his last stand. He still would, but he understood now what a futile gesture it would be. He wished that a stray round or a sniper would relieve him of his disgrace. The demonic noise of pitched battle had fallen back to the sound of scattered, pitiable skirmishes, most of which ended the same way: with that peculiar ripping snarl of a barbarian's rifle as it snuffed out another life.

He could hear the dull chop of their wingless aircraft. The sound seemed to swirl everywhere around him. And now he understood that the high-pitched whine belonged to their tanks.

There wasn't much of his command left. Some of the staff officers had barricaded themselves in on the lower floors and piled up a sizable cache of rifles and grenades. Somebody had even salvaged a Type 97 antitank rifle from somewhere. There were a handful of reports from Luzon and Singapore that it was the only thing short of cannon fire that could punch through the mysterious padded armor worn by the Emergence barbarians. Perhaps they might take one or two with them.

Most likely they would all die in some bizarre cataclysm, such as the firebomb that had annihilated Wakuda's company down by the riverbank.

As he stood at the window, peering into the harsh tropical light, two of the eight-wheeled armored cars rumbled into the street. The turrets traversed with a humming sound he could hear even over the noise of small-scale fighting. The long barrels came to a halt when they had lined up on his building.

So this was it.

Homma unbuttoned the flap on his holster and stepped out onto the little balcony. He raised his pistol to squeeze off six shots. The officers and orderlies on the floor below and in the offices to either side of his opened up with small arms. The antitank rifle sounded with a much deeper boom, and he was sure he saw the round strike the angled glacis plate of the lead vehicle. An extra-long spark streaked off the camouflage paint.

The turret guns erupted, and he was immediately thrown to his feet as the entire building seemed to shudder backwards under the impact. Plaster fell from the ceiling, and windows shattered. The noise was deafening, and painful. It filled the whole world, forcing him to drop his sidearm and jam his hands over his ears.

He could feel the cannon shells demolishing the floors beneath, and expected to die as the building simply fell in on itself.

Instead, he rolled over, ready to crawl downstairs and die with some honor among his comrades, only to find himself staring into the face of his assassin.

The man appeared in the doorway without warning. He looked huge, looming over Homma in his bulky armor. His was white, but most of his face was hidden behind goggles that were so perfectly mirrored, all the general could see in them was a distorted image of himself.

He clawed around for the pistol he'd dropped as the soldier raised one of the two weapons he was carrying. It was black, and oddly shaped, with two metal spikes poking—

He jumped as the spikes fizzed across the room and embedded themselves in his chest. He noticed wires leading back to the device.

And then the world turned black.

. . .

. . .

. . .

. . .

. . .

Homma came to in a different room. No. A tent.

He had no idea of how long he had remained unconscious. The tent was lit by glowing tubes, so perhaps night had fallen.

He lay on a cot. It was a simple structure of canvas and wood, but strange machines sat on a trestle table to his left. Somebody spoke in English. He tried to focus through the pain of a blinding headache and the sudden realization that he was a prisoner.

More shame. *Unending, unutterable shame.*

Hard, callused hands held him down. His head was clamped in a lock and wrenched backwards, exposing his neck. He felt a cool metallic object press against his jugular and then a sharp sting.

He passed into darkness again.

Battalion Intelligence Officer Major Annie Coulthard stepped back from the prisoner.

"Give him a minute or so, sir."

"Thank you, Major," said Colonel Jones.

While they waited, Brigadier Barnes and Colonel Toohey, the Australian commanders, countersigned the data scrip authorizing Homma's field punishment, and handed it to Jones. The Marine Corps officer added his own signature and passed the flexipad back to Corporal Britton.

The clerk saluted and left the five officers alone. Jones, Barnes, Toohey, Coulthard, and Lieutenant Stafford, who would act as interpreter.

"Your people did some good work, today, Mick," said Jones. "It was a hell of a thing, watching those old A-Ones go tear-assing through the brush again. I haven't seen anything like that since Iran. It really took me back."

The Australian brigadier nodded gruffly, but it was clear that he wasn't in the mood for banter. He had just come from the prison camp.

Combat medics had choppered in right behind the assault and set up triage on site. The worst cases were being treated by Marine Corps and 2 Cav medics at the local hospital, but it was unlikely that many of the original inhabitants would survive the ordeal. A couple of hundred at best, out of a town of thirteen thousand. WCIU investigators from the *Clinton* had already begun exhuming the bodies of hundreds of contemporary Allied servicemen and -women who had been exterminated after the fall of Bundaberg, and buried in a series of mass graves some distance outside of town.

Jones could see that Toohey was struggling with the urge to place his gun upside the general's head and just pull the trigger. But although they had already signed the warrant authorizing his execution, it would be some time before Masaharu Homma was taken to the edge of one of those mass graves. He was a high-value prisoner who would spend months being interrogated before meeting his ultimate fate.

"I think we should be okay to start the interrogation, now," announced Major Coulthard.

"Go ahead," Jones told her.

Coulthard turned on the two cameras. She spoke directly into one of them. "I am Major Annie Coulthard, battalion intelligence officer with the eighty-second MEU. With me are my commanding officer, Colonel J. 'Lonesome' Jones, Colonel Michael Toohey, and Brigadier Michael Barnes of the Australian Second Cavalry regiment, and an interpreter from the Southwest Pacific Headquarters, Lieutenant Andrew Stafford, USN, contemporary."

Coulthard moved aside and adjusted the focus to sharpen up the image of the prisoner.

"This is General Masaharu Homma, commander of the Imperial Japanese land forces in Australia. He was captured at the Battle of Bundaberg, on October tenth, nineteen forty-two, at roughly sixteen-thirty hours. Colonel Jones and Colonel Toohey have already authorized Sanction Four summary field punishment of General Homma for crimes against humanity. Execution of the sentence has been delayed to allow the prisoner to be interviewed.

"The prisoner is a Japanese male, age fifty-five, roughly seventy-six kilograms in weight. He was disabled for capture with a one-second minimal charge from a Texas Instruments Model Nine-forty-two taser. At twenty-forty-five hours, on October tenth, nineteen forty-two, I administered ten cc's of Trioxinol Five to the prisoner. It is now twenty-forty-seven hours. The interview has begun. Lieutenant Stafford is working from a list of questions prepared by me in consultation with General MacArthur's Intelligence Liaison at SWPA in Brisbane."

"You are General Masaharu Homma?" asked Lieutenant Stafford in Japanese.

"The black barbarian. The giant," replied Homma in a weak voice.

Stafford repeated the question twice. Homma agreed with him after the second try.

"And you are the officer responsible for the extra-judicial killing of contemporary Allied personnel, and the incarceration and killing of the population of this town?"

Homma shook his head. "I have not killed anyone."

Stafford rephrased the question. "Are you the commander of the Imperial Japanese forces in this town?"

"Yes."

"Did those forces, under your command, execute Allied officers and enlisted men when they took control of the town?"

"Yes."

"Did those forces incarcerate civilians?"

"Yes."

"Did those forces execute civilians?"

At that Homma seemed to lose focus. He closed his eyes and his head drooped to one side. A thin line of drool stretched from the corner of his mouth to the pillow.

Major Coulthard tapped him lightly on the cheek, pushing his face back toward the glo-sticks. "Did Japanese forces execute civilians in this town?"

"There was resistance," Homma whispered, his voice cracked. "Much resistance."

"Did Japanese forces execute civilians because of this resistance?"

"Yes."

The interview continued in this fashion for over an hour. Jones had seen plenty like it before. He knew that if it was him on the cot, with ten cc's of T5 in his bloodstream, he'd be giving up whatever was asked of him, too—state secrets or his wife's bra size, it wouldn't matter.

Just after midnight, Stafford asked Homma about the convoys. "Why did you bring Chinese soldiers to fight here?"

"We did not."

"There were Chinese soldiers on your troopships."

"Not soldiers," said Homma. "Prisoners."

"Why were there Chinese prisoners on your troopships?"

"They were targets," said Homma.

"Decoys?" asked Stafford.

"Targets, for your rockets and death beams."

Stafford translated the reply.

"Decoys," Jones muttered to Brigadier Barnes. "They were never meant to set foot on land."

The Australian just nodded.

Jones leaned over and whispered into Coulthard's ear. "See if you can get him to tell you what the fuck he was doing here, anyway. I think this whole invasion was a fucking sideshow."

Coulthard checked her watch. "I'll need to boost the dose in ten minutes, sir. We should wait until then. He's beginning to resist the drug."

Homma was shaking his head, refusing to talk about the Chinese anymore. Stafford switched the angle of his attack, asking the general why the army had let itself be duped into quitting China.

Homma looked like he was attempting to bristle, but nothing came. Just a sigh. "Yamamoto," he said quietly.

She knew she was going to be haunted by this place for months, if not years to come. Bundaberg was one of the worst atrocities she'd ever been witness to. The tiny hospital was overwhelmed. They'd begun to set up emergency facilities at a nearby high school, but had to find a new location when it became obvious that the Japanese had used the place as a torture and interrogation center.

One civilian health worker, a Rhodesian doctor named Michael Cooper, had survived his imprisonment and proved himself invaluable in triage. He told her of the appalling mistreatment meted out to the most vulnerable members of the community. Hundreds of survivors owed him their lives, but Major Margie Francois knew that wouldn't be enough to save him from himself. He was going to spend the rest of his life mourning the ones he couldn't save. She knew that particular level of hell only too well.

They were standing in the entrance of a giant hospital tent as dusk fell, discussing the likely treatment needs of the surviving locals when a passing corpsman stopped to tell them that the field punishments had already begun.

The major watched as a sickly grimace stole over the doctor's face. His cheeks first drained of color before flushing bright red. His Adam's apple bobbed convulsively as he struggled to say something.

Francois placed a hand on his arm, which was twitching with nervous tension, or possibly exhaustion.

Cooper croaked at her. "We were told that the uh . . . procedure . . . was open to the public."

"Why don't you go have a look, Doc," she said softly. "It helps. Sort of. Helps me sometimes anyway. You've done more than enough here. Go on, if that's what you want."

She gripped his arm a little tighter. "But if I was you, I'd be getting some rest, too. You look like a man on the edge of collapse. You've earned a break."

The Rhodesian shook his head. His eyes were a thousand miles away. "No, Major," he said, "I've earned the right to see justice."

"Okay, then, take this," she said, handing him a stick of gum packed with a very mild stimulant. "It'll get you through the next two hours, but then I'm going to send a corpsman to make sure you get some sleep. Two hours, Doctor. I mean it."

He agreed to follow her instructions, and shambled out into the dark. Francois watched him go.

The snap of gunfire was already drifting over the ruins of the town, from the main enclosure of the liberated prison camp. About two hundred survivors had gathered there to watch the rather unceremonious retribution being exacted on their behalf. She didn't need to see it herself again. She'd briefly attended a Sanction 4 execution earlier in the day.

No drumbeat accompanied the condemned men to their final moment. No holy men of any faith administered the last rites. The prisoners' hands were cuffed behind their backs with plastic ties. They were led or dragged over to a deep trench that had been dug in the center of the playing field by a mechanical excavator. The simple charge of "a crime against humanity" was read out to them. They were forced to kneel at the mouth of the pit, and a single bullet was fired into the back of each prisoner's head by a man or woman, officer or enlisted, who had been rostered onto field punishment detail for that day.

Jones and Barnes divided the task equally between their commands. As a medical officer, Francois was one of the few who had the right to claim exemption from the duty, and as long as she had worthy lives to save, she generally exercised her right.

But later, standing in triage, surrounded by a pile of bloody rags that had been cut from the body of an eight-year-old boy who was now in surgery, having a gangrenous leg amputated, she felt the black heat rising inside her head again. It made her wish she'd gone with Cooper.

What the hell is wrong with people that they'd do these things—to little kids?

It was the same fury that had driven her to the edge of reason back at the prison camp in Cabanatuan, when she'd capped off five Japanese guards and their commander. She'd earned a reprimand from Jones for that— for carrying out a Sanction 4 punishment without a properly cosigned authority. But none of those women was complaining, and she wasn't losing any sleep over it.

"Major Francois. I need your okay to release the battalion store of amoxicillin, ma'am. It's the last we've got."

She wrenched herself out of the spiral of dark thoughts that was threatening to drag her under. A corporal was holding out a flexipad and plastic pen.

"Sure," she muttered, more to herself than to the corporal; then she signed out the last of their broad-spectrum antibiotics. They had originally been intended for the Chinese internees at the caliphate's detention centers on Java, back in twenty-one.

"Major Francois, ma'am," another voice called out, "we just lost those 'temp surgeons flying up out of Brisbane, ma'am. Their plane crashed on takeoff at Archerfield."

Then another: "Major Francois, we're going to need you in surgery, ma'am. That antitank round fucked up Bukowksi a lot worse than we thought."

It felt like she'd stepped through a portal into purgatory: the coppery stink of blood, the stench of putrescent flesh, the stink of voided bowels, the screams, the sobbing, the madness and horror that were her natural working environment.

Her flexipad beeped and pinged with constant messages, queries, demands for action, and solutions to impossible problems.

The human part of her wanted to walk away. But Michael Cooper hadn't given up, and he had faced a much more daunting challenge.

"Get me some more surgeons," she told the orderly who'd delivered the bad news out of Archerfield. "We've been training hundreds of them down in Sydney and Melbourne. We got fuckin' surgeons to burn."

Then she turned to the runner who'd been sent to bring her back to the operating room.

"Tell them I'll suit up in five," she said.

She unclipped the flexipad from her belt and ignored the hundreds of messages stacking up in her in-tray. She fired off quick, brutal messages to half a dozen people who were dragging their feet at various points between here and Brisbane. She told them to get their thumbs out of their asses and send her the drugs, dressings, and personnel she had asked for when the battalion left the Brisbane Line. She threatened to personally shoot anyone who didn't do exactly as she ordered.

The stories about what she'd done at Cabanatuan lent the threat some real heft.

Just before she headed back to the operating theater, she grabbed a passing corpsman and tasked him with finding Dr. Cooper in exactly one hour. "Knock him out with a taser if you have to," she said. "That man needs to get some rest. Hell, we may need him back here before long."

She ignored the insistent beeping of the flexipad. It had been doing that ever since she'd jumped from the rear of the LAV and run toward the first cries of "Medic!" hours earlier.

There were close to nine hundred unanswered routine vidmails and e-mails in the lattice memory of her pad. There was only one she would later regret failing to get to in time.

21

Despite the unmasking of von Stauffenberg and his murderous cabal of plotters, the führer still felt safest at the Wolfschanze. In truth, this was a testament to his personal bravery, and strength of will.

Of course, Himmler mused, the assassin's bomb that would have been planted there in July of '44 would never materialize. He had made sure of that. Anyone even remotely connected with that act of treason had already been killed. As had their extended families, their friends, and any possible accomplices. He had even eliminated some whose names were not found in the Fleetnet files, but upon whom suspicion fell anyway.

His Mercedes hummed through the thick stands of pine and birch that made up the Goerlitz forest, where elk and wild horse still roamed free, through the steep-sided valleys and troughs carved out by massive glaciers in the distant past. As they sped along the road to the bunker complex, the SS chief felt his spirits lifting for the first time in months.

Thankfully, the worst of the traitor-hunt was now behind them. Rebellious elements of the Wehrmacht and the *Kriegsmarine* had been brought to heel with exemplary severity. Some useful men had been lost, it was true. And he was the first to admit that it was more than possible that innocent blood had been spilled. But the revelations furnished by the Emergence demanded resolute action. The vengeance of the Black Angels, falling on those who would have failed the führer, had been swift and terrible to behold—as history demanded that it must be.

And there was still so much to do. There was a war to be won, against much greater odds than anyone would have admitted only a year ago. But just as the Emergence had brought frightful knowledge of criminals acting in league with Jewish and Bolshevik plotters to destroy the führer's legacy, so, too, had it yielded the means of thwarting their schemes—and of defeating the corrupt democracies.

The heavy, armor-plated sedan gracefully powered out of a long, sweeping turn, allowing him to catch sight of Kaltenbrunner's limousine, just a few hundred meters ahead. Himmler still considered his Security Service chief a very lucky man. According to the records, some doubt had hung over his actions at the end of the war in *die andere Zeit*, the other time. Fortunately for Kaltenbrunner, the records were inconclusive, and nobody could pin down quite what he had done. Ultimately, he was saved by his performance on the gallows.

It was an SS researcher who had discovered an electronic magazine article about famous last lines. He had come across a report of Kaltenbrunner's execution by the Allies, in October 1946. Just before the hangman's noose took him, Kaltenbrunner showed a distinct sense of style, saying in a low, calm voice, "Germany, good luck."

That was the sort of Aryan contempt for death that the führer found reassuring in these uncertain of days. So Kaltenbrunner lived. *For now.*

And his tenuous hold on life was driving him more fervently to prove his loyalty. He had accelerated the solution to the Jewish problem, despite the fact that the Allies had stepped up their efforts to bomb the rail lines that led to the camps. He had even taken over the *Abwehr* two years early and had placed it under the supervision of the Reich Central Security Office.

That would have happened in 1944 but—

"Pah!"

Himmler chided himself and waved away these idle thoughts. *Would have, could have, should have, may have . . .* It was all so pointless. What mattered was that they strike a massive coordinated blow against the English-speaking world, to smash them so hard that they would be crippled, if not destroyed altogether.

He knew that Stalin was using the current hiatus to desperately shore up his own defenses, but to no avail—it would never be enough. Russia would burn, and this time they wouldn't make the mistake of sending millions of troops into the wasteland of the steppes.

A thin, contemptuous smile twisted his features as he thought of the eagerness with which Stalin had accepted the terms of the cease-fire.

The small procession of cars motored through the northern gates of the Wolfschanze, past a checkpoint manned by the finest of all German troops, the *Leibstandarte-SS Adolf Hitler*. Himmler nodded approvingly as the men snapped out an extra-crisp salute for his car when it glided past.

The outer ring of the complex, which enclosed an area of two and a half square kilometers, was secured by minefields and a double-apron barbed-wire fence, although that was gradually being replaced with electrified razor wire as it became available. The main bunker was located in the north of the compound and sat within a secondary enclosure.

Thousands of workmen still crawled over the eighty or so fortified structures, hardening them against possible Allied air or missile strikes. Almost no evidence remained of the original wooden buildings, which now formed the inner shell of triple-bunkered concrete blockhouses. Himmler missed the old-world charm of the original design. It had felt like visiting a hunting lodge out here in the woods. But such whimsy was for quieter times.

His driver was forced to stop at the inner ring, as his identity was verified, although that did not take long.

Himmler climbed out of the rear seat as a car pulled up from behind, and the Japanese ambassador arrived. The German waited for Lieutenant General Hiroshi Oshima, not really wanting to talk to Kaltenbrunner.

"*Reichsführer*, a fine day, if a little chilly," said Oshima. "It reminds me of the forests on Hokkaido."

"Herr General," Himmler responded. "Let us hope that the first snows hold off a little while longer, eh?" They shook hands and entered the *Lagebaracke*, where the July Plot would have—

Himmler sighed again.

He really had to concentrate on what was, not on what would have been.

Albert Speer was talking. Another survivor, even though the evidence against him was even more damning than it had been against Kaltenbrunner. The minister of armaments would have survived the war and not been executed, which Himmler found *very* suspicious. Unfortunately, the information available on him was even more sparse, and largely second- or even third-hand. There was one reference to a book about him called *The Good Nazi*, which infuriated Himmler because he couldn't be sure whether the title was meant to be ironic or literal.

But, the führer had intervened—one of the few times he'd done so. Thanking the *Reichsführer-SS* for his diligence, he had suggested that Speer was too valuable to condemn, at least for the moment, when they had already lost so many and faced the immense challenge of the coming months. He argued that Heydrich had been allowed to live, despite his Jewish blood, so Speer should be given a chance to redeem himself by bringing the special projects to fruition. He was on notice, the führer had said, and he'd seen what happened to the others. If he could not be trusted, he could at least be watched.

Himmler privately thought the führer was still upset over the business with Rommel.

So Speer was alive, although he never seemed to look Himmler in the eye. To the *Reichsführer*, he very much appeared to be a man with something to hide.

His turn would come.

"And so, I am afraid the jet program will not reach its maturity in time," said Speer, never once looking up from his notes.

Göring began to grumble, and curse under his breath as Speer carried on.

"So I recommend that while we continue to invest in the development of these jets, there are other, much more pressing programs in need of our resources. The use of radar, to direct antiaircraft fire, has greatly limited the Allies' ability to strike at our preparations for Sea Dragon. But we still lag in this area, and while the productive capacity exists, the program lacks the funding needed to achieve its goals.

"I can add fifty percent to our coverage immediately, if the Chancellery will just release the funds. That extra capacity will be crucial. The RAF has changed its tactics, and has begun striking at our radar sites with these wooden Mosquitoes, flying low and fast and firing a new rocket specifically designed to home in on radar emissions. They, too, have accelerated their weapons-development programs. And they posses the *Trident*, which we do not—"

"We *would* have such a ship, if it weren't for our yellow friends," Göring muttered, a little too volubly.

"Enough," Hitler commanded. "Let Speer continue."

Himmler glanced over at the Japanese ambassador but his face was a marble mask. For once, the SS chief agreed with Göring. He didn't think they should have let the *Dessaix* out of their grasp, either. It would have been invaluable in the coming operation. But the führer had insisted. They would fight this war as a global conflict. The Japanese were closely coordinating their plans with the Reich, and Yamamoto insisted that those plans turned on the *Dessaix*. Besides, she had been stripped nearly bare before being sent to the Pacific. She might not play a direct role in Sea Dragon, but some of her weapons systems would.

Himmler listened as Speer mumbled a thank-you to Hitler and pressed on. *Still refusing to raise his head.*

"The *Panzerfaust* Two-fifty, a great improvement on the model Thirty, will be ready, but in limited numbers," he said. "On current scheduling, twelve hundred will be available in the one-use format. There are also two hundred prototype reusable *Panzerschrecken*, available immediately, with a projected supply of eighteen to nineteen hundred warshots."

Himmler moved his cold gaze away from Speer for a moment to let it rest upon General Ramcke. The paratroop commander had designs on those weapons, along with the body armor and assault rifles under development at Monovitz. Himmler met the man's gaze and held it, forcing the *Fallschirmjäger* to lower his eyes. The new SS special units would be receiving those items. They had been in training with the prototypes and mock-ups from the first day of the project.

He went back to staring impassively at Speer. The armaments minister spoke for another quarter hour, outlining the state of all the accelerated programs for which he was responsible. When he was finished, the führer dismissed him, along with all the other minor functionaries.

The room cleared quickly, until only four men remained besides Himmler and Oshima. The führer of course, *Reichsmarshall* Göring, Herr Doktor Göbbels, and Foreign Minister Ribbentrop, who was one of the few people besides Himmler who had come to enjoy even greater prestige and power since the Emergence. He had negotiated the cease-fire with Stalin, and Hitler considered it to be a master stroke. And more important, like Kaltenbrunner, he had died well in the other history.

Ribbentrop was the first Nazi to hang at Nuremberg, and he had gone out proclaiming his loyalty to the führer. Even Himmler could find no fault in that, although the man remained the most awful preening snob.

With the meeting reduced to the inner core of the Reich, Himmler opened the manila folder that contained his notes. Although he had become comfortable using a flexipad, he still preferred to rely on paper and ink in situations such as this one. It wouldn't do for his briefing to be marred by a misplaced data file or malfunctioning software. He didn't understand how this "Microsoft Corporation" could have become so dominant in *die andere Zeit*. He found their products to be annoying, and entirely unreliable.

"The Demidenko Project proceeds well," he began. "The Bolsheviks have committed enormous resources, and state that they are satisfied with progress, which of course, remains far behind the joint research we are carrying out with the Japanese government. Demidenko has allowed us to test much of the secret theoretical work we have undertaken without the Soviets' knowledge, and even the failures at the test site have proved invaluable in confirming the hypotheses of von Braun's group. While we consider it inevitable that the Politburo will have established their own rocket research, in violation of the cease-fire agreement, we can be confident they possess neither the technical resources nor the skills needed to match our combined efforts."

Oshima bowed his head slightly in acknowledgment.

"On current projections," he continued, "we will have a V-Three rocket capable of striking at all of the main Soviet production and population centers by late nineteen forty-three. Within a year after that, we should be able to launch from land-based systems against the East Coast of the USA. Although, they will have achieved a similar level of development with their own missile programs, and of course, their Manhattan Project should also have come to fruition by then."

Nobody in the room looked comfortable with the idea of an America that would be able to obliterate entire cities in Europe with just a single warhead.

"However," Himmler added, "we do not think they will be able to fit an atomic device onto a missile for some time yet—"

"What do you mean by *some time*?" Göring demanded. "Will it be nineteen forty-five, nineteen forty-six? When?"

The führer didn't slap down his *Luftwaffe* chief this time. Instead, he laid down the pencil with which he had been taking notes. "Yes, Heinrich. This is an important point," he said. "If we allow them to achieve a lead on us, Truman will not make the same mistake twice, assuming that he still succeeds the cripple. If he can develop the same superiority of atomic forces he enjoyed over the Communists in the early days of their Cold War, he will strike us without hesitation. He may even trade one or two of his own cities for all of ours. And if that pig Churchill is still alive, skulking around in exile, he will probably bomb his own countrymen rather than allow us to hold England."

Himmler listened in respectful silence. It was a reasonable question, even if it had been inspired by a very unreasonable and slightly drunken oaf like Göring.

"There are two things to note, *mein* führer. First, Churchill. I have a plan in hand to deal with him during Sea Dragon. I will come to that presently. Second, I must agree that the Americans *will* lead us in rocket technology. They gained a much greater bounty from the Emergence—thousands of personnel, many of them trained technicians, and a wealth of computing power within their ships that unfortunately we can but dream of. The files on the *Sutanto* and the *Nuku* are a very poor substitute. They had very restricted access to Kolhammer's Fleetnet, much of it at the level of the mundane and ridiculous.

"The French vessel has been a treasure trove, by comparison, but of course we have had her for less time, and the vast majority of her crew were uncooperative. Some of those who we'd thought cooperative at first, turned out to be working against us, and they even managed to accomplish quite significant acts of sabotage before they were caught and punished. I can only imagine what information has been lost to us because of that. Another saboteur nearly destroyed the entire vessel when we were removing the Lavals.

"But in executing them, of course, we killed the very men best able to teach us how to use the infinitely more complex devices on that ship. It is the devil's own dilemma."

He could see Göring twisting about like a man whose hide had shrunk in all the wrong places. The *Reichsmarshall* wore the burden of his failures heavily.

He still controlled the Luftwaffe, in a sense, but he was no longer free to determine its destiny. Whereas the German Air Force had once been his personal plaything, it was now simply a tool of the state. He retained his position simply because, of the three services, only the Luftwaffe had shown no evidence that it was a nest of vipers. In Himmler's eyes, loyalty without competence was hardly worth having, but he could understand the führer's need to keep a few of the old comrades around him.

And Göring was manageable, if increasingly irascible. As long as he had his wine and his estates, he could be tolerated. Nonetheless, Himmler spoke a little more forcefully to shut down whatever infantile protests were brewing in the fat toad's skull.

"The Americans have enjoyed other advantages. Their production and population base remains well beyond our reach, and they carry out their research without the handicap of having to do so in secret. We have been forced to maintain a false and deliberately impaired project at Demidenko to throw both the Soviets and the Allies off our trail."

Himmler was one of the few men in the Reich who could speak the blunt truth like this. The führer didn't look happy, but he always appreciated the *Reichsführer*'s refusal to overstate good news or downplay the bad.

He stared up at Himmler, his chin resting mournfully on his chest, his eyes pools of still darkness. "And so, to the counterstroke," said Hitler.

The SS chief nodded. "If we cannot yet defeat the Americans, we can delay the moment just long enough to secure our gains from them. They may well develop the means to destroy us a hundred times over, but we need only have the ability to destroy them once . . . and perhaps not even that. They remain a racially degenerate nation of criminals. They may be willing to lose Miami, for instance, in order to see us defeated. But would they be willing to see another five or six seaboard cities utterly destroyed? Can they live with the prospect of New York, Los Angeles, and San Francisco, all turned into melted glass? I doubt it."

"You aren't telling us anything we don't already know," said Göring. "We need *time*. Yamamoto said the same thing in June, when he presented his plan."

Himmler smiled. "But now I can tell you with certainty that it will work."

Only Oshima and Göbbels did not stir. Oshima already knew, of course, and the propaganda minister was a like a snake, which never moves until it is ready to strike.

"We have wasted a great deal of time and energy, because we did not believe it possible that slow neutron fission could cascade quickly enough to create an explosion," Himmler explained. "We have since learned that this is untrue. We have maintained production at the heavy water plant in Norway, and we are shipping that to Demidenko simply to mislead our enemies.

"In fact, we have shifted the main focus of our efforts into fast fission. For this it has been necessary to secure a supply of graphite uncontaminated by the boron electrodes we have traditionally used in commercial production. We have now secured ongoing supplies from Pargas in Finland, and the Oshirabetsu mine on Hokkaido, but we also took a considerable delivery from the Zavalie deposit in the Ukraine before pulling our forces back to Poland.

"Following this new line of enquiry and using the much more capable *undamaged* computing systems we stripped from the *Dessaix*, I can promise you that the Reich will be in possession of its first nuclear weapon by nineteen forty-five. And that the Soviet Union will cease to exist sometime in nineteen forty-six."

A buzz of excitement greeted the news. The führer's face lit up like the dawn of a new day. Even Göring looked happy.

"There is more to it, of course," said Himmler. "We must now strike at Churchill and secure control of the British Isles. We must bar the Americans from Europe. And Japan must also secure herself in the east. I will have more to add about that, in a few minutes. But I believe General Oshima has a few points to make first.

"Ambassador?"

General Oshima thanked the *Reichsführer* and stood to address the room.

They were a motley collection. Ever since the Emergence, these so-called supermen had indulged themselves in an orgy of self-doubt and preemptive revenge. There had been times since June when he thought that the Reich might just eat itself alive. Tokyo had seriously considered withholding some of the material that had been extracted from the Indonesian computers, simply because every newly translated historical file, no matter how anodyne, seemed to stoke the furnace of Nazi paranoia.

But the peculiar emergence of the *Dessaix* had made such considerations redundant. The French "stealth cruiser" had materialized off the northwestern coast of Africa near the Spanish naval base on the Canary Islands weeks *after* the appearance of Kolhammer's fleet at Midway. A U-boat, which had been secretly refueling there, was quickly sent to investigate the strange reports by Spanish fishermen who'd seen the vessel. With at least a quarter of the crew dead—another unexplained difference—and the rest unconscious as had been the case on the *Sutanto*, the vessel was easily captured. It made Oshima wonder what else might have come through from the future and remained undiscovered, or what might yet arrive.

The *Dessaix* had significantly altered the balance between the two principal Axis powers, leaving Japan reliant on the Reich to deal fairly with the changed circumstances. The ship was almost infinitely more powerful than the two Indonesian vessels that Japan had taken, but then her crew had proved to be much more difficult to manage. Only a handful had agreed to cooperate, and some of them had later been exposed as saboteurs and double-crossers. Removing the land-attack missiles from the ship and re-deploying them to Donzenac had been difficult enough without their inter-ference. The ambassador silently cursed the two-timing Frenchmen even as he stood to address the German leaders.

"Firstly, allow me to extend the thanks of the emperor. He is deeply grateful for the friendship and support of the Reich.

"As *Reichsführer* Himmler has pointed out, if we are to survive this war and correct our histories, we need to confine America behind her ocean walls long enough to develop the means of keeping her there. You will all have seen the news out of Australia. It looks grim, on the face of it, but I can assure you that apart from one or two tactical setbacks, events there proceed exactly as we had planned."

Göbbels, the master of the lie, raised an eyebrow. Oshima bowed in his direction and gave the propaganda minister a brief, knowing smile.

"In dealing with General Homma, we calculate that Kolhammer's land and sea forces in the Southwest Pacific have used up eighty percent of their war stocks. They appear to have overcome some logistical problems, such as fuel supply. But they simply cannot replace the missiles, or shells, or even the bullets they have expended. They do not have the factories to do so, even with the establishment of this Special Zone in California, or the smaller, less significant industrials efforts in the United Kingdom, Canada, New Zealand, and Australia."

General Oshima asked for the lights to be dimmed. He used a small, handheld controller to power up the tiny projector that sat at the end of the conference table. It was no bigger than a packet of cigarettes. Just one of hundreds of marvelous devices taken from the *Dessaix*, it projected a large, crystal-clear movie onto an old roll-down screen.

A computer-generated map of the world appeared. Himmler wondered if there would be a musical soundtrack. On the advice of Fräulein Riefen-stahl, he always had appropriate music composed for his own PowerPoint shows. It soon became apparent that Oshima did not.

The Japanese ambassador brought up four separate windows, showing maps of the English Channel, the Middle East, Hawaii, and the Southwest Pacific.

"You will be more familiar with your own preparations for Sea Dragon than I," he said. "So, too, with Operation *Grün* in the Middle East. With the departure of the *Clinton* for the West Coast of America, Operation H.I. is now under way."

World time clocks ticked away in all the relevant time zones.

"The *Dessaix* will be in position to launch her strike on the U.S. air and naval facilities in Hawaii within twelve hours," Oshima said as another window opened up, featuring video of the amazing French vessel. "Unfortunately, as *Reichsführer* Himmler pointed out, we will not be able to bring the full power of this ship to bear, because of the unwillingness of most of the crew to cooperate, and because of sabotage to some of the important systems by a handful of individuals who misled you into believing they were trustworthy."

Himmler had personally attended the punishment of those swine. The memory was still vivid enough to make him blanch.

"However," Oshima continued, "with the help of a few patriots among the crew, who have helped train enough of your men to form a skeleton crew, along with some of the Indonesian sailors we took off the *Sutanto*, and because of the *Dessaix*'s amazing ability to do so much herself, the grand admiral is confident of success.

"The first shots from Operation H.I. will land on the Americans in less than twelve hours. The Eighty-second Marine Expeditionary Unit in Australia will almost certainly be withdrawn to try to reclaim Hawaii. They may be accompanied by other elements of Kolhammer's Task Force in the Southwest Pacific, but they will have been significantly weakened by the fighting in Australia, and of course, the Australian government may not release any forces to help if they feel they themselves are still threatened."

The cgi window covering the Pacific theater inflated to twice its previous size. Rising sun flags appeared over the harbor of Rabaul in recently conquered New Guinea, and moved southwest, threatening the long, isolated and almost entirely undefended coast of Western Australia.

More flags designating Japanese air units appeared over New Guinea and sortied south, where animated bomb blasts popped up over the Australian cities of Darwin and Cairns. Cartoon parachutes descended on Darwin as landing barges traversed the gap between New Guinea and northern Australia, and larger forces established themselves around the small coastal town of Broome in Western Australia.

Some red arrows then pushed south toward Perth, while others moved inland, across the desert toward a flashing icon that everyone now recognized as the symbol for radioactive material.

"Significant deposits of easily mined uranium lie here and here," said

Oshima, twirling his laser pointer over the center of the Australian continent.

Before he could speak again, the führer interrupted him. "General," he said slowly. "I do not believe you have the capacity to carry out a successful invasion of Hawaii and Australia at the same time."

"No." The ambassador smiled. "We do not. But if the Allies can be misled into thinking that we will attempt a second, coordinated series of landings in Australia, their response to the attack on Hawaii will be affected, perhaps crippled. General Homma was instructed to use the most severe methods to subdue his conquered subjects in Australia. The government there will be loath to release any of their forces, contemporary or otherwise, to the Americans if they think another such campaign is imminent. The effect will be all the more profound, of course, if the Allies suspect we will make an attempt to seize those uranium deposits in the Australian desert. Even the Americans may balk at just handing those to us. The combination of factors might even be enough to tip the balance against an immediate mission to retake Hawaii, allowing Admiral Yamamoto to consolidate our hold there.

"I believe the *Reichsführer* has a plan in hand to help with this."

Oshima bowed slightly in Himmler's direction. They had worked this out between them weeks before.

Himmler nodded briefly. "The *Ausland SD* has successfully inserted a small number of agents into the United States."

An audible gasp sounded from around the table. The führer, who already knew the broad outlines of Himmler's plan merely gestured for him to continue. Oshima was just as keen to hear the details.

Himmler spoke from a handwritten note in front of him. "Three special agents have been in the U.S. for a month, preparing for their mission. They will receive their orders by secure channels just before the attack on Hawaii. They will bomb a number of targets on the East and West Coasts. Herr Göbbels will receive the transcript of a propaganda broadcast I wish him to make after the bombings. The effect will be to sow fear and uncertainty amongst the American populace, causing them to believe an attack on the mainland is imminent. It will further complicate any response to Hawaii."

"But how?" asked Göring with considerable bad grace. "You have never had any success at sabotaging their defense facilities before now."

Himmler smiled. "We won't be hitting airfields or naval bases. Their bombers have been targeting our civilian populace. Now, in a small way, our bombers will be targeting theirs."

"Excellent!" said Hitler, smashing his open palm down on the desk. "You are right, of course, Hermann. They are a degenerate race, and they won't be able to absorb punishment like our own *Volk*. Or even like the Britishers, I'll wager."

The führer chortled. "I shall look forward to hearing more of this when your plan comes to fruition. But now, Mr. Ambassador. Please return to your briefing."

Oshima bowed and worked the controller in his hand. On the screen behind him, the window displaying the Australian theater collapsed into the background, to be replaced by a display hovering over Hawaii, and another with a wider scan of the western Pacific. The latter contained two icons, one representing the *Dessaix* by itself, and another for the Combined Fleet, which was located some two hundred miles to the northwest.

"The force advancing on the Hawaiian Islands is somewhat smaller than the one originally slated for Operation M.I., the invasion of Midway," said Oshima. "But the presence of the *Dessaix* has made up for that. Again, the emperor sends his heartfelt thanks to the führer for his consideration in this matter. Without the help of the Reich, this operation simply could not proceed."

The führer shrugged, but he looked pleased. "This is a struggle for the world, and it must be fought all over the world," he said. "Your efforts in Hawaii over the next twenty-four hours will have a direct bearing on ours in the next week. The emperor has been more than accommodating of our prerogatives, acknowledging Germany's claim over New Guinea, and guaranteeing the security of the German settlers in South Australia. And with the Bolsheviks still holding the British and American ships at Murmansk, we can wait for the *Dessaix* to return."

The führer glowered at Göring before continuing.

"Our engineers have taken the critical systems which we need for Sea Dragon off her, anyway, and without the ability to replenish her rockets, the *Trident* is little more than a floating radar station. We shall deal with her in good time."

Oshima bowed. As he arose, his face was blank. He suspected an unspoken reason for the Germans' generosity was their calculation that a sucessful Japanese invasion of Hawaii would inevitably draw American power farther into the Pacific and away from Europe. The ambassador let none of these thoughts affect his expression. He was still waiting for Hitler to put the final piece of the puzzle in place.

The German leader took a moment to consider the dazzling array of images and data moving around on the old-fashioned movie screen.

"In three days, the tides and the weather will be right," Hitler said. "I shall order the High Command to surge our forces for Operation Sea Dragon. I am afraid that Speer will not have the two months he wants to build up further war stocks. The Luftwaffe will have to do what it can to protect the harbors. Two months would put us into winter, and the opportunity will be lost, probably forever.

"General Oshima, you may tell your superiors that we are with them . . . but, uhm, please use the secure lines."

22

BERLIN, GERMANY

To an educated man of humanist sympathies, Berlin was a perverse caricature of the city Müller knew. A fright mask drawn over a familiar face.

Nazi Germany was every bit as bad as the history teachers had said. A wasting of the soul had taken place here, and darkness had rushed in to fill the void. The fear was tactile and oppressive. It sat on everyone's shoulders like a giant crow, ready to pluck out their eyes if they should look the wrong way.

The SS was everywhere, too. As were the Gestapo. They made no attempt to disguise themselves, and terror surrounded them wherever they went.

Müller had developed painful stomach cramps and a permanent headache within two days of arriving. He was sure the entire nation, possibly all of Europe, felt the same way. He'd used his spinal inserts to dial back the pain, so distracting had it been.

The implants dispensed stimulants, painkillers, and a cocktail of pharmaceuticals to aid concentration, to sharpen the senses, and to control the physical manifestations of fear. He was familiar with the effects and the side effects. He had never known there was a spiritual dimension to fear, however. And there was no drug capable of counteracting its corrosive effect. The hammering pulse, the sweaty palms, and shaking limbs that might give him away in a random street encounter with the Gestapo—these could all be controlled by the pharmacological wonders of implant technology.

But it was beyond the ability of science to ameliorate the psychic pain of having to confront evil cast in his own image. The Germany through which he moved was both familiar and utterly alien. Its people were Nazis, and they loved Adolf Hitler as much as they feared his agents. He had seen the same thing in the next century in what had been North Korea, a sort of national Stockholm syndrome, where the hostage nation had come to love its captor.

His equipment was buried beneath his skin, some of it standard issue from the *Deutsche Marine*, some of it implanted when he began his two-year secondment to the U.S. Navy, and some of it new, fitted in Scotland at Kinlochmoidart. As he sat, drinking a foul-tasting ersatz *kaffee* across the square from his target, a biolocater and feedback chip in his neck maintained a constant link with one of the *Trident*'s high-orbit geostationary drones.

Müller observed the café without watching. He listened to the conversations without hearing. He had learned to filter out the useless residue of everyday life. He was a scanner, sweeping his immediate surrounds for mission-critical data, and not much else.

He lit another cigarette with his free hand. The other was encased in a fake plaster mold, suspended in a sling around his neck. It was part of his cover story; he was a fighter pilot, injured over England, his wrist shattered by a bullet chip, recuperating before shifting to a desk job. It induced a lot of sympathy.

Yes, he had agreed a hundred times, it was a great pity he would never get to fly the new planes they were building. Herr Göbbels says they will sweep the old tin cans of the British out of the skies.

Müller doubted that. The problems with the early German jet program were systemic and resource based. They couldn't be wished away just because you suddenly learned how to build a better ME 262.

The bell attached to the shop door jingled as a rotund man in a uniform entered, trailed by his fat son and equally stout wife. *Party members.* The husband had to be some minor functionary, although Müller had no idea of what ilk. The Nazis were crazy for uniforms. He'd seen dozens of different types since he'd infiltrated the city, most of them unidentifiable. This guy might have been the deputy leader of an *Ortsgruppe*, a small local party unit, or he might have been a Nazi strudel chef.

Possibly the latter, given his imposing frame.

The great oaf was barking like a seal about how much better this café was since it had been taken away from Zelig the Jew, and come to be run by Holz, the Bavarian. "It always smelled like the cream had gone off when Zelig was here."

Müller instantly killed the expression of distaste that wanted to crawl over his face. Two SD goons were sitting at the corner on the far side of the café, smoking cigarettes and spooning lumps of sugar into their cups. The sugar bowl on their table was full, the only one like it in the whole place.

The fat man's voluble beastliness grew louder and even more offensive as he spotted the security men. His dumpy Frau smiled at them, but her eyes were fixed and glassy, and she bustled their child away to a dark corner.

Müller didn't blame her. After the Jews and the gypsies and the cripples, it would only be so long before the fat kids went into the ovens.

He folded his copy of the *Völkischer Beobachter* with the banner where the Nazis could see it, pushed his chair back, and left, nodding briefly to one of the SD agents who caught his eye. One Aryan patriot to another. He looked like a man at ease with the world, a warrior at rest, and they ignored him.

Then Müller put them out of his mind. He had spotted his quarry leaving the apartment across the square. His hand wanted to caress the small pistol concealed under his jacket, but he gave no sign of it as he exited the shop. He fixed his eyes on the target.

Colonel Paul Brasch.

Brasch could hardly breathe by the time he reached his office in the Armaments Ministry. He couldn't swallow, and his heart threatened to burst out of his chest.

Today was the day. The orders for Sea Dragon had arrived by safe-hand courier—as almost all high-security communications did now, with at least two of the *Trident*'s Big Eye drones in stationary position above Europe at any given moment.

Now he had to make his choice. He told his secretary to hold his calls and shut the door behind him. There was nothing unusual about that. All over the Reich, functionaries like him were attending to their duties with increased determination. The next few days would decide the fate of Germany.

He'd noticed the diffuse energy on the streets as he walked to work. Nobody gossiped, not with the Gestapo and the SD everywhere. But he could tell that even in Berlin, hundreds of kilometers from the action, tens of thousands of men and women were to be involved in the attack on Britain. They walked a bit more briskly, kept their backs a little bit straighter, and that fanatic glint of the eye was just a touch madder.

Brasch looked just like them, but for a different reason.

He had been planning and preparing for this specific action for weeks, but in fact, the seeds of betrayal had been planted back in June, in his cramped, steamy cabin on the *Sutanto*, when he'd first read about the Holocaust. His fingers had felt cold and numb as he held the flexipad then, and a similar deadness affected them now. Indeed, whole patches of his body felt that way, as though he was already lingering in a Gestapo cell somewhere.

He hadn't felt so alive since the Eastern Front.

Outside of the marbled glass door that led to his office, he could hear phones ringing and messengers scuffing up and down the corridor. The building, always a hive of industry, was electric with excitement this morning. He had a dozen separate tasks to attend to, but most of them he'd done at home on his flexipad the previous evening. His eyes were hollow with sleeplessness and, he had to admit, with anxiety. Not so much for himself but for his family. Himmler had plowed unknowable numbers of new victims into the earth since the Emergence. A distant relationship with *anyone* who might be implicated in future acts of betrayal was enough to condemn whole branches of some families to the extermination camps.

Brasch let go a shuddering breath at the insanity.

He powered up the flexipad and brought an encrypted compressed file to the front of the little desktop screen. It had taken him a long time to work out how to do this, and even longer to work up the courage to go through with it.

He opened the software that he was certain would provide a link into Fleetnet, if a valid connection could be made. He keyed in the code Moertopo had given him back in Hashirajima, when they'd had made their pact by the light of the burning Japanese ships.

The result was unimpressive, but momentous. The pad chimed, making him jump. He had forgotten to mute the sound, but that was all right. He worked with the device every day.

The file disappeared from the out-tray, and security software wiped every trace of it from the lattice memory.

He couldn't help but glance out of his window, taped to protect against bomb blasts. The sky was completely blocked by low, dark gray clouds. If he had done this correctly, somewhere up there on the edge of space, a surveillance drone was already decoding his microburst package and pulsing it back to the smart-skin arrays of the *Trident*.

HMS *TRIDENT*, THE ENGLISH CHANNEL

It wasn't the first time the ship had played host to royalty. King William and his new wife had toured the stealth destroyer shortly after the ship was commissioned, but that had been an occasion of state, with pomp and circumstance as the order of the day.

The monarch's younger brother was much less disruptive, although word of his arrival still flew belowdecks with the speed of laser-linked gossip. He arrived with a Special Air Service squad and their Norwegian counterparts. Halabi, who knew the mood of her ship as well as she knew her own feelings, sensed that the excitement had more to do with having a Special Forces component on board again than it did with any celebrity aura that hung around Prince Harry.

The SAS and their commando guides pretty much kept to the Air Div hangars at the stern, where they laid out their equipment, checking and rechecking everything. Major Windsor appeared in Planning once, to request permission to load mission prep software into the *Trident*'s Combat Intelligence. The CI could render the mock-up of the heavy water plant with much greater detail than the field server they'd brought with them.

He was most amused to discover that the voice of the ship was a synthetic facsimile of Lady Beckham.

"I met them at the investiture," he told Halabi, smiling broadly at the memory. "She still looked smashing, but I thought poor old David had gone to seed quite badly. He never got over it when supercoach Johnny Warde dropped him from West Brom, did he?"

Halabi was almost unique in twenty-first century Britain, having zero interest in pop music, soccer, or celebrity gossip, so it took her a moment to catch up. "I suppose not," she conceded, without knowing exactly what he was talking about.

Harry quickly returned to the hangar to boot up the V3D mission sim, sparing her any further embarrassment, although she could tell the junior ratings thought she was a bit of a knob for not wanting to talk Posh and Becks with Harry.

When she'd first taken command of the *Trident*, she would probably have retreated into stiff dignity, but three years of constant action had loosened her corset strings, and she let a wry smile play over her features instead. "I'm sure His Royal Highness would like nothing more than to spend the whole day with you lot, plonking on about gormless rejects from the *Hello!* magazine celebrity Deathstar. But he's busy, and so are you. So get your heads down and your arses up, where I can kick them a little more easily."

The sailors returned to their workstations with only pro forma grumbles. They were busily plotting a course that would take them to their insertion point in the Skagerrak, when Halabi's intel boss pinged her on shipnet.

"Better come up to the CIC, Captain. We've got all sorts of things going on here. The birds are picking up indications of massive troop movements on the continent, and comms has detected an encrypted burst. Unscheduled, unauthorized. Completely outside parameters for any of the deep-cover skin jobs we're tracking."

"Sounds like we're game-on, then, Mr. Howard. I'll be there right away. Better set up a laser link connecting us to the Admiralty."

She acknowledged the message and left her ops coordinator to carry on with the mission plot, although she suspected that circumstances might have just cut short their cruise to the Norwegian Sea.

It was a short walk to the CIC, which sat in the *Trident*'s central hull. Sailors and officers bustled through the companionway, already alerted to the possibility of action. Footsteps padded along the composite decking at double time. The rude, northern brogue of her boat chief Dave Wadding-ton could be heard all the way over in the portside hull as he rousted a cou-ple of slackers. The ship herself thrummed as the engine room spooled up in readiness. Halabi listened with approval to the whirr of Metal Storm pods and laser packs deploying from their recessed silos.

Unfortunately the increased tempo also served to remind her of how naked the ship felt. Her offensive capabilities were almost played out. She reminded herself again that she had only six ship-killers and four antisub missiles left. Every station was occupied in the cool blue cavern of the CIC when she arrived. The huge battlespace monitors on the wall at the far side of the room told her that the waiting was over, even before her executive of-ficer arrived to confirm it. Dozens of e-tags on the computer map of Europe were in motion now. Data notes affixed to each tag scrolled through unit designations, capabilities, and the presumed role that unit would play in the coming invasion.

"They're surging," said the XO. "There's a lot of activity on the coast, in the ports, but mostly it's still inland, at least for now, as they're moving into position for the jump-off."

"Thank you, Mr. McTeale. Are we feeding this back to Admiralty?"

"Live and in color, without commercial breaks, ma'am."

"Whom do we have there interpreting for them?"

"Lieutenant Williams, Captain. He just got into London this morning, but he's had a few sessions up there already. They'll listen to him."

"Of course they will," she said. "He took a blue in beer drinking at Eton. Speaking of which, best ping Major Windsor and get him up here. I suspect his little jaunt is about to go wobbly."

"Aye, ma'am," said McTeale. "About that, there's this business of the data burst. I suggest you have a shufti in your ready room, Captain. It might be hot."

Halabi knew better than to second-guess her exec. "Okay. I'll make it quick.

"Mr. Howard," she called out to her intel chief. "You're with me. McTeale, I'll leave you here to keep an eye on all this. Ping me if any more nasty surprises develop. Have Major Windsor join me in the ready room."

"Aye, ma'am."

She spun out of the CIC with Lieutenant Howard in tow. They found the SAS officer waiting at her door with Lieutenant Poulsson, the Norwe-gian commando.

"What is happening, Captain?" asked Poulsson. "Has the invasion begun?"

"Pretty much so, Lieutenant. You'd best join us, too, I suppose. Is that all right, Mr. Howard?"

"Actually, I think Lieutenant Poulsson needs to see this, ma'am. It partly concerns his mission."

They squeezed into the small space, where a flat screen was already displaying some of the data burst that had arrived without warning. Halabi closed the sliding door behind them.

"So what am I looking at, Marc?"

"A rare bounty or a giant con, Skipper. It's a file dump. A big one. There are hundreds of subpackets I still haven't decompressed and decoded. Mostly they're in German, but there was one attachment in English. Here."

The intel boss brought up a simple text message:

Attention *Trident*. Attached you will find information detailing accelerated weapons programs of the Reich Armaments Ministry. Also, some details of Operation Sea Dragon, the early phases of which you will have now detected. Do not contact me. I shall contact you when possible.

"I see," said Halabi. "What's your first reaction Marc? Is it for real?"

Lieutenant Howard chewed his lip. "My gut feeling is yes, it's real. It's come in via a secure Fleetnet channel the Germans *probably* wouldn't know about. I haven't had time to check, but I think it's one of the subroutines we authorized for the *Sutanto*."

"Which the Japanese got."

"Right. And they stripped her. This guy has access to a pad, too. He's figured out how to use the secure links, or somebody's told him. There's no indication of who he is or why he'd do this, but anything's possible. Maybe he was a Rommel fan."

"They're all dead," said Harry.

"I am sorry," Poulsson interjected, "but where do we come in? You said there was something of relevance to our mission."

"My German isn't up to much beyond getting into trouble at Oktoberfest," said Howard, "but one of the highlighted files was this."

A new window jumped to the front of the screen.

"Holy shit," said Harry.

They all turned to him.

"*My* German is fine," he said, "And that's a document about the heavy water plant. Do you mind?"

He took a seat in front of the flatscreen and began to read, and then to scroll down.

"Oh, dear," he said after a minute.

"Major, would you like to share with the other children?" asked Halabi.

Harry turned around on the swivel chair. "If this is good," he said. "Telemark is a no-show. It's sitting there to distract us from a fast-fission program they've set up with the Japs."

"What does that mean?" asked Poulsson.

"Nothing good," said Captain Halabi.

A chime sounded from the monitor, and McTeale appeared in a pop-up window.

"We've got incoming, Captain. Jets again. About twelve of them, this time."

"Sound to general quarters," she ordered before turning to Harry and Poulsson. "Gentlemen, you should continue with your preparation, but I'm afraid I'm going to have to talk to London. I think everything just turned to shit."

Alarms began to blare throughout the ship.

23

PACIFIC THEATER OF OPERATIONS

None of them could be trusted. Hidaka was as sure of that as he was of anything.

The helmsman was probably the most reliable. He seemed a brute, and had become fast friends with some of the Nazis on board. The boy, Danton, looked like he would piss himself to death at the first fall of shot in the water. And Le Roux . . .

Hidaka sighed quietly. It was a difficult thing to accept, that the fate of the empire should rest in the greasy hands of such an ill-bred cretin.

As the magnificent warship known as the *Dessaix* sliced through the long, rolling swell of the Pacific, Hidaka did his best to contain the resentment that was burning in his gut as the slovenly chief petty officer lounged in the commander's chair and held forth about the glories of France.

Hidaka had come across a phrase in an English language journal that he thought better encapsulated the current position of France. *Cheese-eating surrender monkeys.*

"Do you find something funny, Commander?"

"I was just thinking of the look that will appear on Kolhammer's face in about half an hour," he lied.

"Uh-huh," grunted Le Roux, before barking something at Sublieutenant Danton in their native tongue. The boy flinched under the lash of harsh words.

Hidaka was long past being shocked by the lack of respect this oaf showed for his superior. Even though Le Roux was older and vastly more experienced than Danton, Hidaka thought him foolish for taunting the boy in such a fashion. The young man was far and away the most proficient officer on board.

Indeed, he had wondered what had motivated Danton to throw in his lot with Le Roux and the Germans, especially after hearing about the other crewmembers who had offered false allegiances, only to attempt to scuttle the ship at the first opportunity. But Le Roux had vouched for the boy, saying that he had a personal motivation of unquestioned validity. Two American marines had raped and murdered his sister.

The ship burst through the crest of a roller that was significantly bigger than the general run of the swell. Hidaka felt the floor tilt forward as they tipped over the summit and raced down the other side. The blue trough between the waves rushed up to fill the bridge's strip of blast windows. The *Dessaix* handled beautifully in these heavy conditions, steered by her Combat Intelligence, cryptically referred to as Melanie by the Frenchmen. Hidaka still remembered the embarrassment he had felt the first time he heard the ship "speak." He had nearly jumped out of his shoes, unleashing great mirth amongst the Europeans, and even some of the Indonesian sailors.

Danton said something, and Le Roux nodded.

"It is time to get below," he said to Hidaka.

The *Sutanto* had not been run by a Combat Information Center. It had been piloted by men on a bridge, like the ships Hidaka was familiar with.

But he knew the path of life had taken him somewhere very special the first time he'd set foot in the stealth destroyer's CIC. It seemed as if you could control the whole world from in here. There were more glowing screens, of greater size, and computers of infinitely greater complexity in this one room than they'd been able to salvage from both of the Indonesian vessels put together. Even after the Germans had stripped the *Dessaix* to her bare bones for this mission, she remained a wonder.

Again, Hidaka could only mourn the opportunity that had been lost. If this ship had remained undamaged, fully armed, and properly crewed, they would have wielded enough power to lay waste to Hawaii, and then to Los Angeles, and all of Australia and the southern Pacific. Such a great pity.

The Germans and a few Indonesians sat at those workstations that had been left behind. Hidaka had almost no idea of what they were doing, although Le Roux had indicated that their role was ancillary. Melanie, the Combat Intelligence, would launch and control the attack, with Sublieutenant Danton designating the targets. Because they had no satellite cover, or technicians qualified to control a surveillance drone, the CI had been programmed with targeting sequences referenced from her own holomap inventory.

"The Honolulu harbor, she does not move around, no? The airfields of my day, they exist in yours, yes?" Le Roux explained. "So we program the missiles to strike at them as Melanie knows them. It's not perfect, but it does not matter. The targets will be destroyed."

Hidaka and a few of the *Kriegsmarine* officers had watched as Sub-Lieutenant Danton brought up amazing, almost three-dimensional images of a Pearl Harbor and Honolulu that would never exist, the island as it would have been.

The young man's fingers danced across a keyboard. He used a light pen to move strange icons and data tags around the massive panel display. After twenty minutes, it was done. He spoke to Le Roux, who translated for Hidaka. The Germans all spoke French.

"We have designated the Fleet Base at Pearl as a wide-area target box," said Le Roux. "The missiles will travel there, then seek out targets using their own sensors. They will be drawn to dense concentrations of metal. Others will home in on the signature of the Americans' radar installations. Still others will deliver area-denial munitions to the airfields. It will be very messy, I'm afraid. If we had the satellite cover and a few nukes, it would be much easier."

"How will they know where to go?" asked Hidaka. "The Allies always position their spy drones above their targets."

Le Roux rolled his eyes. "Over there, Commander, look. That *Boche* officer is working at the navigation console. We have no GPS fix, but we still know where we are, partly because he is a trained navigator and can tell us, but also because the Americans have placed locator beacons at fixed positions such as Midway, to help them navigate. Those beacons emit their signal, so we can receive them without using an active array to seek the position fix. You understand? Melanie knows where she is in relation to the targets, so she can give them directions? Yes?"

Hidaka was glad that most of the men in the center didn't speak English.

He had never been treated in such a dismissive fashion. Le Roux spoke to him as if he were a slow child, and took a cruel and obvious pleasure in doing so.

A slow, dull, throbbing pain built up behind Hidaka's eyeballs, as he resisted the urge to cut this brute down. Even so, it was a lucky thing his sword was not close at hand. "Chief Petty Officer Le Roux," he said, slowly and quietly, "you forget yourself. You can no more captain this ship than I. You are a simple *mechanic.*"

Hidaka loaded the word with as much contempt as he could muster, and he leaned forward.

"I hope your confidence in your own abilities does not prove to be misplaced. You would not want to disappoint your new masters, I think. They are no more forgiving of failure than I."

Le Roux couldn't help flicking a quick glance at the Germans. The tip of his tongue darted out to lick at dry, cracked lips. A nervous laugh slipped the leash, and escaped from within him. "We won't fuck it up," he promised. But all of a sudden, he didn't sound so sure.

Sub-Lieutenant Philippe Danton hoped that nobody would see how much his hands were shaking. But then, even if they did, they would presume that it was because he was a coward. *Half a man.*

While that pig Le Roux argued with Hidaka, Danton found himself praying that they would come to blows and kill each other. A serious confrontation had been brewing between them from the moment the Japanese had come aboard, in the Southern Ocean.

As they snapped at each other, he told Kruger, one of the Germans, that the CI was asking him to recheck and reenter some of the data.

"Why?"

"She has checked her holomaps and thinks the coordinates should be refined," he said. "See, the airfields at Hickham and Wheeler are much smaller in nineteen forty-two than they will be in twenty twenty-one. Melanie thinks the missiles are likely to land outside of the new target box."

Kruger watched a computer illustration that showed six Laval missiles slamming into empty cane fields. "Ah, I see, yes. Best we correct then. Good work, Lieutenant. I shall tell Le Roux."

Danton snorted in amusement. "Good luck. He doesn't like to be told he is wrong."

Kruger took in the scene of the Japanese commander and the French *premier maître*, arguing over by the weather station.

"No, he doesn't," Kruger agreed. "You had best see to it, then."

"Yes, sir," Danton replied, calling up a window he'd opened earlier, and immediately shuffled to the back of the desktop.

He typed quickly now, trying to appear calm and relaxed, even though he felt like passing out from terror. He shot a quick glance in Le Roux's direction. Hidaka had leaned in close and appeared to be threatening him.

Please, let them keep fighting.

He reprogrammed the weapons in the forward bays. Another window opened up. He reprogrammed the bays amidships.

Hidaka and Le Roux became ominously silent. He tried to catch sight of them in the reflection on his monitor, but the CIC was too dark for that. He forced himself to look bored, like a process worker on the production line at the end of the day. He made a show of stretching his neck to work out a cramp.

Hidaka was stalking away, and Le Roux was about to return.

Damn.

He was out of time. Two key clicks shut down the targeting windows. He'd reset half the missile bays, but the rest were still programmed as Le Roux had wanted them. Except for the last two bays. Those missiles had already been taken off the ship. That still left plenty of punch, though. Twelve subfusion plasma-yield Laval cruise missiles.

He had failed.

He took out the photograph of his sister that he kept in a breast pocket. "I'm sorry, Monique," he whispered.

Le Roux's coarse bark sounded right behind him, making him jump. "Don't cry for her now, boy. She'll have her revenge soon enough, eh?"

"I hope so," said Philippe Danton. He wanted more than anything to kill Le Roux at that moment.

A marine had not raped his sister. In fact, she had married a marine she met in Lebanon, when she had been working there for Médecins Sans Frontiéres. She had loved him, but she had lost him forever.

His name was J. "Lonesome" Jones.

It would be good to get home. They were running low on frozen brioche.

Still, he wouldn't want to miss this for the world. Le Roux wished they had satellite cover, or even a drone. The vision they took from the small cams in the nose of the Lavals was nowhere near adequate. Even with the CI cleaning up the image, it still shook so much that watching for too long was liable to make you feel ill.

He occupied *Capitaine* Goscinny's old chair, and from there he could survey the entire Combat Information Center. The trained apes Hidaka had brought along were proving themselves fast learners. They couldn't match the original crew, of course, but they could be trusted to keep the ship running at a basic level. And the Germans were quite impressive. He couldn't rely on them in combat, but the navigator was good, and the others had adapted to their various roles with great enthusiasm. Within a year, they might just make decent replacements for those idiots rotting in the cells back in Lyon.

Melanie began the ten-second countdown. Even Hidaka, who spoke no French, could tell immediately what was going on. He stood as still as the pitch and yaw of the vessel allowed, and watched the main panel display, which carried vision of the silos on the forward decks.

"Quatre, trois, deux, un . . ."

Le Roux's balls climbed up inside his body as the first salvos soared free. The whole vessel shuddered as the brand-new, French-designed multipurpose missiles scorched away, their scram jets engaging after a less than a minute. Sonic booms reached them through the hull as the atmosphere was ruptured by the passage of the Lavals.

"Sacre merde."

It was done. There was no calling them back now. He wasn't even sure Danton could destroy them in flight, if he had to. Suddenly a flash of blind panic seized him, before subsiding just as quickly. "These will destroy the American's radar stations and, I think, Hickham air base," he said loudly, for the benefit of the others. "Is that correct, Danton?"

"Oui," the surly young man replied.

"Can we see the movies from the missiles themselves?" asked Hidaka.

"Danton?" Le Roux called out.

The sysop blushed and began to fiddle with his station settings. Le Roux rolled his eyes. Hidaka and the Germans waited impatiently. After a minute, the krauts began to mutter among themselves, when the boy was unable to bring up any vision.

"Oh, for fuck's sake," said the chief petty officer. "Let me do it."

As he pushed himself up out of the commander's chair, Danton blanched visibly. He was probably expecting another thrashing, but Le Roux merely pulled him out of his chair as the ship pitched down a large wave. Danton fell heavily into the met station.

Le Roux chuckled at the sight of the young officer's distress. "Fucking four years at the Sorbonne," he said to Hidaka, "And he still can't use a fucking mouse."

As Air Division maintenance chief, Le Roux was intimately familiar with the cam systems on the ship's Eurotigers. The same software controlled the cams in the nose of the Laval missiles. A few clicks, a bit of typing, and the feed was live.

Four windows displayed a blur of indigo as the weapons ripped across the ocean at Mach 5.

"How long?" asked Hidaka.

"Not long at all," said Le Roux.

He hadn't counted on this. He'd hoped he could stall them on the cam feed, perhaps even fob them off altogether. But of course, Le Roux *would* be able to operate that subsystem. He worked with it all the time on the Tigers.

Danton cursed himself as the ship quaked with the second launch. Le Roux was boasting that this salvo would destroy all the major army air bases on the island. But Danton wasn't so sure of that. He'd got to at least half those missiles. He hadn't had enough time to render them completely safe, though. They were going to land somewhere, and do a huge amount of damage. But at least it wouldn't be where the fascists wanted them.

Not all of them, anyway.

As he struggled to his feet in the deepening swell, he found that he was no longer scared. He had made his decision, and knew he was going to die in the next couple of minutes. There was no changing that now. All that mattered was how he went out.

He hadn't been able to hide proof of his interference. When the Lavals began to drop into clear sea and empty fields, they would know what he had done. There was nothing for it. He would have to try destroying the missiles in flight.

The third and final launch roared away as he calmly took in the scene. A couple of Indonesians were watching the cam footage rather than tending to the met station. Hidaka looked as if he might be about to levitate, he was so excited. The Germans were babbling. And Le Roux was bullshitting to anyone who would listen.

It would be only a few minutes until he was discovered. So he made the sign of the cross and said one Hail Mary—apologizing to God for having to whisper—for the lives he could not save, for those he was about to take, and most of all for a steady hand and a good aim. If he wanted to destroy those missiles, he would have to kill everyone in this room first.

". . . Holy Mary, mother of God, pray for us sinners, now, and in the hour of our death. Amen."

"What's that boy? What the—"

Danton smiled at Le Roux over the sight of a Metal Storm VLe 24 he'd smuggled in. Operating on exactly the same principle as the Close-In Weapons System that protected the *Dessaix* from missile swarms, the pistol had no moving parts. The ceramic rounds were stacked in-line in three barrels, hence the three muzzles into which Le Roux's horrified eyes now stared. An electronically fired propellant separated each bullet. The gun could discharge the entire load in one simultaneous burst. Or it could be set to fire single shots. Or three round volleys, as it was now.

"—*hell?*" said the chief petty officer, beginning to drop to his knees, to beg for his life.

Danton squeezed the trigger.

Le Roux's descent meant that the burst took off the top half of his head, rather than all of it. But the end result was the same. The multiple shots sounded like a single discharge. The impact of three ceramic bullets on the traitor's skull was dramatic. It popped open like a rotten piece fruit, the kinetic energy knocking the pig off his feet with enough power to spin the bloated body through the air. Blood, bone chips, and brain frappé splashed across the ceiling.

He flicked the selector to single-shot and began to work the room. Kruger took a round just below the ear. The compressed nanoshards unfurled inside his brainpan and blew out the other side of his head. Danton hadn't minded Kruger, and wanted to spare him any sense of violation and betrayal.

The others were just Nazis, and he calmly put a round into each as they scrambled for their own weapons. The bullets were advertised as one-shot/one-kill, and they worked mostly as advertised. A German lieutenant lost an arm at the shoulder, but the shock wave traveled into his body and killed him a few seconds later. The flat, hollow, painfully loud report of the 24 boomed out again and again.

Danton thought of nothing as he went about his killing. At night, in his cabin, he had always imagined that if it had come to this, he would think of himself as an avenging angel, meting out justice on behalf of his crewmates back in Lyon. Especially on behalf of his best friend, Dominic, who had been caught erasing files and was strangled to death in front of them all.

But now that the moment had arrived, he felt nothing. The carnage around him slowed down, as though he had thumbed the half-speed function on a video stick. His head was light and strange. Everything appeared slightly flat to him.

Someone was firing back at him. A monitor exploded by the side of this head, but it might just as well have been a mile away. A German rushed at him with a chair raised like an unwieldy shield, though he seemed less real than a character in a V3D game like Halo VII.

He fired twice into the backrest, knocking the man to the floor, where the laser designator found him and marked a spot in the center of his body mass. But there was no need. The rounds had begun to unfurl as soon as they hit the chair, but they passed through with enough integrity and velocity to turn his chest into a sucking crater. He was already dead.

As the odds improved, he began to wonder if he might somehow survive. Kill them all, destroy the missiles, and become a hero. He died with that happy thought on his mind.

Hidaka emptied the entire clip of the Luger into the prostrate form of Sub-Lieutenant Danton. The body jumped with each impact, blood already leaking from the first shots he'd pumped into the treacherous dog.

He was speechless with rage that the Germans could have let yet another conspirator slip past their guard. After all of the trouble they'd had with saboteurs and turncoats among the original crew. They should not have been blinded by the familiar extremism of Le Roux. These people weren't to be trusted.

He stumbled against the body of the corpulent chief petty officer. Everything above his nose was gone, as though a shark had clamped its jaws around the top of his head and ripped it away.

Hidaka noticed that he was shaking. Shrugging it off, he kicked Danton's body, but there was no life in there. Only two others had survived in the room, both of them Indonesians who had dived under their consoles. He felt like shooting them, as well, but controlled the urge.

Sparks and flames crackled around him from damaged equipment. In just a few seconds the boy had—

Hidaka cursed and spun around, almost slipping in the fluids that were pooling beneath his boots.

He rushed back to the station where Danton had been working, but the dense mosaic of windows and boxes on the screen meant nothing to him. He yelled at the Indonesians, ordering them to help him, but they were both in shock, too terrified to be of any help.

His heart pounding, he turned instead to the massive flat panel display. Sixteen windows displayed a feed from the nose-cams of the Laval cruise missiles as they screamed in toward Hawaii. The cobalt blur of open sea was the only image in twelve of the windows. But four showed land, buildings, aircraft, and vehicles all rushing to fill the screen.

Hidaka wanted to beat the display with his fists.

He couldn't tell what was happening. It was all too quick.

24

Rosanna Natoli had decided that it just wasn't going to work out with Lieutenant Wally Curtis.

He was sweet and all. Just about the sweetest boy she'd ever met, in fact. But that's exactly what he was—a boy, not a man. He didn't excite, or intrigue, or even annoy her. He didn't even try to seduce her. He'd moved firmly into the friend zone.

But he wasn't very likely to understand that. They didn't seem to have much of a friend zone here in 1942. Meeting somebody for a drink or a bite to eat seemed to imply you were going steady, or keeping company, or something. Her mother would have approved. She, however, wasn't so sure.

She swirled the dregs of her beer and let the pang of homesickness slide on past. She desperately missed her mom, but she was never going to see her again, and unlike so many of the uptimers, she had a large established family she could run to, even if her great-aunts and -uncles and great-grandparents were younger than her now. And of course, there were her earlier forebears, most of whom she had known only through family legend. Here they were in their prime.

Her eyes began to well up as she thought of them. When she'd gone to New York to visit, they'd practically smothered her with their crazy love. She'd always thought of her mom and dad as freakazoid ethnic wannabes, what with all of the public hugging and kissing and haranguing. Turns out, she hadn't known the half of it.

At the moment, she and Curtis were perched at a quiet bar on Diamond Head Road, overlooking the beach, a few miles from Pearl. It wasn't a twenty-first joint, so it remained segregated. But the management had made a few half-assed attempts at drawing some customers from the *Clinton*'s battle group. The jukebox had been restocked with an MOR selection of "golden newbies," as the hits of the future were known. Buffalo wings, satay sticks, and curly fries had crept onto the menu, but Rosanna didn't recognize them when they appeared with her beer.

The beer was a giveaway, too. She didn't drink it much, preferring a dry Californian white if she could get one, but that wasn't the sort of thing they stocked in a joint like this.

The bar was about half-full, mostly with off-duty military types. She was one of the few women, and certainly the only civilian woman in the place. Her white cotton pants, linen shirt, and fuck-me boots weren't endearing her to her fellow femmes, either. She could sympathize with them, having to wear those dowdy 'temp uniforms, but it was hardly her fault.

She wouldn't normally stray into a place like this, but Curtis was on a short leash, and had to get back to his office. He had a new job writing training manuals for 'temps who were posted to twenty-first units. It bored him witless, and he was just marking time until his request for a transfer to the Zone came through. He'd passed the prelims for flight training and was hell-bent to fly jets when they came online. In fact, it was all he could talk about. Rosanna's eyes glazed over as he squirreled on about the new F-86.

". . . . and they're building them with ejector seats and drop tanks. They even reckon they'll have heat seekers ready by the time the first squadrons are . . ."

Rosanna just said, "Uh-hm," and gazed out over the sea. The best thing about this skanky bar was the view. It went on for about a thousand miles, and on a clear day you'd think you could see China if you stood on your chair and squinted. Nodding and smiling and throwing in the occasional comment—*Oh wow, really? That's amazing!*—just to show that she was still actively listening. Really, though, she was just breathing in the fresh air and trying not to let the sun make her too drowsy.

She had a couple of hours of video from Julia to edit that afternoon, for telerecording onto film. They'd cut a deal with Movietone for a one-hour newsreel on MacArthur's Brisbane Line. Rosanna had been worried that they'd end up having to make some tragic fucking forties period piece, complete with a patronizing voice-over and racist stereotyping. But the Movietone guys had been surprisingly cool.

They'd—

She was probably the first one in the bar to see it coming. Her Mambo sunblades completely nixed the glare of the day. A micron-thin layer of polychromatic film in the lens gave her sharper vision than a healthy eagle. First she saw the shock wave blasting across the calm bowl of the ocean, out near the horizon.

"Shit!" she cried out, jumping off her stool and knocking it to the floor. "Get down! *Everyone get the fuck down now! Incoming!*"

She dropped to the floor, pulling Curtis down with her, yelling at him to breathe out, close his eyes, and plug his ears.

"But why—"

"*Just do it!*"

At Mach 5, the pressure wave generated by the Laval swarm could have

demolished the palm-frond-and-bamboo-trunk structure, and killed everyone inside. But the missiles flashed on past, crossing the coast a few miles
away as they headed inland. The sonic boom was still severe enough to
shred the eardrums of everyone who hadn't taken her advice, and even she
could hardly hear the screams of the other patrons thanks to the ringing in
her ears.

Once she was sure the missiles were gone, she grabbed Curtis by the collar of his shirt and dragged him to his feet. "Come on!" she shouted. "We've
got to get going."

Curtis was moving his jaw and slowly squeezing his eyes open and shut.
He had no idea what had just happened. "Did we get bombed again? Did
they come back?"

"Not exactly, Curtis. But you're a lucky guy. I'll bet those missiles are
heading for Pearl."

Then the ground shook with the force of a volcanic event. The sound
rolled over them, like that of a planet cracking open.

"I've got to get back to the base," Curtis cried out.

"Don't bother," said Rosanna. "It's not there anymore."

PACIFIC THEATER OF OPERATIONS

"Hurry up, faster—*schnell, schnell.*"

Hidaka had no idea whether the helmsman, the sole surviving Frenchman on board, understood him or knew what he was doing. The giant barbarian had sworn up a storm when he'd rushed into the CIC.

Three Indonesians and a German lieutenant commander followed on
his heels, all of them pulling up sharply at the sight of the killing room. The
Nazi spoke a little English. Just enough to infuriate Hidaka as he tried to explain that he wanted to slow down the movies from the missiles.

They'd pushed the helmsman into Danton's old seat and the German,
whose name tag identified him as Bremmer, relayed instruction in French.
It might have been laughable, if the fate of the world weren't hanging in the
balance.

The two Europeans bickered and sniped at each other. More of the
screens blinked over to white noise as the missiles detonated. And still
Hidaka couldn't tell whether Danton had interfered with the attack before
attempting to murder them all.

The helmsman directed a spray of unintelligible abuse at Bremmer before waving his arms at the main display. Hidaka's mood went through a
swooping series of dives and loops as he saw that the replays were running

much more slowly, and that some of the missiles seemed to do exactly as they ought. But others appeared to drive themselves into the sides of mountains or open fields.

"Again, *again*," he demanded.

Bremmer relayed the instructions, and the movie was rewound—no, *re-played*, as he corrected himself.

Keeping a much tighter leash on his emotions, this time he was able to see that about half the missiles had gone off course, but not always to ill effect. One that had been heading for the wreck of the *Arizona*, possibly drawn by its magnetic signature, suddenly veered away and dived on a cruiser, one he didn't recognize. Hidaka couldn't tell what sort of damage was done, but unless Danton had somehow defused the warheads, it still would be considerable.

On other screens, airfields and army barracks were certainly hit. But he counted five windows in which nothing—absolutely nothing—of value seemed to have been targeted. One rocket appeared to land on the beach in front of a hotel. He could only hope that a large number of officers were staying there.

His stomach had knotted itself so tightly, he wanted to be sick. But he would not give in to the convulsions that were trying to force his breakfast back up. He took a deep breath, ignoring the sickly sweet, rancid smell of death. This was going to take a while to work out. But he was supposed to signal Yamamoto the instant they had launched. The grand admiral would already be wondering what had happened.

"Play it again," he said. "Slowly."

OAHU, HAWAII

Good luck and bad habits saved Detective Lou "Buster" Cherry. While he'd been on suspension, he'd taken to calling in at a couple of Big Itchy's bars for a liquid lunch—on the house, of course. He often stayed on for dinner, making selections from the same menu. Even after the Bureau had pulled a few strings to get him back his badge and gun, it was a routine he'd been unable—or unwilling—to break.

So noon found him at one of Itchy's new joints, a place called Irish Mike's, where they had those tasty fucking Buffalo wings he loved so much. Apart from beer and whiskey, there was probably nothing else in his bloodstream now. Except nicotine. And he seemed to recall having a doughnut for breakfast sometime last week.

He'd parked himself in the corner of the bar, where he could watch his subjects, some four-eyed Myron and his greasy girl. He wasn't supposed to pick them up until later, to learn whether they slept together. But after a couple of days on their trail, he'd come to know their routine. Chances were they'd end up at Mike's for lunch, which gave him every reason to be at Mike's, too—perhaps even to get there a little early, to set up a comfy surveillance position and to work on his bent elbow. Mike, who was Maori rather than Irish, and whose name was Tui rather than Mike—well, he didn't like customers who wouldn't bend elbow with the best of them.

And Buster Cherry was fine with that.

He licked the spice from his fingers and took a long, cold pull on his beer. A Bud. Not his favorite, but times were tough all over. He stared at the table next to his targets, watching some flyboy and his squeeze, a nurse from over at Pearl. That way he could keep his eyes on Myron and the broad without being so obvious about it. Besides, the nurse had bazongas out to Wednesday, and half the mutts in the joint were staring at them, so it was a good cover.

You could tell Myron's piece of ass was twenty-first, dressed as she was, although he didn't need to be Sherlock Holmes on that score. The feebs had given him some paper on her, and told him to get more. She was a reporter, name of Natoli, and a looker, too, if your tastes ran to foreign ass.

He could tell that Myron—actually, some gimp called Wally Curtis—was boring her silly, which wasn't surprising. The kid was boring him, too, and he couldn't even hear them over the jukebox playing some shit piece of nigger music from the future. The seventies, it sounded like. He was getting better at picking the era. This particular tar boy thought Buster was a "sexy thing" and he really believed in "Milko," whatever the hell that meant. He'd take Glenn Miller or Bing Crosby any day—no matter what they were saying about Bing.

Detective Cherry had just come to the conclusion that he'd grievously miscalculated the amount of beer he'd need to see off the rest of his Buffalo wings when Natoli started screaming at everyone to get down. Nearly twenty years on the job, he didn't need to hear it twice. That broad moved like she knew a thing or two. He was halfway to the floor, frantically scanning the room for a shooter, reaching for his own piece, when he saw that both she and her boyfriend were under the table, thumbs jammed in their ears, mouths wide open like they were fixing to swap spit or something.

It took a second, but he suddenly caught on.

Must be a bomb.

He got his own ears covered and was emptying his lungs when a cataclysmic roar shook the floor, the bar, the whole of fucking Diamond Head.

It was so violent and lasted so long that Cherry thought it might just shake them off the side of the island and down into the sea.

When he was a little kid on the mainland, his old man had taken him up in a clock tower to hear the bell toll twelve. He'd started screaming at the first gong, at the size of it, and the feeling of his insides being shook to jelly. He was back there for a few seconds, until the monstrous rolling thunder trailed off and the sound of a screaming woman cut through the high-pitched whine he just knew he was gonna be hearing all day.

He felt tender inside. Not just his head, which always felt that way, but everywhere, like he was some sort of human fucking cocktail shaker and he'd just made up a couple of hundred daiquiris.

The bar wasn't nearly as badly fucked up as he expected. He'd thought a bomb might have gone off, but apart from a lot of broken glass and some upturned furniture that'd been knocked over by the patrons, there was remarkably little damage. A lot of people were wailing in pain, though, holding their hands over their ears. But there was none of the grotesque carnage he'd witnessed after the Jap attack last December. No severed limbs or chunks of meat hanging from the trees.

He caught sight of Natoli and Curtis busting out of the front door, and he chased after them without thinking about it.

For such a dive, Irish Mike's poorly named bar was superbly located. As soon as he stepped outside and his eyes adjusted to the fierce sunlight, he had a panoramic view back along Waikiki toward the harbor. An enormous cloud, looking just like a big mushroom, had swallowed up half of Honolulu. His balls contracted, and ice water filled his gut. He'd heard about those fucking things. They were bad fucking news. Even the cloud could kill you if you breathed it in or let it touch you.

Nevertheless, he was nailed to the spot, completely unable to move. The whole island seemed to be covered in twisting clouds of smoke. Pearl, Hickham, Schofield Barracks—they were all lost inside the firestorms.

But strangely enough, so were the mountains in the center of the island. And something had obviously exploded with great force a mile or so off Waikiki, where there was nothing but empty water.

"Hey, are you a police officer?"

At first he didn't realize they were talking to him.

"*Hey*, you there, are you a cop?"

Cherry looked up stupidly. His targets were walking toward him. He followed their eyes, looking down and seeing his .38 growing out of his hand like a blue metal tumor. It was so much a part of him that he'd forgotten about pulling it.

"Uh, yeah," he said, knowing that his surveillance was over, if not exactly blown.

"You got a radio? In your car?" Natoli asked. "You still got your car, right? You've been following us in that piece of shit for three days now?"

Blown, all right.

"What? Huh? Oh, yeah. Over there." He waved his gun in the general direction of the car.

"The black Dodge, I know. Do you have a radio?"

"Why?" He couldn't get his brain out of first gear.

"Just come on," said the broad. She raised a dust trail, she moved so quickly. When she reached the Dodge, she wrenched open the door with a yank.

"Hey, you can't do that!" he protested, starting to get his senses back at last. The sound of three gigantic eruptions reached them from the burning maelstrom of Pearl Harbor. He looked away from Natoli and Curtis, but he couldn't see a thing through the smoke.

"Secondary blasts," he said to himself, musing that only a cruiser or a battleship going up would sound like that. He saw the gimp playing with his police radio, and then with the car's own set.

"Get the hell outta there," he called out.

They emerged from the front of the Dodge, but not because of him.

"It's fried," said Curtis. "EMP."

"What?"

"Electromagnetic pulse. Every piece of wiring on the island is probably fused."

"Oh," said Cherry. "That's bad, right?"

PACIFIC THEATER OF OPERATIONS

It wasn't nearly as disastrous as he had feared. Hidaka had watched the footage over and over again. It seemed that Danton had got to the entire opening salvo. One missile had fallen into the ocean and two more had speared uselessly into a mountain range. But one that had been meant to land on Ford Island had instead devastated Honolulu. Half of the city was probably gone, according to the helmsman.

Of the second launch series, only one had been wasted, flying right over the Fleet anchorage and continuing on for another two hundred miles before dropping into the water. The other Lavals had all found their intended marks, or hit near enough as made no difference.

He turned away from the display to take in the slaughterhouse that was the *Dessaix*'s Combat Information Center. There had been no time to clean up yet. The dead lay where they had fallen. This was a disaster, but his attack was not, and the next phase of Operation H.I. could proceed.

Hidaka asked Bremmer to organize the Indonesians to police the mess. Then he moved over to the communications station. This, at least, he had been trained to operate, if only on the most simplistic level. As he opened a secure channel to send a compressed burst to Yamamoto, he wondered how best to present what had happened.

There was no point in avoiding the truth.

He began to type.

Dessaix has launched successfully. Some missiles sabotaged, but strike unaffected. Proceed to next phase. tora. tora. tora.

He read the brief note. There would be a torrent of questions from the Combined Fleet, but Yamamoto knew what he needed to know.

The Hawaiian Islands were defenseless, and awaited the killing stroke.

25

MIAMI, FLORIDA

It had been his idea to come down to Miami early this year. Washington was hell, what with everyone staring at them like circus freaks, and Roosevelt was playing both ends against the middle. Hoover hardly knew where he stood nowadays. Under those circumstances, and with a gloomy winter in the offing, a week or two at the Gulfstream had proved irresistible.

They would normally have traveled across the country to vacation in Southern California, for the racing at Del Mar, but he simply couldn't stand the idea of setting foot on the West Coast again, as long as that power-mad German Jew was running wild out there.

It's a pity, he thought as he snugged the silk kimono around his sturdy frame. They always made him feel so welcome in La Jolla. He and Clyde had first refusal on Bungalow A at the Del Charro, where the management ensured that everything was perfect. He always had direct phone lines to Washington; three ceiling fans, because he hated what the air-conditioning did to his sensitive skin; new bulbs in every lamp and light socket; two rolls of scotch tape; a basket of fresh fruit; and a bottle of Jack Daniel's for himself and Haig & Haig for Clyde—gift-wrapped, of course.

The Gulfstream, down in Miami, was fine, too. Staying there meant being able to use his complimentary box at Hileah whenever there was a race. But it wasn't his first choice, and J. Edgar Hoover was used to getting his way.

"Oh, Clyde," he said irritably, "go put on the gown I bought for you. You look a terrible sight in your socks and boxers."

Tolson was barely speaking to him after the argument they'd had at the track, earlier that day. Hoover was certain that Clyde had been flirting with one of the models who was hanging out with Lewis Rosenstiel, calling her "dearie" and "darling" and patting her on the knee and thigh, which were both scandalously exposed, in the new fashion.

Somebody knocked at the door.

He heard Clyde curse under his breath. The man had a stinking temper when he was cross. And to make it worse, much worse, he was also quite drunk tonight. He stomped over to the door, jerked it open, and stood there in his underwear. "What the hell do you want?" he barked.

Hoover couldn't hear what was said in reply, but Tolson exploded.

"Well, I don't see that that's any of our goddamned business!" he yelled. "Probably some thug from California. I understand that's how they do things in their day. So why don't you just get back in your little car, and get the hell out of here. I'm sure you can find your way out to the Valley. Just follow the army of perverts."

That would normally have been the end of if, but Hoover could still hear the low, insistent murmur coming from the front porch. Clyde started screeching again, unintelligibly this time. He sounded positively unhinged, and Hoover grew concerned that he might lash out. He was a big, powerful man, Clyde.

And it might well be someone important at the door. With all their troubles back home, it wouldn't be very smart to invite even more trouble.

So Hoover grunted with exasperation and the effort of forcing himself up off the chaise after six whiskies and a double helping of dinner at Joe's Stone Crabs.

He grumbled all the way over to the door. "This had better be good," he growled when he caught sight of the pale, trembling figure who was standing there. It was an agent, but not one he recognized. He dealt only with the senior staff when he was here in Florida.

"I'm sorry, sir," the young man stammered, "but we had to contact you immediately, and you left instructions never to call on the phone. The president wants you back in Washington right now. Something terrible has happened."

Hoover could feel a fine head of steam building inside his head. "We are on holiday—"

"Sir, please," the agent interrupted, staggering the FBI director with his impertinence. "It's Pearl Harbor again, sir. And bombs, too, sir. Bombs going off *all* over the country."

". . . Just follow the army of perverts . . ."

Rogas couldn't help grinning at that. They had something like 140 hours of audio-video taken from inside Hoover's love shack now.

"Fucking army of perverts," he chuckled. *"Madre de* fucking *Dios."*

The chief petty officer was nearing the end of his observation shift when the FBI agent interrupted Hoover and Tolson. The others were sleeping, and he sent a soft *ping* to their earbuds to alert them.

The team was located in adjoining suites at the Gulfstream, in a separate wing of the pink U-shaped hotel to the director and his "longtime companion." Rogas was bunking with marine Corporal Harriet "the Chariot" Klausner, while in the next room a fellow SEAL, Chief Petty Officer Bryan Cockerill, had teamed up with a marine Corporal Shelley Horton, who'd done three years undercover in a previous life on the Baltimore PD. They were posing as servicemen on leave with their wives.

It hadn't been possible to get a room near Hoover. They were all kept vacant. But the fucking moron stayed in the same luxury suite every time. So Horton and Cockerill had rented it a few days earlier and installed all the microcams before checking out for a short, fictitious scuba-diving trip down in the Keys.

Rogas had no idea where Kolhammer got his intelligence from, but it was good.

Hoover took the exact room the admiral had said he would on the day he was supposed to.

"Admirals"—the Navy SEAL smiled to himself—"is there anything they can't do?"

"S'up bitch?" asked Klausner, rubbing the sleep out of her eyes as she appeared at his shoulder in the darkened room.

"Dunno," he said. "Some Bureau dude just fronted Tolson with a story about bombs going off somewhere. You might want to check out Fleetnet if you can get a link."

The other two roomies, Horton and Cockerill, appeared from next door. There was a door between the suites, which Rogas assumed was normally locked, until some rich mom and dad needed to rent separate space for their kids.

It was late, and the only light in the room came from the screen Rogas

was watching. The hotel room was rank with the smell of four human beings who hadn't been outside for a long time. Room service trays and dis-
carded junk food artifacts lay everywhere, threatening to pile up into a
couple of serious garbage drifts. The technical specs for the gig had been
minimal. The surveillance rigs and just two data slates to display the take.
They needed to be able to break the observation post down for a quick exit.

Rogas waved Horton and Cockerill over to the table where he had one
slate running live vision from the targets' room.

"What's going on?" asked Horton.

"Bombings or some shit," said Klausner, who was powering up the other
slate to send a query to Fleetnet.

"Anything else?"

"Well," said Rogas. "Edgar and Clyde have been having a tiff, and
Clyde's been hitting the bottle a little too hard. Edgar thinks he should wear
that spanky little kimono he bought for him—"

"The blue one?" asked Horton. "I like that one. I reckon Clyde looks
really edible in that."

"Well, he's just sitting around in his fuckin' crusties for now," said Rogas.
"I thought they were going to have a real catfight over it."

"Talk about your fuckin' funniest home videos," grunted Cockerill.

The mission boss was playing with touch-screen controls while Cocky
spoke, trying to isolate the audio take from the agent at the door.

"Got it!" Klausner called out. "Early reports of half a dozen soft target
bombings in New York. No details yet."

"Shit," said Horton.

They watched as the two men on screen argued with each other. They
dismissed the agent who brought the bad news.

"We have to get back there now," said Tolson after the man had left. *"We'll
get the blame for this."*

Rogas waited for Hoover to reply, but an unusual stillness had come over
the FBI director.

"We'll see," he said at last.

Rogas looked at his watch. They were due to send another data burst in
ninety minutes. He took less than a heartbeat to make his decision.

"Cocky, start compressing the last six hours' feed for a flash traffic burst.
Kolhammer needs to see this now. Shelly, let's get this fucking pigsty policed up. I think we're going to be on the move soon."

If they were going back to Washington, Rogas would need to send an
alert ahead to his advance team.

They needed to finish wiring up Hoover's house and to try to get a surveillance roach into his office.

Again Rogas had no idea how Kolhammer hoped to achieve that. "*Admirals* . . ." He smiled.

NEW YORK

Julia and Dan were in Midtown on a cold autumn evening, walking to dinner and arguing as they huddled in overcoats: his olive drab, hers black leather. The temperature had begun dropping away an hour earlier, and a gray drizzle was threatening to turn to sleet. Dan's mood matched the weather. He wasn't happy about her mixing with the wrong crowd, which in his opinion seemed to account for just about everyone who had ever associated with Slim Jim Davidson.

"If those federal agents were on his case, they probably had good reason to be," he insisted.

"Oh, puh-leeze! Come on, Dan, the good ship *Lollipop* pulled away from the pier a long fucking time ago. Haven't you been paying attention? Hoover is a fucking lunatic and a hypocrite and a screaming bender. He's only been able to hold on to his job because half the fucking country is terrified he's got something on them."

"But Davidson is a known criminal!" her fiancé protested. "He doesn't even try to deny it."

"*Was* a criminal, Dan. But he's super rich now—'legitimate businessman' is now the correct phrase, I believe."

She could see that he was really ticked off, and she knew her gentle flirting with Davidson had probably been the cause. Dan's frown line, which she called the Grand Canyon, was etched deeply into his forehead. It was kind of cute, really, but it would get old if he didn't snap out of it soon. She was about to say so when her flexipad began to chime in a way that signaled a high-priority call from the office.

"Sorry," she said. "I have to take this."

The *Times* had secured two flexipads and one data slate, clearly at great expense. Besides giving them access to Fleetnet's publicly available Web cache, it also meant that Julia was instantly available 24-7, as long as she was within shortcast range here in Manhattan, or jacked into Fleetnet as an embed while on tour. It was rare for them to call, however. The traffic was mostly one way, when she sent in stories after the censors had cleared them.

A bitter wind blew grit into her eyes as she hauled the pad out of her overcoat.

While she was answering, Dan's pad went off, too.

"Shit," said Julia. "I'll bet something's up."

"What makes you—?"

She held up a hand and waved it to indicate that he should take his call. His frown added even more depth to the canyon, but he did as she suggested, wandering into a bookshop where it was little quieter, and probably warmer.

She remained on the sidewalk, oblivious of the passersby who were staring, some even stopping to gawk openly. The signal came through, and Graeme Blundell, the chief of staff, was frowning on Julia's display. A lot of the 'temps did that when they were confronted with the technology.

"What's up, Graeme?"

"Julia, you need to get over to Chambers Street, to the subway station. There's been an explosion. A bomb or something has gone off over there."

"What sort of bomb?" she asked as all of her nerve endings lit up.

"I don't know," he spluttered. "A *big* bomb, from the sound of it. There are a lot of people hurt. And that's not all. The wires are saying there are another dozen or more of these things gone off around the country. And we're getting reports from Hawaii that the Japanese have struck there again."

Julia shooed away a couple of teenaged boys who tried to crowd in for a closer look at the flexipad. "Piss off," she said. "I'm working here. No, not you Graeme, go on. How'd they get near Hawaii? I thought the *Clinton* left the better part of a fighter wing there. Sea Raptors and Hawkeyes."

Blundell threw up his hands. "I don't know, damn it! We don't know much about Pearl yet. It's all too early. But I can tell you, we've got a big story developing over at Chambers Street. And I'm afraid it's right up your alley, Julia. It looks like the sort of thing you say used to happen all the time, back where you came from."

"Yeah, okay," she said. "I'm sorry to hear that. I'll get over there right now. And just so you know, I've got Dan with me. We were heading out to dinner, and he took a call same time as me. That won't be a coincidence. There *are* no coincidences where I come from. If he can tell me anything about Pearl, I'll get back to you with an update."

"Do you think you could send me a briefing note on what you've got off the wires? I can't access them."

She could see Blundell shooting the flexipad at the other end a nervous look. "I'll get Miss Meade to do it. She's much better on these things than me."

"It's because she's a chick, Graeme. We're better at everything, y'know. See you soon."

She cut him off and looked around for Dan. He was still on the pad. If he was talking like that, it meant that Kolhammer had a live link running between the East and West Coasts. They didn't do that very often, because of the amount of dicking around involved in setting up the relay.

The shit had definitely hit the fan.

"Miss, miss, can we have a look at your flexipad, miss?"

It was those kids again. She recognized them as bicycle couriers, a new industry that had taken off in the city about a month ago. Now it seemed as if they were everywhere. Julia had even had a close call with a couple of female riders. At the time she hadn't known whether to be pissed at them for nearly taking her out, or proud of them for having the *cojones* to do the job in the first place. In the end, she'd opted for wry amusement.

There were no Lycra bodysuits, powered helmets, or carbon-fiber bike frames to be had in 1940s New York, but both of those girls had done their best to pull off the look. Julia was sure their raked-back riding helmets were made of papier-mâché, and the sunglasses were strictly Ray-Ban aviators from current stock. But they must have stayed up late for a whole week cutting and sewing their black overalls to have them fit so tightly. And where they got the Day-Glo strips from, she had no idea.

The two boys jumping from foot to foot in front of her hadn't invested nearly so much effort. She looked in on Dan again. He was deep into some unpleasant conversation. Normally she'd have just tapped on the window and waved him good-bye as she rushed off to the job, but she wanted to know what his call was about.

"Okay," she told the kid. "But it'll have to be quick. You wanna music vid? Sativa or J-Two? Or I've got some very old Britney Spears here. I'm guessing you boys would be right into Britney."

"Oh, wow!"

"Awesome!"

"Okay, check it out," she said, bringing up a vid file and glancing at Dan again. "If you try a runner on me, though, I'll shoot you down before you get ten feet away." She let them catch a glimpse of the SIG Sauer in its holster under her leather coat. That seemed to excite them even more than the Ericsson.

As she was waiting for Dan to emerge, growing impatient, she heard the unmistakable rumble of a bomb going off a few blocks away.

SPECIAL ADMINISTRATIVE ZONE, CALIFORNIA

"I need you on the next flight to Washington, Dan," said Kolhammer. "I'll be catching a red-eye myself, when I've wrapped up here. I don't doubt this bombing campaign is related to Pearl and the U.K., but we haven't seen anything to indicate an invasion of the U.S. mainland. Most likely, it's a feint. At any rate, I've got everybody above the level of bird colonel or equivalent hammering me for ray guns and space rockets. I'm afraid you're going to have to be my flak catcher."

Black seemed to be standing in some sort of library. Kolhammer could see shelves full of books behind him. The navy commander made a visible effort to pull himself together.

"I'll just see Jules off, Admiral. I got a feeling she's going to be busy here, anyway. Then I'll get straight out to Idlewild."

"Thanks, Dan. I'll have Liao make sure there's a seat for you."

They signed off, and Kolhammer cut the link.

He brought up the latest flashes on his desktop display panel. Nine bombs had exploded within a twelve-minute period, in three cities. Four in New York. Three in Chicago. Two in Washington. And not one of them had taken out a hard target. Subway cars, trains, buses, and two department stores were reported as having been hit. Civilian deaths were high. Not what he thought of as mass casualties, but it was going to rock the fucking house for the locals.

There was no vision available on Fleetnet just yet, for which he was grateful. He didn't need to see that shit anyway. Arms and legs looked the same the world over when they were blown off with high explosives. And there'd be the usual obscenity of tiny little limbs torn from children's bodies, given the nature of the targets.

He shook his head and suppressed the images for the moment. As horrifying as it was, it wasn't even the crisis of the day for him.

That was over in Hawaii.

He *did* have visuals streaming from there. Mike Judge, still en route to San Diego, was providing the link he needed to see what was happening on Oahu.

A drone on station above Honolulu had recorded the attack, which was lucky in a cold, left-handed way, because there weren't many Task Force assets left to file a report. Hypersonic cruise missiles had wiped out most of Hickham Field, where the F-22s and support craft he'd left in place to secure the island had been destroyed. Slagged by a sunburn missile. A Laval, by all indications.

Other airfields had been partially, or totally, destroyed. And Pearl Harbor looked worse than it had the first time. A low-res, jumpy, live-action feed from the drone showed massive losses. The only saving grace was that it could have been so much worse, if Spruance hadn't been safely tucked away in the southwest Pacific, supporting the *Kandahar*'s battle group.

That was where the counterstrike would have to come from, if they still had the ability to launch one. A dense ball of lead was growing in Kolhammer's stomach as he began to see the outline of Yamamoto's design. And it wasn't just him, of course. He was clearly coordinating his strategy much more closely with the Nazis now, trying to make up for the odds that had been stacked against them.

His teeth ached and his jaw muscles clenched as he bit down on his fury. There was only one place such an attack, with Laval multipurpose cruise missiles, could have originated. The *Dessaix*. No other ship in the Multinational Force was carrying them. They all thought she'd been left behind, until now, but she'd obviously come though the Transition and fallen into the hands of the enemy. He could tell, from the substandard attack profile that the original crew wasn't responsible—or not all of them, anyway. If the *Dessaix* had launched a properly coordinated attack on Hawaii, there'd be nobody left alive.

As it was, the damage was still catastrophic. And it wasn't over yet, either. He'd bet the farm on that.

Admiral Phillip Kolhammer looked at the pictures coming out of Hawaii and he knew in his bones that the Japanese were on their way.

NEW YORK

Julia was alone again. Dan had said his good-byes and gone straight to the airport. She'd caught a cab down Broadway to Chinatown and made the rest of the journey on foot against the flood of pedestrian traffic rushing away from the bombing. Hundreds of sirens filled the air, and occasionally a city worker would stagger past, covered in soot, clothes singed, coughing and crying.

For Julia it was something akin to déjà vu. She supposed if she'd been a bit older, she might have instinctively looked for the old Twin Towers. But the New York she remembered hadn't included them, so the antiquated low-rise buildings—such as City Hall, just ahead of her—didn't seem so out of place. No, the streetscape didn't much affect her, but the victims did. It was their faces.

She'd grown used to thinking of the 'temps as different. Their faces were much more racially homogenous, their bodies oddly shaped. They were neither grotesquely obese nor inhumanly hard—sculpted by drugs and extreme exercise, like something out of one of Spielberg's Draka movies. But running from danger, eyes bulging in terror, they were all of a sudden too painfully familiar to her.

She stopped at the corner of Canal and Broadway, ostensibly to rig her flexipad for the job and to dig out her cardboard press pass, but also to regain her balance. Disorientation threatened to sweep her legs out from under her before she got anywhere near Chambers Street. She took in several long, slow breaths, letting the chill of the early dusk clear her head. Her breath came out in small, quick clouds of steam.

Regaining her center, she pushed on.

Fire trucks and ambulances were gridlocked for a block around the subway station. The approaching night pulsed a deep red from their spinning lights, as though a wound had laid open the city's heart, and the blood was everywhere. Without access to her Sonycam, she had to use the flexipad in its camera mode, taking full-motion video of the scene as she approached.

A block away from the Chambers Street station, hundreds of stretchers covered the grounds of City Hall Park, reminding Julia of the MASH unit she'd visited back on the Brisbane Line. That had been a hell of a lot more organized than this. She couldn't see any sort of system here. There seemed to be four or five competing triage centers. Police, firefighters, and civilian medical teams swarmed everywhere, sometimes rubbing up hard against each other, leading to arguments and even a couple of fights, which she caught on video.

A soldier wandered through, an army lieutenant, a 'temp. His uniform was blackened, and a big, egg-shaped bump had come up on his forehead. But otherwise he seemed fine. Julia grabbed him, identified herself, and got down to work.

"I was going to meet my brother," he said. "He was going to be on the subway—the A train. I was waiting over by the newsstand. I don't know. I don't know what happened. A bomb. I guess. They must have dropped a bomb. I gotta find my brother—"

He wandered off before she could get his name.

She had to get closer to the station, to find somebody who had at least half a clue. So she began to jog over to Chambers Street, stopping to grab a clip of a mother and young daughter—she supposed—dressed for the opera, sitting and hugging each other, shaking violently and not speaking at all. The daughter was moaning.

The pad chimed, and she broke off filming to read an updater from the *Times*. There were three other bomb sites in Manhattan: at Penn Station, Grand Central, and in Macy's. There were fewer casualties at Macy's, which had been closed when the explosion went off. The bombs at the railway stations had seemingly been designed to hit civilians, rather than to damage infrastructure. They'd gone off in the restaurants.

She heard the musical theme from *The Simpsons* and experienced a definite shunt in her mind, as it tried to get traction on a very slippery slope. Then she remembered that was Rosanna's call ID tag.

"Hey, babe. God, am I glad to see you," Julia said with enormous relief. "Dan said you guys were toast."

Rosanna looked fine, if a little shaken. It was still daylight in Hawaii, and she seemed to be outside, with a huge fire burning in the background. "We got hammered," said Rosanna. "It had to be a missile strike, Jules. Nothing else looks like this. There was even an EMP. It fried all my stuff that wasn't hardened to mil-grade. Where the hell are you?"

"I'm home," said Julia. "Well, not at home. The city got parcel-bombed. I'm on it right now. Looks like someone's been doing their homework. They've gone for soft targets, high body counts. Easier than hitting guarded facilities. How long has the laser link been up?"

Rosanna shook her head. "Just a few minutes. I figured they'd use the *Clinton* as a relay soon as I saw how bad it was. I can't say how long it'll stay in place, or how long they'll let us have access. Bandwidth is pretty limited, but I guess they want to know what happened. I've got a highlights package for you. I'm sending it now, compressed in the signal. I've got vision of Pearl, what used to be Hickham, and what's left of Honolulu."

"Hickham? Isn't that where the Raptors are based?"

"Were based. They're fucked."

Julia felt a surge of anxiety in her friend's behalf. "Jesus, Rosanna. Get yourself out of there now. The Japanese are coming for sure."

"I know," said Natoli. "This place is on the edge of a panic spiral. But there's no getting out. It's pure chaos, Jules."

"Is Curtis all right?"

"He's fine. He was with me. And our fat shadow, too."

Julia was going to ask, but Rosanna carried on without a break.

"I'll tell you about that later. Look, I've got to go, Jules. I'll file every three hours, as long as the link is up and I have access. Raw footage. You can produce me for a change."

Rosanna attempted a brave smile, but Julia could tell it was forced. Happiest in an editing suite, her friend wasn't a field reporter. She'd never had embed training. And there she was, stuck in the middle of the ocean, on a small island that was about to become a battleground.

"File every hour," said Julia. "Then I'll know you're okay."

"I'll be fine. I'll see you soon," Rosanna promised; then she cut the link. Somehow, Julia doubted it.

26

THE PACIFIC THEATER OF OPERATIONS

The sight of so many aircraft forming up and heading out, to further reduce the enemy's defenses, should have brought joy to the grand admiral. After all, it was rare in war to be given a second chance.

But Yamamoto had not yet fully recovered from the shock of seeing Hidaka on the little movie screen, disheveled and covered in blood, telling him that one mutinous Frenchman had nearly wrecked the entire plan. Indeed, he may well *have* done so. They hadn't yet determined how much damage this barbarian Danton had wreaked, and they wouldn't know for certain until their own planes flew over the islands and reported back.

Unlike his initial reaction to the Emergence, Yamamoto wasn't incandescent with rage, not this time. For the admiral, rage came from the sudden, unexpected destruction of certainty. And in his heart, he hadn't been at all surprised by this development.

After Midway, nothing seemed to surprise him anymore. If somebody had walked in and told him that Charles Lindbergh had been elected president of the United States, or that a race of super Nazis had suddenly emerged in southern Africa, he doubted he would raise an eyebrow.

So his primary reaction to Hidaka's untimely news was a feeling of sickening free fall, which he fought to keep to himself. He could only wonder if the world would ever return to the certainties of just a few months previous.

The mood on the bridge of the great battleship *Yamato* mirrored his own. Perhaps if Hidaka had been able to report a complete success, it would have been different. The officers and crew might yet have been seized with the fevers of victory, celebrating as they had during the first few months of the war. But now, they all seemed to wonder if their doom was approaching, and whether or not a squadron of F-22s might still come shrieking toward them at two or three times the speed of sound.

Pounding through the Pacific toward their objective, the Combined Fleet looked unstoppable. Yet in the face of the weapons the Americans now possessed, his cruisers and carriers were little better than origami trifles.

The officer of the watch announced that the last squadron of dive-bombers was away. Yamamoto did not bother to get up from his chair to watch them disappear into the vanishing point, far to the east. But he was quietly gratified to see some of the junior officers excitedly whispering to each other and pointing as the attack got under way. Regardless of any trepidation they might be feeling, they could not contain their enthusiasm to have at the Americans.

It was good, he thought. His Majesty would be well served by these new samurai.

Following their example, he put aside his own concerns. The warrior who drew his blade without confidence was doomed. Hidaka said the missile strike had done an enormous amount of damage, and his own air assault would surely add to the Americans' woes.

"Captain," he said, sitting a little straighter in his command chair, "signal the fleet to redouble its vigilance. There will be enemy submarines in front of us. And a counterattack from Midway remains possible."

The bridge crew took their lead from Yamamoto's renewed vigor. Backs straightened. Orders were barked out just a bit more crisply. Everywhere he looked, he saw evidence of Japan's finest young men, willing to die in the service of the empire.

It wasn't right for him to let them down with maudlin displays of anxiety.

Lieutenant Wally Curtis just couldn't believe it. He had thought of the jet planes as indestructible. And yet there they were, every last one of them, totally fubar. A dozen or more piles of burning wreckage.

Hickham Field was littered with scrap metal and human body parts, but most of the crash crews and fire engines were clustered about the tarmac where the F-22s from the *Clinton* had been parked. They were all gone, except for two that had been up in the air when the missiles came over. And he'd heard *they* had been banged up when they had to land on a normal road surface, because there was no undamaged runway anywhere that could take them. The undercarriage of one had collapsed when it fouled in a big pothole, and the other had clipped a power pole and just about torn off a wing.

That was the scuttlebutt, anyway. He hadn't seen it himself, and as Rosanna kept telling him, unless you actually saw it happen, it probably didn't.

Well, he'd seen this happen hadn't he? Curtis had thought he'd never again see anything to equal Midway, but this came close. They'd driven in to Hickham, flashing three different types of ID at the guard post, which was too busy to check them properly, anyhow. The base was a write-off. It was hardly recognizable as a working facility.

Rosanna was too busy filming to answer any of his questions, so he turned to Detective Cherry instead, which was pretty strange when he thought about it, because the policeman was supposed to be following *them*.

"You think the Japs are gonna invade, Detective?"

Cherry laughed, but it was a sour, shriveled-up sound. Curtis didn't think there was any humor in it at all. "Sure, kid. You sucker-punch a guy this good, you gotta give him a good kickin' while he's down. Finish him off if you can. That was their mistake the first time around. They shoulda finished us back in December last year."

"What should we do, then? I tried to get back to my unit, but it's just a big crater now. I couldn't find anyone at Pearl."

"Forget Pearl," Cherry said. "The Japs are gonna be over to bomb the rubble soon enough. You know how to fire a gun, boy?"

"I did basic," Curtis protested, feeling as if Cherry was somehow disregarding his martial prowess.

The detective let go another one of his humorless laughs, as a series of explosions destroyed a hangar full of Wildcat fighters a couple of hundred yards away. Curtis flinched and ducked, but Cherry hardly moved. Rosanna swung her little movie camera around to take in the new action.

"Basic, huh?" Cherry said. "Well, that's good. Killing a man is pretty basic, when you get right down to it. Put a bullet in him. Or a knife. Put your hands around his neck and choke him to death. You think you could handle that, son? Killing a man right up close like that? Smelling him as he shits his pants and calls out for his mama?" Cherry's eyes were lifeless as he spoke. In a way, it was more disturbing than if he'd been ranting.

"I can handle myself," Curtis replied weakly.

An air raid siren began to wail before the cop could reply. Curtis spun around, almost describing a complete circle before he spotted the danger: dozens of planes coming in from the west, diving toward the airfield out of the late afternoon sun.

"Rosanna!" he yelled. "Run."

They all ran, heading for a slit trench twenty yards away. About a hundred others hand the same idea as the first bombs began their whistling descent.

Both Rosanna and Cherry surprised him. She by jumping into the shelter and then popping right back up to film the attack while others cowered on the floor. Cherry by the speed with which he covered the distance to safety, and then by pulling his service revolver and taking potshots at the Japanese planes.

The policeman wasn't the only one doing that. A crackle of rifle and pistol fire grew into a minor torrent as men, and even a few women, opened up with small arms. Curtis felt less than useless, having no weapon to shoot. He crouched and hurried over to Rosanna's side. She had turned, and was now filming down the trench, capturing the resistance to the bombardment.

The fury of the attack increased so much and with such speed that Curtis thought the sound alone was going to kill them. He tried to shout at Rosanna to duck down, but the crash of gunfire and the storm of exploding bombs all around them made it impossible to communicate. Fire trucks that had been pouring water onto the burning SeaRaptors were suddenly obliterated by a stick of bombs. Massive roiling balls of filthy orange flame engulfed the tenders, and the firefighters who had stayed with them. One truck was lifted high into the air, turned over slowly like a spitted hog, and smashed back to earth, crushing two men and a woman who'd been running for cover.

Curtis didn't know what weird sense cut in to save them, but he grabbed Rosanna and pulled her down a split second before a Zero roared overhead, strafing the trench line and turning dozens of defenders into chopped meat and splinters of bone. Rosanna was screaming and clawing at his face, trying to get to her feet again as another Zero on a strafing run chewed up the trench. Hot soil and pieces of tarmac poured in on them as Curtis used his body weight to press down on the reporter and keep her safe.

"You're going to get killed!" he yelled over the uproar.

"We're *all* going to get killed, you stupid sonovabitch," she cried back.

Curtis felt someone grab the collar of his torn shirt and haul him up off Rosanna. He was powerless to fight back.

It was Cherry, passing him a rifle. The stock was shattered and sticky with gore. "I admire your spirit, trying to get laid at a time like this," said the cop, "But your country could use a little help, too, Casanova."

The volume of fire pouring from the trench was a fraction of what it had been, now. Curtis saw why when Cherry turned away. Nearly half the soldiers and air crew were dead, shredded by the cannon and machine-gun fire. The floor of the trench was covered in a thick, semiliquid gruel. Curtis felt his gorge rise and his stomach contract. He vomited up everything he'd eaten for lunch.

"That's the spirit," Cherry called back at him. "Spit in their fucking eyes."

IN TRANSIT TO WASHINGTON

About the only thing to recommend the Connie was the lack of restrictions Eastern had on using electronic equipment while in flight. Kolhammer was able to stay hooked into Fleetnet for most of the trip to Washington. The link was tenuous, and prone to dropouts, but as long as he was content to take compressed data bursts, rather than a live feed, he was fine.

Nothing else was fine, though.

His Secret Service shadows were back. Agents Flint and Stirling, by order of President Roosevelt. At least they didn't crowd him, as they had when he first arrived.

His slate beeped with updates every few minutes. Tellingly, most of them didn't come directly from the remaining Task Force units in Hawaii. There weren't many remaining Task Force units *in* Hawaii. But there were at least ten journalists from the *Clinton* who could provide real-time coverage from the islands, so the link had been maintained largely to provide for them. They were allowed to access Fleetnet to file, but on the condition that their raw footage became the property of the Task Force.

Mike Judge had a team of analysts on the *Clinton* raking the coverage and repackaging it for military use. That was a lot like what used to happen at home, anyway. An almost embarrassing percentage of so-called intelligence was lifted straight from the news media, only to have it returned to them as "inside information."

Kolhammer stretched out his cramped legs in the surprisingly roomy wicker chair of the Lockheed Constellation, and scanned the latest reports from Hawaii. Judge's people had confirmed that Lavals, almost certainly coming from the *Dessaix*, had struck at a number of points around the islands. The missiles hadn't done nearly so much damage as they could have, partly because some had malfunctioned, or been sabotaged, and partly because the rest hadn't been used to their best advantage.

It was a moot point, however. Enough damage had been done to render the island indefensible against any Japanese force that included the *Dessaix* or a ship of similar capability. Follow-up strikes by carrier-based Japanese planes had focused on further degrading the islands' air defense net, but those strikes had been unnecessary, as far as he could tell. The piles of twisted, white hot metal, which had been the *Clinton*'s surviving fighter wing, were all Yamamoto needed to see. With those gone, and the *Dessaix* at large, it was only a matter of time before the Rising Sun flew over Hawaii.

There was little point in turning the *Clinton* around and sending her back. Without a working catapult or fighter wing, she was just a target, not a threat.

The *Kandahar* was an option, but not a great one. Jones's forces were spread over a couple of thousand square miles, and it would take more than a week to gather and embark for any counterstrike, and they were running perilously low on ammunition.

The *Havoc* had run through all her land-attack missiles. She had a small number of ship-killers left, and seemed the obvious choice to hunt for the *Dessaix*, but he was going to have the devil's own job convincing Canberra to release her.

As they approached the Rockies in near total darkness, Phillip Kolhammer examined his options and could find only one viable response to Yamamoto's gambit.

The *Siranui*.

HONOLULU, HAWAII

Every window in her apartment was broken, but at least the building still stood. So much of Honolulu had been flattened that Rosanna hadn't expected to find anything but smoking rubble where her home had been.

Cherry's place was gone, along with his police station. And Curtis had been trying all day to find someone to report to, without any luck. He'd given up for now and decided to stick with her. The three of them pulled up outside her place in the gathering darkness of midevening. Her apartment building stood on the side of a hill, and half the island seemed to be ablaze below them.

The time between the Japanese air raids was becoming noticeably shorter.

"They're closer now," said Curtis as a few pathetic lines of tracer snaked up from the fiery cauldron that had been Pearl Harbor. Irregular flashes from exploding bombs strobed away below them.

"You got anything to eat?" asked Cherry.

"You gotta be kidding," said Curtis.

"No, he's right," Rosanna countered. "If the Japanese get ashore, we don't know when we'll eat again before relief arrives. I've got some leftovers in the icebox, and my oven is gas. We should eat now. We'll need our strength. I want to pick up some batteries for my gear, too. I don't know if we'll get back here again, once we leave."

Curtis looked even more despondent. He stopped halfway up the path that led to the front door of her block. "Do you really think the *Clinton* will come back?" he asked.

Even Cherry seemed interested in her answer.

"No," she said. "The *Clinton*'s out of it for now. But the *Kandahar* isn't. Or that LAS with her, the *Ipswich*. Even if the Japanese take over, they could kick down the door and fight their way in."

"Unless they get sunk," said Cherry, "by whatever hit us."

"Yeah," she agreed, feeling very tired. "But let's not think about that right now. Come on, let's get inside."

There was no electricity to light the place, whether from the effects of the electromagnetic pulse or from direct damage to the power grid, she couldn't tell. It didn't matter. Cherry had brought a hooded oil lamp, looted from God knew where. There was so much smoke and dust in the air that the beam was tightly defined, reminding Rosanna of a light saber. That familiar image from her childhood, which now seemed so much more peaceful than this nightmare, lifted her spirits slightly.

Everything was relative, she told herself as they climbed the stairs to the rooms she occupied on the third floor of the Mission-style building. Curtis thought that she'd grown up in a world full of violent lunatics.

"Miss Natoli, is that you?" a quavering voice asked. Cherry's lamp quickly picked out a small, round white face framed by unruly strands of gray hair, peeking out over the landing above them.

"It's okay, Mrs. Mackellar. Yeah, it's me."

"Oh, dearie, I've been so worried. Mr. Ramsay said the Japanese had landed and were going to kill everyone and—"

Cherry's voice boomed out. "It's all right, Mrs. Mackellar. I'm Detective Cherry, from the Honolulu PD, and I can assure you that everything will be okay. Now you need to go back into your apartment, ma'am, and wait for help to come. Do you have enough food to last a few days?"

"Well, I . . . the delivery boy came this morning, just before the air raid and—oh, I hope he hasn't been hurt—"

"He'll be fine, ma'am," Cherry said, taking the stairs two at a time to get up to her. The oil lamp threw long, swaying shadows as he climbed. Rosanna saw him place a huge paw on the old woman's shoulder and steer her back into her home. "Fill your bath with cold water, Mrs. Mackellar. And your sinks and any pots or pans you have. In case the water gets cut off. And listen to your radio—"

"I can't, Detective. The Japanese broke it."

"What . . . Oh, right. Yeah, Lieutenant Curtis down there told me about that. They had some special bomb fried the electrics. Most of 'em, anyhow. Well, not to worry. A uniformed officer will come around, and tell you when it's safe again. For now, just do as I say. In fact, you might want to go around to the rest of the occupants and tell them the same thing. Can you do that for me, Mrs. Mackellar? Can I deputize that job to you?"

Rosanna found herself touched, and more than a little surprised by Cherry's ability to calm the old lady's nerves. Mrs. Mackellar promised him she would go right away, and instruct the rest of the building to do as he said.

"Well, get yourself a candle or a torch," he cautioned, "and be careful on the stairs in the dark. There isn't going to be any ambulance service for a while."

Cherry came back down and joined them on the lower landing.

"What are you fucking looking at?" he growled at Rosanna.

"You fucking asshole. You're just a pussycat," she said back. "Why can't you be nice like that all the time?"

"Because it hurts my head," he said. "This your place, Natoli? Can we get inside and get some grub now?"

She added the light of her flexipad to his oil lamp, to help find the keyhole.

"Is there a layer of lead or something in there that protected it from the pulse?" asked Curtis.

"Not lead, no," she answered as the key turned. "But most of my stuff is hardened for battlefield use. My watch isn't, though. Look."

She showed him her wristwatch. The alphanumeric display was dead.

"It used to light up," she said. "It had the prettiest blue face."

"Got any booze?" Cherry asked, pushing his way into the living room, where glass crunched underfoot.

"There's champagne in the icebox. That's it, but you're welcome to have some."

"Jesus Christ, lolly water," he muttered.

"Hey, for a guy who was spying on us until this morning, and doing a shit job of it, too, you're a bit of a lippy fucker, aren't you?"

"Calm down, sister," said Cherry. "It's been a long day. Where d'you keep your glasses?"

"Not under my pillow, like you. Try the cupboard over the sink."

Cherry crunched away.

"I'm sorry about your place," Curtis said. Every window seemed to be broken.

"It was always too dark for my tastes, anyhow," she said, shrugging. "You should see the joint I bought in New York, with Julia. Hey, speaking of which, I'd better file."

She set about slotting the flexipad into the drivebay of her personal server. It could run on batteries for three days, and had even better shielding against an EMP than her pad. A row of blinking lights, on a charcoal gray communications cone jacked into the rear of the box, told her that she still had a link to Fleetnet.

"Small fucking mercies," she said to herself.

The screen powered up with its familiar background of family photos. The computer linked automatically to a drone circling high over the island, and a message popped up.

"Hey, you guys had better come and see this," she called out.

Both of them appeared from the kitchen carrying bread and sandwich fillings.

"What's up?" asked Curtis.

"Your friends on their way?" said Cherry.

"Not really."

They leaned in to read the message.

Flash traffic, Fleetnet. All units and ancillary personnel. Japanese invasion of Hawaii imminent. No equipment or data is to be captured by
the Japanese. Repeat, no equipment or data is to be captured by the
Japanese. Destroy all relevant material. By order of Admiral Phillip
Kolhammer.

Outside a lone air raid siren wailed in the night.

27

WASHINGTON, D.C.

The Whitelaw Hotel on the corner of Thirteenth and T wasn't the finest
establishment in Washington, but it was special in a way that a Waldorf-
Astoria could never be.

Built in 1919 in the Italian Renaissance Revival style, the Whitelaw was
the world's most famous African-American hotel. It was a temporary home
in the national capital for entertainers like Duke Ellington, or the leaders of
black organizations like the NAACP, none of whom could rent rooms in the
city's segregated luxury hotels. So it was unusual—almost unprecedented—
for a high-ranking white military man to stay there. Admiral Kolhammer's
PA had standing instructions to book him into the Whitelaw whenever he
traveled to Washington.

He checked in early, straight off the red-eye, before starting a long day
of crisis meetings at the White House and the War Department.

"I need to get some breakfast, have a shower, and change," he told the
front desk. "Then I'm out of here. In fact, if you could have a car waiting for
me at a quarter of nine, my little part of the war effort would run a lot
smoother."

The duty manager was only too happy to help. The Special Administrative Zone put a lot of business through the Whitelaw.

Agents Flint and Stirling hovered nearby, like golems in off-the-rack suits.

"Would you prefer to have breakfast in your room, sir?" the manager asked. "We have a suite ready for you."

"No. I'll just go through to the dining room now. One of my staff is meeting me there. A Commander Daniel Black. Please send him on through when he arrives. He shouldn't be too long."

He turned to his security detail. "We're going to be on the move all day. You guys ought to grab some chow while you can, too."

The agents nodded, and Stirling moved through to check out the room.

A bellhop was summoned to take Kolhammer's baggage, and the kid obviously recognized him. In fact, almost everyone in the large crowded lobby seemed to know who he was, courtesy of four months of blanket coverage in the black press. As he moved through the warm but cavernous space, with strangers pointing and smiling, or just whispering and trying not to look like they were gawking at him, Kolhammer was struck by the thought that this was probably how Spruance had felt when he'd first come aboard the *Clinton* back at Midway.

Well, it was his choice to stay here. In part, it was just petty politics, really. But sometimes that was important, too. He had a lot of officers serving under him who would not be welcome in any of the other, *better* hotels in Washington, simply because God had wrapped them up in the wrong skin color. And to Phillip Kolhammer's way of thinking, that sucked. Back in the twenty-first, a lot of assholes would have thought of his insistence on staying here at the Whitelaw as politically correct grandstanding. But they could go fuck themselves and the horse they rode in on.

Correctness be damned. He simply wouldn't stand for his men and women being treated with anything but the utmost courtesy. If the fucking Ritz or the Savoy wouldn't have, say, Colonel Jones as a customer, then they could damn well get by without Kolhammer's money, as well. He tipped the bellhop and walked through to breakfast.

"You eating, Agent Flint?" he asked.

"No, sir," said Flint. "Stirling's always been more of a chow hound than me. I had a Twizzler on the plane."

A waiter met them at the entrance to the dining room, a huge sumptuous space that was about half-full. Kolhammer took a table and ordered a full hot breakfast with a pot of Jamaican coffee. Flint left him alone, taking up a station where he could see all the entrances and exits. Dan Black arrived just as Kolhammer's first cup of coffee was poured. The man looked like he hadn't slept in three days.

"I haven't, sir," Black said, when the admiral asked him. "Julia believes sleep is for the weak. She'd make a good Nazi, in many ways."

Kolhammer allowed himself a chuckle at that. He had no personal relationship with Duffy, but they had locked horns professionally a couple of times back in the twenty-first. She'd proved herself more than helpful after the Transition, however, and Kolhammer had come to appreciate having an indirect line into the national press via Duffy, through Black. It was amazing, really, the alliances he'd been forced to make.

"Any closer to setting a date for the big day?" he asked.

Black shook his head. "I'm beginning to think she has a—what do you guys call it?—a fear of commitment."

Kolhammer laughed out loud for the first time in days. "We do," he said. "We do. But I don't know if a lack of *commitment* is one of Ms. Duffy's defining character traits, Commander. She's just very focused. I think you'll find that, when the time comes, she'll throw herself into marriage with the same enthusiasm she brings to her work, you poor bastard."

Black looked more than a little worried at that. "You two have crossed swords before, haven't you, Admiral?" he said. "She speaks of you a lot. Calls you the Hammer."

"Yes, but does she say it with respect?"

"You can't have everything, sir."

"And therein lies the sorrow of existence, Commander. At least according to the Buddhists. There's no law says you can't have breakfast, though."

Black ordered bacon and eggs when Kolhammer's order arrived.

"So, you read the files I e-mailed you?"

"Yes, sir," said Black. "Read them on the train coming down. I've already made calls to Patton's staff, and to Eisenhower. Ike's on board, but I suspect that if we delay too long here in Washington, we'll get home to find that General Patton has made off with all of our prototypes and the test crews to drive them, colored or not. I've gone ahead and released the new 'chutes to the Hundred-and-first, though. I didn't think you'd have a problem with that."

Kolhammer chased a piece of sausage around his plate and shook his head. "That's fine. But I'll bet General Lee didn't leave it at that."

"No, sir. He wanted the assault rifles and the grenade launchers, too. They've done some training with the MK-One down in Kentucky. Lee's in town right now, trying to get Marshall to agree to reequip the whole division."

"Jesus Christ," muttered Kolhammer. "They're still months from being combat effective. Okay. Leave that one to me."

"What's your reading, sir, if you don't mind me asking. I've been out of touch."

Kolhammer blew his cheeks out in exasperation. "Well, first up, I don't think there is any chance of an invasion here. I know that makes me a minority of one, but the Axis powers don't have the ability to force a landing on the continental U.S. They *do* have a fair shot at taking Hawaii, and they will throw everything at England."

"Will they win?"

Kolhammer sighed. "They could. The odds are against them. It's the wrong time of year. They don't have air superiority. The Royal Navy can still kick Raeder's ass in a straight-up fight. And of course, there's always Halabi to consider. But it's not going to be a stand-up fight. The *Luftwaffe* can put two thousand aircraft over the Channel, which will severely constrain the British Home fleet, even with the RAF and the Army Air Force ripping into Göring's men. They've been just as busy leapfrogging themselves as quickly as we have."

Black nodded. One of the files Kolhammer had sent him was Captain Halabi's report of the jet and rocket attack on the *Trident*. She described the German weapons as primitive and their tactics nonexistent. But those 262s looked mighty impressive to Black, who'd learned his flying just ten years earlier in a canvas biplane.

"And Hawaii? Australia?"

Kolhammer looked grim as he mulled over his answer. "The signals we're getting from MacArthur about a second assault Down Under are bullshit. The Japanese do not have the depth to pull off two strategic strikes at the same time. But they'll benefit from any doubt they sow in our minds by making a move to surge more of their forces down from New Guinea. It complicates things enormously. The chances of Prime Minister Curtin releasing any forces to help us in retaking Hawaii are slim because of it."

"You think it'll come down to having to retake the islands."

"I'm afraid so," said Kolhammer. "I've got all my intel people working the take from Hawaii, and nothing I'm seeing makes me feel good about this. The Japanese definitely have control of the *Dessaix*, a French ship that was part of my original force. I don't think they have the crew helping them—or not many, anyway. The attack profile was a fucking shambles and seemed to indicate both a very low level of competence by whoever is sailing her, and possibly even active sabotage by somebody on the ship."

Black poked at his breakfast disconsolately. "Well it's not all bad, then."

"No," said Kolhammer. "But there's nothing good about it, either. The enemy won't have sent the *Dessaix* in harm's way without stripping her of everything that wasn't immediately needed for the strike. And that's a lot of technology off a ship like that. It's even possible they've removed whole weapons systems and given them to the Germans. I had to send a burst to Halabi warning her that she could face a missile strike out of France. You see the problem. It's like a demonic butterfly effect."

"A what?" asked Black, looking completely dumbfounded.

"Never mind," said Kolhammer. "Bottom line, things are about to turn to custard everywhere all at once . . . There's something else, too, Dan."

Black's food had arrived, but he really hadn't touched it. He looked up from the plate at the change in Kolhammer's tone.

"I received some information the other day. Through back channels. It's about Hoover."

Black's face was blank.

"We've had a lot of trouble with the Bureau in the Zone, as you know."

The commander nodded. He seemed genuinely in the dark about whatever Kolhammer needed to discuss.

"I was given a list of names, of people the Bureau had recruited or attempted to recruit as informants, provocateurs, and so on. Your name was on the list."

Black's eyes went wide, and he swore. The blood drained from his cheeks and then rushed back in as his whole body seemed to stiffen with an electric shock. "Me? Why me?"

Kolhammer's smile was tired, but real. He had no intention of hooking Black up to a polygraph or asking him to take a shot of T5. His security section had already determined the circumstances of the approach to Black.

"Don't beat yourself up over it, Commander. You were an obvious candidate, and believe me, it is a goddamn tenth-order issue today. They were always going to pick you, and I think you were always going to disappoint them. But you didn't disappoint me."

Black moved around uncomfortably in his uniform. Their presence in the dining room had ceased to be a minor sensation, although a newly arrived group of four men did stop on their way through and pointedly check them out. Black didn't seem to notice them at all.

"It just leaves a sour taste in the mouth is all, Admiral."

"Get over it. They tried it on. They failed. Hoover will keep for the moment. Just be careful about talking to garrulous sheet metal salesmen in the future."

Black's face twisted as he tried to work out the reference.

"The man on your flight over here," Kolhammer said helpfully. "His name really was Dave Hurley, but he wasn't a sheet metal maker. He was FBI. He was trying to get you to compromise yourself, before he put the hook in. It wasn't the first time."

Black's jaw was knotting and clenching furiously. "Damn, Jules was right. I thought it was just her being, you know, twenty-first. All cynical and so on. But she was right about Hoover after all."

Kolhammer shrugged. "Maybe. There's a lot of *unsubstantiated* rumor around Hoover. And the thing about rumors, Commander—as your girlfriend the journalist could tell you if she's any good at her job—is that the rumor you most want to believe is the rumor you should be most skeptical of. Now, if you'll excuse me, I'd better go clean myself up. I feel like a bag of shit. I'll meet you in the lobby in fifteen."

As he stopped to sign his chit on the way out, Kolhammer saw the small group who'd just come in approach Black and engage him in an animated conversation. That was okay. As far as he knew, the FBI didn't have any black field agents at this point in time.

He hurried out of the dining room, with his Secret Service detail falling in behind him.

His hand kept patting the pocket where he had the data stick with the surveillance download from Chief Petty Officer Rogas. Kolhammer hadn't had time to watch the raw footage, but Rogas had cut together a five-minute briefing package that was mercifully free of too much X-rated material.

Kolhammer had no taste for gay porn.

Kolhammer was familiar with both the White House Situation Room in the basement of the West Wing, and the deeply buried tubelike Presidential Emergency Operations Center under the East Wing. In 2021, the meeting he was attending would have been held in one of those two places.

In 1942, however, neither existed. They were about to be built, because one of the more obscure factoids that came through the Transition in the lattice memory of Fleetnet was the information that the White House was structurally unsound and needed to be completely rebuilt from within. The work would have taken place during the Truman Administration, but had been brought forward in light of changed circumstances.

A single bomb could have brought the entire structure down on top of President Franklin D. Roosevelt. He was due to be temporarily shifted across to Blair House, but the move had been delayed by the attack in the Pacific and the bombing campaign at home. Thus Kolhammer and Black found themselves ushered into the old Oval Office by the president's secretary, Ms. Tully.

The room was instantly recognizable, but like so much of the world he moved through nowadays, noticeably different from Kolhammer's memories of the twenty-first century. He'd been in the room three times before.

Some things were reassuring constants, though: the white marble mantel from the original 1909 Oval Office, the presidential seal in the ceiling, the two flags behind the chief executive's desk, and the desk itself, carved from the timbers of the British warship *Resolute*. It was so familiar that he could have felt right at home, were it not for the other men in the room.

Roosevelt was in his wheelchair behind the desk, and he did not stand to greet them, although Kolhammer understood that the treatments he'd received from Task Force medical officers had greatly improved his mobility. The secretary of war, Henry Stimson, was waiting with Marshall and Eisenhower. Ike offered both of the newly arrived officers his cheeky, infectious grin.

Marshall, as ever, remained formidably reserved.

"Admiral Kolhammer," he said in his cold, clipped way. "Commander Black."

Black was mechanically formal in his reply. Kolhammer could afford to unwind a little, although he never called the chief of staff anything other than General or General Marshall. Roosevelt had told him that when he'd first met Marshall, he'd slapped the guy on the back and tried to call him George.

He quickly put me in my place, I can tell you, Roosevelt had said, not altogether fondly.

Admiral King, the navy's senior officer, stood next to one of the two dark studded leather couches, which made the room seem so much darker than Kolhammer remembered. The British ambassador, Lord Halifax, had been talking to the Army Air Force's Commanding General Hap Arnold near the windows overlooking the Rose Garden. Kolhammer could only guess at the unhappy tone of that exchange. There were already calls in Congress for the withdrawal of USAAF's strategic bombing units from the U.K., to prevent them from falling into the hands of the enemy when Britain inevitably fell.

Roosevelt cut though the formalities and asked everyone to "take a pew." He turned first to Kolhammer. "Admiral, I believe you have the most recent report from Hawaii."

Kolhammer thanked him, and inserted a data stick into the flatscreen that had been suspended on the Oval Office wall where Jann Willhelm Rohen's famous oil painting, *The Death of Bin Laden*, would have hung in another world.

"Gentlemen. These first images come from a Big Eye UCAD currently on station above the island of Oahu. It was launched from the *Siranui* last night to provide greater surveillance cover than the smaller multifunction birds we put in place to provide broadband links and basic oversight after the *Clinton* left for San Diego."

When the vision of Pearl Harbor and Ford Island came up, Admiral King let slip a single, sharp curse.

"As you can see," Kolhammer continued, "no significant surface units have survived the missile strike."

It was Hap Arnold's turn to react when similar images of Hickham, Wheeler, and Bellows detailed the utter devastation that had been visited upon those airfields. Kolhammer then switched to a top-down view of Honolulu, showing that approximately three quarters of the city had been razed to the ground.

"Casualties are estimated at twelve thousand dead, and about as many injured. My F-Twenty-twos are gone, save for two that were about a hundred miles south of the islands on Combat Air Patrol at the time of the attack. They had just enough fuel to make it to Midway. General MacArthur has released an in-flight tanker and a Hawkeye from the Southwest Pacific Command to join them. As you know, while in transit the AWACS plane located Yamamoto's Combined Fleet. The Japanese have already begun conventional air attacks and are expected to be in position to force a landing on Oahu in about six hours."

"How long before your jets can hit them?" asked King.

"Two and a half hours. But that strike will have a limited capacity. Each plane is carrying one heavy air-to-surface ship-killer, which, all things being equal, will take out whatever it's aimed at."

"But all things are not equal, are they, Admiral?" said King.

"No," he admitted. "The *Dessaix* appears to have survived and been compromised. She would be capable of negating an attack by the Raptors, and of shooting them down, too. However," he hastened to add, "I can say with certainty that the *Dessaix* is not being crewed by her original complement, and it's doubtful that whoever is in control will be able to use the ship to the best of her abilities."

King pointed at the scenes out of Pearl. "Really, Admiral? Their abilities don't look all that goddamn doubtful to me. Sorry, Mr. President."

Roosevelt waved his apology away, but indicated to Kolhammer that he should carry on.

"If the *Dessaix* had been commanded by Captain Goscinny and crewed by his men, there would be nothing left of Oahu," the admiral said. "The *Clinton* would probably be at the bottom of the ocean, and half of Los Angeles or San Diego would be gone."

"And that's supposed to fill us with confidence?"

"No, but it should forestall any undue panic, if you were so inclined."

"Why, you impertinent son of a—!"

"*Gentlemen!*" The president intervened to defuse the escalating confrontation between the two navy men. Then he continued. "Admiral Kolhammer. Can Hawaii be defended?"

"No, sir."

King threw his hands up in the air. "*You just said—*"

Roosevelt had to hush his naval chief again, before Kolhammer could continue.

"It cannot be defended, but it *can* be retaken, if we move before the Japanese have time to secure their lodgment. The Eighty-second could do it, with some help from the *Siranui*, your marines, and maybe the Second Cavalry."

"Neither Prime Minister Curtin nor General MacArthur are going to trample you with offers of assistance, when they have their own problems to address," said Roosevelt. "I've already had both of them in my ear about a *second* Japanese attack on Australia."

"With all due respect, Mr. President, there won't be a second Japanese attack on Australia. I have seen the sigint take, and my people have been analyzing it, too. It's a diversion. The same sort of thing you would have done before the original D-Day. For the moment, the Australian theater is insignificant. I think the main purpose of the original invasion was to draw my forces down there and to exhaust them. You've seen the briefing note on young Kennedy's mission and Homma's interrogation. *They were drawing our fire.* To some extent that has worked, and so Hawaii is now the main game. If they get a lock on the islands, they can take Australia and New Zealand at their leisure and hold us back from their home islands long enough to develop an atomic deterrent. You can *order* MacArthur to release the Eighty-second, Mr. President. Jones has a degree of autonomy at the operational level, but we've integrated our units into your command structure."

"That's arguable," said King. "The way you run your little duchy over in California—"

Roosevelt interrupted him once more. "Gentlemen, please, let's not fight this one all over again. Unless you want to speed up the integration of your own services, Admiral King. I could sign Truman's Ninety-nine-eighty-one Order today, if you want, rather than continuing with this ridiculous fiction that Admiral Kolhammer is field-testing the concept out in the Zone."

Silence greeted that ultimatum.

"Right. Admiral, please continue with your presentation."

Kolhammer reformatted the big screen to display a world map, with smaller windows open over current flashpoints. "Taken with developments in the European theater and in General MacArthur's area of operations, I believe the Axis powers are attempting to compensate for their long-term strategic vulnerability by swarming us sooner, rather than later. In addition to the movements at Hawaii, off northern Australia, and in France, Lord Halifax confirms that Gibraltar is coming under greatly increased air attack. Wahabi insurgents are fomenting trouble in Egypt, Palestine, and Syria. And Baath Party fascists are in revolt in Iraq. I don't believe any of this is unrelated."

Kolhammer looked to the British ambassador for confirmation.

"I'm afraid that's not all," said Halifax. "We don't have confirmation yet, but Lord Mountbatten has sent word from India that Soviet armor is reportedly pushing down through the Afghan passes. We have no idea whether or not this is true, and if so, whether it presages open cooperation between Berlin and Moscow again, but at any rate it appears the Axis powers are going to attempt to link the Asian and European theaters through the Middle East, while we have our hands full elsewhere."

Roosevelt looked positively ill. "I can't believe Stalin would get back into bed with Hitler," he said. "I suppose I can accept him withdrawing from the alliance. It makes some sense to let us bleed along with the Germans, while he gathers his strength. But I can't imagine anything that would make him trust Hitler again."

Kolhammer spoke up again. "I haven't seen the British material yet, but if Stalin is pushing down through the Afghan passes, we shouldn't assume it's to *help* Hitler and Tojo. He may just be moving to stop them encircling him."

Marshall spoke up from the couch, addressing that point. "Mr. President, Stalin doesn't *need* to trust Hitler. One way or another, we fully expect the Soviets to reenter the war in late 'forty-four, early 'forty-five, but what form that takes will depend on circumstances. Either Hitler will turn around and attack them, having secured his western flank against us. Or if we have beaten Germany, we can expect to have to deal with a Soviet assault into Europe. Atomic weapons or not, Stalin has shown that he won't accept the verdict of history. He knows that if he sits pat, waiting for the correlation of forces or the contradictions of capitalism to deliver him a victory, it all ends with his statues being pulled down and Coke machines being installed in the Kremlin."

"Admiral Kolhammer?" said Roosevelt. "Do you concur, based on the value of hindsight?"

"I do, Mr. President. The Soviets always go long. Stalin was *this* close to going under when Hitler offered him the cease-fire. While he knew he would have come out on top in version one of this war, he knows he can't guarantee that same result in version two. Not with the technology and the forewarnings that the Axis powers now have in their hands.

"So the opportunity to build up his forces while we grapple with Hitler was heaven-sent, even though he knows the Nazis will be back at his throat, given half a chance. Still, I don't think we'll find them in an open alliance with Germany again. Every bullet they have will be needed soon enough. But if this push into Afghanistan plays out, it may be the first move in whatever new game Stalin is playing. At a guess, I'd say he's going to give the Cold War a miss, and get straight down to business when it suits him best. As General Marshall says, sometime in 'fourty-four, or the year after."

"My God," said Roosevelt. "This war could go on for ten years."

Kolhammer nodded. "Or it could all be over—quite literally—much sooner, if the Nazis and the Soviets develop atomic weapons."

The president looked to the British ambassador again. "This new information you have, the files sent to the *Trident*, do we know if they're genuine?"

"There's an enormous volume of information, Mr. President. Our boffins have given it all a tick so far, but I believe Admiral Kolhammer has assigned some of his analysts to the package."

"We have, sir. So far it checks out. The Norwegian heavy water plant, this Demidenko project—they both seem to be blinds for a joint fast-fission project the Nazis are working on with the Japanese, and they very much exclude the Soviets. The other material, the conventional weapons projects, all look kosher to us. Whoever this guy is, he's done us a huge favor."

"Okay, we'll move on to that this afternoon. We're getting off our agenda. Let's talk about these bombs that have been going off here. It's scaring the hell out of people, and beginning to have a real effect on home front morale."

Even though he'd stayed up all night preparing for this meeting, Dan Black wasn't required to speak, for which he'd be saying a special prayer of thanks later that evening. When asked, he provided hard copy and electronic files showing the status of all of the accelerated R & D projects in the Valley. Then he sat back down and watched the show, wondering just how the *hell* an unemployed coal miner turned copper miner turned crop duster had ended up in the Oval Office at a time like this.

His old man wouldn't have believed it in a million years.

He didn't think he'd ever be comfortable in this sort of company. Not like Admiral Kolhammer, who never seemed to take a backwards step, no matter what. Or Admiral King, who looked to be as tough as nails as he stalked around the room like he had an iron poker jammed up his ass. His intolerance of the Multinationals was matched only by his intolerance of the British, in the person of Lord Halifax, and even of the U.S. Army, leading Black to wonder if Marshall and Eisenhower were at the meeting in part to draw fire away from Kolhammer.

As for his own role, Commander Black sat in his chair by the mantelpiece, stiff-backed, unmoving, and trying not to sweat too loudly.

He almost fell over backwards when the president's secretary showed J. Edgar Hoover into the room.

Black couldn't help sneaking a look at the admiral's reaction, but Kolhammer was perfectly amiable. If anything, he greeted the FBI director with more warmth than anyone else in the room. Roosevelt was quite proper, without being warm. Halifax was smooth, as you'd expect of a knighted diplomat. Eishenhower was his usual friendly self, but the other military men were quite chilly. Although, when he thought about it, neither Marshall nor King were particularly friendly with anyone.

Hoover looked terrible. Gray blotchy skin hung in loose bags all over his face, and his watery eyes were sunken inside bruised-looking sockets. He was holding a single sheet of paper that he clung to as though to let go of it was to release his hold on life itself.

"Mr. Hoover," said Roosevelt. "I asked you here to give us the latest on the bombings. What do you have for us?"

Hoover didn't sit, preferring to stand by the president's desk, reading from his notes like a pupil called up to the front of the class. When the famous crime fighter spoke, Black had trouble following the rapid-fire delivery, although it sounded as if he didn't have much to say, anyway.

"Fifteen bombs have now gone off on both the eastern and western seaboards," Hoover said. "No war industries or elements of the infrastructure have been damaged, due I believe to the work of my agents in securing these facilities of vital national importance against the depredations of saboteurs and enemy sympathizers."

He shot Kolhammer a scowl at that point, but the commander of the Special Administrative Zone lobbed back a totally anodyne smile.

An uncomfortable silence enveloped the men in the room. As the seconds ticked by, it became quite excruciating.

"Is that it?" asked Henry Stimson.

Hoover's bulldoglike face flushed a deep crimson. "Mr. Secretary, my agents are shaking the trees and crawling down the darkest rat holes at this very moment in order to catch the vile malcontents responsible for these outrages. I think it ill behooves us to cast aspersions on their performance at this time. If there have been any slipups, you can rest assured I will find out about them."

Dan Black felt a sudden urge to leap from his seat and shout down the hypocritical little prick. He felt Kolhammer's cool gaze settle on him, however, so he reined in his indignation.

"I see," said Roosevelt, his voice as empty as an abandoned house. "Do you have any casualty figures, Mr. Hoover?"

The director stumbled for a moment. "Uhm, I believe one of my assistant directors is preparing those as we speak, Mr. President. I didn't think it would be advisable to come here with incomplete or misleading facts for you."

"All right, then, you get yourself back to your office and get me those figures, and when you come back, I'd like to know who's been setting these bombs, how they did it, and what you're going to do about catching them. People are beginning to panic, Mr. Hoover. They think this is some sort of prelude to an invasion. We have to convince them otherwise."

"If I may, Mr. President?" said Hoover.

Roosevelt's head tilted, and his bifocals caught the light at just the right angle to completely obscure his eyes. It was an eerie effect, since it made him look quite inhuman. Dan sensed that a trap was opening up in front of Hoover, but the FBI boss couldn't see it.

"I think they're right, Mr. President," he offered. "I think this may well be the work of a fifth column smuggled into the country through California, from South America. I intend no insult to Admiral *Kölhammer* . . ."

Black wasn't sure if Hoover had intentionally used the Germanic pronunciation, but again it seemed to roll off the admiral without effect. On the other hand, General Eisenhower did not seem at all impressed.

Hoover pressed on, seemingly oblivious. "But I am afraid things are very lax in California, from a security standpoint, Mr. President. Very lax, indeed. The laws of the country are flouted openly and at every turn. Simply uncountable numbers of undesirables and subversive types have set up shop in the shadow of this 'Special Administration' Zone. Enemy aliens are free to wander about unmolested. Some of them, I am duty-bound to point out, are men and even women who arrived with Admiral Kölhammer with the most advanced military training, and some of them having special training above and beyond that in *exactly* the sort of covert operations which have taken place in New York, and now in Los Angeles—which of course, is so close to the Special Zone that it would be remiss of me not to follow up that line of inquiry."

Hoover's excitement had got away from him. He was like a race caller at the derby now, so quickly did each sentence tumble out over the last.

"And of course, there are still 531,882 registered enemy aliens in that state who have not been interned, another 1,234,995 free in New York, and plenty more in between. If you would be willing to indulge me, Mr. President, I feel we can get right to the bottom of this situation. I have taken the liberty, which I'm sure you'll understand given the current exigencies, of having the Bureau's legal section draft a proposed executive order which would give the FBI the powers it needs to effectively deal with this immediate threat to our cherished freedoms and—"

"Enough, enough, Edgar. Just leave it behind on your way out," said Roosevelt. "I'll have Francis Biddle review it, later."

Hoover looked stunned. His mouth opened and closed twice without a sound coming out.

"That'll be all, Edgar."

The FBI director seemed incapable of movement. It was as though he had gripped a naked electric wire, and couldn't let go.

A Secret Service agent appeared through the Oval Office door.

He whispered something in Hoover's ear and gently took his elbow, guiding him toward the door. With only two exceptions, everybody in the room found something fascinating to look at, somewhere off in the middle distance. The exceptions were President Roosevelt and Admiral Kolhammer.

Black could have sworn that a flicker of a smile played across the president's face. And Kolhammer had somehow positioned himself near the exit without Black ever seeing him move there. He leaned over to give Hoover a comradely, reassuring pat on the back as he passed by. It looked like a genuinely compassionate gesture by the admiral, unless you heard what he actually said, as only Dan Black could.

"Hey, Edna. Loved the kimono."

"Have you ever considered a career in politics, Admiral?" Roosevelt kept the grin from his face as he asked, but the tone of his question was playful.

Kolhammer played it straight down the line. "I really don't believe it's appropriate for serving military officers to publicly involve themselves in the political process, Mr. President."

"Really?"

The Oval Office was empty, save for the two of them. The others had all left some twenty minutes earlier. A storm front was coming in from the west. Gusts of wind pasted wet leaves against the windows. Roosevelt wondered whether Kolhammer was just being polite. He might well be a registered Republican.

"You don't think that was politics, Admiral? Sandbagging Hoover like that? Is it common practice for the military in your day to put spies on the tail of civil servants they don't like?"

A smile crinkled a fine network of wrinkles at the corner of Kolhammer's eyes. "We've had some trouble with apparent espionage efforts in the Zone, Mr. President. It's what you'd expect, with so much advanced R and D going on there now. So it was only natural for my security to mount an effort to close down the operation."

"On your own."

"We had interagency help. From the Secret Service and the OSS. You can imagine our surprise when the trail led us to a hotel room in Florida. And the terrible shock of finding Mr. Hoover there. In a kimono."

Roosevelt snorted, unable to contain himself. "I think he'd call it a bathrobe. Tell me, Admiral, what was the Secret Service and Colonel Donovan doing offering *interagency* help for a domestic security matter? That's not within their fief?"

"Nobody knew that, until they knew it, sir," the admiral replied. Completely deadpan. "When I received the data from my security people—" He nodded at the video stick Roosevelt was rolling around in his palm. "—I immediately informed the other services that we had a problem. It was the considered opinion of us all that the only way to resolve the matter was to take it to the chief executive."

"I'll bet it was," said Roosevelt. His mouth felt like it was full of dry leaves and dust. He wanted to know a lot more about these "security people" of Kolhammer's who'd caught the FBI director with his pants down. They didn't sound like your run-of-the-mill night watchmen. Still, if there were problems here, there was also opportunity. An especially strong gust of wind threw a heavy twig into the window behind him. He expected to hear thunder start up in the next few minutes.

The admiral remained sitting at ease in front of him, giving nothing away.

"I imagine you'll want to know what I'm going to do about this?" said Roosevelt.

"It's really none of my business, except where it impinges upon the security of the Special Administrative Zone, Mr. President."

"No," Roosevelt agreed. "It's not."

He said nothing else, expecting to draw Kolhammer out with his silence. But the admiral remained po-faced. "Well, I'm not going to sack him today, if that's what you were hoping. But then as I understand it, in your day, what a man does in the privacy of his own home is his own business. Is that right?"

"It is, Mr. President. In his home . . . or his motel room."

Roosevelt contained a chuckle with only the fiercest of efforts. He wondered how on earth Kolhammer did it.

He placed the video stick into a desk drawer.

"What matters now are results, Admiral. Mr. Hoover knows I want results on the questions of who set those bombs, and how they managed it. If he is to have a future as director of the FBI, he'll get me those results."

For the first time Kolhammer offered something without being asked. "He'd get them a lot quicker if he didn't have so many agents crawling around the Zone. Or following your wife, with all due respect, Mr. President."

Roosevelt used his tongue to work free a piece of meat that stuck between his teeth during lunch. It covered his reaction to Kolhammer's comment about Eleanor. He'd been livid when he'd seen the data about how Hoover had been opening her mail and having her followed around. But he wasn't about to lay that card on the table. As much as he'd come to respect and even like Phillip Kolhammer, he still wasn't a hundred percent sure about him. After all, he could well be a Republican, couldn't he?

"I'll make sure the Bureau stops wasting its time in California, Admiral. You can be certain of that."

"I'd like to be, Mr. President."

Roosevelt patted the desk where he'd deposited the data stick. "You can."

28

LOS ANGELES, CALIFORNIA

True Grit was the best goddamn movie Eddie Mohr had ever seen. It was a hell of a shock, seeing John Wayne all fat and old and grizzled, but Mohr had seen enough birthdays to have no trouble imagining himself like that, so it wasn't entirely a bad thing. After all, even missing one eye and carrying a huge spare tire, Rooster Cogburn didn't give much away in the ass-kickin' stakes.

Mohr had seen the movie five times now: two times for free on the base up at San Diego, and three times on his own dollar at a theater in downtown L.A., where he was now. The youngsters, they all preferred that *Star Wars* shit, but it just left him cold. How you could get into something that was so far removed from reality, he just didn't know. But *True Grit* was as real a story as he'd ever seen, even the bit at the end with John Wayne doing his one-man cavalry charge, reins between his teeth, six-shooter in one hand

and Winchester in the other. That was a great fucking ending, not like that dumbass *Apocalypse Now*. He'd had to see that one in the Zone, because it was banned everywhere else, and he wondered why the hell he'd bothered when that bald bastard chopped up that poor fucking cow.

Mohr shook the image from his head as Marshal Cogburn yelled at the bad guys to fill their hands. After three weeks without a break, he was gonna enjoy—

"Oh, *goddamn*. What now?"

The lights in the theater came up, and the management came on over the PA, telling everyone they had to get out in a fast but orderly fashion. Luckily Grauman's Egyptian Theater, a less famous cousin to Grauman's Chinese a few blocks west, was only a third full, because there was nothing orderly about the way most of the patrons suddenly flew for the exits. Some idiot even shouted that there had to be a bomb in the joint.

Mohr rolled his eyes to heaven. He dawdled at the rear of the crush, ready to start pulling people off each other if it got out of hand. But the ushers and the good sense of a couple of other customers prevented a serious bottleneck from building up. As the choke point cleared, he saw a couple of AF uniforms at the exit. A black airman and a white sailor.

"Hey, you guys know what's up?" he asked.

The black guy, a flight sergeant, inclined his head toward the manager in the lobby, who was quickly handing out refunds and trying to hurry the stragglers outside. "He said a bomb went off on a trolley car over at Van Nuys. The city is shutting down the electric railway and all sorts of stuff. Like theaters, I guess."

"Oh, for fuck's sake," said Mohr.

"Hey, chief, how we gonna get back if they shut down the rail?" asked the sailor, a young middie whose name tag read LINTHICUM.

"Initiative, Mr. Linthicum. Let's get out of here and find a bus. You coming with us, Sarge?"

Fight Sergeant Lloyd thought it best if he did.

They collected their refunds and stepped out into the bright light of a warm autumn morning. Mohr was still squinting into the sun when the tomato hit him.

"What the fuck?"

A rotting apple struck Lloyd on the head.

The fruit came from a rowdy group across the street, which he'd mistaken for disgruntled movie patrons. They were bunched up where roadworks partly blocked the footpath. Looking at them now, Mohr could tell that they were off-duty sailors and soldiers, all 'temps. There were about fifteen or twenty of them, and the way they'd gathered around in a tight group, all turned inward, he could tell somebody was about to get the shit kicked out of him.

A cruising police car slowed down as it passed by; then it sped up and disappeared around the block.

"Shit," said Mohr. "You guys gonna back me up?"

He headed across without waiting for their reply. Lloyd fell in beside him, with Linthicum bringing up the rear.

As they got closer, dodging in between the traffic, he heard somebody call out, "Hey, it's the nigger lovers and their *boy*."

With that, it didn't matter that they were outnumbered. Mohr was past thinking rationally. He grabbed a steel picket and wrenched it out of a pile of earth and broken asphalt.

A corporal came at him with his fists up, but Mohr just swung the heavy iron bar into his face with such casual violence that he might have been taking the top off a boiled egg. The corporal's head snapped back with a wet crack and three or four teeth flew out. As he dropped, Mohr swung an overhand blow onto his shoulder, feeling it break like a soft twig.

The dark energy holding the group together drained away instantly, allowing him to get a better look at what had been happening. A kid in a torn AF uniform was down, already unconscious and covered in blood. Half his faced had been pulped. Mohr didn't know him, but he looked like some sort of Mexican.

"He's a fucking zoot-suiter, Chief. He deserved it."

Mohr turned a pitiless eye on the man who'd spoken, a big dumb bastard in an army uniform. "You want some of this, shit head?" He held up the steel rod, which was noticeably stained with the corporal's blood.

The private backed down. "No, sir."

"Do you think you could help him up, Mr. Linthicum?" Mohr asked the midshipman he'd met inside.

The young man nodded. He and Lloyd pushed their way in through the crowd. It was then that Eddie Mohr finally realized there was something else wrong. He hadn't paid attention to the sound of sirens when they'd emerged on the street, but now that he did, they were everywhere. And at least five or six columns of smoke were visible rising over the city.

"What the fuck's been going on here?" he asked.

WASHINGTON, D.C.

"More bombs?" asked Kolhammer.

"No, sir," said Black. "Riots. Both in Chicago and L.A."

They'd moved from the White House to the War Department offices in the Munitions Building on Constitution Avenue, for a smaller meeting. Just the two of them with Eisenhower, and his secretary to take notes. Kolhammer had wondered whether they might meet Kay Summersby, but then remembered that Ike himself wouldn't meet her until he got to England. Who knew if that would ever happen now.

He'd been waiting on Eisenhower, dwelling on the ripples of blood and consequence his arrival had created, when both his and Commander Black's flexipads beeped with incoming traffic.

Black scanned the message first and told him what had happened. "It's weird, sir. It looks like your zoot suit riot in L.A., and the black riot that would have happened in Chicago in your nineteen forty-three. They're early, though. And quite a few of our people have been caught up in the violence, back in L.A."

"Have they been specifically targeted?"

Black frowned and read more of the message from the Zone. "Hard to say. There's some guy in a hospital, one of your sailors off the *Leyte Gulf,* says he was attacked by a mob which blamed him for Hawaii and the bombings and for the Japs invading. But the police radio is carrying lots more reports of sailors and soldiers ganging up on the local pachucos."

"And in Chicago?"

"Straight out black-and-white race riot. A big one. But nothing on why yet."

Kolhammer had his own ideas about why, but he kept them to himself for the moment.

Eisenhower turned up at that point. They'd scheduled this meeting to discuss what role Kolhammer's units out West would play in the wider global conflict.

"Let's talk worst-case scenarios first, Admiral," he said. "What can you give me right now?"

Kolhammer beamed the relevant files across to Ike's flexipad before passing across a hard copy. "There's a test squadron of Sabers out at Muroc, which I'd be happy to certify as battle ready. Two prototype midair refuelers are good to go, which means we can get those planes over Hawaii if you choose. Of course, they won't have a lot of payloads to deliver. The rockets are still in beta phase, but the cannons are fine. We've got ten thousand MK-One assault rifles, with grenade launchers, but we don't have ground forces ready to deploy with them. Colonel Jones gave up a significant number of his people to supply training cadre, but it's a slow business, and sending them now really means killing most of them, for no appreciable return."

Eisenhower turned the problem over in his mind. "What about the First Marine Division?"

Kolhammer had hoped he might suggest that option. The First had never made it to Guadalcanal. The destruction of the Fleet at Midway had robbed the Allies of any means of getting them there, and Yamamoto had seized the opportunity as part of his mad dash south to take a stranglehold on the island, at the same time as he pushed nine divisions into New Guinea through Rabaul.

"MacArthur's blooded them on the Brisbane Line," said Kolhammer. "They've been working in with the Eighty-second, so they'd be familiar with our methods. The Aussies have been replacing their Lee Enfields with a thirty-aught-six Kalashnikov variant that's a close copy of our MK-One. So the marines could train with them down there. I'd say they're good to go."

"MacArthur will scream blue murder. As will Curtin, and with good reason."

"If the Japanese take Hawaii and keep it, Australia will go down, and New Zealand with it. We'll be boxed in on the Pacific. And then the Atlantic, if England falls."

Eisenhower turned around in his old, wooden swivel chair to look at the map that hung on the wall behind his head. "Okay. Leave the politics to me," he said at last. "I'll get the First marines ready for redeployment. Which raises the question of how we get them to Pearl with that rogue ship of yours lurking around."

"The *Siranui* can escort them, if we turn her around right now. The *Clinton*'s close enough to San Diego that we can cover her with the Raptors we've got on shore."

"How many Japanese do you have left on that vessel, Admiral? The *Siranui*?"

"Nine. All volunteers. They've been helping with the changeover to the *Leyte Gulf*'s crew. We couldn't have done it without them. All of the software was in *kanji* script."

"Good for them, but I'm afraid they'll have to sit this one out."

Kolhammer didn't reply immediately. He'd fought very hard to keep his "enemy alien" personnel out of prison, and just as hard to protect the *Siranui*'s crew from the prejudices of the 'temps. He trusted each of them with his life, but he could understand Eisenhower's point, and he could tell there'd be no shifting him on it.

"Okay," he agreed reluctantly. "We can cross-deck them to the *Clinton*, for now. The software changeover is complete, anyway. But they're going to be assigned to active duty under my command, General. I'll not have them treated with a lack of honor."

Eisenhower didn't seem put out by that. Instead he threw Kolhammer off balance with a pause and a change of tack. "I thought you handled that scene in the Oval Office very well, Admiral. Hoover was really gunning for you."

"He's been gunning for all of us, from day one," said Kolhammer. "Well, maybe day two, when he figured out that he had no secrets from us."

"Rumors have been swirling around him for years," said Eisenhower. "But he's wounded, not crippled, Admiral. You'll want to watch yourself."

"I have bigger problems than that fruit and nut bar," said Kolhammer.

"For now you do. That won't always be the case." Eisenhower waved a hand toward the map on the wall. "This isn't the only war you're fighting, Admiral. Don't make the mistake of assuming you have to fight every battle on your own. Not everybody in this country is as frightened of the future as Mr. Hoover."

"They should be," replied Kolhammer. But he regretted doing so.

LOS ANGELES, CALIFORNIA

The guy in the back of the car was beginning to spasm and vomit up bile. Mohr thought they might lose him before they made it to the hospital. The driver, some Good Samaritan who'd surprised the hell out of Eddie by pulling over and offering to help, kept veering into the oncoming traffic as he craned around to ask if the kid was going to make it.

"I don't know," said Eddie. "They fucked him up pretty good."

Flight Sergeant Lloyd was in the front passenger seat, while in the back Mohr and Linthicum nursed the unconscious victim of the mob attack. The chief had been forced to crack another one of those losers across the head with his makeshift club to get them to break it up. He'd belted a sailor with blood on his bell-bottoms, figuring that was as good as a guilty verdict in a proper court.

"And the rest of you can fuck off right now, unless you're hungry for some of this, too," he'd growled, waving the steel picket around.

They hadn't argued.

Mohr and Lloyd had been trying to rig up a litter to transport their patient when a black Packard Clipper, driven by a silver-haired gent called Max, pulled over and offered them a lift. Frankly, Max looked like he had the sort of old money that'd make Scrooge McDuck seem hard up for a buck, but he didn't even take off his expensive suit jacket when he helped pick up the kid. He just mucked right in and got blood all over it.

"I know a private clinic we can take him to," Max said, almost swerving into the path of a fire engine as it shot past in a red blur. "The big emergency wards are all going to be stretched past what they can handle, anyway. This madness is all over the city. And you can take it from me, the police aren't making it any better."

"You a doctor, Max?" Mohr called out over the muted roar of the Packard's 356-cubic-inch straight-eight.

"Hell, no. My family's in oil. You boys are with the Zone, right? Your friend there, too."

"We are," Mohr confirmed, "but we don't know this guy. We just found him."

Max took them out of the city, driving hard past mobs of drunken servicemen and small groups of angry-looking Mexican kids in ridiculously oversized suits. Half of Bunker Hill looked like it had been set ablaze, and they saw a huge mob at war with itself a few blocks down Third Street, near the tunnel entrance.

At times, Mohr was sure they reached a hundred miles per hour, an insane speed, but Max stayed hunched over the wheel, all the way up into the hills. A motorcycle cop seemed to think about giving chase at one point, but the dispatchers must have had something better for him to do, because he peeled away almost immediately.

"Those assholes are just letting this happen," said Max. "And you can bet there's a reason behind it. Did you hear? The same thing's happening in Chicago, with the blacks over there, of course. Mark my words, gentlemen, some baby-fascist like Anslinger or Hoover will get their grubby little mitts all over this."

"Jeez, Max, you sound more like a Wobbly than an oil man," Mohr said, smiling for the first time since they'd left the theater.

"Like I said, my family's in oil, Chief. But I'm not. I had enough of that in the Great War. Drove a St. Chamond tank with the French at Laffaux Mill. Damn thing turned over in a ditch and caught fire. I swear, I could still smell burning Frenchmen a year later. Never again, Chief. This car is my one indulgence. The rest of my life I try to live according to the teachings of Henry Thoreau. You know him?'

"Another French tanker?"

Max burst out laughing, and nearly put himself into a ditch again. "Not likely. Okay, we're here. Let's get your friend seen to."

Max took them off the street and through a grand, gated entrance into what looked like a mansion.

"It's a private facility," he said as they slid to a halt on the gravel driveway. "Half of Hollywood comes here to dry out, but they have a fully equipped emergency ward, too. You never know when Veronica Lake is going to turn up."

"Uhm, do you think they'll let us in?" Flight Sergeant Lloyd asked doubtfully.

"Don't worry, son. The only color that counts here is money. My family's probably built a whole wing onto this place over the years. They'll let us in, all right. Let's go."

Two white-suited orderlies carrying a stretcher were hurrying toward them, down a sweeping staircase that led up into a blindingly white building. They didn't even break stride when Mohr and his motley band emerged from the car covered in blood.

"Hello, Mr. Ambrose," they called out simultaneously.

"Hello, Louis. Mandy," Max answered. "I wonder if you could see to my young friend here. He's in some distress."

They relieved Mohr and Linthicum of their burden, placed the kid on the stretcher, and disappeared back up the stairs without another word. The chief didn't know what to say. He had never, in his whole life, been witness to such a thing. He'd always thought it was compulsory to be a complete asshole once you got to be rich enough to get away with it.

But Max was already climbing back into the car, saying there'd be other people downtown who needed his help. "Are you coming?" he asked.

"I guess so," said Eddie Mohr. His companions just nodded.

29

BERLIN, GERMANY

In many ways, Sea Dragon was a blessing in disguise for Captain Müller.

The titanic effort required of the Nazi superstate to rise up and throw itself across the English Channel inevitably focused the energies of the Reich in northern France. The Gestapo and the SS were both kept busy trying to suppress the French resistance, which was sacrificing itself in a desperate assault on German preparations for the invasion of Great Britain.

Thousands of Frenchmen and -women would die in the next few days to give their traditional enemies, the English, a fighting chance against Jürgen Müller's countrymen. He pondered the ironies as he polished his great-grandfather's war watch and wondered what role his forebear would play in the crusade of the coming days. In Müller's universe, he'd been a company commander in the *Gross Deutschland* Division. His ancestor had been executed for holding a river crossing against the Red Army during the retreat from Moscow. Saving the lives of hundreds of his men was considered defeatist, and had cost Heinrich Müller his own life.

His family had gone into the camps shortly after.

This same watch still sat in his great-grandfather's breast pocket somewhere. Probably in a forward depot near the French coastline, where the *Gross Deutschland* would await transport to Britain, should the airborne assault gain a foothold. Holding the watch gingerly in his "injured" hand—the one encased in a fake plaster cast—Müller rubbed at the glass face with a handkerchief. Apart from that glass face, which had been replaced sometime in the 1960s, this timepiece was the same one his ancestor carried, right down to the subatomic level.

Müller could only wish that human nature could be as constant.

He had volunteered for this mission, knowing that he would most likely not return from his personal journey into the darkness of Hitler's Germany. But that didn't concern him. If captured, he was wetwired, not just to resist the pain of torture, but to laugh in the face of his tormentors. However, there was no spinal insert that would dull the horror of seeing the children he had really come to save. He wasn't supposed to seek them out—in fact, he had been specifically ordered to avoid them at all costs.

But Müller had come fully intending to disobey his controllers. He would carry out his primary mission: the capture, hostile debriefing, and termination of Colonel Paul Brasch. But once that was done, he would be a free agent. And then he intended to save his family.

Unfortunately, it wasn't turning out to be so simple. He wasn't concerned about Brasch. No, that would run smoothly. But as he obsessively polished Heinrich Müller's watch, sitting in the small park across from the apartment block of his prime target, he felt like a man who was slowly being drained of life by a succubus. His eyes were hollow and his soul withdrawn. He appeared haunted and lost, which was to his advantage, in one sense. It fit perfectly with his cover.

But it wasn't an act. For he had broken the one promise he'd made to himself—that he would execute the mission first.

Müller had been unable to resist the urge to seek out his family, just to catch a glimpse of the children. Of Hans, who would be beaten to death protecting his little brother, Erwin, from a homosexual rapist. Of little Erwin, gunned down without reason by an SS guard. He had seen them with their sisters, Lotti and Ingrid, but it had been a terrible mistake.

To his horror Hans was dressed in the uniform of the Hitler youth, and as Müller had stood there, completely numb, they had all skipped past, laughing merrily at the eldest boy's story of having chased and kicked an old Jew, while away at camp.

Müller was so lost in his dark thoughts that he almost missed Brasch, exiting the door of his building and hurrying off to catch the tram to work.

He hadn't needed the overcoat. It was, unfortunately, an unseasonably warm day.

Brasch had been praying for foul weather, for anything that might hinder the success of Sea Dragon. He had done what he could to, at great risk to his family's survival. Now it was down to Providence, and the Allies.

He still found it hard to believe that he—a winner of the Iron Cross—had actually betrayed his homeland to them. As he made his way into the foyer of the Armaments Ministry, through the hive of National Socialists and their Wehrmacht mercenaries, he wondered if any of the self-doubt and fear showed on his face. He knew it was a common conceit of the treacherous that they stood at the center of events, and thought themselves to be the object of everyone's attention. But he was a rational man, with enough strength of will to be able to avoid that potentially fatal self-absorption.

Colonel Brasch returned each of his colleagues' greetings with an appropriately enthusiastic *"Sieg Heil."* He maintained his facade of dour industry as he climbed up to his second-floor office. And he tried to brick off that small part of his mind that constantly screamed at him, expecting to open his marbled glass office door and find half a dozen Gestapo men waiting for him with guns and rubber truncheons.

"Good morning, Herr *Oberst.*" His secretary smiled in her anteroom office.

"Good morning, Frau Schlüter," he replied. "No calls for an hour, please. I shall be very busy."

Brasch closed the door on her answer and collapsed into his chair, shaking and sweating. He recognized the scent of his own terror, a really foul, sour sort of rankness. He opened the windows as far they would go and sat on the ledge, hoping the slightly cooler air outside might clear his head and remove the fug of anxiety that seemed to hang in the room.

On the desk, his flexipad beeped, causing his heart to skip. Then he calmed down. Only a few high officials had access to the devices, and *Reichsführers* didn't ordinarily bother themselves with low-level administrative tasks such as calling traitors in for questioning.

Brasch picked up the pad, expecting to find a small envelope, the standard icon of a text message. He was amazed to discover full-motion video on screen—the Reich did not have the bandwidth that would allow for such indulgences.

His surprise was quickly supplanted by panic and confusion as he observed the content of the movie.

His wife and son were gagged, and bound to kitchen chairs in the apartment, their eyes bulging in fear while a man he vaguely recognized stood behind them.

The image disappeared, and was replaced by a text screen.

i will kill them if you are not home in fifteen minutes. i will kill them if you come armed or with company.

The connection dropped out—just as the world dropped out from under his feet. Brasch grabbed at the edge of his desk to stop himself collapsing to the floor. Gray spots bloomed in front of his eyes, threatening to join together and drag him down into unconsciousness.

He had to tell himself to breathe, mechanically forcing his lungs to draw in air. He spun around and lunged for the open window, leaning on the sill and dragging in long drafts of fresh air.

His eyes throbbed and tornadoes blew through his head.

Who could it be? *The Gestapo?* Had they discovered his treason? *But no, if that had happened, I would not be alive.*

Then who? Where had he seen that man before?

Willie's wide eyes and Little Manny's white, terrified face loomed out of the gray spots that still lurked in his peripheral vision. When he was almost sure he could walk without getting tangled up in the wet spaghetti strands of his own legs, he grabbed the flexipad, attempted to compose himself, and headed out the door.

"Herr *Oberst?*" said Frau Schlüter. "Is there anything—?"

"No," he croaked, waving the pad at her. "I simply forgot a meeting at OKH. I am late. I shall be back later today."

"But there is no meeting at—"

"I got the message last night," he called back over his shoulder, as he left the office. "It was too late to call you. Please carry on updating the Two Sixty-two files."

He broke into a trot in the corridor, almost knocking a *Kriegsmarine* officer off his feet as he hurtled around a corner.

"Excuse me," he called out as he dashed past the elevators, which were notoriously slow. He headed straight for the stairwell instead, trying to get out of the building as quickly as possible, without looking like a madman.

Others were also hurrying about, no doubt on important state business, so no one paid him any mind.

Brasch hit the street and ran for a tram that was pulling up a hundred yards away. As he struggled to put his flexipad away, he realized he had no change for the fare, but rushed on anyway, leaping onto the bottom step just as the streetcar began to move.

A conductor began to amble toward him as he puffed and prepared to browbeat the man into letting him ride for free. But as he began the pantomime of searching his pockets for coins he knew weren't there, the man nodded at the Iron Cross on his breast and turned away.

Brasch examined the decoration somewhat dubiously. So it had a use after all.

He rode the entire way home, bunching the muscles in his legs, silently urging the driver to hurry up. He checked his watch at least twice every minute, cursing himself for not noting what time the message had come in. Would he make it in fifteen minutes?

Would a delay of a minute or two cause the man to kill his wife and child?

Behind of all this lay the bigger question: Who was their captor? Which master had sent him?

The more he thought about it, Brasch didn't think the man was an SD agent. The state had no need to play games like this. If they had wanted him, they would have marched a squad of goons into the office and simply taken him. So, too, with his family.

He realized with a flutter of his already churning stomach that he still wore his Luger. The instructions had been quite explicit. He was to come alone—and unarmed.

Thus as he jumped from the trolley at the stop nearest his home, and half walked, half jogged the rest of the way, Brasch unbuttoned the clasp on his holster. His soldier's training tried to assert itself, pushing him toward action. But his rational mind checked the warrior spirit.

This bastard wanted him, for whatever reason. If he had been an assassin, he wouldn't have bothered with Willie and Manfred. No, the prize was Brasch, not his corpse.

He fumbled with his keys at the building entrance, and again at the door to their rooms. "It's me," he called out, closing the door behind him. The kitchen was at the end of a long corridor. He unloaded the Luger and slid it along the carpeted floor with an underarm throw.

"There," he called out, "it is as you wished. And I am alone."

A German voice replied. "I know. I can see. Come into the kitchen, slowly."

When he was halfway down the hall, the voice spoke again. "Turn around, place your hands on your head, and walk the rest of the way back-wards."

Brasch did as he was told.

Müller watched the engineer as he felt his way into the small kitchen. When Brasch was a few feet from the table, Müller told him to stop and turn around.

"Bind your hands to the table leg with those plasteel cuffs," he ordered, pointing to the objects on the table. "I'm sure you know what I mean, so don't fuck around or I will put a bullet into your son. This pistol is silenced. Nobody will hear."

He spoke in English, to spare the boy any more distress than was neces-sary. Even so, he fought to keep the disgust off his face and out of his voice. This wasn't how he had imagined himself when he had enlisted, twelve years earlier. No, this was the moral equivalent of the evil he had volun-teered to fight, although he had no real intention of murdering the boy or the woman.

Brasch however, could well be spending his last day on earth. When the engineer had cuffed himself to the table, Müller moved around to a spot where he could see the man's hands.

"You have brought your flexipad, I see. Good, Herr *Oberst*. I will remove it now and place it on the table. My gun will be at your head the entire time. I doubt you will want your son to watch as his papa's brains are blown out."

Brasch was shaking with coiled tension as Müller removed the device, powered it up, and laid it next to his own on the table. He keyed in the com-mand set that would effect a laser link transfer of all the data.

"What are you doing?" asked Brasch. "You're not Gestapo, are you? You're one of them. From the future?"

"Yes," Müller admitted. "And I'm saving Germany from herself."

"You *idiot*!" Brasch spat. "Why did you have to do this to my family? Look at little Manny—he is shaking with terror. You have tortured him, and all for nothing. I sent you everything I know. Everything! And *this* is my re-ward? What sort of a barbarian are you?"

Müller had no idea what the man was talking about. His mission brief had been simple. Brasch was one of the critical players in the Nazi's acceler-ated weapons program. So Müller had been sent in to determine how much they had accomplished, and to liquidate Brasch once he had the informa-tion. The engineer's outburst made no sense.

"Where do you think the data burst came from, on the Demidenko Cen-ter, the fast-fission project, the SS special-weapons directorate," Brasch hissed, glancing around as if afraid they might be overheard.

"Just shut up, and slow down," Müller barked when he finally recovered his wits. "What are you talking about? What burst?"

"It was yesterday! I sent a compressed, encrypted burst to the British ship, the *Trident*. It took me *months* to work out how to do so, without being caught. I sent everything I had on the special projects, and on Sea Dragon. Have they told you nothing?"

"Did you identify yourself?" asked Müller as he tried to understand what was happening. It was like wrestling with blocks of smoke.

"Of *course* not. Do you think I'm insane? I took enough of a risk, just sending the information as I did."

Müller glanced at the wife. She must speak English, too, he guessed. He'd spoken to her only in German before. Her eyes registered a renewed shock—something beyond the trauma of being taken hostage.

He tried to think it through as quickly as possible. If Brasch had sent such a burst, but hadn't identified himself, there would be no immediate reason for the special ops executive to contact Müller. Particularly if there was any risk of compromising the source of such valuable new information.

"Shit," he muttered as he scooped up his own flexipad. He dropped the file transfer into the background and brought up the communicator, scribbling out a quick message.

He needed to check out Brasch's story.

HMS *TRIDENT*, THE ENGLISH CHANNEL

The *Trident*'s defensive stocks had dropped to 13 percent of capacity. The previous day's attack by ME 262s had sliced through the destroyer screen and pressed in on the ship, requiring her Close-In Weapons Systems to respond.

The Metal Storm pods had chewed up the incoming fighters in less than four seconds, but all the defensive sysops in the ship's Combat Information Center had red warning lights displayed on their screens. Ammunition for the pods had dropped past the critical line. Back home, the *Trident* would have been assigned protected status, and would have been shielded by other ships connected via the Cooperative Battle Link. Or she would have withdrawn from hostilities altogether.

Neither of those options was available to Halabi now.

She caught herself chewing at her bottom lip as she reviewed the situation. It wouldn't do to look as though circumstance had the better of her. But she was growing concerned that that was exactly the case. News of the missile strike on Hawaii had jolted the ship's complement, but not as much as the message from Kolhammer that arrived shortly afterwards, warning her that the *Trident* might come under attack from weapons stripped off the French cruiser. It was unlikely, but it forced her to revise down their chances of survival. How difficult could it be to remove a cruise missile from the *Dessaix* and rig it up for a land-based launch against her command? Very difficult, she supposed, but not impossible if a few key crew members had helped out.

And the chances of that?

She had no idea.

She could feel the increased tension in her CIC. Nerves had been stretched to the breaking point. The first blows of Sea Dragon had already been struck. The two attempts by the Luftwaffe could no longer be seen as probes. They were hammering at Britain's shield. The Wehrmacht was moving into position for an assault across the Channel.

Thousands of men dueled and died in the skies above them as the RAF and the Luftwaffe clawed at each other for supremacy. Neither side had unleashed any additional jet fighters, since the ME 262s had been destroyed attacking her ship, but there had been some nasty surprises for everyone, nonetheless.

Some of the conventional German fighters had been modified to allow them much more time to wreak havoc over England. ME 109s with modified propellers, drop tanks, and even a few with DKM-type rotary engines had been shot down and recovered. Some carried primitive radar-seeking missiles.

In reply, Spitfires with mods designed by her own engineers had climbed into the air to meet them. Bomber Command sent waves of B-17s and Lancasters across the Channel to rain high explosives down on the staging ports and airfields of northern France. Radar-controlled triple-A raked them from the sky.

Halabi had slept four hours in the last thirty-six. *Thank God for stims.* The *Trident* remained poised to deliver Prince Harry and his commandos to Norway, but they hadn't moved away from the Solent, waiting while London tried to decide whether or not to scrub the mission.

It seemed to her that the stealth cruiser was needed more right here, to help coordinate the immediate defense of the realm. Sixteen newcomers had invaded her CIC. Top brass from the Admiralty, the RAF, and General Staff, all of them blundering about, getting underfoot, and generally hampering the very effort they had come to "supervise."

She was just about to ask a knighted rear admiral to get his fat arse out of her way when the intel section reported incoming traffic, for her eyes only.

"To my viewscreen, then, Mr. Howard."

"Right you are, ma'am."

It was a short text message from a skin job. Müller.

Target Brasch acquired. Claims to have delivered data by encrypted subroutine in the last twenty-four hours. Please advise.

Halabi had to call up his mission profile, and that required her DNA key for access. She placed her palm on the reader and waited for the ship's Combat Intelligence to unlock the data.

"Access granted," said Posh.

"What the hell's going on here," asked an air vice marshal.

Halabi couldn't remember his name. She held up one hand to silence him while she skimmed the mission brief.

"Don't you wave me away, young lady!" he blustered. "I've got every fighter wing in the country up there right now. If the fat's in the fire, I need to know."

"Mr. McTeale," she called out, trying to concentrate on the screen in front of her.

Her executive officer appeared at the shoulder of the RAF man. "The captain is extremely busy, sir. Please step away from her station."

Halabi typed out a quick reply to Müller.

Transmission confirmed. Stand by.

"Mr. Howard, to the ops room, please."

As her intelligence boss left his station, McTeale struggled briefly with the RAF officer. Air Vice Marshal Simon Caterson, she now recalled—a bit of a prat with an irritating habit of holding forth on all manner of topics, whether he knew anything about them or not.

"Air Vice Marshal, you *will* restrain yourself, or I will have Mr. McTeale turn you over to the SAS lads, to use as a practice dummy. They broke their last one."

With that, she headed for ops. She was certain she heard Caterson say, "Wretched woman," as she left.

Howard joined her there, a few steps down the corridor in the central hull. It was a smaller version of the CIC, with backups for many of the same systems. It was also mercifully free of 'temps.

"You're familiar with the Müller jacket, Mr. Howard?"

He nodded. Howard was responsible for tracking all the skin jobs on their bionet. Thirteen in all. "He was going after an engineer. One of the brighter kiddies."

"Well, he found him," said Halabi. "And this guy claims to be our secret admirer from yesterday. Do you think it's possible?"

"Brasch?" The lieutenant commander thought it over. "It's definitely possible. The project data we received matches up with his AOR. But it matches a couple of others, too."

"How many?"

"Two. An admiral in the *Kriegsmarine*, and a Luftwaffe colonel."

"What're Müller's mission specs?" she asked.

"Quick and dirty. A hostile debrief, followed by Sanction Two."

"Really?" said Halabi. "I thought Müller was a pilot. He's not really trained for that sort of business, is he?"

"Jacket says he volunteered. He's a Jerry. Figured he'd fit right in."

Halabi, who had an intimate understanding of cultural dislocation, doubted that, but she didn't have time to debate the point.

"Excuse me, ma'am," the comm operator called over, interrupting the discussion. "Eyes only again, for you."

Halabi took the message on the nearest screen. She had a feeling it was Müller again.

She was right. It was a one-line message, but it cut through the Rubik's Cube of possibilities she'd just been playing with.

Brasch requests extraction.

"Better get the War Ministry for me," she told her comm officer.

"Captain! We have incoming. Sorry, no, we don't. London does."

"What do you mean?" she asked. "More jets."

"No, ma'am. Missiles. Cruise missiles."

30

NORWAY

These were the finest men Aryan blood had to offer, and he was immensely proud of them. There were only eight of them, two units of four men each, something they had learned from England's much-vaunted Special Air Service. The SS wasn't so arrogant as its opponents imagined. It was more than willing to adapt and improve upon their ideas. But if they wanted to think of his troops as mindless automatons, then let them.

He would laugh on their graves.

It felt strange, however, to be standing in front of an American aeroplane—a Douglas Dakota, they called it, captured in North Africa. Stranger still to be addressing men dressed in the uniforms of the enemy.

As the moment finally arrived, and Operation Sea Dragon began to unfold, *Reichsführer* Heinrich Himmler could have been at the missile base in Donzenac, or with his new airborne regiment at Zaandam. These eight men, however, were about to embark on a personal odyssey entirely of his own design. They were going to drive a dagger into the heart of England, and so he had chosen to join them on a small, nameless airfield at the edge of the North Sea.

Three of them spoke English perfectly; most of the others with a slight accent, hence the uniforms, which identified them as Free Polish forces. Englanders thought of all Europeans as essentially the same. Wogs or wops or some such insulting nonsense. That ill-considered sense of superiority would cost them dearly over the next few days.

Only Colonel Skorzeny, the commander of the group, would proceed without a thorough mastery of English. But he was the one man Himmler knew he could trust with a job like this. Given the need, he would walk through mountains if they stood in his way. The *Reichsführer*'s only regret was that he wouldn't personally get to watch as Skorzeny completed his mission. But if the colonel survived, he would entertain everyone at the Wolfschanze with his vivid tales of the adventure.

The giant storm trooper, who was dressed as a simple corporal, stomped up and down in front of his men as they stood in line like carven marble statues. "So who amongst you will slaughter this fat pig for the führer?" he roared at them.

"I will, sir!" they all chorused in return.

"No," he boomed back, laughing like an elder God. "*I* will choke the life out of him, and you shall do nothing more than gather around to slap me on the back, and tell me what a fine fellow I am. Are we understood?"

"*Jawohl, Herr Korporal!*"

Skorzeny seemed to find that immensely funny, and another gale of his rich laughter peeled away into the night sky. It was uncomfortably chilly on the runway, which had been carved out of an ancient birch forest high above the waters of the Skagerrak, and Himmler wrapped himself more deeply into his greatcoat. He would never share the bond Skorzeny had with these men, the easy familiarity they had with each other and with the likelihood of their own deaths. But he could appreciate their camaraderie, and even Skorzeny's high spirits.

He coughed loudly, and the colonel yelled at the men to attend to his words.

"Please, please, stand at ease," said Himmler.

They unbent just a fraction.

"You men make me proud to be German," he said. "You have all volunteered for this most dangerous mission, and it will take you into the deepest recesses of the enemy's lair. You are few in number, but the effect of your actions will be unmeasurable. To me, you personify all that is great in our party. You are supermen, and my best wishes go with you. *Heil Hitler!*"

"*Heil Hitler!*"

Himmler bowed his head slightly in acknowledgment, and Skorzeny yelled at the pilots to spool up the Dakota's two engines. As they coughed into life, thick smoke and blue flame belched from the cowlings. Skorzeny slapped the first man in line on the shoulder and he turned with mechanical precision to climb into the cabin. The others followed, until only Skorzeny was left.

"The führer has much to occupy him right now," said Himmler, "but he wanted me to tell you that he will be thinking of you and your men especially."

An uncharacteristic solemnity came over the SS colonel. "Thank you. That is most gracious, Herr *Reichsführer*. We shall earn that honor, or die to a man in trying."

They saluted, and Skorzeny disappeared in through the darkened door of the plane.

MOSCOW, USSR

The lights hadn't been put out in the Little Corner for nearly a week. Even with Hitler's attention elsewhere, this was a very dangerous time for the Soviet Union. Josef Stalin had napped only fitfully during the last three days, although physically he felt fine, thanks to the medicines his physician had been given from the British ship named *Vanguard*.

Sitting in his office, the Soviet leader allowed himself a rare moment of relaxation, sipping from a long glass of hot tea, as he contemplated a world remade in his own image. It might take another ten years, and it would without a doubt be a bloody business. But at the end of it, the revolution would be safe from fascists like Hitler, traitors like Khrushchev, and imperialists like Churchill and Roosevelt.

There would never come a day when his statues were tipped over and melted down for scrap. Indeed, he amused himself by imagining a statue large enough to replace the Washington Monument. A great towering Comrade Stalin to keep a stern watch over the liberated workers of the United Soviet States of Amerika.

"More tea, Comrade?" asked Poskrebyshev. "Before the others arrive?"

"No, I will need a bucket under the desk, if I drink any more."

Stalin stretched his tired frame. A light dusting of snow lay on the cold stone laneways of the Kremlin, outside his window. He knew he would feel more secure once that white blanket was properly draped over the Motherland. Zhukov was doing wonders with the Red Army, now that he had time to train and equip his divisions properly. When the thaw came, no matter what the correlation of forces in the West, the Soviet Union would be safe behind an Iron Curtain.

That phrase, which Beria had taught him, was most appealing. Having faced annihilation at the hands of the fascists a few short months ago, Josef Stalin was much taken with the image of an iron curtain falling across the frontier with Germany, no matter who controlled it.

He suspected that it would be the Allies. Their industrial capacity supplied them with an advantage that would be nearly impossible to overcome. And now, augmented with the wonders of the next century, they would surely triumph over the fascists.

But he would not be helping them. Not if that support meant the eventual collapse of the revolution. Or the conquest of the Rodina by a— What was Beria's phrase? *A digital Hitler.* The situation had been so finely balanced that when that mincing dandy Ribbentrop had offered a cease-fire, he had not dared let the opportunity slip by. Not when the reports from the Pacific illustrated how powerful the weapons were that the fascists had obtained. For one very tense week, he'd actually expected Himmler's storm troopers to crash in through his windows at any moment, cocooned in armor that made them virtually invulnerable.

Of course, he'd been wrong about that. As it had turned out, those bastards had only picked up the table scraps, while the bulk of the windfall had gone to Roosevelt and his allies.

But that didn't matter now.

Stalin placed his empty drinking glass on a silver coaster and leaned forward to pick up the model again.

The NKVD had retrieved it from the *Vanguard*. It was a model of the ship that had materialized at the edge of the Siberian ice pack. A beautiful weapon; unusual, with its three hulls and featureless deck, but deadly looking nonetheless. Like an assassin's dagger. How strange that it had arrived a whole day *before* the Pacific Emergence.

Stalin wished for just a moment that the burdens of state didn't have to lie so heavily on his shoulders. He would have loved to make the journey to the special facilities that were being constructed around the ship, just to see it with his own eyes. But such things were not possible.

Then he snorted in amusement. Was there anything that could be called impossible nowadays?

"*Vozhd?*" his secretary asked. "Something amuses you?"

"Life amuses me, Poskrebyshev. Life, and everything about it. Tell me, are they here yet?"

"Yes. They are waiting outside."

"Well, bring them in, bring them in."

Poskrebyshev carried his narrow-shouldered, slightly hunched frame out of the room. He'd never really been the same since the NKVD had executed his wife. He had an impressively ugly countenance, which Stalin admired because it frightened visitors who came to the Little Corner. That countenance wore a perpetual scowl.

He reappeared, with Beria and Molotov in tow. The secret policeman seemed as chipper as ever, which was to say not at all, but at least relentless morbidity was his natural state of being. Molotov, like everyone in high office these days, looked as though the executioner stalked his every move.

They sat in hard wooden chairs in front of Stalin's desk. He spoke first to Molotov. "So, Vyacheslav Mikhaylovich, we have acceded to the fascists' request for assistance on this one little matter, and I can see that you are still not happy."

"I doubt the British will see it as such a trifle," said Molotov. "They are rather fond of Churchill, and will not appreciate the fact that we have helped the fascists to kill him."

"Yet our involvement is quite deniable," said Beria. "Our man should be able to get himself out to Ireland, and then home when he is done."

Stalin, like his foreign minister, still was not sure.

Britain had come close to declaring war on Russia when he'd impounded the ships of convoy PQ 17 at Murmansk, just before signing the cease-fire with Germany. Their anger was quite reasonable, he admitted. With one backhanded sweep, he had done more to damage the Royal Navy than Hitler's oafish admirals had managed in two and a half years.

The vessels were still there: thirty-five merchantmen and their escorts, including four destroyers, ten corvettes, two antiaircraft auxiliaries, and four cruisers. He had been scrupulously fair, refusing every German entreaty to turn the ships over to the *Kriegsmarine*. And the crews were being held in relative comfort, given the deprivations of wartime Russia.

But it was important that he maintain the facade of neutrality, and that meant detaining the combatants. The matériel in the holds of the ships had always been meant for his country, so he kept the hundreds of tanks and bombers, the thousands of trucks and other cargo. The trucks, in particular, had been very useful, when it became obvious that the *Vanguard* could not be moved. He stroked the model of the trihulled warship.

The Nazis, with their pathetic attempt to deceive him with the Demidenko project, would have fainted dead away if they could see what Kaganovich and Zhdanov had built around the *Vanguard*. Well, they would know soon enough. His country might be poor, but it was still a giant, and vast amounts of her resources were now being directed to exploiting the windfall of the *Vanguard*. If he could just keep the fascists and the capitalist gangsters at war with each other, and away from his own jugular for a little while longer, he would soon be able to strike at them both, and set history right.

The Nazis dismal efforts at *maskirovka* would come back to haunt them, for while it was true that Demidenko was draining much-needed men and matériel from his real efforts, it was also costing Hitler and Himmler an unknowable amount of treasure to maintain the facade of rapprochement. And his Soviet engineers were ingenious enough to quietly learn enough from the "mistakes" at Demidenko to advance the *Vanguard* project all the much more quickly. If only they'd been able to take and keep more of the crew alive . . .

But as dialectical materialists, they would work with what was, not what he might wish to be.

"All right, Beria," said Stalin. "Your man is cleared to help the fascists, but there must be no way of tracing our involvement. Do you understand?"

"I will take all necessary measures," Beria replied.

HMS *TRIDENT*, THE ENGLISH CHANNEL

"They're coming," said Halabi.

The giant battlespace monitor, which covered two walls of the *Trident's* hexagonal-shaped Combat Information Center, swarmed with hostile contacts. Thousands of them. So many, in fact, that although Posh could track each individual enemy unit, her human operators had no chance of keeping up.

Thus most of the smaller contacts were simply tagged with a number and buried under layers of more pertinent data, such as the flight of hundreds of slow transports making their way across the air–sea gap between the eastern coast of the British Isles and a series of airfields in Norway.

The highest priority contact, however, was a formation of three blinking red triangles screaming across the French countryside from an originating point just north of a village called Donzenac.

They were hypersonic Laval GA cruise missiles, and the ship's Combat Intelligence had calculated that they would impact somewhere in the U.K. in approximately four minutes. They were even curving around through Belgium and the Netherlands to put themselves well out of reach of any possible countermeasures she might have deployed. Not that there was any need. The *Trident* could have dealt with them had they been aimed right at her. Her Metal Storm and laser pack weapons systems were specifically designed to neutralize such threats. But there was nothing they could do from hundreds of kilometers away.

"Weapons, can we get an intercept lock?"

"Negative, Captain."

That was the answer Halabi expected. "Mr. Howard, does Posh have an attack profile yet?'

"They're ground-attack variants, Skipper. Almost certainly taken off the *Dessaix* at some point, and transferred to a makeshift launch tube. They may have even dismantled part of her VLS and used that."

"Doubtful," she mused.

"No projections on likely targets yet, ma'am, but if it was me I'd hit the key sector stations—Biggin Hill, Hornchurch, Debden, and North Weald. Luftwaffe's been leaving them alone, concentrating their bombers on Croydon, Rochford, and the others. Those stations are near critical, and a lot of capacity's been shifted to the undamaged fields. A hammerhead run would knock the RAF out of southern England."

"Comms, you got that?" Halabi asked. Air Vice Marshal Caterson and a couple of the other tourists began to advance on her command station. She ignored them for the moment. "Better give them a heads-up on shore. They're about to get the shit kicked out of them."

"I think you'd best explain what the hell is going on," Caterson demanded.

"Three ground-attack missiles are heading toward England at over five thousand miles an hour," she said, without betraying any emotion. "We cannot stop them. We don't know where they're going to hit, but whatever the target is, it will be gone very soon. My intelligence chief has indicated that

the most likely targets are your main sector stations. There's only three missiles, but they're carrying enough submunitions to destroy all four airfields,
and then some."

"I see," Caterson said quietly. "And having brought this upon us, what
are you going to do about it?"

Halabi ignored the baited hook. "We're going to do exactly as we
planned and stay here, providing battlespace management data, waiting for
the German surface assets to attempt the crossing."

"*Damn* you, and your crew," he spat. "What sort of a captain are you,
anyway, Halabi? Get out there and *do* something. You've got this God-
almighty ship of yours, but you're hiding behind those destroyers that're
out there protecting your worthless black hide.

"Get—out—there—and—*do something!*"

The CIC crew maintained their stations. Nobody as much as turned in
their direction. But the buzz of discussion dropped away, and Halabi could
feel it as everybody in the room shifted their attention onto her.

"Mr. McTeale," she said, fighting to keep a quaver away from her voice.
"Call Chief Waddington, and have him come up here with a security detachment. If the Air Vice Marshal Caterson opens his mouth again, have
him removed."

"Very good, ma'am."

Before Caterson could do anything to get himself thrown out, her chief
defensive sysop called out. "Captain! One of the Lavals has splashed. And
another has just corkscrewed off course over the North Sea."

Halabi, McTeale, and all the 'temps searched the main viewscreens. Indeed, one of the red triangles *had* disappeared, and the other was moving
erratically. The *Trident*'s captain remained outwardly unmoved, but inside
her a little cartoon Halabi was leaping up and down, punching a fist in the
air. Kolhammer had reported that many of the missiles fired on Hawaii had
malfunctioned, probably through sabotage. She'd been praying to a God
she'd never really believed in, hoping beyond hope that whichever of the
Dessaix's crew had been responsible for that sabotage may have been able to
get to these missiles, too.

But there was still one French hammerhead streaking in toward London.

"What's happened, Captain?" asked an army brigadier named Beaumont.
She didn't mind him as much as Caterson. An old India hand, he'd once or
twice shown himself to be more accepting of her command, and of those
members of her crew whose bloodlines didn't necessarily go all the way back
to pre-Norman England.

"At first blush, sir," she said, pointedly paying respect to his rank, "it would seem as if somebody on the *Dessaix* doubled-crossed the Germans. Two of the missiles appear to have been sabotaged."

"Splash two, Captain."

"There," she said, pointing at the flashing red triangle before it blinked out. "The second Laval has gone down."

"But not the third?"

"No, sir. I'm afraid not. And if it hasn't shown any signs by now, it probably won't."

The ship's defensive sysop spoke up. "Posh has determined that Biggin Hill is the most likely target."

"Captain, we have significant movement out of Calais, Dieppe, Cherbourg, and Rotterdam."

"Captain?" asked Beaumont.

Halabi took a few seconds to digest everything on the big screen: the developing airborne assault out of Norway, the strategic campaign against the islands' air defense net, the naval forces now surging out of the continent. It was cack-handed and primitive and barely coordinated, by the standards of her day, but she recognized the underlying principle.

"It's called a horizontal and vertical envelopment, Brigadier. *Swarming*, to use the vernacular. Although I believe the old-fashioned term *invasion* probably covers it all.

"*Gentlemen,*" she said, raising her voice slightly to grab the attention of all the 'temps. "We're game-on. My intelligence division will monitor the assault as it develops, and keep you updated with the attack profile. We're already streaming data to London via laser relay. If you'll examine the big screen, you'll see the German capital ships swinging into the Channel from the north. I need to move out in order to engage this group with my remaining ship-killers.

"We will be offloading Major Windsor's men by helicopter. I suggest you take the opportunity to get back on shore, as well. You will be needed there."

Beaumont saluted, as did a couple of his fellow officers. Most however, did not.

"Mr. McTeale, please escort our guests to the hangars."

"Yes, ma'am."

"Comms, inform the destroyer screen that we'll deploy in forty minutes."

"Aye, Captain."

Halabi watched the dozen or so staff officers troop out after her exec. She walled off her personal feelings at the affront handed to both her and the crew by Caterson and his colleagues. It was lucky, she thought, that she knew what sort of enemy they were *really* fighting today. Otherwise she might have wondered whether their lives were worth it.

The Cabinet War Rooms lay deep under the streets of London, beyond the reach of Göring's bombers. Churchill remembered the many late nights they'd spent here during the blitz and the Battle of Britain. He recalled the way the shock waves from an especially close hit traveled up through the wooden frame of the chair he now sat in, in front of the old-fashioned world map, at the head of the Cabinet table. Almost everything was as it had been. Sweating brick walls the color of spoiled cream. The massive red steel girders running across the ceiling. The ashen gray faces of his advisers. The stale air. Only the rumble and deep, tectonic shudder of Nazi bombing was absent.

The Luftwaffe had been concentrating on the RAF's airfields, radar stations, and, of course, on the *Trident* for three months now. The city had been spared, but for what, he wondered. Was it now to be destroyed in a cataclysmic battle, street by street, a thousand years of history and culture reduced to rubble and ash?

Not if he could help it.

"Well, gentleman," the prime minister said after everyone had taken their seats. "The darkest of days is upon us, but if we are marked to die, we are enough to do our country loss; and if to live, the fewer men the greater share of honor."

Shakespeare's words fell though four hundreds years into the taut silence of the room.

Churchill waited on somebody to speak. But his generals and admirals were silent. Before the moment could become uncomfortable, the PM continued. "Well, then, let's us stiffen the sinews and summon up the blood. Lieutenant Williams, if you will?"

The young officer, one of Captain Halabi's people, came to his feet. "Thank you, Prime Minister."

He pointed a control stick at the wide screen that had been affixed to the brick wall less than a week earlier. Everyone turned toward it as the display winked into life and a map of the British Isles and Western Europe appeared. It was always a marvel to see these things, but Churchill was frustrated by the size of the screen. He privately felt that he could get a much better appreciation of developments on the old plotting table.

"Real-time drone surveillance and signals intercepts indicate that German forces are moving rapidly into final position for an assault on the British Isles. Army Group Central is on the move out of Tours, Orleans, and

Lemours. Army Group North is consolidating rapidly in Caen, Dieppe, and Calais."

As Lieutenant Williams spoke, icons depicting the various units began to move north toward the Channel.

"The Luftwaffe has ninety percent of its five operational air fleets either up or in preflight. Some formations are already moving into position for raids on all air-defense-sector assets. Allied air units are being vectored on to the incoming hostiles by Fighter Command via *Trident*'s battlespace management system."

Churchill saw Air Chief Marshal Portal nod vigorously.

"*Kriegsmarine* capital ships are moving out of Norwegian waters at full steam. At least sixty U-boats are converging on the Channel from the North Sea ahead of them, taking up a position between the *Tirpitz* battle group and the Royal Navy's Home Fleet."

The lieutenant flicked his controller at the screen again. As Churchill watched, a mosaic of smaller windows filled the screen. They seemed to show movies of airfields with transport planes banked up.

"The first German forces we can expect to directly engage will be airborne units. The *Fallschirmjäger* which dropped onto Crete. They have regrouped and will most likely be joined by specialist Waffen-SS airborne units which have been hastily put together in the last few months. At this stage, we cannot provide a projected drop zone with any certainty. But there are a limited number of options. It appears the assault will go ahead without the Luftwaffe establishing air superiority . . ."

A chorus of mumbled astonishment greeted that statement of the obvious. It was a measure of Hitler's desperation that he would persist in the face of such odds. A measure of his criminal insanity, too, thought Churchill.

"Taken in concert with the capture of multinational elements and technology by the Axis powers, it does raise the prospect that the Germans have rushed the development of some weapons systems with which they hope to tip the balance in their favor. As of this moment, however, none of our sigint or Elint scans have returned data which would help clarify that issue."

"Thank you, Lieutenant," said Churchill, who did not wish the meeting to descend into an undergraduate bull session about the specter of Nazi superweapons. "And so to our reply, General?"

General Wavell, recently returned from North Africa with General Montgomery to coordinate the defense of the British Isles, got to his feet.

He turned to an old-fashioned map at the opposite end of the room to the PM.

"We expect a seaborne assault across the narrowest section of the Channel, landing at Dover, probably near Ramsgate and Margate. Army Group Central is expected to make their attempt between Weymouth and Sidmouth, placing immediate pressure on the defensive position to the south of Birmingham and Wolverhampton. These are the logical avenues of German advance and we have prepared our response accordingly . . ."

Wavell frowned and seemed to lose himself in the map for a moment.

"Of course," he resumed, "it is entirely possible that the attack will not follow a logical course. Many of the Wehrmacht's better commanders have been lost to the purges since the Transition. We shall not have to face Rommel on our own turf, but Field Marshal Kesselring will probably do just as well. And while the Germans do not have our advantage in drone technology, they have had enough old-fashioned planes flying overhead to make a reasonable guess about our preparations. With this in mind, and given that they can probably only get four divisions ashore in the first wave—"

Churchill sighed audibly at that. *Only four divisions!*

"—we will hold in reserve the Canadian First Army, Free French Second Armored, and American infantry divisions on the GHQ Line, with our XXX Corps armored and infantry units advanced to engage the enemy at the bridgehead, wherever that may be."

Wavell swept his hand across the breadth of the map covering all of the southern counties.

"The imponderable question is where General Ramcke's paratroopers will land. Here I think we find the hinge of victory or defeat. Without control of the air or the sea-lanes, the Germans must plan on massive losses for their seaborne forces. We know they have made a massive investment in rebuilding the *Fallschirmjäger*, and Himmler has personally overseen the creation of a Waffen-SS air-assault division. Wherever they land, we must fix them and destroy them. To this end, I am holding in reserve the Guards Armored and the First Infantry Divisions."

Wavell, who had been reading from a paper on the table in front of him, looked up from his eyebrows at Lieutenant Williams.

"For what it's worth, the SAS Regiment has been attached to the First Infantry and will do whatever it is they do when we know where Ramcke has set down."

Churchill ignored Wavell's bad grace. He had faith in the young prince and his merry men. They seemed just the right sort of bastards to turn loose on the Nazis.

31

RAF Biggin Hill in the London borough of Bromley was one of the most important airfields in the defense of London during the Battle of Britain. Built at the end of the First World War, it sat on high ground above the village of the same name. The first RAF flights controlled by radio flew out of there, and the first kill of the Second World War was credited to a fighter from Biggin Hill. It had been the object of endless attacks during the Battle of Britain, suffering massive damage, which almost but never quite closed down its operations.

Three of Halabi's crew were quartered there, coordinating battlespace management with the 'temps, and supervising a number of experimental programs, such as the Super Spitfire night fighter squadron. Those twelve prototype planes were located in hardened bunkers at the eastern end of the airfield, protected by radar-controlled Bofors guns. They weren't specifically targeted, but they were amongst the first casualties of the incoming strike.

Of the *Trident* crew on station at Biggin Hill that morning, only Petty Officer Fiona Hobbins was on duty. The others, a flight sergeant and a pilot officer with an advanced electrical engineering degree, were both asleep in their billets down in the village. Both had worked through the previous thirty-six hours.

The *Trident* flashed an alert to all her shore-based personnel, twenty-nine officers and others of various rank, as soon as the threat of the incoming missile strike was detected. When Hobbins's flexipad began screeching, she was lying on a gurney under one of the Spitfires. She didn't even bother to look at the screen—she'd been through hundreds of drills, and five actual alerts. She just spun off the gurney and started yelling as loudly as she could.

"Incoming! Get out. Get out! *Move! Move! Move!*"

Five seconds later, sirens began to wail all over the base.

Twenty-two men and women had been working in the hardened hangar when the alert came through. That had surprised Petty Officer Hobbins at first. She'd come to Biggin Hill expecting to find an exclusively male domain, but had been chuffed to discover a large number of women "auxiliaries." Equal opportunity debates were by the by now, though.

Everyone was running for their lives.

Hobbins hammered out of the aircraft shelter, overtaking a couple of lead-footed 'temps who'd spent a few too many quid on the real ale down at the Black Horse in the village.

"Move your fat arses," she yelled at them.

Hundreds of ground crew, technicians, and even pilots who'd been enjoying the warm autumn day were hurrying for slit trenches and sandbagged antiair mounts. Hobbins felt rather than saw it when the tarmac changed to grass beneath her pounding boots. A zigzag trench line beckoned, and some finely honed instinct made her dive for it rather than running and climbing in. That jump saved her life.

A grotesquely loud shriek, whoosh, and roar signaled the arrival of the hypersonic Laval over the base. The shock wave burst the eardrums of everyone within eight or nine hundred meters, including Hobbins, who screamed as it felt like long metal skewers were being driven into her head.

Unlike the American hammerhead-type missiles, the French weapon didn't need to open a bay door on its underside. Two hundred mini-silos were built into the fuselage, and those spat out submunitions of fused DU and SRDX accelerant. Rendered deaf, Hobbins was unable to register the impact of the first bomblets as they went tearing into the hardened concrete bunker, shredding it like crepe paper.

The rolling percussion of primary and secondary explosions registered as dull mallet blows somewhere outside her head. The Laval screamed past, far enough away that she survived the impact of the small front of violently compressed air that was trailing the rocket at five thousand kilometers an hour. Unprotected, the two crewmen she'd passed earlier flew apart as though hit by a speeding locomotive when the wave struck them.

A blizzard of offal poured into the slit trench, which threatened to collapse as the rest of RAF Biggin Hill was destroyed.

Petty Officer Fiona Hobbins curled up at the foot of the trench and waited to die. But the final eruption never came.

HMS *TRIDENT*, THE ENGLISH CHANNEL

There was no live video feed available, for which Harry was grateful. He didn't need to see what happened when you unleashed a Multipurpose Augmented Ground Attack device on a target that wasn't prepared for it. He'd been amongst the first troops into Algiers after the French Mediterranean Fleet "reduced" the city in retaliation for the radiological attack on Marseilles. Biggin Hill was a little sturdier than the mud brick capital of Algeria, but not so much as made any difference.

The SAS men and their Norwegian colleagues had cheered when the screen in the *Trident*'s main hangar had shown the first two Lavals veering off course. But the cheering had died out as it became obvious there'd be no reprieve from the third missile. Harry had turned away from the screen, and was busying himself checking their gear for the short hop back to Portsmouth when Sergeant St. Clair called out.

"Look, guv, the primary didn't go off."

Harry looked up and was amazed to discover that his RSM was right. The Combat Intelligence indicated that the submunitions had fired, but not the main warhead. That would have excavated about three quarters of Biggin Hill down to a depth of thirty meters in less than one second.

"Has it moved on to a secondary target?" he asked. A part of him was afraid that the Germans had figured out how to program the missile to strike at multiple points, as it was meant to do.

But no. A flashing dialog box indicted that the ship's Nemesis arrays were no longer tracking the weapon, and hadn't registered any primary detonation of the Laval's subfusion plasma yield warhead.

Most likely it had simply crashed somewhere.

"*Vive la France*," Harry murmured. Whoever had been able to dicker with the first two shots, he must have been interrupted before he could finish with number three. The SAS commander wished him—or her—good luck, wherever they were.

Even so, Biggin Hill was a write-off. But he wondered if the Germans knew what had happened.

THE WOLFSCHANZE, EAST PRUSSIA

"We shall have crushed the life out of them by the time nightfall arrives," boasted Göring.

Himmler thought the führer seemed less sanguine, having been here before with his Luftwaffe chief, but the reports were good.

In war, it was always advisable to discount the best and the worst of everything one heard. But the news coming out of the firestorm they'd unleashed over England was encouraging. Three experienced pilots had radioed back reports of a catastrophe engulfing the RAF station called Biggin Hill, a name they had all come to loathe back in late 1940.

Two others reported identical results over Croydon and Hornchurch.

It was frustrating that they couldn't duplicate the surveillance the British enjoyed thanks to the *Trident*. They would all have been much happier, seeing the results of the missile attack for themselves. But as the führer rightly pointed out, what did it matter if the British had a perfect view of their doom as it came rushing at them? It was still *their doom*.

The *Reichsführer-SS* had flown straight back to the Wolfschanze, having watched Skorzeny depart, and he had been quietly amazed to see how far and how rapidly the situation had developed.

Defeatists and cowards within the High Command had balked at Operation Sea Dragon, even questioning the führer's judgment. But their craven attitude was no longer a consideration. There was a phrase from the future that Himmler quite liked, and which described them perfectly. *Oxygen thieves*. Well, they weren't stealing any of the führer's oxygen now. The only pity was that they weren't alive to see how wrong they'd been.

The Operations Room was crowded with personnel. The large central table, inlaid with a huge map of western Europe, was covered with hundreds of small wooden markers. These were constantly being pushed toward their objective by junior staff members carrying long, thin poles.

A young female *Oberleutnant* moved several little wooden blocks, signifying the *Tirpitz's* battle group, a few miles farther down the Norwegian coastline. A Luftwaffe *Hauptmann* needed two long pointers to reposition all the airborne forces that were now winging their way toward the east coast of England. Dozens of markers showed Wehrmacht and Waffen-SS divisions converging on the embarkation ports, while dozens more denoted the thousands of Luftwaffe planes that engaged the Royal Air Force over the Channel, or bombed airfields in the southern counties. These measures protected the invasion fleet as it set out from France, and harassed the Royal Navy's squadrons as they moved to intervene.

"Savor this moment, gentlemen," the führer declared as he slowly circled the Ops Room, followed by his entourage. "There has never been a greater force assembled in the history of human conflict. And there has never been a heavier blow landed on that little island. We are not just remaking history today. We are smashing it into a thousand pieces."

HMS *TRIDENT*, THE ENGLISH CHANNEL

"Good luck, Major Windsor."

"Thank you, Captain Halabi. Better luck next time, eh?"

The commander of the *Trident* and the SAS officer saluted each other. Harry's was the last group to be lifted off the destroyer. The observer group, for the most part, had been put ashore, with just two liaison officers remaining. Harry was lifting with his squad and their equipment for a fast, nap of the Earth flight to London, from where he was to link up with the regiment. Nobody yet knew where that might be. It would depend on the Germans to a large extent.

Weak gray sunlight poured in through the hangar roof. The sky was a shroud, the color of dirty washing water. It was a high ceiling, however, and it seemed as if hundreds of planes dueled beneath the clouds. Here and there, puffs of smoke and flame marked the end of the fight for somebody. Parachutes billowed occasionally, but not always, and once or twice he heard the crackle of laser fire burning the air around the ship as a Stuka or a Heinkel pressed home a suicidal attack.

No jets had as yet reappeared. Halabi had told him she expected they'd be back when her antiair stocks were demonstrably empty.

She didn't even wait for the elevator to lift them clear of the hangar, returning to her station as soon as they began the ascent. A couple of the Air Div crew waved him off, and Harry replied with a thumbs-up. But he felt a lot less jaunty than the gesture implied.

The Germans were attempting a multidimensional assault right out of the twenty-first-century playbook. Their coordination was hopeless, and a lot of the technology they needed simply did not exist yet. A couple of hastily built, poorly flown ME 262s just didn't count.

But having secured their eastern flank, they seemed to be bringing the entire weight of their continental war machine to bear on the south of England.

Every now and then, when the pounding of the five-inch guns and ack-ack mounts abated, he could hear the much deeper, more sonorous bass note rumble of ten thousand engines. Of twenty thousand guns, and high-explosive shells, and dumb iron bombs detonating for hundreds of miles around. It was the sound of two worlds grinding against each other, and even with his years of service, he'd never known anything like it.

St. Clair sat across from him, sphinxlike and withdrawn. His sergeant major was always like that, on the edge of battle.

The chopper's engines hummed into life as the elevator lifted them clear of the hangars and into the daylight. His six troopers reacted in character. Some simply adjusted their Bergens and checked their weapons. Some leaned forward in their seats to catch whatever glimpse they could of the world outside, a slate gray tableau of small, antique warships tossed on heaving seas.

One man, Gibbs, slept with his head cushioned by a life jacket.

"Sergeant Major, what's our current strength at Kinlochmoidart?"

"One hundred and twenty-five officers and other ranks, sir. Captain

Fraser's already got them turned out and kitted up. They're waiting for movement orders."

"Very good."

The Eurocopter cycled up to full power as Harry felt the *Trident* come around. They began to dip and rise on the confused swell and crosscurrents where the waters of the Solent met those of the Channel. The rotor's down blast tugged at his battle dress and made it difficult to communicate without shouting. He signaled to St. Clair to engage tac net. Everyone who hadn't already done so fitted combat goggles and earbuds before powering up their helmets.

Over the years, Harry had trained his software to the point where it was virtually an extension of his own psyche. Without being instructed, it brought up eight separate windows, biofeedback from his men and himself. Instinctively he scanned the squad, looking for signs of combat fatigue, developing psychoses, exhaustion, or any of the myriad symptoms that stalked everyone who did this sort of work for too long.

They all checked out.

A link to the helicopter's on-board systems provided a V3D holomap of their flight plan, while an outside link to the *Trident* added relevant battlespace data. Harry hummed quietly as he took in the information. In truth, there was no safe route they could take to the drop-off. Hundreds of 109s and 110s infested the airspace around them. It was going to be like flying through a hailstorm, trying to avoid the stones.

They lifted off, and he acknowledged a couple of crew on the deck of the cruiser who paused to wave them away.

"Right, everyone, I'll keep this short."

Halabi's voice was broadcast throughout the vessel via shipnet, emerging from speakers and screens on all the decks, from bow to stern.

"The Admiralty have assigned us two objectives. First, a strategic strike on the *Tirpitz* group, which is now sortieing into the Channel to cover the invasion fleet. And second, battlespace management for sectors One through Four.

"We will need to move west to bring the *Tirpitz* within range. We shall be doing so without the company of our destroyer screen. They simply can't move as quickly as we can. Posh calculates that we have enough antiair stocks to return with a three percent reserve. The RAF will provide continuous cover during the run. We will need the reserve, given the new threat of missile strike from the continent. I don't want to overstate the danger. Even if a number of missiles have been removed from the *Dessaix* for use against us, the ship herself is not here and the enemy will thus be striking blind. Nonetheless we need to be aware of the risk and ready to respond."

The *Trident*'s captain paused. The CIC crew watched her in person. The rest of her men and women craned upward to follow the speech on screen, or listened over shipnet speakers where no screens were available.

"While we are fighting to achieve our goals, the enemy will fight just as hard to destroy us. There are hundreds of pilots aloft now, with even more climbing into their cockpits. Their only goal today is to sink this ship. There are commanders of U-boats and torpedo boats, destroyers, cruisers, and even a few battleships who have probably been personally ordered by Adolf Hitler to ensure that we do not see out this day. Some of them are good men. Some are evil. They are almost all brave and well trained, and they will not hesitate to do whatever it takes to win this battle, and enslave our countrymen."

She paused again, to let her words sink in.

"That doesn't really matter," she continued, *"Because we are going to kill them all."*

At that, a rousing, full-throated cheer filled the Combat Information Center, and sounded more distantly throughout the rest of the ship.

Halabi looked over to the antisat station, where the two contemporary navy men had been corralled. They were cheering along with the rest, and every bit as enthusiastically.

"Thank you, I expect you will all do your best."

She switched off the shipnet and turned to her executive officer.

"Mr. McTeale, all ahead full. Engage the S-Cav system. Assign Autonomy Level One to the Combat Intelligence for defensive measures."

"Aye, ma'am."

"Comms, signal Stanmore that we are guns free and running west."

"Fighter Command report that Three-oh-three Squadron have scrambled and will rendezvous with us in six minutes."

"Excellent," said Halabi. "Let's test their VHF sets now."

The 303 was a Polish squadron, and she had specifically requested them for this operation. Certain pinheaded elements within Fighter Command at Stanmore were dismissive of the Polish pilots, ignoring the fact that pilot training had been extensive and advanced in that country before the war. And, of course, that the Poles had more experience than anyone in scrapping with the Luftwaffe.

Even though they hadn't joined the Battle of Britain until a few months after it started, 303 Squadron was responsible for downing more of Göring's precious aircraft than any other single squadron. Flying augmented Spitfires with the new VHF radio sets, they had been training for this operation since shortly after the *Trident*'s arrival.

"Three-oh-three on line, Captain. Squadron Leader Zumbach sends his compliments."

"My greetings to Jan," she said. "Put them in holding, and slave them to air control. We'll vector them down as needed."

Halabi rolled her shoulders and settled into her command seat. She had never seen the battlespace display so densely filled with information. It was an almost impenetrable wall of data and imagery that was beyond the ability of one individual to fully comprehend. It wasn't beyond Posh, however. The ship's Combat Intelligence tracked every return from her Nemesis arrays and low-orbit drones, sorting the raw intelligence into a coherent narrative that her human controllers might have some hope of understanding.

"Helm, Captain. Course plotted. Supercavitating systems engaged."

As the trimaran's aquajets began to shoot out enormous volumes of seawater, pressurised to 60,000 psi, billions of microscopic pores in the nanotube-sheathing of her three hulls opened to vent a fine mist of compressed air bubbles into the surrounding water. With the drag on her keel reduced to a small percentage of its normal coefficient of viscosity, the ship began to accelerate to speeds that left her escorts standing still by comparison.

"CI has the helm, ma'am."

"Thank you," Halabi acknowledged.

With her speed leaping up to well over 140 knots, it wasn't feasible for a human being to steer the *Trident* through the labyrinth of hazards that lay ahead of her in the Channel. They were now in the hands of the Combat Intelligence they called Posh.

32

TOWNSVILLE, SOUTHWEST PACIFIC AREA

It didn't *look* like a weapon of mass destruction, but that's how Colonel J. "Lonesome" Jones thought of it. He hefted the gun, which was still slightly oily from the packing grease. It looked and felt pretty much as he remembered.

The AK-47, he thought. *Killed more people than the atom bomb and the automobile put together.*

They weren't calling it a Kalashnikov or an AK down here, though. In Australia it was known as a Lysaght submachine gun, after the firm that had the contract to turn them out. He knew that in the U.S. it had been designated the MK-1. And in Canada and the UK, the prototypes were called, rather unimaginatively, AW/GLs, for Automatic Weapon and Grenade Launching system.

Jones thought he'd stick with *AK*. It was like Coke or Pepsi. Why fuck around with the original?

"Thank you, soldier," he said, handing the weapon back to the quartermaster with very mixed feelings. He'd only been issued with his G4 on the eve of deployment to Timor, but he was getting ready to miss it like hell. It was a magnificent killing piece, but there was no point in even thinking about trying to build one here. They were going to be years just getting the electronics up to speed. Not to mention the ceramics, the alloys, all the materials science that was thus far beyond the abilities of a *very* primitive industrial base.

Hence the AK-47, preferred weapon of rag-headed punks from southern Thailand to Addis Abbaba.

It was a depressing thought.

The supply sergeant just saluted and disappeared out of the tent, into the harsh light and subtropical humidity of Townsville. This was another place Jones had thought himself familiar with. Up in the twenty-first, he'd transited the joint a couple of times a year on his way to and from Southeast Asia. The Marine Corps had leased a massive training range nearby, and from 2010 onward, an MEU had been rotated through the Townsville barracks every two years.

This Townsville had been a sleepy backwater, a cattle town and a minor port before the Japanese had taken it. Now it was just another burnt-out ruin. The airstrip and the docks had been repaired, though, and the *Kandahar*'s battle group lay just a few miles offshore—although *battle group* was probably too dignified a phrase for the sorry collection of odds and ends gathered around the slab-sided assault ship and her tenders.

The *Enterprise* was out there, still sailing under Spruance, along with the old cruisers *Pensacola* and *Salt Lake City*, the Littoral Assault Ship *Ipswich* and a destroyer screen stitched together from surviving U.S., Free French, and British Commonwealth forces. Jones had known shower curtains that'd offer more protection. But if Hawaii was going to be retaken, those ships would have to be the ones to do it.

Their chances would be greatly improved when the *Siranui* arrived in twelve days.

He pulled his cap down over his eyes, wrapped a pair of sunglasses around his face, and tried not to think of what might happen on the islands over the course of twelve days. He also tried not to think about the news that his brother-in-law might have come through the Transition on the *Dessaix*. He'd only met Philippe Danton once, at the wedding, but he'd seemed a nice enough lad. He couldn't bear thinking about him getting caught up in this unholy mess. Was he still on the ship? Jones hadn't even known he'd been part of the Task Force until this morning. Was he helping the Japs? Or did he have a hand in the obvious sabotage of the Lavals? This bullshit was now a personal fucking nightmare as well as a professional one. The colonel pushed his doubts down to where they couldn't bother him anymore. It wouldn't do to waste time worrying about shit he couldn't change. If Danton had come through alive, chances were he was part of the reason the *Dessaix*'s missile strike had aborted, at least in part. The Eighty-second's commander had more pressing issues to deal with. As he emerged from the supply tent, the two guards—both 'temps—snapped to attention.

Very few civilians remained in Townsville. A massive garrison was growing quickly on the ashes of the old town, however. Acres of tents breathed slowly in the hot, humid air, which smelled of diesel, sweat, and burnt offerings. A "Negro" battalion, the Ninety-first Engineers, was busily running up more permanent structures, adding the sound of their hammers and tools to the grunt of bulldozers clearing away rubble, deuce-and-a-halves delivering men and matériel, choppers thudding back and forth to the Task Force, and men and women cursing and laughing, shouting orders, and talking shit.

Jones returned the sharp salutes of a couple of privates from the Ninety-first as they passed by. He wasn't sure, but he suspected they'd gone out of their way to cross his path and get his attention. Behind the mirrored blades, his face was unmoved as he walked on, but he couldn't help the stirring beneath his breastbone. Those men were proud, and not just of their uniforms. His company clerk had to field hundreds of requests every day for transfer into the Eighty-second, from men like that. He was sorry that he couldn't take them, but they would need at least two years of retraining before they were ready to join a squad and carry a G4.

Or an AK-47.

Jones arrived at his Humvee, still shaking his head.

"Aerodrome, Colonel?" his driver asked.

"Thanks, Shauna. But we need to swing by Second Cav and pick up Colonel Toohey first. I'm giving him a lift to Brisbane."

Jones allowed the motion of the vehicle to lull him into a drowsy state as they motored over to the Australian camp. He'd been off the stim for a couple of days, but his sleep patterns would take another week to settle down. He'd almost dozed off when his flexipad began to ping at him. He nearly missed the call, as he started to half dream about a pinball game he used to play on his old Pentium as a teenager.

"Sir. Colonel Jones, sir. You've got a call coming in."

Jones was a little embarrassed to be caught out, and found himself uncharacteristically apologizing to the driver. He must have been *really* out of it.

He shook his head to clear the cobwebs and took the call, a live link from the *Kandahar*. It was Major Francois, the battalion surgeon.

"'S'up Margie?" he asked.

"We got him, Colonel. We got the fucker who killed Anderson and Miyazaki, back in Pearl."

Suddenly Jones was wide awake.

"I can't believe I missed this!" she said angrily. "I set this whole *fucking* system up just to scan for this one thing, this one *fucking* thing, and then when it works, I'm too *fucking* lazy to check back and see. Meantime this asshole's been living high on the hog. I just can't believe it."

"Don't beat yourself up, Doc," said Jones, looking over her shoulder at the computer screen in her quarters back on the *Kandahar*. "It looks like you've got, what, four and a half thousand messages there, and eight hundred are marked priority one. You were busying saving lives. The dead can wait."

She looked like she was about to beat on herself some more.

"I knew Anderson," he said, cutting her off. "She'd come back from the grave and give you an ass-kickin' if she thought you put a Band-Aid on someone with anything less than perfect care, just because of her."

"Well, what are we going to do, then?" Francois asked, turning self-recrimination into angry indignation.

Jones looked at the name on screen, and was lost for an immediate answer. "I don't know. At least not right now. It's going to be sticky. We'll need to talk to Kolhammer first."

Francois looked as if she was going to go for his throat. Or someone else's—

"Belay that, Major," he warned her. "You go taking a potshot at this guy before you've got him dead in your sights, and he *will* get clean away. You're not the person to do this, anyway. Not after Cabanatuan. You're compromised."

The surgeon's face flushed bright red and then drained of all color as her anger imploded into a small, dense ball of rage. Jones knew his chief medical officer all too well.

"Listen, *I* know you were the ranking officer. And *I* know you exercised your prerogatives under Sanction Four. But then, I know what that means, and accept it as valid. Almost nobody outside the Task Force will agree, Margie."

"That's just fucking politics, and you know it, Lonesome."

"That's right, and if we're not careful, politics are going to fuck us just as surely as bombs and bullets. We *are* going to deal with this, but not by charging in and capping this asshole as though we've got a perfect right to do so."

"But we do!"

"Not here, we don't. Now, sit down, chill out, and give me some time to think this through. I'm already late for a meeting with MacArthur. We'll talk about this tomorrow. But we do not, *under any circumstances*, go off the reservation with this. You understand?"

"Yes, sir," she grumbled.

It was the grumble that let him know he'd convinced her. She was always a sore loser.

SOUTHWEST PACIFIC AREA HEADQUARTERS

His old man always said, never do someone a really big favor—they'll never forgive you for it. Jones had reason to recall that pearl of wisdom as he listened to MacArthur in the old sandstone bank building that housed the HQ of the Southwest Pacific Area Command.

The *Über-temp* looked like he was going to bite right through the stem of his corncob pipe when he greeted the Multinational Force leaders who'd flown in for the crisis talks. Thirty or more officers squeezed into the bank's former boardroom. They represented all the services of all the different Allied Forces in the Pacific theater. And they mixed more readily with the men and women of Kolhammer's Task Force than would have been the case a few months earlier. There was nothing like spilling a little blood to bring people together.

But MacArthur didn't share the mood of reconciliation. Jones suspected he was pissed that the coup de grâce had been delivered to Homma by Kolhammer's forces, even if they were nominally under Mac's command now. And Jones knew for a righteous certainty that the general was *seriously* pissed at the deployment order withdrawing the *Kandahar* and her group from the Australian theater, for a counterstrike against the Japanese in Hawaii. MacArthur probably thought he'd never get them back again.

Jones had already noticed one glaring absence. Captain Willet of the *Havoc* was nowhere to be seen. He hoped that meant the submarine had gone hunting for the *Dessaix*. Even if the stealth destroyer *was* crewed by a scratch team of half-assed try-hards, he didn't fancy trying to force a landing on Oahu with that ship hanging around.

The colonel felt a hand on his upper arm and was surprised to find

Prime Minister Curtin standing beside him wearing a dark, slightly crumpled suit. Jones hadn't known he was going to be there, and hadn't seen him enter the room.

"Mr. Prime Minister, you should try out for the SAS, sir, the way you spook about."

Curtin, who looked about five years younger than he had the last time they'd met, took Jones's hand and pumped it a few times. "Labor Party conferences are blood sport enough for me, Colonel. Anyway, I just wanted to say thank you."

"You should be thanking your men, Barnes and Toohey, sir. They made the case for the counteroffensive."

Curtin nodded. His eyes were watery, but that could have been from all the cigarette smoke. These people lived in a permanent fog of nicotine and free-floating carcinogens. "I've already spoken to Mick Barnes," the prime minister said. "But I wanted to be sure of catching you, too. I'm not staying for your meeting. It's all operational stuff. I have to get back to Canberra, and I wanted to visit some of your wounded before I flew out. I understand they're at the Royal Brisbane."

"They are, sir," said Jones. "Major Francois is setting up shop there."

"So I hear. My scientific adviser tells me she's rewritten the texts for our medical schools."

"I think she probably just copied some new ones out, sir." Jones smiled.

"Well, we're very grateful for everything you've done, Colonel. If there's anything we can do for you . . ."

Jones didn't openly point out MacArthur, but he did let his eyes rest on the fuming supremo for a second. "Well, not everyone is happy about our redeployment, Prime Minister. I imagine you've had some experience at smoothing ruffled feathers."

Curtin sighed, "I'm the veteran of ten thousand conferences, Colonel Jones, but this may be beyond my limits. Nevertheless, I'll see what I can do."

"There is one other thing, Prime Minister."

"Yes?"

"I can understand," said Jones, "that you'd want to keep Second Cav here, but it would make my job a lot easier if they were with me in Hawaii."

Curtin held the big marine's level stare for a long time. Jones realized then and there that he wouldn't want to play poker against the man.

Eventually though, his head bobbed up and down, just fractionally. "There's no point in being a ninety percent ally, is there, Colonel?"

"No, sir, there's not. And neither Admiral Kolhammer nor I, nor Brigadier Barnes, for that matter, think there is a realistic chance that the Japanese can make another landing in force here in Australia. We've got long-range aerial surveillance covering your northern approaches, and nothing is lighting up the threat boards."

Curtin took that in and gave Jones a flat, calculating look. "But your own signals-interception people tell us there is a lot of talk on the Japanese radio channels about a second invasion."

"Talk is cheap, Prime Minster. Men and ships and planes are not. You need a lot of them to pull off an invasion, and best we can tell, Yamamoto has all his eggs in one basket. Hawaii."

"Do you really think you'd be able to take the islands back from the Japs? They'll have had at least three weeks to dig in, by the time you get there."

"That'll just mean there's a nicer gravesite ready for them," promised Jones.

HIJMS YAMATO, THE PACIFIC THEATER OF OPERATIONS

He could not see the prize he had come to take. It was obscured by the smoke of his own giant guns, and by the burning of so many buildings and fields. But Oahu was definitely there, just ten miles off starboard, the whole island shaking under the thunder of bombardment.

The commander of the Combined Fleet did not let his feelings escape. He maintained a stern countenance and refused to join in the celebrations. But he did let his men applaud as reports came back of a sea of fire, engulfing the remains of Nimitz's fleet at Pearl Harbor, and of airfields reduced to smoking rubble and twisted, red hot metal. Indeed, they had earned the right.

The great iron behemoth of the battleship *Yamato* shuddered again as her eighteen-inch batteries fired a broadside into the gray shroud that hung over the Americans' Pacific bastion. Using the newly installed German range-finding equipment, the ship's gunnery officers could be certain of landing their shots with remarkable accuracy. Only the *Yamato* had been fitted out so far, but with every volley, she sent tons of high explosives screaming through the air, to land on the heads of the defenders.

Above him, lost in the glare of the equatorial sun, hundreds of bombers and fighters pressed their attacks, sweeping in toward their prey and then returning home to the decks of his carriers by an elliptical route that kept them from being destroyed by the cannon fire of their own ships.

If Yamamoto had one regret, it was that the *Dessaix*'s attack had been so successful, despite the attempted sabotage. As a result, he would never engage in a decisive match with the American fleet. The U.S. would survive this defeat, and would rebuild their navy. Indeed, it would probably be infinitely more powerful than the force he had set out to destroy in December 1941. But it would do them no good. By then, they would be on the wrong side of history, and the next fifty years would tell the story of their unavoidable decline.

Another broadside. Another volley of massive, three-thousand-pound shells.

The decking tilted beneath him, and he felt the sudden overpressure as a discomforting sensation—not just in his ears, but throughout his whole body.

It felt splendid.

Yamamoto accepted a cup of green tea offered by a young officer. The steaming liquid vibrated inside the bone china cup, a small and delicate manifestation of the insensate violence tearing at the world around him.

"General Tanaga reports that the first transports are successfully away, Admiral," said the duty radio operator.

Yamamoto thanked the lieutenant and sipped at his tea.

He was content with the progress of the assault, but privately anxious that the army should get ashore and establish control as quickly as possible. Much of the contemporary U.S. naval power had been destroyed for now, but there remained significant forces from the group that had come through at Midway. Battle damage had negated some of the threat. The *Clinton*, for instance, had not been able to repair her catapult system with the tools at hand, and had been retired to the West Coast, perhaps to be stripped, perhaps to be refitted. He did not know.

What was important was that she had gone. The *Trident* was on the other side of the world; Kolhammer's "stealth" cruiser, the *Leyte Gulf*, was confirmed sunk. And the stocks of advanced weapons on the remaining ships were surely close to running out.

That was the gamble he had chosen to take.

Yamamoto closed his eyes and remembered the sacrifice made by Homma and the many navy men who had died off Australia, simply to exhaust Kolhammer's store of weapons. For a month now, no IJN ship had disappeared inside the infernal white fire of a "plasma yield" rocket, or had been torn to pieces by hundreds of tiny bombs spat out of the belly of a "hammerhead." None of his colleagues had been claimed by the barbarian woman on the submarine *Havoc* with her torpedoes that seemed to run as quickly through the water as a Zero flew through the sky.

And of course, the *Dessaix* had turned the *Clinton*'s surviving Raptors into metal confetti.

Even so, he thought, as another thirty thousand pounds of high explosive erupted from the mouth of the ship's main batteries, he would have been happier to have delayed this moment until he could be sure. The *Sira-nui* and her treacherous crew still gave their loyalty to Kolhammer. And although the archival data indicated that the *Kandahar*'s air wing was not equipped with antiship missiles, how could he be sure without being able to walk through the vessel's armory to check for himself? Midway had taught him that nothing was certain.

Unfortunately, nothing was perfect, either, and the warrior who waited until he had conditions exactly as he wanted them was in the end no warrior at all. He was a coward who would never know triumph.

"Torpedoes in the water! Off the port side."

Yamamoto did not react. This was not his battleship to command. So he very deliberately raised his cup and slowly drank the rest of the tea, without even looking out the window, like so many others who were searching for the telltale streak just beneath the ocean's surface. Captain Takayanagi would see them through this, or not. Yamamoto concentrated on drawing a slow, deep breath and focusing on the center of his being, his *hara*.

In spite of his outwardly unmoved appearance, however, the cry of *torpedo* had been a nasty jolt. Until he realized that it could not be the *Havoc*. Her torpedoes ran deep, and so swiftly that the first you knew of them was when your ship was disintegrating around you like an exploding star.

No, this would be an American submarine, firing torpedoes that hardly ever worked, assuming the U.S. Navy had not yet to come to its senses. Yamamoto didn't know why it was taking the Americans so long to fix their torpedoes, now that they must surely know of their defects. Perhaps they weren't listening quite so closely to Kolhammer as he would have, in their position.

The grand admiral tilted his head in a figurative gesture of peering into the sky, where he knew that robot planes were watching everything. He finished the tea, while around him sailors and their superiors shouted orders and acknowledgment back and forth as Takayanagi attempted to move the *Yamato*'s seventy-thousand-ton bulk out of harm's way.

"Look!" someone shouted, and a strangled cheer arose, then quickly died as a little destroyer raced across the torpedoes' track. There were two explosions, and twin geysers of white water bracketed her, at stem and stern. The *Yamato* continued to pour on steam, leaning over at a noticeable angle, fighting to drag herself out of the path of any more enemy attacks.

Four other destroyers raced toward their crippled sister ship, popping depth charges as they sliced through the waves and sea spray.

Yamamoto sent a silent prayer of thanks to the ancestors of the men who had just perished on the little ship that had sacrificed herself in his behalf.

No, he thought, nothing was certain but death.

33

A lone Wildcat had appeared out of nowhere and strafed Corporal Yutaka Nanten's landing barge, turning it into a slaughtering pen. Cannon and machine-gun fire killed three quarters of his platoon, the first pass by the fighter scything them down, another pass pulverizing their remains into a scarlet gravy while Nanten screamed and screamed.

Three Zeros came and drove the demon away, but by then it was too late. Even the helmsman was dead; all that was left was one disembodied hand, still clutching at the steering wheel. Nanten himself was unharmed, except for a small sliver of bone that had pierced his left cheek. With tremors shaking his entire body, he pulled it out like a splinter, expecting half his face to come away. But the bone fragment wasn't even his.

As reason began to reassert itself, he realized he was not completely alone. Not everyone had been killed. He could hear three other men moaning or screaming over the sounds of the engine and the thump of the hull on the waves, as the helmsman's hand steered them ever farther from the other boats.

Nanten's limbs shook so much that he couldn't manage to drag himself up out of the bloody gruel that was sloshing up and down the length of the barge as they plunged through the swell.

The night before, as they had waited to transfer from the troopship, there had been a great deal of nervous talk concerning the time travelers they might encounter, and what weapons they might wield. Many of their greatest fears seemed to be centered on the lost souls of the *ronin*, those Japanese warriors who had come back with the magician Kolhammer. They were thought to be the most fearsome of all the time travelers, armed with "chaos blades" that could slice through the barrel of a tank. Since they had turned their backs on the emperor, the *ronin* had clearly gone mad.

Nanten himself felt madness gnawing at the edge of his mind.

Who needed chaos blades and lost souls, when a simple aeroplane could do this?

He wiped the blood from his eyes with one shaking hand and took in the ruin of his platoon. What he saw caused him to retch uncontrollably. He had no way of reaching the rail, so his vomit became a part of the foul mixture that filled the bottom of the barge.

The platoon had been together since the Nanking campaign, and now in a sense they would be together forevermore. One of the other survivors stopped screaming, but Nanten did not know why, and did not go to investigate. He did not wish to raise himself, lest another plane dive in to finish the job.

His fear began to shift, and his stomach knotted with fury. They had told him there were no American aircraft left. No rocket planes, or even any of the older types. He tried to wipe more blood from his eyes, but it only made things worse. His face was sticky with the remains of his friends.

Nanten craned his head skyward and slitted his eyes against the sun's glare. It was a hot, gray day, and it felt like he was sitting in an oven. Ammunition popped and burned around him. The moaning stopped, and he knew he was finally alone.

It seemed perversely safe inside this little ghost ship now. The war was a distant murmur. Surely nobody would fire upon a vessel full of dead bodies. Even the gaijin were not that uncivilized. Although, given the rumors he'd heard of their atrocities in Australia, perhaps they were.

Seagulls began to gather now, and they shrieked and swooped down to feed on the rich pickings. Yutaka Nanten felt outrage boil up inside him. He was preparing to shoot at the nearest bird, which was attempting to tear a strip of meat away from the charred rump of a comrade, when the barge hit something with a grinding clang and a great lurch sideways.

The boat tipped over about twenty degrees, as the keel scraped across sand, and possibly a coral bottom. He had been so conditioned to leap forward when he heard those sounds that the failure of the bow doors to drop actually surprised him. But then he remembered that there was no one to operate the lever.

The boat slewed around, beginning to rock along its axis, as it turned side-on to the surf.

Nanten's eyes opened wide, cracking the thin crust of dried blood that had formed in the folds of his skin. Big waves bore down on him. Big enough to see over the side of the boat. For some reason that terrified him even more than the strafing of the fighter plane. The barge rolled to and fro, tipping itself toward the swell like an open bowl. A breaker slammed into the seaward side with a sound as loud as a small shell going off. At least two feet of water poured in on top of the corpses.

It was too much to bear.

Without thinking he scrambled to his feet and over the side that seemed closest to shore. Another wave struck as he attempted to get free, threatening to tip everything over on top of him. A pitiable sound crawled up out of Nanten, a mewling animalistic protest against the fates. And then he was thrown free. He sailed through the air, hit the water, and tumbled over and over without a hint of control. Salt water rushed in through his nose and down his throat, and he began to cough and choke, which caused him to suck in even more water. His arms and legs, no longer shaking, scrambled for purchase, but he could not touch bottom. In the swirling chaos, he wasn't even sure which way was up and which way was down.

His feet struck out on their own accord, desperate to find something solid from which they might propel him to safety. He was vaguely aware that the water was turning pink, and then red. His head broke surface just long enough for him to grab one precious mouthful of air, and then he was under again, tossed about like flotsam.

His left toe touched something.

And then he felt sand underfoot. He pushed off and broke free of the surf again. Sucked in clean air. Once . . . twice. A wave slammed him, but this time when he went under, gritty sand scraped at his face. His hands and knees touched bottom.

He beetled forward, riding in on a small pink wave of mutilation and blood froth.

But he was safe. He had made land.

Nanten crawled up from the water's edge. The sea rushed up the incline of the beach, and flowed back again, sucking the sand out from beneath his hands. Despite the contamination of the water, from the contents of the barge, he'd never felt cleaner. The awful gummy sensation of being bathed in human blood was gone. The sun was warm on his neck. The sand hot beneath his hands.

"Going somewhere, Tojo?"

But Corporal Yutaka Nanten was beyond the point where his heart could possibly leap in fright. It had been racing so fast, for so long, that the meaningless words actually seemed to *slow* his pulse.

Then he looked up.

Three gaijin stood in front of him. Two men and one woman. The woman was pointing something at him that could only be a gun from the future. She was going to disintegrate him, turn him into dust that would blow away on the breeze.

"I said, *going somewhere?*"

Nanten turned his head slightly toward the larger of the men, the one who had spoken. He looked like a civilian, dressed in a business suit, which struck the corporal as funny, down here on the sand, with the remains of his platoon bobbing around him on the tide.

The businessman was also carrying a gun, but it was a standard contemporary weapon. A shotgun of some sort. The muzzle stared back at him, a circle of darkness. Eternity.

Suddenly it flashed white . . .

Rosanna Natoli jumped as the shotgun went off. She hadn't expected Cherry to actually *kill* the guy. She hadn't really expected anybody to crawl out of the barge when they'd seen it wash up on the beach. It'd been shot to pieces long before they got to it.

Nobody said anything, though. A day or two back, Curtis might have protested, but they were all well past that sort of bullshit now. None of them were going to risk leaving a wounded survivor in the barge who might later bring them undone.

She filmed Cherry as he bent forward and unhitched four grenades from the dead man's webbing. The detective passed one to Curtis, kept one in his hand, and pocketed the other two.

"On my count," he said.

The young officer nodded.

"One . . . two . . . three . . ."

They pulled the pins—actually they looked like pieces of string to Rosanna—and lobbed the grenades, one after the other, into the barge. The muffled crump of detonation came a few seconds later, as they hurried back up the sand to the walking track that passed through the dunes. They'd given up on cars after the last one had been strafed by a Zero.

"You getting a signal?" Curtis asked as they pushed back into the thick growth from which they'd emerged to check on the barge.

"Yep," she said. "Still there."

They were all curiously comforted by the continued presence of the Big Eye drones that were circling over the island. They were so high up, it'd be impossible to spot them—or to shoot them down—and they weren't armed, as far as she knew. So there was nothing the drones could do to help, really. But just the knowledge that they were there, that the Multination Force could still keep tabs on them—that was enough to make them feel as if they weren't completely alone. And it gave them faint hope that they might be rescued.

"How're your batteries?" asked Cherry.

"Good," she said. "These babies were approved by the Energizer Bunny himself. They'll be sweet for another couple of days."

The looks on their faces told her that neither man knew what the hell she was talking about.

Another ten minutes of walking through the scrub brought them to the tree-shaded hollow where they'd made their camp. Though it was pretty generous to call it a camp. Three folding cots under a canvas tarp. A solar sheet to recharge Rosanna's battery packs. Big cans of fresh water. Five days' worth of canned food looted on Cherry's say-so from an abandoned shop in town.

"There's a lot of other barges coming ashore," said Natoli. "You think we should get out of here?"

Cherry dropped onto a foldaway cot, grunting with exhaustion. "We'll be all right, sister. They're beaching around the point. The way the land lies, they'll move inland away from us, not toward us. I say we lay up until dark, and then see if we can move back over to the Koolaus. Get you a better vantage point to film what's happening at Pearl."

"The Japs are going to be all over the roads by now," said Curtis. "How do you plan on getting past them?"

Cherry rubbed at the back of his neck as he rooted through the pile of tins for something to eat. "People I used to know, Lieutenant. They did most of their business out of plain sight."

They were all tired, so they left it at that, and sat around in silence. Cherry opened a can of baked beans and ate them cold, sitting on the edge of his cot. Curtis washed down a Hershey bar with a cup of water.

Rosanna linked the Sonycam to her slate and transferred her files for editing. She had about an hour and twenty minutes to work on, including the footage she'd taken of the barge. She hadn't been able to bring herself to follow Kolhammer's instructions to destroy all her twenty-first tech. Most of it, she'd hidden in a spot Cherry had shown her, a buried ammo locker just off the road in the foothills of the Koolaus. There'd been two pistols in there. "Throw downs," he called them. And about $2,300 in cash. She didn't ask him about the stash.

Curtis had, though.

"That's my retirement fund and insurance policy, Lieutenant," was all the cop would say.

Rosanna figured she'd increased the value of his glory box about a thousand times over, just by dropping her flexipad and powered sunglasses in there. She figured she could put a bullet into the slate and the Sonycam, if they came close to being captured.

For now, though, she used the touch screen to package a burst for Julia back in New York. The live link was gone. A message had come in on Fleetnet ordering all the surviving embeds and 21C personnel to switch to compressed burst, to reduce the possibility that the transmissions might be traced.

That had been a heavy blow. Julia had a lot more experience with this sort of shit, and as long as they'd been able to talk to her, she'd been a serious source of reassurance. Especially when the first Japanese ships had appeared on the horizon. Even Cherry had listened to everything she told them to do.

Now they couldn't communicate in real time, and it felt as though darkness had drawn itself that much closer around them.

Cherry was sleeping quietly. Rosanna had insisted he spray himself with Snore-eze.

Curtis came over and sat next to her on the cot. "Do you mind?" he asked.

"Nah. It's cool."

Rosanna was only half listening to him, though. She might have been clueless in a firefight, but she could use an editing program in her sleep. With the slate balanced on her lap, she sent her fingers dancing over the screen, cutting, splicing, and juxtaposing images while she and Curtis talked.

"Do you think we're going to get out of this?" he asked.

Rosanna chopped twelve seconds from a long shot of Japanese dive-bombers working over the wreckage of Ford Island. Even pulled in as tight as she could, they weren't individually identifiable. *Damn.*

"I doubt it," she said.

"You don't think we can hide out up here, until help arrives?"

She tidied up a jumpy bit of footage of half a dozen landing barges beaching themselves on the island's eastern shore. They were the main body of the force from which the wrecked barge had been detached.

"Wally, maybe we could, you know, in the movies. But this is real life, buddy. Nothing good happens in real life. Not in wartime, anyway. Like this," she said, bringing up a vid of Cherry killing the Japanese soldier on the beach.

Then Curtis watched as he and the detective used the grenades to make sure nobody else crawled out of the barge.

"There's nothing good here, Wally. We're killing them. They're killing us. It's old news."

"You can't really believe that," he said, sounding almost offended. "You know what these guys are like. The Japs and the Nazis, they're in your history books. Beating them is the most important thing in world."

A smile softened her face. "I'm sorry. You're right. It is, but—"

Rosanna was never able to figure out whether she heard the shot or saw the impact of the bullet first.

Curtis was already flying backwards, tumbling over, blood spraying back in her face, when she became aware that she couldn't hear herself screaming for the sound of rifles discharging all around them.

Julia had often said that time became elastic under fire. A few seconds might stretch themselves out over what felt like half a day, or whole hours might disappear in a glimmer of compressed, accelerated activity. For Rosanna, it happened both ways.

Curtis airborne, slowly turning and twisting like an Olympic diver, his body jolting as more bullets struck home, bright red pearls of blood sailing away. And then Cherry, twice as big as she remembered him, suddenly on top of her, knocking her down, filling the whole world, a riot gun in his hands, the muzzle barking and shooting flames and sparks and smoke.

Japanese soldiers everywhere, some leaping from the brush in a twinkling, others charging at her in such drawn out, slow-mo that if they kept running and running for a thousand years, she doubted they would cross the little clearing to reach her.

A bloodied steel spike—a bayonet—emerged through Cherry's shoulder. He roared and spun, and a Japanese soldier with a comically surprised expression was taken off balance by the momentum. She saw a huge pistol in Cherry's hand. It fired twice, and Rosanna was somehow aware of a man *behind* her being killed, his head taken off by the twin blasts. A sickening wet, crunching sound. Three more bayonets driven into Cherry's body. Fists and boots hammering at him as he went down. A single pistol shot. A soldier falling away, clutching at his shattered jaw as it hung from his face by tendrils and skin.

Something slammed into her head, and she fell into darkness.

OSWEGO, NEW YORK

Julia couldn't believe she'd been suckered into this. It wasn't like she had nothing else to do.

Car bombs and parcel bombs were still going off all over the country. The Japanese were on Oahu. She was overdue to download Rosanna's latest package. And the *Times* had finally agreed to give her a team to run a three-part investigation of Hoover's FBI.

But here she was, stuck on a platform in a town hall that had rats in the rafters, in some pissant burg in upstate New York, selling fucking *war bonds*. At least the turnout was healthy. The hall probably held about 150 people, but at least three times that had spilled out into the night, wrapped up in mufflers and heavy coats, listening to this circus over an antique PA system that lost about half of everything that was said. The whine of the feedback was giving her a headache.

She felt like gagging on the cigarette smoke, and couldn't believe that people would allow their children to breathe in the stuff. But dozens of kids were dotted throughout the audience, many of them dressed for bed in slippers, winter pajamas, and long woolen robes.

She'd originally agreed to do the gig because Ronald Reagan was supposed to be on stage, along with the monkey from *Bedtime for Bonzo*. Well, actually, it wasn't the real monkey, which probably hadn't been born yet. *Bedtime* was originally filmed in 1951. Instead, it had been telerecorded onto celluloid by Universal Studios, and it was one of the most popular movies of the year.

Now Reagan couldn't get in from the West Coast, what with all the terrorist bombings, so Edward Gargan, who played Policeman Bill in *Bedtime*, had been sent in his place.

But there was another reason Julia had been dragooned into this animal act, and he was sitting next to her on the hard wooden bench: Sergeant Snider, of the USMC. He was in line for a Medal of Honor, or at least a Silver Star, for his bravery on the Brisbane Line.

Julia didn't hold it against him, though. Snider was all right, and she couldn't begrudge him living off the publicity tit. He'd done more than his fair share, and he was never going to walk freely again, thanks to his wounds. It was just that she had better things to be doing than entertaining a room full of hicks in order to get them to fork over—what, ten or twenty bucks each for the war effort?

There was no getting out of it, though. Her chief of staff, Blundell, said that if she was going to be a "celebrity reporter," there were certain obligations that came with the job. She wasn't sure whether he was insulting her with that "celebrity" stuff. She knew there were plenty on the paper who resented it. Harold Denny, one of the other war correspondents, had told her to her face that she was "all surface, even at the core."

She'd punched him out.

Maybe that was why she'd been sent upstate. As punishment.

Her flexipad was set to silent mode, and it began to vibrate on her hip. She considered faking an emergency to take the call and escape, but before she could do that, Policeman Bill had finished up, and she was being called to the podium to tell her stories about how Sergeant Snider had saved the world.

Two hours later, the hall was emptying of people. She'd been signing autographs and answering questions and was actually starting to dig the whole thing. She took a particular delight in telling a couple of teenaged girls to forget about boys and to concentrate on their studies, and to see if they could get a copy of de Beauvoir's *The Second Sex* or Greer's *The Female Eu-*

nuch from one of the mail-order companies that were springing up in the Zone.

Later on, she could remember Snider asking her if she wanted to get a cup of joe before she drove back to Manhattan, but she couldn't recall powering up the Ericsson and finding the message from Rosanna.

Except it wasn't from Rosanna. It was from a well-spoken Japanese Navy officer who identified himself in perfect English as Commander Jisaku Hidaka, interim military governor of Hawaii.

He was standing in a bare room.

Rosanna was seated in front of him, sobbing.

"Miss Duffy," he said. "You will relay this message to your leaders. Hawaii is under the control of the Imperial Japanese Navy. Your countrymen are being well treated. If there is any attempt to retake the island, however, every man and woman and child will be executed. This is not an empty threat."

And with that he drew his pistol and shot her friend in the head.

For the first time in her life, Julia Duffy fainted.

34

ALRESFORD AERODROME, HAMPSHIRE, ENGLAND

They hadn't even finished transferring their kit to the jeep when the copilot broke in over tac net.

"Excuse me, gentlemen. German air assault, gliders and Junkers, twenty-one minutes out. CI had confirmed this field as the likely DZ."

Harry told his men to finish up as quickly as they could. He climbed up into the jeep, standing in the rear with one boot on the spare tire. This airfield wasn't a major facility. It was a dispersal point, a place to hide precious fighters to protect them from bombing raids on the main centers like Biggin Hill. Mostly it consisted of a small control tower, a couple of Nissan huts, and a grass runway. There were no serviceable aircraft on the ground at the moment. Almost all the RAF and its Allied Air Forces were aloft.

That was probably why the Jerries were planning to use it as a landing field. Nice location, no resistance to speak of.

The aerodrome was set amongst farmland just over a hundred miles to the southwest of London. The nearest settlement was a village, which had grown up around a Norman-era church. There were no major military bases nearby. The full complement of the airfield came to 129 ground crew, air defense guards, and administrative staff. Some two dozen of them had gathered a short distance away to watch the helicopter land and disembark its passengers.

Harry called over his two demolition specialists. Bolt and Akerman.

"Andy, Piers, you've got fifteen minutes to turn that runway into a serious hazard to human life. Go!"

The troopers snatched up a couple of backpacks and dashed away enthusiastically.

The base commander was a one-legged Australian named Fitzsimons. He'd played test rugby in the 1930s before volunteering for the Empire Air Training Scheme. He'd taken a desk job after losing his leg, and that had turned a lot of his muscle to fat. But he still looked like a powerful man.

"Anything I should know, Major Windsor?" Fitzsimons asked as Bolt and Akerman moved ominously toward his runway.

"Yes," said Harry. "I'm afraid you're about to have some unwanted visitors. Jerry has decided he wants your lovely little airfield for his own. I'd put away the good silver, if I were you, Mr. Fitzsimons. German gliders and Junkers—probably with paratroops are on their way. Enough of them so that it looks like a battalion to me. They will probably have some fighters escorting them, too."

"Ah, I see. Well, then, what do you think we should do?"

"We shall tell them to keep their filthy fucking paws off the place, I imagine."

The remainder of the SAS squad was standing ready next to the jeeps.

"Okay, lads," he said, turning around to include them all. "Adolf wants this field as one end of an air bridge. That makes sense. There are no likely defenders around to see them off. It's a handy distance from London. But then, he doesn't know we're here, does he? Fitzsimons, you need to get your people together. Arm all of them, women and cooks included. Can you do that?"

"I can."

"Excellent. Did you play off the bench by the way, or did you run on for the Wallabies."

The base commander stood about three inches taller. "I ran on. Every game. Seven test matches. Could have been more. Plenty more actually, but—"

"Excellent. You know your own people. Leave me your airfield defenders. You take your bench players, divide them into three fire teams and get them up into that little copse of trees on the hill just off the north end of the runway. I think the gliders are going to put down over that way. Don't open fire until they're on the ground. Have each team concentrate on one glider at a time. Try to kill them inside, while they're all bunched up."

He turned back to his own troopers, finding his sniper, Corporal Fontaine, sitting on the bonnet of one of the jeeps.

"Angus. You go with these guys. Take Austin as your spotter. Take out the NCOs first, then the officers. Then anybody looks like they might be setting up a crew-served weapon."

"Come on, then, Stevo," said Fontaine, and they immediately began to unpack some of the kit they'd just finished stowing in the jeeps.

Fitzsimons was already bellowing orders, hurrying away on his wooden leg.

Harry walked over to the chopper to speak to the pilot. "Lieutenant Hay?"

"Sir."

"Ashley, wasn't it? Listen Ash, you need to get clear for the next twenty minutes. These characters will come in with fighter cover, if they're any good—"

"CI confirms that, Major."

"I thought as much," Harry said. "Do you have a full weapons load?"

"Autocannon is at a hundred percent. But only one rocket pod's working. We haven't had a chance to put the other into the shop."

"One will have to do. Can you bring up a holomap for me? The threat bubble out to fifty thousand meters."

He pulled his goggles down from where they'd been resting on his helmet. Flight Lieutenant Hay initiated a laser link to the *Trident* via the nearest low-orbit drone, then downloaded an edited V3D holomap of this part of the English countryside. Harry had to ignore much of the detail, such as eight-lane freeways, which simply hadn't been built yet. But he was betting that the landscape hadn't changed much.

"Lieutenant, can you park yourself in that blind river valley, about fifteen klicks to the north? We may have to call on you if we need close air support."

"Well, it's not in my job description, but I'll see what I can do."

"Best move out, then," Harry said.

The massive drooping composite blades of the NH 91 began to turn as Hay fed power from the Alfa Romeo/GE turbocells into the titanium rotor hub.

"*Viv!*" Harry shouted over the strengthening roar of the chopper, as he bent over and hurried back to the jeep. "I want you to take Chris and Frank down to the village. Set yourselves up with the Scorpions. Take out the fighter cover first. If you have any shots left when that's done, knock off the Junkers. They'll be a little ways behind. Then haul it back up here in the jeep. I'll need help."

"Right you are, guv," St. Clair replied. "Trooper Pearson, you silly old poof, you heard the heir to the throne, didn't you? Well, what are you fuckin' waiting for, then? Trooper Devine, let's go. Or should I get you a fucking walking frame, too?"

The towering Jamaican and his two off-siders quickly repacked one of the jeeps and lit out toward the sound of pealing church bells.

The Eurocopter lifted off and banked away to the north.

As the rotorwash died down, Harry found himself alone for a moment. Several soldiers dressed in khaki were double-timing his way. The airfield-defense unit. Men and a few women in RAF blue were emerging from the Nissan huts and control tower, under Fitzsimons's supervision. All of them were carrying old-fashioned rifles.

Harry looked at his watch.

Fourteen minutes.

The battalion had suffered nearly 12 percent casualties before they'd even crossed the Channel. RAF Hurricanes had ripped into them, diving out of the sun and slashing through the tight formation of transports and the gliders they were towing.

Their escorts, a squadron of standard 109s, had finally beaten off the defenders, but not before six Junkers had dropped away, trailing smoke and flame. Colonel Albrechtson tried not to imagine what it would be like, dying in such a fashion.

His men all wore the same expression. Thin lipped, gray faced, but resolute. The fucking SS with their pantomime costumes and superior bullshit—they liked to think of themselves as the elite. But Albrechtson knew that the best soldiers in the world were here in these planes with him. The *Fallschirmjäger*. Germany's airborne warriors.

The hollow bass notes of exploding flak reached him through the corrugated metal skin of the JU-52, but it was distant. The entire coastline of southern Britain was ablaze with gunfire. Thousands of planes dueled in the sky, and hundreds of ships pounded away at each other down below. It was a titanic struggle, but for the moment, it was a contest of machines.

In a few minutes he and his men would contend in blood. Their strength and their will against their offspring of this failed, bankrupt empire. Albrechtson didn't know if he would survive. But he was certain that Germany herself would triumph.

The drone of the engines made it impossible to hear anything but shouts, so there was no point saying any last words to the men. They didn't need speeches, anyway. All they needed was the jump light. He took a sip of water from his canteen and stroked the wooden stock of his trusty Mauser. It wasn't as fancy as the new automatic assault rifles issued to the SS, but it had served him well on Crete and in the Ukraine. He was happy to have it along, as an old friend.

He took the last few minutes to inspect his men. They looked magnificent, but he wasn't so foolish as to imagine that would last. He'd fought the British on Crete. Although that had been a victory, it was a bloodbath, as well. There had been talk that the führer would never allow an airborne assault again, yet here they were. At least a third of these men had jumped into Crete with him, falling amongst the savages of the Maori Battalion and their New Zealand slavers. It had been a slaughter from which normal soldiers would not have recovered.

But his *Fallschirmjäger* had regrouped after crippling losses, and in the end they had taken the island.

They would take this island, too.

Harry instructed his makeshift platoon to take up positions in a series of slit trenches that offered fire lanes that converged with Fitzsimons's fire teams on the hill at the end of the runway. He had no illusions about the kind of fire support he could expect from them, but you have to cut the cloth to suit your budget, as his grandfather used to say.

He heard Sergeant St. Clair's thick East End accent, booming through the speakers of his helmet. "Target lock, guvnor. Confirmed as eight ME One-oh-nines. Five thousand meters out. Launching."

"Acknowledged," said Harry before he muted the channel back to his antiair team.

"Listen up," he called down the trench line. "Escort fighters are coming in. Eight Messerschmitts. They're about three miles away now, but I want you to watch what happens. Keep watching in the direction of the village."

The men—they were all men—studied the tree line behind him.

"Cor blimey, wozzat!" cried one of them.

Eight thin tendrils of white exhaust smoke shot up from the hollow and rocketed away.

"Those are Scorpion ground-to-air missiles," Harry informed them. "They will destroy every Messerschmitt that's currently heading toward this airfield, hoping to shoot the crapper out of you."

He watched as their heads turned to track the flight path of the missiles.

A few began pointing in excitement. A cluster of small black dots, the fighters, had become visible to the south. The Scorpions ate up the distance to their targets at a phenomenal rate.

Eight balls of fire filled the sky where the aircraft had been.

Lusty shouts of approval arose from the trenches, and Harry was sure he could hear something similar coming from Fitzsimons's hill. His demo specialists, Bolt and Akerman, dropped into the shelter beside him, having just finished a rush job of mining the runway.

"Whizzbangs are ready, Captain," Bolt announced.

"We set a few claymores, too. Had 'em for securing the lay-up point in Norway. They're about halfway out to the runway."

Another six contrails whooshed away from the village.

"Is that more fighters, sir?" asked a private with an amazingly shiny hairdo.

Brylcreem, thought Harry.

"No, Private," he answered, checking the heads-up display in his goggles. "My sergeant is aiming for some troop transports. You can't see them yet, but he can. They'll all be shot down long before they get here."

There was no cheering this time. Some nodding, a few murmurs of appreciation, but no cheering.

"Are there going to be any left for us to get, Major?" asked the Brylcreem boy.

"Oh, yes," replied Harry. "I'm afraid so."

Something had gone wrong.

The pilots were shouting. The aircraft swooped and climbed and dropped down violently, throwing Albrechtson and men around the cabin. One man had already broken his arm, and the colonel himself would have been knocked out had he not been wearing a helmet.

Six loud flak bursts had gone off all around them, and it sounded as if every single shot had scored a hit. There was a terrible sound when a plane took a direct hit—all that metal and fuel and ammunition going up simultaneously. It was a much denser report than the slightly empty boom of a near miss.

He began to feel just how painfully slow the JU-52 was—that was why they stopped using them as bombers in the first place. Fighters and ack-ack guns picked them off too easily.

Every muscle in his body was clenched, urging them on to the drop point just that little bit faster. The rapid *pom-pom-pom* sound of Bofors shells going off all around them told him that their fighter escorts hadn't dealt with the enemy's antiaircraft emplacements. The transport bucked and jolted alarmingly as near misses buffeted them. Some of his men began exchanging worried glances. A young paratrooper at the far end of the cabin vomited over his boots. Another man, two places down from him, was suddenly thrown forward and dropped to floor, his parachute shredded and smoking, blood leaking out of his tunic.

The jump light turned red. The men all held up their hooks for the static line.

"Up!" he called out, checking his helmet strap.

The men arose as one, even the kid who had been puking his guts out.

"Hook up!"

Standing by the open door, Albrechtson felt the tug of the slipstream. The rushing air added a constant roar to the crash of exploding shells as his seventeen surviving men hooked their chutes onto the line. Some tumbled over, cursing, as a volley exploded over the wing, punching the plane down and to the left. Albrechtson saw three lines of tracer converge on another Junkers two hundreds away. The portside engine blew up and sheared off the wing.

"Equipment check," he yelled over the noise.

Each paratrooper patted and pulled at the man in front him, checking for faults that might kill a man before he had a chance to fight.

"Sound off!"

They counted themselves down, halting temporarily at the ninth man, as two windows shattered and somebody screamed.

"It's Dietz. He's gone."

The puking kid was dead.

The count continued, as the men on either side of Dietz cleared his body from the lineup.

Albrechtson called out that he was clear as the red light turned green.

He grabbed the frame of the exit and thrust himself out. He felt the shock of hitting the airstream at speed and heard the *zip-zip-zip* of bullets passing by his head. His chute deployed, and his boots swung up with the jerk of interrupted momentum.

It was peaceful then, dropping through the autumnal sky, no longer trapped in the corrugated metal coffin. He could see the airfield below, and the gliders dropping gracefully toward their landing zone.

But his stomach lurched as he searched the sky for the transports that were carrying his *Fallschirmjäger*. There were so few left. He knew they'd taken casualties before the escorts had driven off or—more likely—destroyed their attackers. But it seemed as though only a handful of 52s had made it through.

As he glided down, Albrechtson frantically searched for his binoculars, a small pair of Zeiss glasses he kept in a breast pocket. He found them, then nearly dropped them, before finally managing to turn them toward the target. He expected to find massed flak batteries down there. Or evidence of a squadron that had been missed by the *Abwehr*. There was no sign of either. Yet half his command had already been destroyed.

This was going to be like Crete all over again.

Prince Harry calculated that about 210 paratroopers had popped chutes overhead. Trooper Akerman said 220. Bolt put his money on around two hundred.

"We'll count them afterwards," Harry decided as he fixed a microlight targeting dot on the chest of a descending paratrooper.

"A fiver on the result." Bolt just wouldn't let it go.

The German appeared at a virtual distance of ten meters in Harry's goggles, although he was actually a good four hundred meters away. Harry exhaled slowly and applied smooth, even pressure to the trigger, until his rifle kicked back with a loud, flat bang.

In one of those post-Transition ironies, the venerable German firm of Heckler and Koch had manufactured his weapon, an M12 carbine. Made entirely of composites, it was a lightweight assault rifle of the old school. It didn't electronically fire caseless ceramic ammunition, instead feeding 5.56 mm augmented bullets from a thirty-six-round magazine, and 20 mm programmable grenades from an in-line stacker.

The German, who had been holding tightly to his risers, scanning the ground as it rushed toward him, jerked as the round hit. Harry didn't bother to put another shot in. He was firing shredders, which disassembled themselves inside the target before emerging at 940 meters per second, dragging about a kilogram of human tissue behind them.

He squeezed off another three shots as the troopers on either side of him did the same. The airfield defenders banged away enthusiastically with a variety of weapons, mostly Lee Enfield rifles and Tommy guns.

The crackle of small arms from Fitzsimons's three squads reached them. A glider broke up as a Bofors crew took it under direct fire.

"Nasty," hissed Bolt.

But the sheer weight of the German assault began to tell. Paratroopers made it to the ground and disengaged their chutes, running for cover. Some tumbled and spun, as the snipers began to pick them off. Even so, small groups of three and four, then larger parties of eight or nine survivors banded together and went to work.

"Over there, sir," Bolt cried as an antiaircraft redoubt came under assault. Five Germans charged it, firing rapidly, one of them hosing down the position with a Schmeisser.

"Bugger," Harry said as the volume of incoming fire stepped up a notch. Rounds whistled close by, kicked up clods of dirt, and occasionally thumped into the chest or splattered the head of a 'temp in the slit trench. He tried to draw a bead on the paratroopers who'd taken over the big gun, but they were at least seven hundreds meters away. His first shot burst a sandbag; the next caromed off the gun itself. He dialed up his sniper team on tac net.

"Angus, Stevo. You need to get busy, or you're going to get chopped into dog meat."

"Sorry, Skip," came Fontaine's reply. "I can't get a clear shot at them."

Harry examined the AAA site again. Pulling in as much as he could. The Germans zoomed in to fill his visual field. But it was difficult to stay focused, since every movement of his head was amplified a hundredfold. Bullets chewed up the sandbags, and one struck a paratrooper in the shoulder, but they stuck to the job of trying to get the gun depressed far enough to use it as a weapon against his people.

Harry was turning that over in his mind when Trooper Bolt suddenly pushed him down.

The ground seemed to shake with a volcanic eruption.

"The runway charges!" he cried.

Harry peeped up in time to see tons of dirt and broken bodies and the smashed up remains of a couple of gliders dropping back to earth. Four more gliders tried to avoid the crater, but it was too late. They went in nose-first, with a bone-jarring crack and the crunch of splintered wood.

The Prince made a few quick calculations. "Fire the claymores, Andy."

Bolt did as he was ordered, even though no Germans were approaching. Two of the antipersonnel mines had been set close to the runway and had gone up with the demolition charges. The other six fired with a thunderclap and instantly peppered three of the wrecked gliders with thousands of steel balls.

"*Fix bayonets!*" yelled Harry.

He heard the rasp and click of nearly two dozen old-fashioned bayonets, as his own men quickly fitted their sawback fighting knifes.

"Follow me, gentlemen. *Let's clean them out.*"

The war cry started amongst the 'temps, a guttural sound building into a full-throated highland scream as they charged across the grass toward the shattered gliders and deep, smoking holes excavated by Bolt and Akerman's shaped charges. Harry flipped his selector to three round bursts as he ran, snapping the M12 up to finish off a few lonesome parachutists who were still wafting down to the ground.

He heard the muffled *whump* of a grenade launcher. It was Bolt, sending a frag into the shallow pit where the glider with the least amount of damage had finished up. A German soldier had been emerging shakily from a huge tear in the rear of the plane, and he was blown back inside.

Whump. Whump.

Twin explosions split the glider into three sections, and Harry flipped his weapon to full auto, sending a stream of 5.56 mm into the crippled airframe. The industrial hammering of the other M12 assault rifles, the crash of grenades and small arms, all served to isolate Harry, almost cocooning him from the wider battle. But he had to press on, to get close enough to that Bofors pit to bring it under fire by grenade launcher.

He heard Akerman grunt and drop. A flashing red icon on his HUD told him the trooper had fallen off the tac net. He was dead. Harry didn't have time to check on why. A lucky shot, perhaps.

He held the M12 level now, the point of his bayonet leading him into the no-man's land of the ruined airstrip, the screams of berserkers all around.

They'd done it.

Albrechtson wanted to hug the men who'd risked all to capture that anti-aircraft gun and turn it on the Tommies. They raked the tree line on the little hill where the enemy had deployed at least three of four separate sections to pour fire down on his men.

The Bofors mount had a direct line of sight that allowed them to target only half the ridgeline, being partially blocked by a crashed glider and a burning British truck. But the explosive ordnance had a dramatic and immediate effect, anyway, shredding the cover and chewing up huge gouts of soil and turf on that part of the hill that it could engage.

The volume of fire from that area dropped away almost completely.

Three more gliders touched down in the safety of the next field, and with only a handful of casualties, most probably from a sniper. Those men disembarked at a run.

A perimeter was established, and they began to work on the British flank, targeting those defenders who were protected from the ack-ack gun. He recognized the sweet sound of an MG42, so much like ripping cloth.

A second Spandau opened up.

A sergeant rolled into the small crater where Albrechtson had taken shelter. He had six other paratroopers with him, to add to the five the colonel had gathered together. Almost the makings of a platoon. If they could just—

"*Get up!*" he barked at them. "*Now!*"

.   .   .

A second German came at Harry as he struggled to withdraw his bayonet from the first, who was still thrashing about like a speared trout. He squeezed off a round, using the recoil and the hydrostatic shock to help him wrench free the blade.

But it was too late. He couldn't possibly turn around in time. His attacker was crazed. Eyes rolled back in his head, frothing at the mouth, tendrils of ragged flesh and khaki swinging from the bloodied spike that was attached to his Mauser.

Harry turned his hips, taking himself out of the line of attack and simultaneously parrying the bayonet thrust with the muzzle of his M12. He summoned a *kiai* from deep within his gut. The focused war shout directed his energies and disrupted the flow of his would-be killer. Without thought, without aim, he snapped out a side kick, driving his boot into and through the most vulnerable point, the German's kneecap, with all the force he could muster, pivoting on his other leg to deliver extra torque.

He felt and heard the joint disintegrate with a sickeningly wet crunch.

The man dropped, screaming, until the butt of Harry's carbine smashed into the bridge of his nose with such power that it destroyed the sinus cavities and caved in the frontal lobes. He was dead before he'd fallen all the way to the ground.

Men tore at each other like animals. So closely enmeshed were attackers and defenders that Harry couldn't fire his weapon normally, for fear of killing one of his own. Combatants shrieked and howled and sank their teeth into each other's throats. In the midst of this psychotic delirium, he and the other SAS man stood out for their economy of movement, and the efficiency with which they dispatched their victims. A knife-hand strike to the throat, a twisting lock that snapped the head free of the spine, the thumb driven into an eye socket, to distract before a fighting knife severed the carotid artery and windpipe.

With two decades of the close-quarter fighting between them, from the Tora Bora Mountains to the alleyways of Surabaya, they drew on a wealth of memory and experience about how best to kill a man when he's close enough to exhale his last ragged breath into your face.

A sledgehammer hit him in the shoulder, knocking him to the ground. He thought he heard the rifle shot a second later, but of course that couldn't be so.

Harry hit the ground and rolled. The pain of the impact was enormous and crippling, even though he'd been saved by the reactive matrix weave of his body armor. Burnt earth, coppery with blood, filled his mouth. When the world stopped spiraling about him, he rolled onto his back, his pistol in hand. A German officer was standing ten feet away, frantically working the bolt on his rifle.

The Prince's arm was numb with shock. He had to tell his fingers to squeeze the trigger, cursing them as they refused to obey him.

The German raised the rifle.

Harry felt like his teeth might shatter, so hard was he biting down with the effort of just trying to pull the damned trigger.

The gun jumped, and the German spun into the ground.

Harry felt the familiar tingle of spinal inserts as they began squirting their contents into his nervous system. Some feeling returned to the arm; renewed energy coursed through his body. He levered himself up.

Two shots sounded nearby, then silence. Or at least relative silence. The Bofors gun still pounded away over the compressed roar of the German machine guns, which reminded him a lot of the old American M60. As he got to his feet, he saw the cost of the ground they had taken. There were no Germans left alive, but only six of his men remained, including Bolt, who had taken a bullet in the mouth and was now missing half his jaw. He was down, feet splayed, his back leaned up against the severed tail section of a German glider. His eyes had the far-away look that told of a massive drug dose washing through his system.

Harry was still stunned and trying to gather his wits when he realized he could hear the dull thud of rotor blades. Two contrails whooshed directly overhead, followed by the *crump* of detonation as a pair of Hellfire missiles stuck home.

The chopper was back, the earsplitting mechanical stammer of its auto-cannon a symphony of deliverance.

35

HMS *TRIDENT*, ENGLISH CHANNEL

"I can't believe this," Halabi said. "What a bloody dog's breakfast."

She was strapped into her command chair. Indeed, everyone in the stealth cruiser's CIC was secured at their stations against the violent, high-speed course changes with which the *Trident*'s Combat Intelligence guided them through the battle for the English Channel.

The main display teemed with thousands of contacts, friendly and hostile. The quantum processors and software of the *Trident*'s Nemesis Battle-space Management System was busy collecting, analyzing, and disseminating terabytes of data every second. Posh broke down the attack into manageable chunks of information not just for the thirty-five dedicated sysops on board the *Trident*, but also for hundreds of newly trained shore-based officers who were laser-linked to the ship via the drones, which floated safely at the edge of the stratosphere.

As they watched, a wall of blue triangles moved across the computer-generated map of Suffolk toward the main German lodgment. Four larger, slower icons trailed behind them.

"Are those the Specter variants, Mr. Howard?"

"Aye, ma'am. But they call them Cyclones here."

Halabi nodded. Two of her engineers from the ship's Air Division had worked as advisers on the project, the fitting out of four Douglas Dakotas as gunships with electric miniguns firing out of two rear windows and the side cargo door. Each gun had been hand-tooled at a small factory in Scotland, and all used components stripped from various ships of the Multinational Force. Like their "forebear," the AC 47 gunship of the Vietnam War era, the Cyclones carried more than twenty-four thousand rounds of ammunition, and could plow up an area the size of a football field in a few seconds.

Halabi keyed in a request for a live feed from the Big Eye, with a footprint over the area.

Before she had a chance to take advantage of the feed, however, her weapons sysop called out. "Coming into range for launch on the *Tirpitz* group, ma'am."

She didn't need to request vision of the German battleship and its escorts, forging into the Channel. One panel of the main display had been devoted to their primary target all along. She heard the jackhammer of the *Trident*'s Metal Storm pods as they lashed out at an air threat that had broken through the protective screen of 303 Squadron. A quick check revealed that they were down to 4.5 percent of their war stocks.

It was getting very tight.

"Targets designated, Captain."

Halabi scanned the main display, looking for the main body of the British Home Fleet that was moving down from the north to engage Admiral Raeder.

"Launch," she ordered.

She heard the ignition of the missiles in their silos, but could feel nothing because of the ship's extreme speed and the violence of the maneuvers the CI was using to protect them.

Deck-cams showed the last of her combat maces lifting away on white exhaust plumes. As soon as they cleared the tubes, the CI threw the ship into a tight turn, the Metal Storm pods drumming away again. Halabi checked the threat boards: 163 German aircraft were attempting to sink her, although it looked like some of them had broken off in a hopeless attempt to intercept the sunburn missiles that were now accelerating away to the east.

Her second defensive sysop, Lieutenant Anne Davis, reported that the laser packs were now "nonfunctional."

"Thank you, Ms. Davis. Comms, how are Three-oh-three doing?"

"Down to sixty percent strength, ma'am. RCAF Four-oh-one and Two Squadrons are set to arrive in three minutes."

Metal Storm roared out again, reducing its stocks to 4.3 percent.

Halabi was beginning to feel decidedly uncomfortable. Her last offensive weapons were speeding away at Mach 6. Her ability to defend the ship and its crew was degrading with every minute that passed.

A sudden lurch to starboard nearly wrenched her shoulder out.

"Sorry, ma'am," said her countermeasures chief, Lieutenant David Loomes. "Posh detected a torpedo launch. Dolphins away."

Down beneath the waterline on the port-side hull, bay doors slid open and two black lozenges spat out into the foam skirt that surrounded the ship when the Super-Cavitating System was engaged. Seeker heads powered up, aqua-jets engaged, the Tenix-ADI Dolphin's own SCS came online, and the weapons shot away from the *Trident* at a speed of 280 knots.

Twenty-three seconds later, there came a dull thud from the speaker system at the subsurface threats station as the first Dolphin intercepted the U-boat that had fired on them. With a final burst of acceleration, the super-hard, nonexplosive warhead simply punched through the thin skin of the submarine, exiting the hull on the other side, leaving two gaping holes.

The sound of the torpedo intercept didn't register against the incredible amount of background noise, but the Nemesis arrays recorded a kill and then reported that both Dolphins were seeking new targets.

"Thank you, Mr. Loomes," said Halabi.

Her six ship-killers, the last of her missiles, were tracking past Calais, ripping along forty meters off the deck, through the obstacle course of ships and even the occasional slow, low flying plane. Halabi's eye was drawn back to the main display for a moment, where the Cyclone gunships had begun their run.

SUFFOLK, ENGLAND

In the end, the rush to finish fitting out the Cyclones had become so frenzied that there'd been no chance to test them properly. McGregor had no idea whether the airframe would even hold together when they triggered the "miniguns." The whole fucking thing might just fall to pieces in midair. If they even made it to the target.

The skies were alive with thousands of aircraft, friendly and hostile, all of them seemingly twisting and turning and roaring in chaotic dogfights around his flight of slow, lumbering transporters.

His headphones crackled with the voice of his copilot. Tight, strangled words gave away how scared his copilot Barry Divola was. They were all frightened. Flight Lieutenant Philip McGregor felt like his balls had crawled up somewhere inside his rib cage.

"Pathfinders dropping smoke. Green smoke," said Divola.

"I see green smoke," McGregor confirmed.

He began to haul the C-47 around, pitting his strength against the machine. He'd heard that you just had to nudge the stick in one of those twenty-first planes and the thing would dance all over the sky. That must be why women could fly them. He had to move this flying pig the old-fashioned way, by wrestling it through every turn and dip.

He gripped the controls and felt the flaps bite into the slipstream as he brought them around for the payload run. The other three converted Dakotas followed his lead. There was no flak, thank God, but his jaws and teeth hurt anyway because he'd been grinding them together so hard. German fighters had attacked them three times since they'd taken off, and three times they been beaten back by their escorts, a squadron of the new Super Spitfires, sooled on the Messerschmitts by some talking box on the *Trident*.

Or at least, he vaguely assumed that's what had happened. He was too busy keeping them alive and on course to think about anything other than the immediate demands of the situation.

"Guns hot," came a voice in his phones.

"Guns hot," he acknowledged. "Commencing final approach."

The engines howled a little louder as the props bit into the air and the Dakota tilted along its axis. McGregor was glad he wasn't responsible for lining up the weapons, the crew chief who'd come aboard back at Debden was using some magic box to do that. The first he'd know about it would be when—

"Firing in three, two, one—"

"Shit!"

McGregor had been prepared for a surprise. After all, they'd told him the electronically powered guns could put a bullet into every square inch of a footy field in just a few seconds. Intellectually, he could appreciate that meant a lot of bullets leaving his plane very quickly, but the reality of it was still a shock. The whole aircraft seemed to lurch sideways through space as though it had been slapped. A terrible, head-splitting metallic ripping sound filled the world, and McGregor felt as though he was on the receiving end of the strafing run, so violently did the C-47 rattle and shake.

"Fuck me blind!" cried Divola. "Did you see that, Skipper?"

McGregor risked a quick glance down at the target area, a densely wooded copse of trees a few hundred yards from a smoking, shell-damaged church. All four Cyclones were pouring solid rivers of fire into the woods, which were literally disintegrating under the effects. A few small, dark black-clad figures emerged at a run from the disappearing cover. Most escaped, but two burst into pink mist.

"Sweet Jesus," breathed the pilot.

Three companies of SS *Sonderaktiontruppe* had been sheltering in the small forest, which was now just a smoking mound of shattered splinters, drifting leaves, and—he supposed—tiny bite-sized pieces of Aryan supermen.

HMS *TRIDENT*, THE ENGLISH CHANNEL

There was no audio track, of course, for which Halabi was quietly grateful. Five or six hundred men being turned to offal was unlikely to make for easy listening. The top-down view, from a virtual height of five hundred meters, was more than graphic enough. The Cyclones began to turn for home. As if in counterpoint to silent carnage, the ship's CIWS fired again, a couple of long, growling bursts.

"Metal Storm down to three-point-nine percent, Captain."

"Thank you, Ms. Morgan. Lieutenant Davis, how's our air cover?"

"Changing over now, Captain. But Squadron Leader Zumbach's men are refusing to withdraw. They're staying until they run out of fuel. One of them has just tried to ram a One-oh-nine."

Halabi rolled her eyes skyward, but could see only ducts, composite paneling, and fiber-optic cable. She could still wonder at what it must be like up there, in primitive planes that probably wouldn't even get a safety clearance in her day. If this were a movie or a cheap, particularly stupid novel, it was the point at which she would call up Jan Zumbach and order him to get his crazy-arse Poles back to base.

But the readout on her personal display told her that she would soon be completely vulnerable to the scores of Luftwaffe planes that continued to press in on her, no matter what losses they sustained.

Metal Storm barked twice more.

"Very good, Ms. Davis," said Captain Halabi.

The main display reformatted as the volley of missiles closed with their prey. One giant window was filled with the image of the *Tirptiz;* two smaller pop-ups, with the pocket battleships *Admiral Scheer* and *Lützow.* Fighter escorts buzzed around them like insects, and a dozen smaller vessels raced along in attendance.

"What on earth are they doing, Marc?" Halabi asked as the entire battle group began to swing around.

Her intelligence boss, Lieutenant Commander Howard, leaned forward, as if to study the screen more closely. "I—I think they're coming around to present a broadside, Skipper?"

"To the missiles?"

"I think so. They've probably had radio reports, by now."

He called out across the CIC to the sigint station. "Do we have any breakdown of the radio traffic to the *Tirpitz?*"

"Working on it now, sir," replied a striking black woman with a thick Glaswegian accent.

"They're firing blind," said Halabi, and it seemed as if every gun on the port side of the *Tirpitz* and her escorts opened up. The missiles were still a hundred miles away, but moving so swiftly that they would close the distance to impact in less than one minute.

As she watched, the fighter escorts broke away and began to race into the west, sparkling points of light on their wings indicating that they, too, were attempting to throw a wall of lead into the path of her missiles.

"Weapons. What chance do they have of intercepting our—?"

"Splash one already, Captain. Attack reformatting."

One of the missiles had been destroyed when it flew into a cloud of shrapnel thrown out by the massive main guns of the *Tirpitz,* which was firing time-fused shells. With the missiles moving at hypersonic speed, there was nothing she could do. Everything happened so quickly that only the Combat Intelligence had time to respond, as another two precious missiles died in midair.

The CI flashed out instructions to the surviving weapons, reassigning one each to the German capital ships. The maces dipped down to wave height and separated. Before Halabi could say another word, could draw breath, or even feel her next heartbeat, three silent white blooms of light consumed the ironclads. The missiles were carrying subfusion plasma-yield warheads that detonated like miniature supernovae deep inside their targets.

Admiral Scheer and *Lützow* exploded and broke up an instant later. Halabi's stomach did a slow backflip as she watched the *Tirpitz* emerge from the plasma effect. The mace had done a huge amount of damage amidships, but the great warship continued on as though shrugging off a peashooter.

"Damn," she cursed, just as the bow of the *Tirpitz* suddenly bent back on itself and began to dig into the North Sea like a plow.

A few of the CIC crew swore at the amazing sight, and then it was gone. A rapid series of secondary explosions ripped her apart, destroying a couple of escorts that had raced in to help.

"Message to the Admiralty, Ms. Davis. All targets serviced. No survivors anticipated."

"Aye, Captain. Allied armored units are moving to encircle the main German airborne assault at Wickham Market, ma'am, and Lieutenant Hay reports that Major Windsor's troops have secured the airfield at Alresford."

"Thank you, Comms."

Halabi could see that another two squadrons of Allied planes were now swarming the German aircraft that had been attempting to kill her. Americans this time, some of them flying prototype Mustangs that hadn't even been painted yet. She didn't presume to retake the helm from Posh, however. Hundreds of vessels still fought in the narrows of the English Channel, and it was beyond her abilities to safely navigate a passage home, particularly at their current speed.

A Metal Storm pod erupted briefly, to emphasize the point that she wasn't yet out of trouble.

HMS *JAVELIN*, THE ENGLISH CHANNEL

Sub-Lieutenant Philip Mountbatten did not have a chance to meet his famous grandson. After fighting her back from Alexandria, HMS *Javelin*, his latest berth, had gone straight into the *Trident*'s air defense screen. With a pair of the ship's two-pounder poms-poms to run, Mountbatten had barely had time to sleep or eat. Socializing wasn't an issue.

"Stukas, sir! Three of them at ten o'clock," cried Seaman Bob Nicklin.

"Good work, Nicklin," Mountbatten yelled over the roar of battle. "On my mark, wait for it—*Fire!*"

The guns began their furious drumbeat, throwing up to 140 high-explosive rounds a minute at the screaming dive-bombers. Dirty, roiling balls of smoke and flame boxed in the lead aircraft. Mountbatten fancied that he could see the single bomb beneath the undercarriage. Two small, stuttering starbursts of light erupted on the inverted gull wings as the German lashed at them with his machine guns.

The sea all around them was a vast enraged cauldron on which thousands of men fought and died. Beyond the deafening sound of every gun on board the *Javelin* firing at once, there lay a deeper, infinitely more savage uproar as hundreds of ships and possibly thousands of planes raked at each other in mortal combat.

"Look out!" yelled Nicklin as the bomb detached itself from the underside of the Stuka like a fat black pearl, an instant before two distinct explosions punched the aircraft into three pieces. The wings twirled away like falling leaves caught on a gusting wind, while the nose of the aircraft, trailing a long tail of flame and smoke, described a fatal arc, which carried it over their heads to explode in the Channel somewhere on the far side of the ship.

Mountbatten watched, in thrall to his own fate as the bomb seemed not so much to drop toward them as to simply get bigger and bigger. The gun was still hammering away at the other bombers, just like every other mount on the destroyer. But Mountbatten's men knew that unlike the other men, they had no chance of surviving beyond the next few seconds.

So completely had the young officer given himself over to the end that he didn't notice the radical tilt of the deck as the helm laid hard a-port and the engine room poured every ounce of power into the ship's geared turbines, pushing her out to her top speed of thirty-six knots and slewing the stern around so violently that tons of cold brine piled up against the armor plating and then spilled over the rear deck, threatening to wash away half a dozen sailors.

The ear-piercing whistle of the Stuka's single 500 kg bomb, the last sound he'd thought he would ever hear, abruptly vanished inside a rolling thunderclap as an enormous geyser of gray-green seawater erupted from the churning waves and climbed high above them. Mountbatten and his men were drenched as the fountain spent its energy and collapsed on top of them.

He heard cheering, and thought it was his own men, celebrating their survival but it came from farther astern, where the *Javelin*'s other Bofors mount had accounted for another plane. The third pulled away, having missed, and was raked by streams of tracer fire not just from his ship's machine guns but by the AA fire of at least two other destroyers in the *Trident*'s screen.

The Trident!

With his life and his ship in no immediate danger again, Mountbatten cast around for her. He'd heard a rumor that the prince was on board and could only wonder what that might mean.

It was phenomenally queer for a chap to have a grandson who was already nearly twice his own age, but that wasn't the weirdest thing to have come out of the last few months. There was his own future, of course, or possible future. It had been judged too indiscreet to allow him to meet his wife-to-be just yet. After all she was still only—what?—sixteen years old? And who was to say she would still be his? And that he would still become the consort of Elizabeth II. It was all too horribly vexing.

Shooting down the bloody Hun was much simpler.

"There she is, sir. Over there. Cor! Look at 'er fuckin' go!"

Mountbatten followed the man's pointed finger.

Sure enough, three giant fantails of sea spray marked the passage of the supership.

"She must be going a hundred!" yelled Nicklin over the din.

"A hundred and thirty knots at top speed, I hear," said Mountbatten, and that settled the question for everyone.

The three fans of water at the stern of the magnificent arrow-shaped vessel pivoted as she came hard a-port to avoid some unseen obstacle. Her destroyer screen, the *Javelin* included, had kept up for less than a minute. She was already drawing away from their protective umbrella—although it was astonishing to think that such a powerful craft needed looking after. Even as he watched, five German planes disintegrated as they pressed in on her. It was as if they had passed through some threshold that marked the point at which the *Trident* could no longer tolerate their existence. And so they had ceased to exist.

Mountbatten could not pick out which of the hundreds of fighters dueling above her were specifically assigned to her air screen, but he'd heard that three full squadrons attended her every move. At least they would be able to keep up, wherever she was going.

Probably to engage the *Tirpitz*, he thought, and instantly wished he could've seen that battle. Although again, from all he'd heard, she would probably strike the German capital ships from hundreds of miles away.

A hand smacked down on his shoulder, and he turned to find Lieutenant Jeffers, who yelled in his ear. "Check your loads, Phil! We're moving into the Channel. Hunting e-boats and troop barges. You're going to get busy."

"Thanks, Bruce," he called back.

As Jeffers moved on, Sub-Lieutenant Mountbatten patted each of his men on the back. "Well done, lads. Well done. No time for a lie-down yet, though. We're getting out of this backwater and into the real fighting."

36

THE ENGLISH CHANNEL

Untersturmführer Gelder was beginning to wish that he was still playing wet nurse to that broken-down cot case of an engineer. Brasch was quite unpleasant company at the best of times, with his mood swings and a dangerous habit of speaking his mind. But shadowing the engineer around

Demidenko to ensure that he was never exposed to the attentions of the NKVD was an altogether more agreeable experience than bouncing across the English Channel in the cramped hold of a *Schnellboot* while all hell raged around him.

They had to be making well over forty knots. The torpedo boat's three diesel engines howled like Valkyrie gone mad, not so much driving them through the rough swell and cross-chop as flinging the one-hundred-ton vessel from the crest of one wave to the next. Each leap ended with a terrifying *boom* as the hull slammed into the water, the impact compressing Gelder's spine, and once causing him to bite down painfully on his tongue. He was wretched with seasickness and tried to climb up, out into the fresh air.

The passage of the boat was so violent, he wrenched his shoulder and nearly broke an arm just getting up the stairwell. When he finally made the wheelhouse, he cursed himself for having been so stupid. The sea was not his natural realm. Just as the führer once admitted of himself, Gelder was a lion on land, but not so much on water. The sight that greeted him as he hauled himself into the tiny enclosed bridge space was enough to rob any man of his courage.

The Channel was nearly dammed up with shipping, all of it charging about at top speed, either making for the English coast like his boat, or dashing into the body of the German invasion fleet. Like the two British destroyers he could see bearing down on them. The thunder of battle was beyond deafening. It did not just hurt his ears. It pressed in hard upon his mind with such a crushing weight that he thought his sanity might just give out under the barrage. The sea was a maelstrom, seemingly whipped into a storm-tossed frenzy not by the weather, which was only mildly gray and unsettled, but by the violent action of so many men and ships locked in bloody contention.

Not two hundred yards away, a shell or a torpedo or perhaps even a rocket struck a barge, packed with soldiers. It suddenly leapt out of the water, flying apart as the warhead detonated, sending men flying everywhere like the flaming fragments of a Chinese firecracker.

"God help us," Gelder cried as one torn-up, smoking corpse twisted through the air and onto the deck of their boat, where the dead man—*surely he must be dead*—slammed into the metal vent that scooped clean air down into their lower decks. Despite the awful roar and pandemonium, Gelder distinctly heard the dull thud of impact, which all but crushed the vent. The body, which was missing a leg and most of everything else above the shoulders rolled to the deck—and then mercifully disappeared over the side as they pitched into a turn and slewed down the side of a rogue wave.

The skipper swore and smacked the helmsman on the back as two shells crashed into the wave top they had just vacated, raising evil green eruptions of seawater. Gelder's stomach knotted, and he dry-heaved repeatedly, bracing himself into a corner of the wheelhouse.

"Don't worry, Herr *Untersturmführer*, we shall get you there alive, yes. Maybe nobody else will survive this fucking crossing, but you're with the best fucking crew in the *Kriegsmarine*." The man sounded genuinely crazy.

How could anyone survive this? Another barge was destroyed, this time a hundred yards in front of them. It didn't go up in a spectacular detonation like the last one. A diving Spitfire poured hundreds of rounds of tracer into the luckless men trapped in the slow-moving, bucket. Iron splinters and hot flakes of metal erupted from stem to stern, but they were mostly lost in a storm of body parts and bloody ruin that had been an infantry company a few seconds earlier.

Gelder squeezed his eyes shut and tried to focus on his own purpose in being here. He mechanically ran through the mission brief.

He would set down on the coast of Kent. He would make contact with the agent Blair. Blair would take him to a safe house, where he would meet with others sympathetic to the National Socialist cause. Gelder would liaise between them and the SS Sonderaktiontruppen *to liberate the leadership cadre of the British Union of Fascists from Holloway Prison.*

Falling shells bracketed the speeding *Schnellboot*, slamming Gelder into a bulkhead and then throwing him to the floor.

He would set down on the coast of Kent. He would make contact . . .

A flash.

A roar.

And then.

. . .

. . .

. . .

Nothing.

HMS *TRIDENT,* THE ENGLISH CHANNEL

"My God," said Halabi. "It's a slaughter. The purest sort of slaughter."

"Aye, ma'am," said McTeale, her XO, as they sped back toward the relative safety of the English coast.

It was impossible to make any sense of the main display in the CIC. There were thousands of individual contacts throughout the battlespace. The ship's Combat Intelligence was still tracking and analyzing every return. Her human operators were still assigning targets to the defenders forces' as quickly as they could. But to have any chance of understanding what was happening on a human scale, you had to turn away from the electronic version of the battle—a vast, hypercomplex simulacrum of cascading data tags—and attend to the simple things.

The drone footage of a Heinkel breaking up in midair, punched apart by a four-inch shell.

The vision of a parachute half-deployed, trailing fire behind a plummeting body, spearing down into the pebbles and limestone scree at the base of the White Cliffs of Dover.

The distant bump and thump of floating corpses as they struck the carbon composite sheath armor of the *Trident* at 120 knots.

"Metal Storm at one-point-three percent, Captain."

"Thank you, Mr. McTeale. Advise the Admiralty that we shall be withdrawing toward Plymouth and will need extra air cover, I think."

"Fighter Command has already assigned three USAAF squadrons to cover us, ma'am. They'll relieve the Canadians in eight minutes."

"Very good, then. I think we're past the worst of it, don't you?"

Halabi and her executive officer stared at the main display. The red icons denoting German surface units were beginning to pile up in the southern half of the Channel. More and more blue triangles, marking Allied air units were streaming down from the northern airfields.

"For now, Captain," said McTeale. "For now."

BERLIN

"Tell me, Brasch, would you have turned traitor if it were not for your son?"

"Ha! You're a fine one to talk, Müller. If I am a traitor, what are you? Skulking about in your stupid disguise. An assassin, that's all."

Müller sipped from the fine bone china cup. Coffee with real cream. Because of his trusted position, Brasch would enjoy many privileges denied to ordinary Germans. The full pound of Italian roasted coffee beans his wife had produced from a cupboard was undoubtedly one. The dollops of rich cream another. Manfred, the engineer's boy, was no longer with them. He'd been put to bed an hour earlier. The three adults—Müller, Brasch, and his plump, pretty hausfrau Willie—all hunkered over the kitchen table, like card players protecting a hand.

They heard the muffled crump of far-off bombs only as an echo of thunder.

"So, Brasch. What say you?"

Müller did not mean the question to be insulting. He was genuinely interested, and Brasch seemed to be genuinely sincere in trying to answer. The play of emotions across his haggard face gave away his conflicted feelings. "I don't know," he said. "I think so. Perhaps I would not have been so quick in my betrayal. Perhaps I was ready to throw it in after the Eastern Front. I don't know, Müller. I did not have the luxury of growing up in your world."

Willie patted his arm. "You were very sick, when you returned from Belgorod. That medal they pinned on you was supposed to make everything better. Men are full of such foolishness, Herr Müller. But not my Paul. He is a good man. We are good Germans."

Müller controlled the sick sneer that threatened to crawl across his lips at the old phrase. "You are." He nodded and waved his flexipad in their direction. "I have convinced my controllers of that. Although, it was the information you sent, Brasch, which has saved your hides."

The engineer flushed with anger. "That is not why I sent it, as you well know. I have saved the hides of my enemy, and condemned thousands of my comrades. I did so without knowing that you were coming for me. I did so knowing that it probably meant the deaths of my wife and child when—not if, but *when* I was found out. So you can cram your insinuations back into your arse, where they came from, Herr *Kapitän*."

"Paul, please," Willie pleaded.

Müller smiled and shook his head. "No, Frau Brasch, your husband is right. I should not pick at this scab. He has done a great service, not just for the world, but Germany herself."

"And so my reward is to be abandoned here," said Brasch.

"Left, not abandoned," Müller corrected. "Your wife and son will be smuggled out, and their disappearance covered up by the bombing raid in two days' time. You, however, must stay. Like me. There is more work to be done."

Brasch's wife gripped her husband's arm tightly. "But they will know, Paul. They will search the rubble and find we are not here, and they will think we have escaped."

"There will be bodies to find," said Müller, pushing on over the woman's objections. "Don't concern yourself with details. The Reich is full of bodies."

"But our neighbors. They will all be killed."

Müller shrugged. "This area of Berlin was taken by the Soviets at the end of my war. They are better off dead. And anyway, I have observed your neighbors these last few weeks. Some of them deserve everything they get."

Tears welled up in her eyes, and Müller regretted his harsh words, but he did not soften them. If this woman and her son were to survive, they would need to toughen up.

"So two days," said Brasch, bringing them back to business.

Müller scanned the latest data burst from Fleetnet. Sea Dragon was failing, the assault collapsing in on itself. Some German units had successfully landed on British soil, but the follow-on forces had been blocked. Raeder's most powerful ships were scrap metal. And the Luftwaffe was being pounded out of the sky.

"Two days will mark the point of maximum confusion," said Müller. "As the two army groups are forced to pull back from the French coast or be annihilated by the Allied air forces. In two days, a thousand British and American heavy bombers will strike at Berlin, to emphasize the scale of Hitler's failure. A few of them, specially adapted for the mission, will bomb this neighborhood into rubble, to cover your escape."

Müller let his eyes freeze on Willie Brasch.

"Do not warn anyone. You are already traitors to the Reich. Like me."

"But there are children . . . ," cried Willie.

"I know," Müller shot back, suddenly giving vent to his own suppressed rage. "Some of them are my family."

HMS *TRIDENT*, ENGLISH CHANNEL

"Outstanding work, Captain Halabi."

"Thank you, Admiral. I'll make sure to pass your compliments on to my crew. What would really make them happy, though, are some more Metal Storm loads."

Kolhammer disappeared inside a cloud of white noise for a moment before his image winked back into clarity. The encrypted vidlink to Washington was very shaky.

"I'm sorry," Kolhammer said. "I think you were asking for MS reloads. There's a seaplane on its way now, should be there in seventeen hours. It's carrying a pallet of ammo from the *Clinton*. That should take you back to twelve percent. After that, I'm afraid we're tapped out. We're going to need everything we've got for Hawaii. But the first hand-tooled Vulcans should be ready for air shipment to you in a fortnight. It's not Metal Storm, but it's a hell of a lot better than a couple of goddamned pom-poms."

Halabi smiled. "It will be, sir. About Hawaii, sir—will you be needing me to prepare for redeployment? It's going to be a very unpleasant business taking those islands back. Especially with the *Dessaix* on the loose."

Kolhammer must have worked through his plans for the campaign already. He shook his head emphatically. "We'll deal with the *Dessaix* first," he said. "And we'll need to redouble our efforts to determine whether any Task Force assets have fallen into enemy hands. The Soviets, for instance.

But for now, you're best off staying right where you are. The Hawaiian mission will be run by the locals, with input from us. But it's their show, and they've agreed to leave the *Trident* in place."

Halabi found herself in two minds. She agreed that the best role for the *Trident* was as a floating early-warning center. But she felt isolated here in her own country, and the brief prospect of rejoining the community of Multinational Force ships was quietly appealing.

She had retired to her ready room and suddenly realized it was the first time in over a day and a half she'd been alone. Kolhammer looked tired, but not as tired as she felt.

"I'm sorry, sir. Excuse me," she said, stifling a yawn.

"That's all right, Captain. You've earned some rack time."

"Soon enough, Admiral. The Germans are in retreat. The bulk of their invasion fleet didn't make it past the halfway point. And they're not reinforcing the airborne forces that did land."

"I read the last burst," said Kolhammer. "There's some hard fighting around *Ipswich*. But infantry against armor? It won't last."

Halabi frowned. "Your burst is a bit out of date, I'm afraid, sir. The British First Armored had to pull back. The Germans were a mix of *Fallschirmjäger* and SS Special Forces. They were pretty well equipped with portable antiarmor systems. Panzerfaust Two-fifties, I think. Or a variation on that theme, anyway. A lot of them had good, basic body armor and they were all packing assault rifles with an over-under grenade launcher. They chewed up a lot of our men."

Kolhammer's mouth was set in a grim line. "So what's happening? Do they have any kind of squad-level antiair systems?"

Halabi shook her head. "No, sir. So that's what's happening. The RAF have regained tactical control of our airspace, and those Cyclone gunships are near permanent fixtures above the German strongpoints."

"I see. How's their ammunition holding up?"

"I think we'll run out of Germans before we run out of ammo, sir."

Kolhammer sighed. "Well, we can't do much better than that."

The link dropped out.

Halabi stared at the wall of static for a full minute, wondering if the admiral might reconnect, but he didn't.

She rubbed her eyes, which felt as though they'd been baking inside a pizza oven. She sent a quick note to McTeale, updating him on the schedule for Metal Storm reloads. The *Trident* hummed under her feet. They'd withdrawn into the comparatively safer waters south of Ireland. It meant that the ship's own sensors weren't available to directly monitor the main battlespace over the Channel and the southern counties, but the Admiralty had decided that with the German attack effectively broken, they could afford to downgrade to drone cover only.

Halabi chuckled: a dry, mirthless sound.

A few months ago, the 'temps wouldn't have thought of drone coverage as a "downgrade." It would have been a bloody miracle.

Indeed, it was a bloody miracle, in the literal sense of the phrase, and it had saved her homeland.

As she slumped into her bunk, she refused to think about the fact that some people didn't agree it was her home at all.

COMMAND BUNKER, RASTENBURG, EAST PRUSSIA

It took many hours for the true state of affairs to emerge, but the *Reichsführer* had begun to suspect that Sea Dragon might fail when his own contribution, the *Sonderaktiontruppen*, were shattered before they had even reached the British Isles.

Reports had to be filed via landline, because of the Allies' ability to read and decode all the Reich's radio traffic. When Himmler finally got word that over half his own airborne regiment had been annihilated in transit, the magnitude of the disaster was already coming into focus.

Nearly two hundred Allied fighter planes had drilled right through the insane confusion of the air battle over the seas around England to attack the transports carrying the SS regiment. It was as though a vengeful God had lead them there. But he knew better. The *Trident* had guided them onto the target. He'd known the ship had that capability. But how had it known which flight, out of the many thousands of sorties flown today, had been the crucial one? There was only one answer to that. A very old-fashioned answer.

Treachery.

"It is just not possible. How dare they, how *dare* they?" the führer raged.

The atmosphere in the command bunker was bleak, tending toward ominous. There would be many, many people to punish for this calamitous failure. Himmler's unforgiving gaze fell upon Göring. He was drunk and blustering about the large numbers of Spitfires and Hurricanes his men had shot down. That may well be, but the RAF's air defense net was nowhere near as badly degraded as the Luftwaffe chief had insisted. And the *Trident* had survived every attack thrown against it with apparent ease.

Yes, it was the führer himself who had downplayed the importance of the ship's electronic senses. What had he said?

What did it matter if the British had a perfect view of their doom as it came rushing at them? It was still their doom.

Well, that was hardly his fault. The führer had repeatedly stated that he had no feel for naval combat. It had been Raeder's job to advise him on those matters. The senior *Kriegsmarine* officer hadn't spoken since news of the *Tirpitz* had come in via safe-hand courier. *Preparing his excuses*, thought Himmler.

Hitler alternated between screaming at his subordinates—ordering them to deploy units already confirmed as lost—and muttering to himself about the depth of betrayal he had been forced to endure.

Himmler kept to himself, wondering what could be salvaged.

All his hopes now lay with Skorzeny.

37

CAMBRIDGESHIRE, ENGLAND

Stealing the truck had been remarkably simple. Tens of thousands of military vehicles were on the move, and contrary to the comic book school of war, not everything ran smoothly. Vehicles broke down. Drivers didn't know which turn to take. Whole divisions got lost. Convoys were attacked and shot up from the air. Many trucks were abandoned, pushed off the road, simply because their drivers knew nothing about them beyond how to start the ignition.

Harold Philby wasn't much of a mechanic himself, but two of Skorzeny's men were. They had the broken down deuce-and-a-half running again within fifteen minutes. As a bonus, it was fitted out as a medical transport, with a red cross painted prominently on the canvas tarpaulin that covered the rear bed. After a hurried conference with the German commander, it was agreed that this would provide even better cover than a normal military truck, in which they ran the risk of being commandeered and attached to any combat unit they might run into.

Skorzeny had his men wrap themselves in the bloodied uniforms and bandages of the previous, missing occupants. Then they all piled into litters in the back. One of the most fluent English speakers was nominated as their "medic" to attend the wounded.

"Let's go then, tovarich." Skorzeny grinned.

He reminded Philby of a fox licking shit from a wire brush. The traitor put aside his visceral dislike of the fascist and gunned the engine. It kicked over after two attempts, and he pulled back onto the road.

They were well north of London, with at least half a day's travel in front of them and absolutely no guarantee of surviving it. He doubted that *he* would survive, even if they made the objective. Number Five had been quite explicit about the steps he should take to escape when he'd delivered Skorzeny, but after six months on the run, the rogue spy knew just how hard it was going to be to avoid detection once he'd put his head up. Unlike Burgess and Maclean, he'd gone to ground immediately upon learning of the Transition, and he was still alive because of it. The others, he had no idea. They could be dead, or more likely they were being detained somewhere by the SIS, tortured with the drugs and interrogation machines that were said to have arrived with the dark woman and the *Trident*.

"What is this marshland, tovarich?" Skorzeny asked as they rumbled along. "I thought Cambridge was a university, not a swamp."

"This is Cambridgeshire," Philby explained. "Specifically we're in the Ouse Washes, a floodplain between the Old and New Bedford rivers, drained by the Fourth Earl of Bedford in the sixteen—"

"A swamp, then, as I said."

Philby exhaled slowly.

If he ever made it to Moscow, he was going to get a medal for this.

A flight of American planes screamed overhead, wagging their wings just for him.

Biggin Hill was unrecognizable.

Actually, that was untrue. Harry had seen damage like this on many occasions. So many over the years that he'd lost count.

"Hammerhead run," said Sergeant St. Clair as the Eurocopter settled on its wheels.

"Looks like," the prince agreed. "Not well directed, though."

"Well enough, guv."

Harry's face twisted as he allowed the point. There were buildings and hangars standing, untouched, and runways that had been excavated in cross section rather than along their entire length. But the damage was still massive and crippling. Twelve hundred dead, they'd told him on the way in, including two members of Halabi's crew who'd died when their billet, a nearby village inn, had been destroyed by a wayward packet of submunitions.

"Can you refuel, here?" asked Harry as the rotors began to wind down.

The voice of Flight Lieutenant Ashley Hay responded in his earbud. "Our fuel stores weren't touched, Major. We'll top up and get back to *Trident* ASAP, if you don't mind."

"Okay. Thanks again for your help back there, Ash. Smashing effort."

"Thank you, sir."

His half-troop, minus the casualties Akerman and Bolt, were already unloading kit from the NH91 into a couple of vintage jeeps with .50 cal. mounts for the drive north, where they would meet up with the regiment, which was prepping for a night assault into Aldringham, one of the Suffolk villages still held by the *Fallschirmjäger*.

Harry waved off the chopper, bent over, and hurried to his men in the jeeps. Fires burned all around them, and as he was climbing into the lead vehicle, he noticed a disembodied human thumb lying by the rear wheel.

"Your Highness," said his driver, a whey-faced lad just as Harry had once been.

"None of that, son. Major will do. You know where you're going? You won't get lost?"

"Ipswich, sir, via the city. Done it a hundred times."

"Good lad." Harry clapped him on the back, announcing with faux high humor, "And you shall know us by the trail of our dead."

"Excuse me, Major?" asked the 'temp, who now looked worried.

"Nah, excuse the guvnor," said St. Clair as he stowed his weapon in a gun rack on the dashboard. "He's got a very sad weakness for postpunk allusions, and it comes out when he's under pressure."

The wheels spun on grass, and they leapt away. Harry settled back and hauled out his flexipad, pulling down the latest sit rep from the *Trident*.

As soon as the unit linked to Fleetnet, a Priority 1 e-mail unfolded itself on screen.

"Trouble, guv?" St. Clair asked.

"Not really," Harry replied. "Good news, actually. The Aldringham job's a blow out. Seems they love their new gunships so much, we're all being pensioned off, and the rest of the war is going to be won by dicing up the krauts with miniguns."

"Fucking corker!" St. Clair grinned. "We still going to London, though?"

"Yep. I've still got to meet the PM for tea and biscuits."

"You'll want to make yourself beautiful, then, guv. You're a right fuckin' sight, you are."

He was, but there was nothing for it but a cat's lick and promise, as grandma used to say. He wondered where she was right now. The firm had decided to stay in London, come what may. He couldn't imagine that some precautions hadn't been taken, however. Then again, last he'd heard, they pitched poor old granddad right into the thick of it in the Channel. Harry had no idea what ship he was on, or whether he'd even made it.

What a fucking mess.

He was going to drink an unhealthy number of lagers when this was all over.

The prince settled back into the seat and caught up with the latest burst.

Halabi had made it through without significant damage, although she was now bereft of any force-projection capability, having fired the last shots in her locker.

The German invasion fleet was piled up on the French side of the Channel, unable to make any headway against the Allied air forces or Royal Navy. The *Kriegsmarine* had pretty much ceased to function as a blue-water surface fleet, with the destruction of the *Tirpitz* battle group, although that had been a close-run thing. The Germans had put up a reasonably effective antimissile screen simply by filling the air in front of them with a storm front of shrapnel and high explosives. A bit like the jihadi in his own day, Harry mused.

Flight ops hadn't resumed from Biggin Hill, and probably wouldn't for a few weeks, given the extent of the damage. But the sky was still crowded with aircraft from other airfields. As they drove away from the ruined sector station, Harry stretched his cramped neck muscles by craning his head right back and scanning the dull gray skies. The traffic was all one way, heading out. Whereas a few hours earlier, it had been an unholy mess up there, with incredible numbers of aircraft twisting and turning in massive dogfights, now the skies looked more like a superhighway delivering massed columns of fighters and bombers over the Channel.

"What were they fuckin' thinkin', d'you reckon, guv?" asked St. Clair as Harry read a couple more E-mails, which came in as flash traffic.

"The Nazis? They weren't thinking at all, Viv. That's the problem with leadership cults. They're red hot on getting shit done, once the big man has spoken, but not so good at weighing up whether that shit should have been done in the first place."

He had an e-mail from the War Ministry with details of the briefing he was to attend at Whitehall, before continuing on to Ipswich. And a quick personal note from Churchill, personally thanking him and his men for their efforts at Alresford.

Harry checked his watch. They'd be another hour or two getting there, and probably an hour delayed while he was at the briefing. "Viv," he said, leaning forward, "you and the lads should chase up some hot nosh when we're in the city. It's going to be a while before they get another sit-down feed."

Their driver piped up. "Begging your pardon, sir, but I know a good chippy near Whitehall, if your lads wouldn't mind."

Harry smiled. "How do you think the lads would feel about some fish and chips, Sergeant Major?"

"I suspect they could murder a feed, guv."

"What's your name, son?" asked Harry, shouting over the engine noise and the rush of air.

"Corporal Draper, sir. Peter Draper."

"Well, young Pete. I like the cut of your jib. That's the sort of initiative which built the British Empire. Drop me at the Ministry, and get my boys some hot tucker—my shout."

Harry passed over a ten-pound note.

"And keep the change."

They almost ran off the road. He'd forgotten that Corporal Draper had probably never seen so much money in one place.

Philby maintained a safe house in London that hadn't been discovered following the Transition. A professor of economics at Trinity College, Cambridge, owned it—a man he had recruited as a talent-spotter for the Russians just before the war began.

He was now in the Pacific, working as a Naval attaché in Melbourne, and Philby presumed upon their relationship to borrow the house as a hideout. Built in the 1700s, it had a coach house around the rear, large enough to conceal the truck they had stolen; London was in such a state of upheaval, with the streets full of military vehicles, the emergency services, and commandeered civilian transport, that one wayward truck was unlikely to arouse much suspicion, if they moved quickly.

Only Philby and the two fluent speakers raised their voices as the squad disembarked from the truck, still pretending to be wounded soldiers. Philby ordered them into the house and loudly announced that they'd be staying there until beds could be found for them at a military hospital.

Once inside, the men stripped off their bandages and bloodied rags, resuming their counterfeit roles as soldiers from Holland and Denmark. They unpacked their kit, checked weapons, and waited for the call.

It came within two hours.

Draper's chippy was a short walk from old Scotland Yard, off the northeastern end of Whitehall, and it proved more convenient to drop Viv and the others there before he and Harry continued on to the Ministry alone.

Hundreds of barrage balloons floated on tethers above the city, over which lay a dense blanket of smoke from the fires started by German bombing raids. Sirens still blared constantly, although the conflict's center of gravity was well away from the city, south in the Channel and northeast in Suffolk. Harry was just indulging in a moment of self-pity that he wouldn't get to sit down with a nice chip butty and a cup of tea when a sixth sense began to scream at him.

He snapped out of his reverie and took a sight picture of the scene in front of them. Draper was motoring down Whitehall at about thirty miles an hour. They'd just passed the Admiralty and the headquarters of the Horse Guards, and were coming up on the War Ministry. A black Bentley was parked in front of the Ministry, its driver moving around to open the back door.

A truck marked as a medical transport was pulling up on the other side of the street, and British soldiers were jumping down from the rear.

They were all bandaged as though badly wounded, but they were still armed, and judging from the way they moved, they weren't injured at all.

"Speed up, speed up *now*," ordered Harry as he reached for his M12.

Corporal Draper stepped on the gas, but not without asking what was up. The rattle of small-arms fire reached them.

The Bentley's driver fell to the cobblestones, and Harry could hear the telltale impact of bullets on metal and armored glass. He flicked the power switch on the rifle's underslung grenade launcher and dialed up a firing sequence. Three fragmentation rounds and two incendiary. Bracing the gun on his knee he sent the five fat 20 mm programmable grenades on their way.

"Hey! That's Mr. Churchill's car, that is," protested Draper.

"I know," said Harry as the tiny bomblets dropped in pattern, the frags bursting on the blind side of the truck, to protect the Bentley from their blast effect. The incendiaries dropped onto the lorry and in amongst the knot of men. They were grouped at the rear of the vehicle to fire on Churchill's car and the guards rushing out of the Ministry.

The deuce-and-a-half rocked on its axle as the HE rounds went off, scattering most of the assassins like bowling pins. Two bright, white flashes followed immediately, setting alight the truck's canvas tarpaulin and the uniforms of the men Harry had targeted.

The jeep was bouncing so roughly that he couldn't be sure of hitting anything with his carbine, so he leapt into the rear of the vehicle and unsafed the .50-caliber mount. For an antique, the big gun was still an awesome piece of fighting machinery.

Harry had to fire in short bursts, lest he demolish the Bentley with a badly aimed volley. They'd begun to take fire now, bullets pinging off the metalwork and cracking the windshield. Draper simply sped up, hunching over the wheel and pointing the car directly at the screaming, burning troops. Harry squeezed out two more bursts, chopping a couple of his targets in half, before he snatched up his carbine again as they drew too close to depress the barrel of the huge machine gun any further.

Time stretched and pulled. They hit a chunk of road excavated by the grenades he had fired, and the jeep lifted off for a short flight through clean air, slamming into the bodies of four burning Germans—at least he hoped they were Germans. One of them flew apart into half a dozen flaming chunks of roadkill.

Then he was down, in amongst them, the rifle firing single shots. Return fire zipped and whistled past his head.

He heard the deep boom of a Webley revolver and saw Draper out of the corner of his eye, dueling with two men. One was missing an arm below the elbow, and both were singed and smoking. The driver killed them and hurried over to the Bentley.

Harry smashed the butt of his M12 into the blackened face of a man dressed in a contemporary British sergeant's uniform, who was swearing at him in low German.

And then nothing for a few seconds.

Silence.

. . .

. . .

. . .

His spinal inserts began to feed beta-blockers into his central nervous system, forestalling the tremors and shock that might otherwise have attended such an unexpected and violent incident.

Everything was rendered into hard clarity: the taste of the scorched air; the hundreds of pockmarks in the body of the prime minister's car; the sizzle and spitting of burning rubber as the truck settled on the steel rims of its wheels; the sound of Corporal Draper, retching in the gutter; the flat, hollow crack of another pistol.

Harry spun and saw a slant scar-faced man advancing on them, firing a Luger. He whipped up his M12, but the trigger pulled back without response. It was empty.

Another bullet cracked past his head. His fighting knife was in his hands as though he had wished it there. Without conscious thought, he threw the dagger as he had so many thousands of times in practice. It embedded itself in the shoulder of the last attacker. The man's face registered the pain as he attempted to wrench it out, but the serrated teeth on the inside of the blade stopped him.

And then he and Harry were on each other.

Iron knuckle-dusters slammed into Harry's chest, breaking a couple of ribs that had already taken some terrible punishment in the fight at Alresford. He spun with the direction of the blow anyway, looping his hand around the other man's forearm and pivoting quickly to bring force to bear on the vulnerable elbow. He heard the man gasp, but he was well trained, and accelerated his own movement in the same direction, speeding up to break free of the hold.

Harry grabbed the hilt of his fighting knife and reefed it free with a wet, tearing sound as they separated. The German grunted in pain, but no more. A shortened bayonet had appeared in his hand.

Both of them were breathing heavily, circling each other like caged wolves.

The man's eyes narrowed, and he smiled. "Prince Harold, if I am right? Not wearing your swastika today, then, Your Highness? Oh, dear? Have I missed the party season?"

Harry didn't respond. He was concentrating on the man's defenses, looking for an avenue of attack.

"My name is Skorzeny. Colonel Otto Skorzeny," he said. "And you are in my way."

Skorzeny struck out with a quick slash at Harry's knife hand, but the SAS officer was ready for that and withdrew the arm, which he'd hung out as a lure. He snapped a kick out, aiming for the colonel's knee, but the German, too, was ready, and he rotated just far enough to allow the blow to glance off.

They slashed at each other three or four times, close enough now to drive in a killing blow, except that neither could penetrate the other's defenses.

"Major Windsor, get out of the way, sir. Give me a clear shot."

It was Draper, nursing an arm shattered by a bullet from Skorzeny's pistol, aiming the Webley uncertainly with his other hand.

Harry heard a car door open behind him, and the thunder of boots on the steps of the Ministry.

Skorzeny smiled and plucked two grenades from his webbing, pulling the pin with his teeth, and dropping them on the ground. "Until next time," he said, spinning around as rifle fire snapped past Harry's head again.

"Grenade!" he yelled, turning to find Churchill emerging from the car without so much as a scratch on him yet.

Harry dived at the prime minister, slamming into him like the champion rugby player he'd once been, and driving the portly old man back into the relative safety of the armored car. A curse, a tangle of arms and legs, and then two explosions that shook the Bentley and peppered the interior with shrapnel through the still-open door. Harry felt some of it hit his body armor, and a hot shooting pain in his calf told him at least one piece had struck home.

Churchill heaved him off, and Harry backed out of the car, looking for Skorzeny.

A platoon or more of real British troops had arrived from within the Ministry building, and more were running up from the Horse Guards.

"He got away," said Draper, appearing from around the other side of the Bentley.

The familiar voice of the British prime minister rode in over the top of him. "You know, Your Highness, we once had a civil war in this country to put the royal family in its place, and that place was *not* on top of the prime minister . . . but thank you, anyway."

Harry took the PM's outstretched hand, still looking for Skorzeny.

But he was gone.

EPILOGUE

The Quiet Room had no physical presence. There was no room, as such. The Quiet Room was a set of protocols, a number of agents, and an expression of will.

Admiral Phillip Kolhammer's will.

He was not an autocrat. He consulted with those he trusted. Men like Captain Judge and Colonel Jones, or women such as Karen Halabi. But when it came time to make a call, the responsibility fell on him alone.

Kolhammer scanned the read-once-only report from one of his best agents. They sat in a nondescript conference room on campus in the Zone. The woman was dressed in civilian clothes. An expensive suit, cut in a twenty-first style by a local tailor who was becoming rich because of his ability to reproduce the designs of Zegna, Armani, and their contemporaries from magazine photographs that came through the Transition.

The woman was wealthy in her own right now. She worked for herself, but she answered to a higher purpose.

"You've done excellent work, Ms. O'Brien," said Kolhammer. And he was impressed. She effectively ran a dozen large and rapidly growing enterprises on behalf of her clients. They'd come to trust her advice without reservation, so successful had she been in advancing their interests. Some of the clients were complex entities, corporate concerns with claims over intellectual property not yet existent in this universe. Some were individuals, such as Slim Jim Davidson.

As long as their wealth continued to grow at a staggering pace, Maria O'Brien's clients asked her very few questions about the vast and ever-growing discretionary funds she invested on their behalf.

Kolhammer grinned at the thought of what an asshole like Davidson would think of his ill-gotten gains being channeled into something like the establishment of the Southern Christian Leadership Conference fifteen years before its time. Not much, he supposed, unless he could see a dollar in it—in which case, he probably couldn't care less.

"I see you've gifted Bryn Mawr's Library fund rather generously," he said, raising one eyebrow.

"Yes." O'Brien nodded.

"You're an alumna of Denbigh Hall, if I recall correctly."

"You do, sir. So I know how much they need the money."

Kolhammer handed her the flexipad, deleting the read-once file as he did so. "Be careful with the political donations, Ms. O'Brien. Hoover's men are all over Congress. They'll pick up any whiff of us playing favorites."

"They won't, Admiral. I know my job."

"I believe you do," said Kolhammer, handing her back the flexipad with a new read-once file, a list of trust funds, individuals, and organizations he wanted her to fund. O'Brien took a few minutes' pace around the bare room, committing the list to memory before she deleted it.

"So," he said when she had circled back to a spot in front of him. "How's civilian life treating you?"

O'Brien relaxed a little. She was no longer in the corps, but old habits died hard. "I don't have to get up early. That's pretty cool," she said. "And, you know, I'm actually loving the work. Not just for you, but for my clients. It's exciting . . ." She seemed to falter at something.

"But?"

"But," she said with the air of someone about to make a confession. "It's really hard here, sir. The rednecks and the assholes I can handle, if you'll pardon my French. A guy like Slim Jim, he's a pussycat. But I'll tell you what hurts. It's the way women resent me, and everything I stand for. The way they look at me when I enter a room, or walk down the street. Like I'm some sort of five-dollar whore turning tricks at their bake-off."

"Not all of them, surely."

"No. But enough." Tears began to well up in her eyes. "There isn't a day I don't wish I could just go home," she said as her voice cracked.

Kolhammer passed her a handkerchief. "You leave anyone special behind?"

O'Brien dabbed her eyes and pulled herself together. "No husband or kids, if that's what you mean. But I was very close to my sister."

"I'm sorry, Maria. Have you been in contact with your family here? Grandparents, or anything?"

She shook her head. "I . . . I don't know how they'd react to me. I don't—"

Kolhammer stood up and gripped her shoulder. "Why don't you find out?"

O'Brien sniffed. "Thank you, sir. I might. I have traced some people on my mother's side. I'm sorry, I don't normally blubber. Marines aren't allowed to."

"You're not a marine anymore. Blubber away. That's an order."

They began to walk toward the door. Kolhammer gave her a fatherly pat on the back of her exquisitely cut suit. "You go get 'em, tiger. I'm sure they'll be proud of you."

"They'll probably hit me up for a loan," she half laughed, half sobbed.

"You can afford it."

They shook hands, and she left. Kolhammer checked his watch. He had another meeting in his office in ten minutes. He turned out the lights and left, walking out of the building into a night so cold and clear, it seemed as if you could see to the end of time out there in the stars.

As he walked back, he tried to keep a whole world in his head. Everything from the planning of the assault to retake Hawaii, to the names of the FBI agents who tried to use Davidson as a pawn. A frost had formed on the turf laid out between the campus buildings. It crunched underfoot as he cut across a section that had been laid just that afternoon. The strips of grass shifted under his feet.

He wondered what he was going to find when Ivanov sent his scheduled data burst from Siberia tomorrow. Assuming he sent anything at all. He wondered if Wild Bill Donovan had made contact with Ho Chi Minh yet, with a promise to supply all the arms the Viet Minh would need to make the Japanese occupation of Indochina a grinding nightmare. He wondered if Roosevelt would accept his argument that rather than fighting the Communist north after the war, they should bury them in aid and consumer goods. As he climbed the steps of the building that housed his office, he thought about the latest reports of out of the Middle East, about the Baath Party uprising in Syria and the Wahabi Intifada in Egypt.

He wondered if his uncle has been sent to the death camps yet and whether another round of horror stories in the broadsheet press might shame Churchill and Roosevelt into assigning more assets to bombing the rail links into Poland. He made a note to ask Dan Black to speak to Julia Duffy about that. She'd been more than helpful that way in the past.

As he saluted the guards at the entry foyer and marched down the corridor to his office, thoughts of Duffy led naturally to the horrible footage of that Natoli girl being murdered. A slow burn began in his gut, and he felt his gorge rising with his anger. He returned the salutes of the three men waiting for him.

Hidaka, the Japanese "governor" of Hawaii, had lied. He'd said that the Allied prisoners, both military and civilian, were being well treated. But the evidence on the flatscreen in Kolhammer's office said differently.

Nobody spoke as they watched the video of the executions. Kolhammer had seen it five times now, and counted 123 victims, all of them beheaded. Even though he'd lost count of the number of times he'd seen people die like this, there was still something about it that froze the soul.

He thumbed the remote to freeze the footage before they had to watch the gruesome scene of Bill Halsey's death again.

"So who is this asshole?" he rumbled.

"Commander Jisaku Hidaka, Admiral. Interim military governor—"

"I know that, Chief. He told me that himself, on the vid, just before he capped that poor girl. I want to know more. You open a file, in the Room. And we'll close it when the protocols are carried out."

"Sanction Four, sir?"

"No," said Kolhammer. "I don't think so. Do you?"

Chief Petty Officer Vincente Rogas shook his head. "I guess not."

Kolhammer regarded the image on the screen with a cold, flat lack of feeling. "Sanction Five," he said.

ABOUT THE AUTHOR

Australian author JOHN BIRMINGHAM, whose book *Leviathan* won the National Award for Non-fiction at the Adelaide Festival of the Arts 2002, "tells stories for a living." For doing so he has been paid by the *Sydney Morning Herald, Rolling Stone, Penthouse, Playboy*, and numerous other magazines. He has also been published, but not paid, by the *Long Bay Prison News*. Some of his stories have won prizes, including the George Munster prize for Freelance Story of the Year and the Carlton United Sports Writing Prize. *Leviathan*, John's fifth book, was first published in Knopf (Australia) hardback in 1999, and is the "unauthorized biography of Sydney," Australia. His earlier works are *He Died with a Felafel in His Hand*, made into a feature film by Noah Taylor, *The Tasmanian Babes Fiasco, How to Be a Man, The Search for Savage Henry*, and *Weapons of Choice*. He lives at the beach with his wife, young daughter, baby son, and two cats. He is not looking for any more flatmates.

www.birmo.journalspace.com

ABOUT THE TYPE

The text of this book was set in Janson, a typeface designed in about 1690 by Nicholas Kis—a Hungarian living in Amsterdam—and for many years mistakenly attributed to the Dutch printer Anton Janson. In 1919, the matrices became the property of the Stempel Foundry in Frankfurt. It is an old-style book face of excellent clarity and sharpness. Janson serifs are concave and splayed; the contrast between thick and thin strokes is marked.